★ ★ ★ ★ ★

# Celia Garth

★ ★ ★ ★ ★

# Celia Garth

GWEN BRISTOW

CHICAGO
REVIEW
PRESS

*By the Author*

DEEP SUMMER

THE HANDSOME ROAD

THIS SIDE OF GLORY

TOMORROW IS FOREVER

JUBILEE TRAIL

CELIA GARTH

CALICO PALACE

GOLDEN DREAMS

*Except for historical personages referred to by their own names, all characters in this book are fictitious.*

Cover design: Sarah Olson
Cover image: Marie Louise Elisabeth Vigée-Le Brun, French, 1755–1842. Portrait of a Young Woman (detail), about 1797 (Oil on canvas). Museum of Fine Arts, Boston, Robert Dawson Evans Collection. © 2008 Museum of Fine Arts, Boston. All rights reserved.

The print of Charleston in 1780 that appears on the title page shows three famous buildings which play an important part in the story of Celia Garth: St. Michael's Church (with steeple, at left), still standing; The Exchange (to the right of the page fold), now a historical museum; and St. Philip's Church (to the right, with parapet), which burned down about 1840. Another St. Philip's Church was built on this site, so that the Charleston skyline, seen from the harbor, still shows these three buildings as in 1780.

This unabridged edition is reprinted by arrangement with the author's estate.
Copyright © 1959 by Gwen Bristow
Copyright © renewed 1987 by Louis Bristow
Foreword © 2009 by Sara Donati
All rights reserved
This edition published in 2009 by
Chicago Review Press, Incorporated
814 North Franklin Street
Chicago, Illinois 60610
ISBN 978-1-55652-787-6
Printed in the United States of America
5 4 3 2

# FOREWORD

*A*T AGE THIRTEEN I discovered historical fiction by means of Gwen Bristow's *Jubilee Trail*, and so began a lifelong preoccupation with stories set in the past.

By the time I was seventeen I had read hundreds of novels about civil wars (British and American), the Revolution, the Anglo-Saxons and the Norman Invasion, and ancient Rome and Greece. I considered myself something of a connoisseur, someone who could tell her Mary Renault from her James Michener. The stories I liked best were the ones that focused on the lives of women, who were so often banished to the periphery of the historical fiction bestsellers. Even at a young age I was skeptical of James Fenimore Cooper's portrayal of the women struggling to survive on the New York frontier.

My impression was that male authors didn't really know how to write female characters, and didn't particularly regret that shortcoming. Women were wonderful for filling in detail and establishing background—a man had to have a family to fight for, after all—but the most a reader could hope for was a female with grit, that stock character who knows how to shoot a gun and speaks her mind now and then, but isn't really fulfilled until she embraces her feminine nature.

Even female authors fell into this trap. Scarlett O'Hara is a strong-willed, spoiled, manipulative, vain wretch who wrestles her fate to the ground and holds it there determined to get what she believes she deserves. Except, of course, she fails, because Scarlett doesn't know what she wants. She rejects the love of a good man, and is doomed to unhappiness.

Gwen Bristow took a different approach. Her female characters may be introduced to us as young and inexperienced; they may even be naive. But they are serious-minded individuals with strong feelings about matters other than engaging the interest of men.

This is certainly true of Celia Garth. A young woman with few family ties, she is ambitious and proud of her skills as a seamstress. She depends on her own intelligence and sense of self, and unlike many primary characters in early historical novels, she does not fling herself into harm's way. Harm comes, nevertheless, in the form of a war for independence and a British army bent on not only subduing but also mastering and humiliating a rebel colony.

Celia has a strong sense of what it means to be a Southerner (first) and an American (second) in occupied Charleston. She does fall in love, but her choice is a good man with a family that loves and respects her. The conflict is not an internal one for Celia; she does not doubt her choices. The force that moves her story along is external: when the marauding British army takes everything she holds dear, the Revolution is no longer academic for Celia. Step by step she becomes more involved, of her own free will. Her love story, as touching as it is, is secondary to the role she takes for herself as a spy.

Bristow takes great pains to re-create eighteenth century Charleston as a war zone. Celia and those close to her are shaken, again and again, by the constant barrage of artillery fired from British ships in the harbor. The Revolution is not a sanitized affair; there is loss of property and injury and death, despair and grievous insult and loss of hope. There is division within the community; Celia's cousin takes the king's side and shows no empathy for Celia even in her worst days. The stories of the many secondary characters, good, indifferent, and bad, come together to bring wartime Charleston into three full dimensions.

Bristow was a proud native of the South. Her love for South Carolina and Charleston is palpable. Thus it isn't surprising that in trying both to tell a true story and to honor her home she does in fact sidestep the issue of slavery. There is no contemplation of that institution; it just is. The many slaves in the story hate the British as much as their owners do. Readers may consider this a simplification or even an act of denial on Bristow's part—or simply a realistic representation of how Celia sees and understands her world.

For Celia, as for many of Bristow's female characters, personal happiness—family, marriage, children—is a byproduct of a life lived on a wider plane. Celia Garth strives for personal fulfillment in a whole range of ways, and by overcoming her many challenges, she earns her happy ending.

There may well have been real young women who lived lives like Celia's, spying for the colonial forces during the Revolution. But these women's stories have been forgotten. If there are records of their acts, the details will be spotty and open to interpretation; the historical record is what it is, and it doesn't strive to convince anybody of the facts or even to make them palatable or believable.

The novelist does bear that burden, and Bristow is equal to the challenge. With *Celia Garth* she gives us a complex, ambitious young woman living in Charleston during the American Revolution—a setting as extraordinary as Celia herself.

SARA DONATI

*To my mother*

CAROLINE WINKLER BRISTOW

*who first told me about*

*her Revolutionary ancestor*

NICHOLAS WINKLER

*one of Marion's men*

# CHAPTER I

*C*ELIA GARTH had blond hair and brown eyes. Her hair was a thick fluffy gold; her eyes were dark, and they looked at the world with brisk attention. She had a good figure, and she was proud of it and carried herself well. Celia's face was lively and irregular: stubborn mouth, pert square chin, straight nose with freckles. It was not a classic face, but it had verve and twinkling humor—a sassy face.

Celia was twenty years old. In September, 1779, she had been for three months an apprentice at Mrs. Thorley's sewing shop in Charleston, South Carolina. When she went into Mrs. Thorley's office before breakfast that morning to get her orders for the day, Celia was trying to look meek. She did not succeed, but she did look interesting.

Her blond hair was brushed up from her forehead and topped with a perky little cap of white lawn. Around her shoulders she wore a white kerchief, knotted on her bosom. Her dress was homespun linen. This linen, woven by the flax-growers of Kingstree and sent down to Charleston in bales, was sturdy, cheap, and ordinary. But on Celia it did not look that way.

The natural color of this cloth was a harsh hickory-brown, but Celia had washed and sunned it till it faded to a creamy tan, becoming to her dark eyes and light hair. Below the white kerchief her bodice clung like satin to her midriff. The sleeves had deep white frills, rippling halfway to her wrists. Her skirt flared backward, graceful as a flower, and short enough to show an inch of her white stockings and her black buckled shoes. Celia had never had an expensive costume in her life, but she loved clothes and she loved her pretty self and she never looked frowsy.

The owner of the sewing shop, Mrs. Thorley, sat at her desk. Celia stood before her, saying "Yes ma'am" whenever Mrs. Thorley paused. But behind her sassy face, Celia was having sassy thoughts. She was trying to imagine Mrs. Thorley being kissed by a man. Of course she must have been kissed, for she was *Mrs.* Thorley, but Celia could not get the picture in her mind. Mrs. Thorley was a dame of massive build; her starched gray dress stood upon her like a suit of armor, and her starched white cap rode stiffly on her head. She had blue eyes and slate-gray hair and a deep rumbly voice. Celia wondered what Mrs. Thorley's husband had been like. No matter, the idea of Mrs. Thorley's being embraced by any man at all was just outrageous.

Celia had been kissed, several times, but not during the months she had been working here. Mrs. Thorley was strict. She employed only girls from respectable families, and those who did not live with their own people in town lived here in the shop, where they were guarded like the pupils of a boarding-school. Mrs. Thorley was proud of the care she gave her girls. (She always spoke of them as "girls" or "young ladies," though several of the senior dressmakers were past forty.)

She was telling Celia to go to Mr. Bernard's warehouse and pick up some rolls of silk gauze. Gauze was rare and costly these days. It had to be imported, and now that the Thirteen Colonies were in rebellion against the king, the trading ships ran the risk of being captured by the king's navy. But a ship of Mr. Bernard's had just come in from the West Indies, loaded with fascinating stuff.

"Now, Miss Garth, before you start for the warehouse," said Mrs. Thorley, "go up to the sewing room. Miss Loring will give you a piece of heavy cloth to wrap the gauze."

"Yes ma'am," said Celia. She was noticing that Mrs. Thorley had quite a lot of hairs on her upper lip. A kiss from her would be scratchy, like a kiss from a man who needed a shave.

"After breakfast," continued Mrs. Thorley, "you will open the parlor." Celia wondered if her voice had always been as deep as it was now. Imagine such a voice saying "I love you" to a man. Mrs. Thorley rumbled on. "There will probably be more visitors than usual, because of the new displays. I announced in the *Gazette* that they could be seen today."

"Yes ma'am," said Celia.

"Several ladies have left orders for gauze caps," said Mrs. Thorley. "So if anyone asks you, say the gauze has arrived."

"Yes ma'am—and oh please, Mrs. Thorley—" Celia's eagerness cracked through her effort to be sweetly respectful. But before she could go on, Mrs. Thorley interrupted with astonishment.

"What is it, Miss Garth?"

"Please ma'am, can't I make one of those caps? I can do beautiful stitching on gauze, really I can, if you'll just let me show you—"

"Miss Garth, you have your work assigned to you," said Mrs. Thorley. She was not angry. Her voice merely had its usual determination. She asked, "Have you finished sewing the buttons on those shirts for Captain Rand?"

"No ma'am, but I can sew on the buttons in the evenings after supper, I won't mind the extra time, please let me—"

"Go on with the work you have been given, Miss Garth. Now if you need any help in the parlor today, tell Miss Loring."

"Yes ma'am," said Celia. It was no use. They were not going to let her prove herself. All they would give her was work so simple that she could have done it when she was six years old. Sewing on buttons!

"That is all, Miss Garth," said Mrs. Thorley.

Celia curtsied. Mrs. Thorley turned to her desk, opened a ledger, and set to work on her accounts. The light from the window showed up the hairs on her lip. "I don't believe he *enjoyed* kissing her," Celia thought.

She went upstairs to the sewing room. This was a large room, well lighted, with plenty of space for the twenty seamstresses who worked here. Mrs. Thorley was not especially tenderhearted, but she knew that people did better work if they were comfortable. A Negro housemaid was dusting, and a man was emptying the trash-boxes where the girls threw scraps of cloth too frayed or too soiled to be of further use. These would go to the *Gazette*, for papermaking. Nothing at Mrs. Thorley's was ever wasted.

The girls were not at work yet, but the two supervisors, Miss Loring and Miss Perry, were already busy. Miss Loring sat by a table, writing; Miss Perry was bustling around, pulling curtains and opening and shutting drawers. Celia went to the table and stood there politely until Miss Loring looked up to say,

"Yes, yes, what is it?"

Miss Loring was thin and tense. She always looked as if she had more things to do than she could possibly get done. Already, though she had not been dressed for more than twenty minutes, her hair was coming down and her cap was crooked on her head. Celia wondered if Miss Loring had ever been kissed. Probably not. Some of the girls said Miss Loring had once had a beau, but he had died. Celia did not believe them. It just did not seem possible that any man could have felt romantic about that scrawny fussbudget. Celia asked for the wrapping-cloth.

"Cloth?" said Miss Loring. She scowled as if she had never heard the word before, then she remembered. "Oh yes, yes, for the gauze, in just a minute, but—" she held out the slate she had been writing on—"this is the list of people who have appointments today. I'll put it in the drawer of your table." She tapped her fingers on the slate and turned her head toward Miss Perry. "Oh Matilda, will you hand me that cloth right there, on the shelf by you?"

Miss Perry was a round, chubby little woman with a shiny pink face. Saying, "Pleased to oblige," she trotted over with the cloth, a piece of heavy unbleached muslin compactly folded.

"Thank you, Miss Perry," said Celia. "I'll go now."

Miss Perry patted Celia's arm, smiling brightly. She looked like a middle-aged cherub. "Well, well, we're going to have a nice walk before breakfast, aren't we?"

Celia said "Yes ma'am." She wondered how it felt to be like Miss Loring and Miss Perry, old maids who weren't ever going to have any fun. Well, she wouldn't be like that. Exciting things were going to happen to her, because she intended to see to it that they did.

She ran downstairs and came out on the front steps. Oh, it was lovely outdoors. The time was a little before six and the sun had not quite risen, but you could tell it was going to be a shining day.

The street was pearly in the morning light. Celia smelt a whiff of geranium from the bush by the steps, and heard the bells of St. Michael's ripple in the air. A little wind blew in from the sea, fluffing her skirt and lifting the tendrils of hair about her forehead. The wind brought her the odors of the waterfront—salt and tar, coffee and molasses and rum. Over the housetops she could see the tall masts of the ships. Some of them had foreign flags, others the new flag of the American rebels. The rebels had been using this flag only about two years and it still looked odd, though Celia thought the design was quite pretty: thirteen red and white stripes for the Thirteen States, and one corner blue with thirteen white stars.

As the church bells fell silent she heard the birds twittering, and the rustle of wind in the palmetto trees along the sidewalk. Two soldiers came down the street, handsome in their blue uniforms. These uniforms were neither dark blue nor light, but what people called "rebel blue," a clear medium shade with facings of buff-color. When the men saw Celia they swept off their smart three-cornered hats—rebel blue like their coats, with rosettes of buff ribbon—and bowed to her, exclaiming, "Morning, ma'am!"

Celia smiled and said "Good morning," but then she looked down and became busy straightening the folded muslin she carried under her arm. You certainly could not be annoyed when handsome soldiers reminded you that you had blond hair and brown eyes and a tempting figure, but there were those unkissed old maids and the unkissable Mrs. Thorley, who might be looking out of the windows. And next week her apprenticeship would be up, and they would tell her whether or not she had given satisfaction. If she had, she could stay here, with the glitter and excitement of the fashionable world around her. If she had not, Mrs. Thorley would tell her to go back to the country and live with her Aunt Louisa and Uncle William and her stuck-up cousin Roy Garth.

"I won't go back!" Celia told herself fiercely. "They can't make me!" But even as she said it she knew they *could* make her, because she was only twenty years old and until her next birthday other people would have the right to boss her around. "Please Lord," Celia whispered, "let me stay in Charleston!"

Turning her head she looked up at the shop. Mrs. Thorley occupied a stately three-story corner building on Lamboll Street, in the aristocratic southern tip of town. This house had formerly been a residence, and still looked like one, except for a small neat sign over the door saying "Amelia Thorley, Sewing." A larger sign would have been out of keeping with the tone of the establishment. It would also have been unnecessary. Everybody knew Mrs. Thorley's shop. Not only was it the most fashionable place in town to have clothes made, but also it was the place where the smartest people gathered to flirt and gossip and hear the news. Besides women's clothes Mrs. Thorley took orders for men's shirts and cravats, so both ladies and gentlemen came to her shop. More than one romance had blossomed there.

As Celia had been to a good school and had graceful manners, she had been chosen to act as reception clerk—they called it "minding the parlor." She loved it. In the parlor she heard the talk of the town and she met so many people—admiring men, and women who thought Mrs. Thorley should choose someone "more settled" to receive callers, and young girls who carefully paid her no attention. Some of these girls were former schoolmates of hers. But that was when Celia had been Miss Garth of Kensaw Plantation. Now that she was a sewing-girl they found that they did not remember her very well; they explained that at school Celia had gone around with another crowd entirely.

But in spite of such annoyances, working at Mrs. Thorley's was fun.

Celia started toward Mr. Bernard's warehouse, on the waterfront. She would know next week if they were going to let her stay. Next week, next week—her footsteps beat it out on the brick sidewalk. All her life Celia had had a keen sense of the future, maybe because her present had never been exciting enough to match her dreams. Now this awareness of tomorrow pushed on her and threatened her. If they would only let her show them! The day she was five years old, Celia's Aunt Louisa had given her a needle and told her it was time she learned to make stitches. That day, Celia had found her talent. She could sew.

Now at twenty she could sew better than most women twice her age. She knew it, but nobody else in the shop knew it and she could not persuade them to let her prove it. Mrs. Thorley, though a competent woman of business, did not have a flexible mind. To her, an apprentice was a beginner who pulled bastings and sewed on buttons and did other dull little jobs that nobody else wanted. Celia felt a helpless anger as she walked along. She prayed again, "Please, *please* let me stay!"

She glanced toward the spire of St. Michael's. "Faith without works is dead." How often she had heard that text read in church. "All right, I'll do something about it," Celia told herself. "I'm not going back to the country and be a poor relation the rest of my life." At that minute the sun popped out, straight ahead of her, and struck her in the eyes with the promise of a golden day. Celia laughed softly. The world was full of promises, and if you put your mind to it you could make them real.

Lamboll Street was coming to life. In front of one residence a Negro boy was sweeping the sidewalk, at another a man was polishing the knocker on the door. Farther down the street a colored girl, gilt rings in her ears and a red kerchief on her head, was scrubbing the front steps. The soapsuds had a fresh clean smell. As she passed, Celia said "Good morning," and the Negroes answered, "Mornin', miss, happy day."

"Happy day to you," said Celia. She turned from Lamboll Street toward the wharfs along the Cooper River.

Early as it was, the waterfront was clackety with business. Men were going down to buy goods brought by the ships, or to load rice and timber to be sent out; women both white and colored were on their way to the fish-stalls to get their choice of the morning catch; sailors hurried about, their pigtails bobbing and their wide breeches flapping around their knees. Soldiers in rebel blue were scrambling into rowboats, which would carry them to the harbor forts for guard duty. Celia wondered why they were so careful to keep guards at those forts. Now in the fall of 1779 the war had been going on nearly five years and everybody knew it was practically over. But the men were good-looking in their bright blue coats, with their guns catching the light. They were having a fine time, too, shouting greetings from boat to boat and waving at pretty women along the wharfs.

Except for their officers, these fellows were mostly very young. Many of them were boys in their teens. Crack marksmen, they had been hunting in the woods and swamps around Charleston all their lives, though few of them had ever shot at anything that could shoot back. They were not part of the Continental troops, but the state militia. The Continentals were full-time soldiers in the national army commanded by General Washington; the militia were volunteers who did regular shifts of duty but between shifts went on with their usual business.

There were not many Continentals left now in South Carolina. Early in the war, before the men in Congress had signed the Declaration of Independence, the British had tried to take Charleston. They had made a thundering attack on Fort Moultrie, out there at the harbor entrance. Celia had not been in town then, but she had heard so much about the battle that she felt as if she had seen it. Fort Moultrie was manned by the Second South Carolina Regiment. Like the fellows yonder in the rowboats, most of those men had never seen a battle, but they fought one nobody would ever forget. They tore the British ships to pieces.

Next morning, the ships that could still move limped out of sight. From that day to this—more than three years now—nobody in Charleston had heard a British gun. Once the British had come close on the land side, but they had thought better of it and slipped away in the middle of the night.

For some time the South Carolina Continentals had kept guard at Fort Moultrie, under command of Lieutenant-Colonel Francis Marion. But as no attack had come, Marion and his regiment had been sent out of the state to points where they were more needed.

Meanwhile, Charleston had become the gateway for the whole Revolution. The rebels held several other seaports, and tradesmen in Europe would have been glad to sell them goods. But the king's navy patrolled the sea-lanes, and the king's seamen were so alert that few ships could come directly from Europe to America.

Charleston, however, did not depend on ships that crossed the ocean. Close to Charleston, in the southern sea, were the West Indies. In those rich islands lived hundreds of merchants—Dutchmen, Frenchmen, Portuguese, even some Englishmen—willing to sell anything to anybody.

Ships from their own countries brought goods to these island merchants. Other ships left Charleston loaded with rice and timber and indigo. The Charleston shipmasters traded in the islands, then they scurried back home. They brought guns for the fighting men, plows and tools for the homefolks, silks and looking-glasses for people rich enough to ignore the war.

Part of their merchandise they sold to people who lived in Charleston. But most of it went at high prices to another group of daredevils, this time men who worked on land. These fellows loaded wagons and drove north. Some of them carried luxuries, which they sold to rich people in towns behind the king's blockade; others took supplies to Washington's army, and got nothing in return but thanks.

It was a dangerous business. The king's navy kept a lookout for the Indies ships, and his army tried to catch the wagons. Some ships were taken, some men who started up the wagon track were never heard from again. But there were so many islands, so many crooked ways up the coast, and such bold men in the trade, that a surprising lot of stuff did get through.

One of the most enterprising of the shipowners bringing goods from the Indies was Godfrey Bernard, to whose warehouse Celia was going now. The warehouse was a brick building near the wharf where the boys were pushing off. As Celia approached, the sun caught her white kerchief and sleeve-ruffles till she fairly shone. The boys in the boats shouted at her and threw kisses over the water. Celia laughed, and as Mrs. Thorley was not here to see her, she tossed kisses back to them.

The heavy double doors of the warehouse stood open, and she went in. The entry was a small room, about fifteen feet wide and ten feet from the front door to another door at the back, which led to a storeroom. Facing the front was a counter on which stood a pair of scales, several account-books, and an inkpot with a tray of quills. Behind the counter, next to a window, a young man sat reading the *Gazette*. He was Darren Bernard, a cousin of Godfrey's who worked for the great man in a miscellaneous capacity. Darren and Celia were good friends.

As he heard footsteps Darren glanced up, then recognizing Celia he sprang to his feet, letting the newspaper fall into the chair behind him. "It's starting off to be a good day!" he greeted her. "You're here for the gauze?" He came toward the counter. Darren was a beautiful youth, strong and well made. His wavy brown hair was tied at the back of his neck with a ribbon bow. Always well dressed, today he wore a dark brown coat and light brown knee-breeches, with a white lawn cravat rippling down the front of his shirt. His white stockings fitted with hardly a wrinkle, and his knee-buckles and shoe-buckles were polished copper. Though Darren had nothing besides what he earned, he was such a likable fellow that he dined out nearly every day; and with all those free meals he could afford to dress like a gentleman of fashion.

Darren had been born of well-to-do parents, but his mother had died young, his father had drunk and gambled away all he owned and finally had been killed in a duel. When Darren was sixteen years old he had had to leave school and look for work. Since he wrote a good hand, his cousin Godfrey had given him a job keeping records. That was six years ago. His salary provided him with a room at an inn, a horse, and a servant who took care of his beautiful clothes. If anybody asked him what he did for a living, he replied good-naturedly, "I'm errand boy for my rich cousin." He showed no resentment of his father's profligate ways, and no ambition to mend his fortunes. Winsome and merry-minded, Darren enjoyed each day as it came and worried about tomorrow not at all.

He asked Celia if she had had breakfast, and she shook her head. "There's a kettle on the fire in back," Darren said. "Have you any scruples about drinking tea?"

"I'd love it!" she exclaimed.

Darren liked comfort. When it was his turn to mind the warehouse in the early morning he always had a hot drink on the fire. "I don't know why anybody should mind drinking tea," he remarked. "It's all smuggled in these days, it's not paying any tax to King George. Here's the gauze—you can look at it while I'm bringing the tray."

Dragging a chest from under the counter he took out seven rolls of gauze in different colors. Celia spread out her wrapping-cloth, and when he had laid the rolls on it Darren went into the back room, leaving her to gasp with pleasure at the lovely silk.

The gauze came in strips a yard wide and about thirty yards long, rolled on wooden rods like broomsticks. The colors were beautiful—dawn-pink and blue, green and greenish gold, red and orange and black—and the silk was so sheer that she could have read a book through it. One by one, Celia loosened the rolls and let the gauze flow through her fingers. Darren came in with a tea-tray, and as he set it on the counter she murmured, "Oh Darren, this is exquisite!"

He agreed, and asked, "What are you going to make with it?"

Celia picked up the teacup, tasted the tea, and felt a knot in her throat as she answered, "Nothing. It makes me so mad—" She broke off, looking up at his blithesome face. "I don't think," she added, "that you'd understand."

"Why not?" he asked genially.

"You're so content the way you are. Oh Darren, don't you ever want to—to *be* somebody?"

Darren chuckled. "I am somebody. I'm an appreciator."

"A what?"

"An appreciator," said Darren. "A person who appreciates things." He grinned. "People who do things need other people to appreciate them. Don't they?"

In spite of her worriment Celia began to laugh. Darren went on.

"I'm fairly bright and I've got pretty good taste. I can ap-preciate books and music, and good clothes, and good food and wine—why Celia, I'm mighty important in the world."

She agreed that he was. But Darren noticed that she was finger-ing the gauze again, and now there was such wistfulness in her look that he spoke to her with real concern. "Celia, what's the trouble?"

Celia looked up. "Maybe you won't understand, but I'm going to tell you anyhow. Talking will clear up my thoughts."

Darren crossed his arms on the counter. "Go ahead."

Celia told him her trial period was nearly over and she was afraid they might not give her a permanent job. "Or if they do," she said, "they'll keep me at buttons and bastings for years—till somebody dies or gets married or something like that. I'm the best dressmaker in town," she exclaimed, "and nobody knows it but me. Darren, I can sew like a dream! But how, oh how can I prove it?"

Darren reflected. "Could you buy some fine cloth and make a dress, in your own time?"

"Buy it? With what? Apprentices don't get wages, just their room and board. When I came to town last spring my uncle gave me ten dollars in paper money, for little things I might need. I've got four dollars left. Stuff like this—" she touched the gauze —"costs eighteen dollars a yard."

"Wrong," said Darren. "It costs thirty dollars a yard in paper money now. So much stuff is going up the wagon track, it makes things scarce in Charleston, and expensive. Yes, I see what you mean."

"And it takes more than cloth to make a dress, Darren. It takes tools for measuring and cutting, and I haven't any. And it takes time. Thousands of stitches to be set, one by one, and I have just an hour or two after supper. Oh, I've been thinking all over my mind! I *could* get some money if that was all. I've got some keepsakes that belonged to my mother. Her silver pins and earrings, and her silver shoe-buckles, and an old family necklace my father gave her when they were married—"

"But you wouldn't sell those!" he exclaimed. A sentimental fellow, Darren spoke with dismay.

"Oh yes I would," Celia retorted. "I'm not going back to the country and be bored to death. I'm staying here. And I *can* sew."

Behind her, from the doorway, she heard a man's voice.

"Can you make a dress that *really* fits?"

Celia spun around; Darren, who had been watching her and not the door, jerked up his head; then as they recognized a friend they both relaxed. The newcomer, Captain Jimmy Rand of the state militia, stood leaning his shoulder on the side of the doorway. As Celia turned he took off his hat, and the sun glistened on his black hair. With a lazy stretch as though he had nothing on earth to do, Jimmy strolled in. He gave a casual salute to Darren —who did a shift of militia duty once a week—and resting his elbow on the counter he turned to Celia. His mouth had a quiver of mischief.

# CHAPTER 2

*J*IMMY'S FULL NAME was Captain James de Courcey Rand.
Tall and lean and dark, he looked leaner and darker than ever
in his smart blue uniform. He had an ugly, engaging face, scooped
at the temples, bony at the jaw, with a wide mouth and a look of
being amused by life in general.

Jimmy lived in town with his widowed mother. His father
had been a rice planter, and Jimmy was the younger of two sons.
Being the younger son he had not inherited much when his father died, and he had his own way to make in the world. But unlike Darren, Jimmy was ambitious: he had studied law in England,
and was now working in an office on Broad Street, where it was
said he had a future bright enough to make up for his misfortune
in having been born after his brother.

His brother was Miles Rand of Bellwood Plantation. Though
they had shared the family fortune like the lion and the mouse,
Miles and Jimmy were good friends. Miles was married and was
soon to have an heir—Celia knew this because Mrs. Miles Rand
had sent an order for baby-clothes to Mrs. Thorley's. This was
another reason Celia liked working there, you knew what was
going on.

Darren had known Jimmy all his life; Celia had known him
since one day about a month ago when Jimmy came into the

shop to order some shirts, and lingered to look at samples of linen in one of the parlor cabinets. It was a rainy day and there were no other visitors, so in a little while Celia and Jimmy found themselves talking to each other. Jimmy seemed quite unaware that a sewing-girl was not usually considered the social equal of a planter's son, and before long they were having a fine time. Since that day he had dropped in often.

Now as he leaned on the counter beside her, Jimmy did not immediately go on with the question he had asked from the doorway. Instead, with his usual lazy manner, he said,

"You look mighty pretty this morning, my brown-eyed blonde. Mighty agreeable picture for a man who's been on guard duty all night." Glancing at her empty cup he added, "Darren, I've just come from Fort Moultrie, and I dropped in because you always have something hot on the fire."

Darren said he would brew a fresh pot of tea. He went to get it, and Jimmy turned back to Celia, his sunburnt cheeks creasing in a grin. Jimmy needed a shave, but otherwise he showed no ill effect of his vigil.

"Tell me something," he began. "You were saying that you'd sell your mother's necklace before you'd go home."

He was speaking soberly now. During their brief acquaintance Jimmy and Celia had met only in the shop or in some public place such as this. They liked each other, but they had never discussed their personal affairs. Celia looked at him directly. "Did that shock you, Jimmy? It shocked Darren."

Jimmy had a keen sense of family, she knew. But he smiled and shook his head. "No, it didn't shock me. I figured you had a reason."

"Of course I've got a reason," she returned. She reflected that Darren was sweet and a darling, but Jimmy had sense.

There was a pause. Celia noticed Jimmy's hand as it lay on the counter, very brown against his blue sleeve. He was not drumming his fingers nor fiddling with anything. His hand looked strong and relaxed. Jimmy said, "Do you want to tell us about it?"

"I'd like to," said Celia.

Darren brought the tea and filled cups for them all. While they drank it, Celia told him and Jimmy about her uncle and aunt and her cousin Roy.

.⌣.

Celia's uncle, William Garth, owned a rice plantation which he had inherited from his father. The plantation—called Kensaw for an Indian tribe that used to hunt there—was pleasantly situated on a little stream that ran into the Ashley River. Though not large, it was well organized and prosperous. But under William's management it did not stay that way.

Poor William went through life in a state of gentle bewilderment. His head was full of cobwebby learning; he knew Greek and Latin, and he could tell you all about the kings of ancient history, but he did not know how to raise and market a crop. He did not know how, and he could not learn. Kensaw Plantation slackened, got out of order; William bumbled along. He married and had two children, and his life turned into a struggle to make his slipshod property give them the advantages his wife thought they ought to have.

William's younger brother Edward, Celia's father, was more enterprising. Since he had no land, Edward became an accountant in the office of a rice broker in Charleston. He married an orphan girl who brought him a good dowry, and when Celia was born her future looked promising.

But when Celia was a year old, about the time that George the Third was crowned king, there was an epidemic in Charleston and both her parents died. Celia's only relative was her Uncle William, who now came to town to look after her affairs.

He did so with a good deal of dismay. William had been fond of his brother, but he expected his brother's child to be a burden on him, and if there was one thing William did not want, it was any more burdens. But when he reached Charleston William found out what a good businessman Celia's father had been. Not only was her mother's dowry intact, but Edward had added to it from his earnings. William took Celia to Kensaw, and told his wife Louisa that Celia would be no expense to them. Louisa drew a breath of relief.

Celia grew up with her cousins. The elder cousin was Roy,

four years older than she was and the pride of Louisa's heart. Though Roy was both clever and handsome Celia did not like him, because he was also a spoilt brat who thought that wherever he was standing, there was the middle of the world. But she did not have to put up with him much. When Roy was eight years old he went to live with Louisa's brother in Georgetown so he could go to the excellent school established there by the indigo planters, and he was at home only on his vacations. Several years later Roy was sent to school in England. William could not afford this, but people expected a planter to send his son to school in England, and here as elsewhere William tried to do what was expected of him. Nobody could ever say of William that he did not try.

The other cousin was a girl, Harriet, a shy little thing who had no distinction at all. She and Celia got along well enough, for Celia felt sorry for her, and treated her gently.

Between the two girls Louisa showed no favoritism. They had the same toys, the same number of new dresses, the same holiday visits to their friends; and Louisa gave them the same training in housewifery and good manners. If she did not give them much tenderness, it was because she did not have much to give. Louisa was fond of her husband in a protective sort of way, and she adored Roy, but this used up her stock of affection. She did her duty by the girls. Louisa always did her duty.

Since William was not practical, Louisa thought this made it important that she should be. She managed her affairs with grim competence. Her house was so neat you would hardly have thought anybody lived there. Meals were served on time. The food was wholesome and they used all leftovers. And in spite of William's haziness in money matters, by her own stern scrimping Louisa managed to send Roy a generous allowance and put aside something every year toward a dowry for Harriet.

Louisa taught the girls to read and write, to spin and sew. Then, when Celia was ten years old and Harriet nine, Louisa sent them to school in Charleston. Here they had lessons in dancing, fine needlework, and other accomplishments expected of gentlewomen. After three years they came home. Now they had nothing to do but grow up and get married.

The war began when Celia was sixteen. Roy had finished his English school and was making a tour of France, but the outbreak of war caused a financial panic in the Colonies and Louisa could no longer keep up his allowance. Roy had to come home. Handsome, well dressed, with polished manners and expensive tastes, he arrived at Kensaw Plantation.

He was appalled at the rundown state of the place. Roy had always thought of himself as a rich young man. But unlike his father, Roy was not vague. He determined to repair his fortunes, and he decided that an important step in this direction would be to get the girls well married.

He set out to make himself agreeable to every girl in the neighborhood who had an eligible brother. He filled the house with well-to-do unmarried men. Before long Harriet was engaged to a young man named Ogden. Young Mr. Ogden had pale eyes, a hawk nose, and a receding chin, and in profile he looked like a fish, but he was the eldest son of a family who had a broad plantation farther up the Ashley River. Roy had his mother's talent for getting things done.

But though Roy did everything he could for Celia, she turned down two good offers. She said both men were perfectly impossible. The first was named Mr. Hawkins. He was rich, but he was also a tightwad. Mr. Hawkins made some fumbling attempts to be romantic, but Celia was pretty sure he had observed that besides her dowry she had rare ability to spin and sew, and he figured her skill would save him more than the cost of her keep. She said no.

Her other admirer, Mr. McArdle, was a widower with three small children. Again Celia declined. She was not fond of babies, and she thought minding her own would be bother enough without minding somebody else's too.

Celia was in no hurry to get married. She knew that a girl whose parents had left her well off would always have beaus on the porch.

She worked hard on Harriet's trousseau. She did not mind, for she liked to sew and she expected to have an equally elaborate pile of clothes when she got married. The wedding was beautiful. It was not until afterward, when the bills came, that William or Roy, or even Louisa, realized how much this happy event had cost.

Finally, Roy told his parents that Celia simply had to hear the facts. So one afternoon a maid came to Celia's room to say that her uncle and aunt wanted to see her in William's study downstairs.

In the study Louisa and William sat side by side. Louisa had an account-book on her knee; William was tying knots in his handkerchief. Louisa looked grim, William looked miserable. Louisa did the talking.

She said the worthy widower, Mr. McArdle, had been distressed when Celia refused him. Louisa thought Mr. McArdle would renew his offer if Celia's guardians should hint that she had changed her mind.

Astonished, Celia said she certainly had not changed her mind. All Mr. McArdle wanted was a nursemaid, and it would be mighty convenient to get a nursemaid who would bring him a dowry.

With a sigh and a shake of her head, Aunt Louisa said Roy was right. It was their duty to tell her.

•~•

When she got this far in her narrative, Celia paused. She took a sip of tea, set the cup in the saucer, and looked thoughtfully at Darren and Jimmy.

"I didn't have any dowry," she said.

Jimmy nodded sagely, as if he had expected this. But Darren demanded, "You mean they had taken it?"

"Oh no. It was just used up. Aunt Louisa had the accounts. She had spent it on my clothes, books, school fees, things like that. She said she had hoped she wouldn't have to tell me. She had hoped I would get married to some man who would love me for myself alone. Because they couldn't afford to give me anything."

Celia paused again. The men were listening with interest, and she went on.

"Well, I knew I wasn't going to marry Mr. McArdle. So I decided to get a job. They didn't like that idea at all. Especially Roy didn't like it. He knew people would smile, and say it seemed the

Garths weren't as well off as they'd been pretending. But I said if they didn't let me get a job now I'd get one as soon as I came of age. And the bills for the wedding kept on coming. So finally Roy said they might as well give in. I think he figured I was going to be an old maid, and dressmaking is genteel work and it keeps an old maid from being dependent on her kinfolks. So Uncle William brought me to town and apprenticed me to Mrs. Thorley."

Celia shrugged, laughing a little.

"Poor Uncle William, he did hate it so. I think he was ashamed of them all. Before we left home he asked me to walk with him down by the river. He gave me the jewelry and told me to take care of it, especially the necklace. That's an heirloom. He wasn't sure how old it was, but the first Garths who came from England about a hundred years ago brought it with them. Uncle William said it had come to my father by my grandfather's will, so now it was mine.

"I'd hate to sell the necklace. But I'm not going back there. Understand?"

"Yes I do," said Darren, and Jimmy remarked,

"You're not of age yet, are you?"

"Not for another seven months—next April."

"Then you couldn't sell the necklace before April," said Jimmy, "even if you wanted to. But you needn't worry about that. Remember what I asked you when I came in?"

Celia nodded. "You asked if I could make a dress that would *really* fit." She said emphatically, "Yes I can."

Jimmy reached for the teapot. "Couple of days ago," he said in his lazy drawl, "I heard a lady say there wasn't a dressmaker in Charleston who could do that."

"I can!" Celia insisted.

Jimmy raised his hard brown hand in a gesture of caution. Again she saw that quirk of mischief at the corner of his mouth. "The lady I have in mind," he warned, "is not easy to please."

"Let me try, Jimmy!"

Calmly, Jimmy continued. "She's very rich. She's used to having her clothes made in Paris."

Out of the corner of her eye Celia caught a glimpse of Darren, who stood on the opposite side of the counter, his chin on his fists. Over Darren's face was creeping a look of astonished recognition.

If Jimmy had noticed Darren's expression he gave no sign of it. "Now this lady I'm talking about," Jimmy went on, "has just lately come to town from her country place. The other evening Mother and I were having supper with her, and she was lamenting about her trouble. Because of the war, it's five years since she's been to Paris. She has tried dressmakers on this side, but none of them has quite suited her."

"Not even Mrs. Thorley?"

Jimmy shook his head. "And she claimed to be in great distress because her old clothes were falling apart. They didn't look it to me, they looked beautiful and I told her so."

"What did she say?"

"She said I was a silly-billy who wouldn't know a dress from a dishrag. Now would you like—"

"Look out, Celia!" said Darren.

His voice was so sharp that she turned quickly. "Why? Do you know who Jimmy's talking about?"

"Yes," said Darren. "He's talking about Vivian Lacy."

Jimmy laughed under his breath. Celia asked Darren, "Who's that?"

"Mrs. Herbert Lacy of Sea Garden," said Darren. "Jimmy's got no business—well at least, Jimmy, you ought to tell her something about Vivian first!"

Jimmy was still chuckling. Celia said to Darren, "You tell me. Is she—what is she like?"

"Well, let's see," said Darren. "She's at least sixty-five years old, maybe more."

Celia felt a touch of disappointment. It would certainly have been more interesting to make clothes for a woman who was young and pretty. But she answered brightly, "Oh, that doesn't matter. I like nice old ladies."

Darren groaned. Jimmy laughed out loud.

"Celia," Jimmy said frankly, "let's get this straight right now. Vivian is not a 'nice old lady.'"

"But—?"

"She's had her own way," said Jimmy, "every day of her life."

"How long have you known her?" Celia asked. She could not help feeling apprehensive.

"I've always known her," Jimmy answered. "My father was related to one of her husbands."

"*One* of her husbands? How many has she had?"

"Five," Jimmy said, laughing as Darren added,

"And every one of them, when he died, left her richer than she was before. Except Mr. Lacy—he's rich, but he's still around."

"Are you related to her too?"

"By marriage I am," said Darren. "Another husband. She's Godfrey Bernard's mother."

Celia looked wonderingly at Darren and then at Jimmy. "What happened to all those husbands? Did she poison them?"

"Oh no," Jimmy returned. "If Vivian felt like killing a man she'd do it, but she wouldn't use anything sneaky like poison. Vivian would shoot him in the middle of Broad Street." He continued more seriously. "Maybe Darren is right, Celia, and you shouldn't try to work for her. It won't be easy."

But Celia doubled up her fists. "I don't care if she's the devil's grandmother. This very morning I made up my mind that I was going to do something about keeping a steady job. And now if I've got a chance I'm not going to miss it."

Jimmy gave her an understanding smile, though he warned her, "I can't promise anything. But I'll tell Vivian there's a new girl at Mrs. Thorley's, a girl who can really fit clothes. Then maybe —just maybe—she'll send word to Mrs. Thorley that she'd like to see you."

Celia felt a lump of excitement in her stomach. Just then she heard the bells of St. Michael's. "Oh my goodness, is that seven o'clock? Wrap up the gauze, Darren, I've got to get back."

Jimmy took the package, saying he would walk with her to the shop. Celia was fairly tingling with eagerness.

"When can you see Mrs. Lacy?" she asked as they walked along Lamboll Street.

"At *her* pleasure," Jimmy answered. "Celia my dear," he explained mirthfully, "people don't drop in on Vivian. They send over to ask when they can call."

"Oh," Celia said faintly. But she could not help admiring anybody who could arrange her life so exactly to suit herself. As they reached the shop Jimmy handed her the bundle of gauze. "I'll go home now and see Mother," he said, "and pat my dog, and get some sleep. But before the day's over I'll send a note to Vivian. And here," he added, "I'll let you have this." He unfastened a silver chain attached to a button on his vest, and drew the other end of the chain from his vest pocket. At the free end was a rabbit's foot. "This is the left hind foot of a rabbit," Jimmy said with a grin, "shot on a Friday the thirteenth."

"That's just right!" Celia exclaimed. "I was born on a Friday the thirteenth."

"Then by all means you must have this. My colored boy Amos shot this rabbit and gave me the two hind feet for luck. I put one on my dog's collar and I've carried the other myself."

He put the rabbit's foot into her hand. "I'll carry it every minute," said Celia.

They laughed at each other. Jimmy was not a handsome man, but as she looked up at him Celia thought he was an impressive one, with his strong lean face and his coat bright blue in the sunshine. The black bristles stood out on his jaw.

Jimmy gave a squeeze to her hand as it held the rabbit's foot, and went off toward home.

# CHAPTER 3

*T*HE BREAKFAST BELL rang while Celia was delivering the gauze to Miss Loring in the sewing room. The girls, who had been at work for an hour while breakfast was being prepared, joyfully took off their thimbles and trooped downstairs.

The dining room was on the first floor, behind the parlor. There was a long table with Mrs. Thorley's armchair at the head. On either side of Mrs. Thorley were the seats of Miss Loring and Miss Perry, and below them came the others in order of importance. Celia's place was down near the foot.

The girls stood behind their chairs, and the two colored maids stood by the door, all waiting for Mrs. Thorley. In their white caps and kerchiefs and their fresh homespun dresses, unbleached brown or dyed blue with Carolina indigo, they made a pretty group. Through the doorway came the sound and smell of sizzling ham.

Beside each plate was a glass of milk. Mrs. Thorley served neither tea nor coffee. This was part of her policy of not taking sides in the war.

The people of Charleston were divided in their opinions. The majority of them were rebels, but there were a good many Tories, still loyal to the king. In South Carolina as in the other colonies the Tories had organized their own green-coated regiments to serve alongside the redcoats of the king's army. If anybody asked Mrs. Thorley which of these parties she favored, Mrs. Thorley replied that she was a simple dressmaker, willing to leave such weighty matters to weighty minds. She did not discuss the war and she forbade the girls to do so. Taking no sides, she kept her customers. If she had served either tea or coffee, that would have been taking sides.

Some of the rebels drank tea, but the most violent of them did not. Remembering the tax on tea at the start of the war, they regarded tea as a symbol of British tyranny and refused to touch it. They drank coffee instead, and called it Liberty Tea. But since hardly anybody in Charleston had served coffee at breakfast before the war, serving it now would have marked Mrs. Thorley as a rebel.

On the other hand, the Tories, bent on proving their loyalty to Britain and King George, drank tea on every possible occasion. If Mrs. Thorley had served tea people would have said she was a Tory. So Mrs. Thorley served milk.

Celia thought this a sensible arrangement. The war was nearly over and the rebels were winning—the *Gazette* said so every week—but in the meantime the shop had to stay open. Celia was glad the rebels were winning, because Darren and Jimmy were on that side and they were her best friends, but she really could not see that it would make any difference to her whether the country was run by King George or the Continental Congress. She was concerned with other matters. Now this rich old Mrs. Lacy—

The thought of Mrs. Lacy struck sparks in her mind. If she won the favor of a rich customer her job would be sure, and she would be independent of Roy. I don't care if she is an old crosspatch, Celia thought, her hands tightening on the back of her chair. I'll put up with anything.

Mrs. Thorley appeared at the dining room door. The two maids stepped aside. Mrs. Thorley came in, carrying her Bible with a ribbon marking a place between the leaves. The voices of the girls dwindled into silence. For a moment Mrs. Thorley stood by her chair, tall, broad, starched. Then with ponderous piety she opened the Bible at the place marked by the ribbon, and in her deep voice she read them a passage from the Psalms. When she closed the book the girls and servants bowed their heads and recited the Lord's Prayer. Then the chairs scraped back, the girls sat down, and their talk rose again as the maids passed the dishes.

For breakfast they had ham, hominy grits with butter, hot cornbread, and the glasses of milk. Ham-and-hominy was Celia's favorite breakfast, but this morning she hardly noticed what she was eating. I wonder why Mrs. Lacy is so hard to sew for, she thought. Probably she's stooped—most old women are, and it's hard to make clothes look well over a hump. Or maybe her stomach sticks out—

Celia heard her name, and started. The girl next to her was saying something. This girl was Agnes Kennedy, one of three girls with whom Celia shared a bedroom on the third floor. Agnes Kennedy had blue eyes and brown hair and a sweet disposition. "Your mind is a thousand miles away," she reproved Celia gently.

"I'm sorry. What were you asking me?"

Agnes answered with a sweet smile. She was so sweet that sometimes Celia wanted to slap her. Agnes said, "I wasn't asking anything. Becky was."

Becky Duren, another of Celia's roommates, was watching her with a gay teasing smile. Becky was a curly-headed flibbertigibbet who seldom thought about anything but men. The daughter of a small farmer near Moncks Corner, Becky had been taught to sew by her German grandmother and she was good at it, but she was not interested in sewing. She had come to town because she wanted to get married, and in spite of Mrs. Thorley's strict rules Becky had met dozens of men in Charleston and was now engaged to three of them. She was going to get married as soon as she could make up her mind among her adorers; meanwhile she stitched dutifully and dreamed up new ways to tease them. "I was just asking," Becky said merrily to Celia, "who's your beau?"

Celia stopped short, her glass of milk halfway to her lips. "Don't be silly. I haven't got a beau."

"Oooh!" said Becky. "There was a tall dark man in rebel blue walking with you this morning—I saw him—I was opening a window—"

"Oh for pity's sake," snapped Celia. "Captain Rand is just one of the customers."

"Oh now Celia," murmured Agnes, "Becky didn't mean anything."

One of the older girls, Ruth Elbert, asked Celia what names were on the appointment list today. Ruth Elbert was about twenty-eight years old, tall and thin, with a sharp chin and beaky nose. She had a brother in the Continental Army, and Ruth herself was an ardent rebel. Addressing her as "Miss Elbert" (for Ruth had been here ten years and was a person of some influence in the shop), Celia said she had not read the list yet.

"Mrs. Kirby's going to be here," said Becky Duren. "I heard her say so yesterday."

"That chatterbox!" said Ruth. "She talks and talks, she stays forever. Who's making her dress?"

"I am," said a girl across the table, named Pearl Todd, a pretty creature with light brown hair and a creamy skin. She was Celia's third roommate. Pearl added, "I like Mrs. Kirby."

"Oh yes," Ruth said acidly, "of course *you* do."

There was a sudden silence. Mrs. Kirby was a Tory, and always wore a touch of Tory green somewhere about her costume, partly to show which side she was on and partly because green was so becoming to her red hair and green eyes. Pearl Todd had Tory sympathies too. There was even a rumor that she was engaged to a greenjacket. As Ruth spoke, Pearl gave her an angry look, while one or two other girls who were hotly rebel glared at Pearl, and for a moment it seemed that there might be a dispute that would bring stern words from Mrs. Thorley. But before anybody could say anything more, Agnes Kennedy interposed brightly, "It's going to be the nicest day! Don't you love this weather?"

Some day, Celia thought, I'm going to really try to make her mad. Just to see if it can be done.

But the others seemed glad Agnes had changed the subject. The conversation went on, about the shop and the day ahead. Celia glanced at Agnes, serenely finishing her ham. Agnes always looked serene. She had her life all planned. Her father was one of the Scotch-Irish farmers who grew flax in the Williamsburg district, and Agnes had grown up in the country near Kingstree. She was engaged to a smart young farmer named Robert Mac-Nair, and they were going to be married when he got his place in order for a family.

Robert would raise flax while Agnes and her maidservants would spin linen yarn. Twice a year Robert and Agnes would take the yarn to Kingstree, to the weaver. These trips to Kingstree would be the high spots of the year for them; they would stay a week or more, visiting friends, meeting strangers, hearing the news. Between trips they would live peacefully, working six days a week and going to the Presbyterian Church on Sundays. They would have a house with wide fireplaces, and a pantry full of good food, and a cat with kittens, and a family of nice children. Agnes was not much interested in the war, and neither was young Mr. MacNair. Those flax-growers around Kingstree were busy and prosperous; they had no quarrel with anybody.

Maybe I could be as calm as she is, thought Celia, if I was content to spend my life spinning flax. But I'm not. I want things to happen to me!

Mrs. Thorley tapped her spoon on the side of her glass. The girls fell silent, and Mrs. Thorley rose to make the announcements.

Miss Duren was to report for a special assignment. Miss Todd would relieve Miss Garth in the parlor during the dinner hour. Miss Kennedy was to go on an errand at nine o'clock. These errands were carefully allotted, for Mrs. Thorley said young people needed exercise and worked better for it. The announcements over, she tapped the glass again and the girls left the dining room to go on with the day.

Celia opened the parlor. This was a pleasant room, with flower prints on the walls and white curtains at the windows, and chairs and sofas inviting callers to pass the time. In the best-lighted spots were cabinets with glass doors where Mrs. Thorley showed her wares. There were buckles and feathers, laces and hair ornaments, a pair of gentlemen's stockings knitted of white silk thread on needles finer than the finest hairpins. Women's stockings were not important, since you saw so little of them. But a man's stockings, visible from his knee to his ankle, were a conspicuous part of his costume. When a man wore handmade silk hose like these, the chances were that they had cost him more than his coat.

In the largest cabinet Mrs. Thorley had placed four fashion dolls, twenty inches high, dressed like ladies and gentlemen in the newest styles. One lady doll wore blue silk, the other white and gold; they had powdered hair and they carried little fans. The man dolls wore white wigs. One of them had on a purple coat and tan knee-breeches, the other a black velvet suit with lace cuffs. The both wore white stockings and buckled shoes.

Celia drew a chair up to her worktable, and while she waited for callers she began sewing a button on one of Jimmy's new shirts.

There could hardly be any news from Jimmy for several days, she reflected. He had a lot to do; his employer, Mr. Carter, was an elderly man, and more and more was leaving details in Jimmy's hands. Besides, Jimmy had said he could not see Mrs. Lacy until she felt like seeing him. Celia felt a shiver of suspense run down her back. "I'll just have to be patient!" she reminded herself impatiently. She had never felt so impatient in her life.

•❦•

She had to wait three days. Then Jimmy came in to tell her the matter was arranged: Mrs. Lacy had agreed to send for her.

He did not have a chance to tell her much else, for the parlor was full of visitors and they all wanted something. A fidgety girl asked Celia to draw a curtain; a short-tempered fat man sent her up to the fitting-room to tell his wife he didn't have all day to sit here; another man asked her to bring him the *Gazette* to read while he waited; two women from out of town, enraptured by the displays, wanted to know the price of everything; and Mrs. Kirby, the pretty redheaded Tory, asked for a glass of water. When Celia came back with the glass of water Mrs. Kirby was telling Jimmy about the remarkable cleverness of her little boy George (named for his majesty, she explained, *not* Mr. Washington).

Mrs. Kirby was careful to say "Mr." Washington instead of "General" Washington. The British and Tories all did that. They held that the rebels, in revolt against their lawful government, had no right to military titles. As Jimmy wore a business suit today, Mrs. Kirby could pretend not to know which side he was on. This she was glad to do, since there was no other attractive young man in the room for her to talk to.

Another lady came in. Her name was Mrs. Baxter, she was a rebel, and she proclaimed it by wearing a blue velvet hat with a buff plume. Mrs. Baxter greeted Jimmy with a smile, but she gave Mrs. Kirby the icy stare she gave any woman who wore a kerchief of Tory green. She told Celia she had come to look at the new gauzes, and would Celia please run upstairs and tell Miss Loring? Oh but first, exclaimed Mrs. Baxter, she simply must see that fashion doll in blue. While Celia was upstairs, would she ask Miss Loring how long it would take to make a dress like this?

Celia said "Yes ma'am," and started toward the door that opened on the staircase. At that moment a maid entered to tell Mrs. Kirby she could come up now for her fitting. Mrs. Kirby went upstairs, Celia following to report the wants of Mrs. Baxter. When Celia came back to the parlor she found that now Mrs. Baxter had taken possession of Jimmy and was telling him about *her* little boy George (named for *General* Washington, she explained, not that stupid old king).

Jimmy had an appointment with a client. By the time the maid summoned Mrs. Baxter, it was time for him to leave. Celia was straightening some samples of goods in a showcase. Jimmy came over, looked with apparent interest at the samples, then turning his back to the room he spoke in an undertone. "Did you know your cousin Roy was about to be married?"

Interested, Celia shook her head.

"Our office handles your uncle's affairs," Jimmy continued, "and Mrs. Carter got a letter this morning. Roy's marrying a girl named Sophie Torrance."

"Who's Sophie Torrance?"

"I've never met her. But the Torrances are planters on Goose Creek."

"Rich?"

"Pretty well off."

"He would," said Celia.

Jimmy chuckled. "Well anyway, you'll hear from Vivian Lacy in a day or two. Got the rabbit's foot?"

"In my pocket."

"Rub it hard. I'll rub the one on Rosco's collar soon as I get home."

He went out. Celia slipped her hand into her pocket and gave the rabbit's foot a pinch.

This was Friday. She hoped a message would come Saturday from Mrs. Lacy, but nothing happened. Jimmy had told her she might get a glimpse of Mrs. Lacy Sunday at St. Michael's, but again she was disappointed, for though there were several old ladies in the congregation they were all customers she had met in the shop.

No word came Monday. Nothing came Tuesday or Wednesday.

Too restless to keep still, when she went up to the bedroom Wednesday night Celia decided to give her hair a good brushing. She brushed so long and so hard that even gentle Agnes protested, "If you don't stop you're going to pull your hair right off your head!" Agnes sat by the candle, writing to Robert MacNair. Celia's other two roommates, Becky and Pearl, were downstairs entertaining boy-friends in the little parlor where the girls received callers after working hours.

Celia said she felt like taking a turn in the hall, to stretch her legs before bedtime. She went out and walked up and down. It had been five days now since Jimmy's visit to the parlor. What was the matter with Mrs. Lacy? Maybe she had changed her mind. Maybe she had decided not to have any clothes made till she could go to Paris again.

Here on the third-floor hall there was a window opening on the front of the house. Celia pushed up the sash and looked out.

Below her lay Charleston, glistening between two rivers. Charleston was built on a little peninsula shaped like Florida, and the shop was at the south end. At Celia's left, on the west side, was the Ashley River, and on her right the Cooper; far ahead of her was the narrow neck of land that joined Charleston to the mainland; and behind her, where the two rivers met, there was the sea.

Toward her right, by the Cooper River, she could see the big dark block of the Exchange. This was the customhouse, post office, and business center where men gathered to talk about trade. Under the Exchange was the vault where they had locked up the first shipload of tea that came bearing the king's tax.

Most people had not yet gone to bed, and the streets were lined with lighted windows. Jimmy had said Mrs. Lacy's house was on Meeting Street near Tradd. Celia could see both streets clearly: Meeting Street ran north and south, halfway between the rivers, while Tradd Street reached from river to river across town. A block above Tradd she saw Broad Street and St. Michael's. In the spire of St. Michael's was a beacon light that guided ships to Charleston and lit the whole neighborhood around the church.

In the street before the church, where carriages had to go around it, stood the statue of William Pitt. The people had put it there to honor Mr. Pitt for persuading the British Parliament to repeal the Stamp Act. The Stamp Act trouble had occurred when Celia was six years old and she did not know much about it, but she thought the statue of Mr. Pitt was the silliest thing she had ever seen. It had been made in England, where the sculptor had had a notion that an English hero ought to look like a man from ancient Rome, so instead of showing Mr. Pitt in his own clothes this artist had dressed him in a Roman toga. The effect was as if the great man had heard a noise in the night and had rushed out with a sheet wrapped around him.

Behind her, Celia heard a door opening. A candle cast a glow on the wall, and she heard the jangle of a bell. Plump little Miss Perry, holding a dressing-gown around her, was giving notice that it was nearly nine o'clock and if you weren't ready for bed you'd better hurry. Celia turned toward her room, and Miss Perry smiled at her brightly. Celia was too impatient to feel amiable; however, since Miss Perry was a supervisor she smiled back.

But the next day, Thursday, when they had finished their midday dinner and Mrs. Thorley rose to make the announcements, she said, "Miss Duren will relieve Miss Garth in the parlor at four. At that time Miss Garth will report to my office."

Celia felt a little jump in her throat.

Across the table Becky whispered, "What does she want with you?"

Celia managed to shrug. "How would I know?"

It was not quite four when Becky came to take her place. Becky loved minding the parlor. You never could tell what interesting men might drop in.

Celia dashed up to her room to make sure her cap and kerchief were straight, then down again to Mrs. Thorley's door. Steadying herself with a long breath, she knocked, and Mrs. Thorley's deep voice bade her enter.

Mrs. Thorley sat at her desk, a large solid block of authority in gray linen. Celia curtsied, and as she did so she found herself wondering what Mrs. Thorley looked like without any clothes on. Stop this, she warned herself, you must not be having sassy thoughts now. Keep your mind on pleasing that old lady from Sea Garden.

"Sit down, Miss Garth," said Mrs. Thorley. Her voice sounded like a roll of drums.

"Thank you ma'am," said Celia. She sat down, crossed her ankles, and laced her fingers on her lap. It was a pretty posture.

"I am happy to tell you, Miss Garth," said Mrs. Thorley, "that your work here has been satisfactory."

"Thank you, Mrs. Thorley." (Is that all she wants? Hasn't she heard from the old witch?)

"As you probably recall," said Mrs. Thorley, "your term of apprenticeship will expire at the end of this week. I shall be glad to have you continue as before."

"Thank you ma'am. I'm glad you're pleased with me." (Just as I thought. She expects me to go on "as before"—pulling bastings and sewing on buttons—of course any job is better than no job, but oh Lord, please! Celia slid her hand into her pocket and rubbed the rabbit's foot. Was it wicked to pray with your mind and rub a rabbit's foot with your hand? She did not know, but she kept on doing both.)

Mrs. Thorley was saying that besides her room and board,

Celia would now receive an allowance of eight dollars a month in South Carolina currency. Celia murmured something, she never remembered what, because just then Mrs. Thorley added, "Now I have another matter to discuss."

There was a sudden sharpness in her voice. For some reason Mrs. Thorley was not pleased.

"Miss Garth," said Mrs. Thorley, "are you acquainted with Mrs. Herbert Lacy?"

"No ma'am," said Celia. Her hand, out of sight in her pocket, closed around the rabbit's foot.

"You have heard of her, I suppose?"

"I've heard of her, yes ma'am."

"This morning," Mrs. Thorley said crisply, "I received a note from Mrs. Lacy, asking that you call to discuss some dress-making."

Celia wondered what made Mrs. Thorley so snappish. You'd think she'd be glad this rich woman wanted to patronize her shop.

"Miss Garth," said Mrs. Thorley, "did you know Mrs. Lacy was going to write to me?" She sounded as if she thought somebody had been up to something behind her back.

Her hand in her pocket, Celia crossed her fingers. "No ma'am," she returned. (Well, I didn't *know* she was going to write! I just hoped she would and was scared she wouldn't.)

There was a brief pause. Celia tried to look relaxed and intelligent, and not sassy.

"Have you any idea," Mrs. Thorley asked her sternly, "why Mrs. Lacy should want you to do her sewing?"

Celia had planned an answer for this one. "I made a lot of dresses at home. She might know somebody who likes my work."

"Possibly," said Mrs. Thorley. She glanced down at her own large strong hands, folded on the desk. Mrs. Lacy's request had surprised her, and Mrs. Thorley did not like to be surprised. After a moment's thought she looked up. "Miss Garth," she said suddenly, "do you want to accept this assignment?"

It was the first time since she came to the shop that anybody had asked Celia if she wanted to do anything. Smiling with astonishment and pleasure, she exclaimed, "Oh yes ma'am! Yes!"

Again, Mrs. Thorley considered before she spoke. "Generally," she said, "when a customer makes a request for one of the young ladies, I am happy to grant it." She looked at Celia directly. "In this case, however, I believe it would be unwise to do so. Mrs. Lacy is—"

"Oh please, Mrs. Thorley!"

Mrs. Thorley was not used to being interrupted. She went on as though Celia had not spoken. "Mrs. Lacy is exacting in her requirements."

(If you mean she's an old crank, thought Celia, I've heard that already.)

"The friend who recommended you," Mrs. Thorley went on, "has no doubt exaggerated your ability. I am afraid, Miss Garth, that you exaggerate it yourself. Sewing for your family at home is quite different from sewing for a woman like Mrs. Lacy." She paused again, to let that sink in. "Therefore, Miss Garth, I believe you will be wise not to undertake it. If this is your decision, I will write to Mrs. Lacy and offer to send her a dressmaker of more experience."

This time she waited for an answer. (The thought flashed into Celia's head—I understand. She doesn't dare say no to Mrs. Lacy. So she wants me to do it. Well, I won't.) Aloud she said, "I'd like to try it, Mrs. Thorley."

Mrs. Thorley unclasped her hands and clasped them again. There was a rustle of starched linen as she changed her position in her chair. It struck Celia that even Mrs. Thorley's clothes sounded stern. "Very well," said Mrs. Thorley. "I shall speak to you in plain words."

Celia felt a quake in her middle.

"This shop," said Mrs. Thorley, "has always guaranteed its work." Her steel-blue eyes looked at Celia straight and hard. "Understand me, Miss Garth. We do not apologize for poor work. We simply do not tolerate it."

"Yes ma'am," Celia said faintly.

"Since Mrs. Lacy has asked for you, I shall not refuse. But I do not feel that I can recommend you. If you insist on sewing for Mrs. Lacy you may do so. But if she is not satisfied, your employment here will be at an end."

Again, Mrs. Thorley waited.

Celia was scared. She thought she could sew, but now she wondered—how could she be sure? Mrs. Thorley had offered her a good safe job, which at least meant that she would not have to go back and be Roy's poor relation. And if she didn't please Mrs. Lacy—then what? She could not sell her heirloom necklace until she was of age, and anyway she had no idea how you went about selling such a thing. No, if she failed here Mrs. Thorley would merely send her back home, to live on Roy's unwilling charity until she married some worthy clodhopper.

But if she should turn down this chance, she might be stuck with buttons and bastings for years. Maybe for the rest of her life. She might turn into one of those respectable drudges known as "an old and valued employee," plodding her way to the graveyard.

Celia doubled her hands into fists and said abruptly, "I want to work for Mrs. Lacy."

Mrs. Thorley nodded. She rarely displayed emotion before her help. Reaching across her desk she took a pen out of her quillholder. "Very well. Please ring for the maid."

Glad of the chance to move, Celia went over and pulled the bellcord. Mrs. Thorley spoke to the maid who came in answer.

"Tell Miss Loring to send me one of the young ladies who has not had a walk today. I need her to deliver a note." She turned to Celia. "Mrs. Lacy wants to see you at half-past five tomorrow. One of the other girls will relieve you in time for you to change your dress."

"Yes ma'am."

"That is all, Miss Garth."

Celia curtsied and went out. Oh Jimmy, she thought as she closed the door, oh Jimmy, maybe you've gotten me into a dreadful mess.

# CHAPTER 4

$\mathcal{S}$HE LIVED through the next day somehow, until Miss Loring
sent Agnes to take her place in the parlor. Celia hurried upstairs
to dress.

At length, in front of her glass, she looked herself over: her
eager dark eyes and her light hair, her well-made homespun dress,
her cap and kerchief crisp as frost. In her pocket her clean handkerchief and the rabbit's foot. Yes, she did look well. With a
smile of good-by to the mirror she turned and went down the
stairs, and let herself out by a side door.

As she walked up Meeting Street the town was golden in the
late sun. The sidewalk was full of people. Soldiers and sailors
roamed about seeing the sights; colored women sat by the curb
selling asters and goldenrod and late roses; fine ladies and gentlemen were out making calls, gay in their many-hued clothes. Men
of business, more sedate in dark suits, hurried on their errands
while they discussed the ships from the Indies and trade on the
wagon track. Ahead of her Celia could see the shining white spire
of St. Michael's.

Oh, it was a merry day, a laughing day, a day to feel sure of
yourself. Celia walked fast, taking deep breaths of the tangy air.
A man in a wine-colored coat swept off his hat and gave her a
smile of admiration. He was a big rugged fellow with bright blue

eyes and a sun-browned face, and down his cheeks two creases that looked as if they had been put there by a thousand smiles at pretty women. Celia liked the audacious air of him, and she smiled back.

Now she was coming near the corner of Tradd Street, and here was the town house of Mr. and Mrs. Herbert Lacy.

The Lacys lived in a tall narrow brick house with white woodwork, and steps coming down to the sidewalk. Their garden was on the south side, divided from the sidewalk by a brick wall and a wrought-iron gate. There was nothing pretentious about the place, but Celia thought its very simplicity made it imposing. You knew when you saw it that the people who lived here did not need to prove anything about themselves.

She felt a tremor like a trickle of cold water down her back. Maybe she had been a fool to come here and risk her destiny with a grumpy old woman, instead of taking the sensible job Mrs. Thorley had offered her. If she should turn back now, and say she had changed her mind—

Quickly, before she could do any such thing, she put her hand on the brass knocker. As she heard it strike she had a sense of relief. Now then. She couldn't turn back.

The door was opened by a colored girl in a neat blue homespun dress with white cap and kerchief. Celia gave her name, and the girl curtsied.

"Good evening, miss. I'm Marietta. Miss Vivian's having her hair done and she's not quite ready. You'll come this way, please?"

Marietta's voice was low and pleasant, and she spoke good plain English with the ease of one who is not used to hearing any other kind. She showed Celia into a formal reception room with mahogany furniture and a marble mantelpiece. As Celia sat down Marietta said,

"Maybe while you're waiting you'd like a glass of water?"

"Oh yes I would," Celia agreed, for her throat was dry with excitement. Marietta went out, and a moment later she brought in a glass on a tray. As Celia sipped gratefully Marietta asked,

"Is there anything else I can do for you, miss?"

She was so friendly that Celia was emboldened to ask advice.

"I wish you'd tell me something about Mrs. Lacy. I do want to please her."

(What a nuisance, always studying how to please other people. Some day, thought Celia, I'm going to be like Mrs. Lacy, and have my own way all the time.)

Marietta was answering. "Well ma'am, she wants everybody to be very neat and clean, but you shouldn't bother, you look nice. And she's very particular about having things done right."

Celia nodded. "Do you know what sort of clothes she's planning for me to make?"

Marietta wasn't sure. She did know Miss Vivian had just gotten a lot of new materials from her son Mr. Godfrey Bernard. The mention of his name reminded Celia of Vivian's many marriages, and she ventured,

"Marietta, tell me some more about the Lacys. They—they're quite an unusual family, isn't that right?"

Marietta said yes ma'am, they were. Miss Vivian had had five husbands and six children. Only four of her children were still living, three sons and a daughter, but they all had different names. She and Mr. Lacy had no children, but Mr. Lacy had been married before and had a son of his own—oh, sometimes things got right confusing around here. Celia could not help laughing, and she was glad to see that Marietta was laughing too. Marietta had turned her head toward the door, and now Celia realized that they were hearing music from the back of the house. "That's Miss Vivian," said Marietta, "playing the spinet. I guess Mr. Hugo is through with her hair. We can see her now."

Celia stood up, hoping she looked more calm than she felt. Slipping her hand into her pocket she stroked the rabbit's foot, and thought of Jimmy's likable ugly face and his grin and the way he looked down at her when he put the rabbit's foot into her hand, his eyes merry and encouraging under the black eyebrows.

Marietta was holding the door open. As she crossed the room Celia glanced at a mirror on the wall. She did look nice; she thought so, and Marietta thought so, and that brown young man in the street, he had certainly thought so. Marietta was saying that Miss Vivian was in her private sitting room.

She led Celia down the hall, past several open doors. The house was lovely. Everything Celia could see had a costly simplicity that appealed to her sense of good taste.

The tinkle of the spinet was clear now, a gay, rippling little tune. Marietta paused at a door that stood slightly ajar. She said in an undertone, "We'll go in, miss, but don't speak to her till she's finished the piece she's playing." Celia nodded, and Marietta touched the door.

The door swung inward, silently. Celia remembered that every door she had seen in this house had been silent, no squeaks and squawks about them. She and Marietta stepped over the threshold. There was a rug just inside and their footsteps made no sound.

The music went on. The spinet stood on the other side of the room, and evidently Mrs. Lacy had not heard them come in. Celia was glad of this, for it gave her time to draw some deep breaths and calm her heartquakes.

The room was dim, for the curtains were drawn and there was not much light from outside. The only other light came from a stand of candles beyond the spinet, placed so that they shone on the sheet of music set there. It took a moment for Celia to get used to the glow and shadows, but she looked as hard as she could.

She was in a lady's boudoir, and the room was as dainty as a fine lady herself. The wallpaper was printed with tiny pink and blue flowers. Celia saw a writing-desk; she saw a little table on which stood an hourglass with a silver base; scattered here and there she saw several delicate chairs and a sofa; and at the far end of the room, seated before the little rosewood spinet, she saw Vivian Lacy.

She could tell that Mrs. Lacy was playing the spinet with skill and enjoyment. But since the light was on the other side of the spinet, the great lady's face and figure were in shadow, and it took a moment for Celia to get a good look. So instead of one general impression she had several impressions, one after another.

As she saw Mrs. Lacy silhouetted against the light Celia's first thought was,

"She sits up straight. Not bent like most old women."

This was good. Celia remembered how she had dreaded trying

to make a dress look well over an old-age stoop. As her eyes went up and down Mrs. Lacy's figure her dressmaker's instinct further observed,

"She's kept herself little in the middle."

This too was gratifying. Whatever her age, a woman who had a waistline looked better in her clothes than a woman who had none. Gradually, as her eyes moved upward past Mrs. Lacy's shoulders, Celia thought,

"She holds her head well. She's got a good regular profile."

And then, as Celia began to see in more detail, her breath caught in her throat. She was so startled that for a moment she did not even believe herself, as the fact slipped into her mind and took form in words:

"She—it can't be so—it *is* so—she—she's beautiful!"

Along with the shock of discovery, Celia felt a twinge of shame. She might have known that a woman who could get five rich husbands must have *something*.

◦～◦

Vivian had not tried to cover up her age. On the contrary, she gave the impression that she had taken advantage of it. She had kept her figure and she was well dressed, but her real distinction was her look of being at ease in the world. You felt when you saw her that she had lived deeply and had grown more worldly-wise with every year of her life, until now her assurance was like a glow around her.

On the bench in front of the spinet Vivian sat erect, her head well balanced on her shoulders and every line of her body in harmony. Her white hair was piled up high, with a decoration of three little pink plumes held by a jeweled pin.

Her face had lines, but they seemed not to matter because her skin was like fine white silk and her features were clear-cut and firm. There was a droop under her chin, but this seemed not to matter either because she held her head so proudly. Around her throat she wore a band of black velvet with one square jewel.

She was dressed in a shimmer of pink. Her dress was satin, and below the hem Celia could see her foot, in a pink satin slipper with a gold buckle, touching the pedal of the spinet as she played.

Vivian came to the end of the tune, and moved the sheet of music to one side. Marietta stepped forward. Glancing around, Vivian said, "Oh yes, Marietta. And you are Celia Garth? Come in."

Her voice was low and her words were clear, no mumbling like some people. As she turned, the candlelight caught the jewel at her throat. The jewel too was pink. Maybe a pink sapphire, thought Celia; she had heard of pink sapphires but had never seen one.

Marietta curtsied. "Miss Vivian, Mr. Lacy told me to ask you first if you had answered Mr. Burton Dale's letter."

"Letter?" Vivian repeated. "What letter now?"

"About Mr. Dale asking you to stay with him when you went up to Miss Torrance's wedding."

"I'll answer right this minute," said Vivian. Without moving from the music-bench she added, "Come here, Miss Garth."

Astonished, Celia stepped forward too, and curtsied. "Yes ma'am?"

"Do you write a good hand?"

"Why—I believe so, ma'am."

"Write a letter for me. There, on the desk—show her, Marietta."

Trying not to look as puzzled as she felt, Celia sat down in the chair by the desk. But Marietta did not seem surprised. As smoothly as if Celia were a secretary who worked here every day, Marietta handed her a quill, took the top off the inkhorn, and opened a portfolio holding writing paper.

"Ready?" Vivian asked. "All right. Mr. Burton Dale, Gaylawn Plantation, parish of St. James Goose Creek." She dictated clearly, spelling the proper names. "My dear son, I am not going to Sophie Torrance's wedding or anybody else's wedding. Weddings and funerals are all alike and they bore me silly. Since I am now old enough to do as I please, I am never going to another wedding or another funeral unless I am the bride or the corpse. Your affectionate mother—now bring that here and I'll sign it."

Celia had almost forgotten that Roy was about to marry a girl named Sophie Torrance. Hearing his wedding treated with such disrespect gave her a wicked joy. Keeping her face demure, she brought the letter and quill to the spinet. Vivian wore no glasses, but now she took up a lorgnette that lay on the music rack.

"You write very nicely," she commented. Changing the lorgnette to her left hand she took the quill and signed "Vivian Lacy" in a swift dashing script. In a lower corner of the sheet she added "Charles Town, 17 September 1779," then held it out to Marietta. "Here, seal this and send it out with the next mail, and tell Mr. Lacy it's done. Now turn the glass. Let me know when the sand has run down."

Celia felt confused. Nothing so far had been what she expected. For reassurance she slipped her hand into her pocket and touched the rabbit's foot.

Vivian stood up. She did not push herself up with her hands, like an old woman; she simply stood up, like a young one. For a moment Celia had an impression of height, then she noticed with surprise that Vivian was not tall. She was, in fact, rather smaller than the average, but she held herself so well that she looked stately. Touching the back of a chair she said, "Marietta, I'll sit here. Bring the light."

It was Vivian's left hand that touched the chair-back, and Celia noticed a wedding ring. She wondered if Vivian got a new ring with each husband and what she did with the old ones.

Marietta moved the candle-stand and stepped aside. Vivian sat down. The candlelight glimmered over her soft fine skin and her jeweled hair. The chair she had chosen was upholstered in sea-green damask, a perfect background for her pink dress. She leaned back gracefully, one hand on the arm of the chair and the other in her lap holding the lorgnette by its long silver handle. "Will you come closer, Miss Garth," she asked, "into the light?"

"Yes ma'am," said Celia.

She moved into the full glow of the candles and stood there, her right hand at her side and the left in her pocket. She expected that now Vivian would start asking questions. How old are you? Where did you go to school? Who taught you to sew? What sort of clothes have you made? Can you do drawnwork? Quilting? Embroidery?

But Vivian merely looked. Her eyes were dark, almost black, and they moved quickly, like young eyes. She looked up and down Celia's figure, along her shoulders, across her waistline. She looked until Celia felt like something put up for auction.

At last Vivian spoke. "Hold up your arms. No, not out from your shoulders, just away from your skirt—understand?"

"Yes ma'am," said Celia.

She stood like a doll, her arms held stiffly, her hands about six inches from her skirt at each side.

"Turn around," said Vivian. "Slowly. Keep your arms out."

"Yes ma'am," said Celia.

She thought she had never felt so foolish. When she had turned around twice Vivian said,

"That will do, you can put your arms down now. Come nearer."

"Yes ma'am," said Celia.

She came and stood by Vivian's knee. Holding the lorgnette to her eyes Vivian examined the stitching of Celia's dress; she ran her fingers along the seams, and took a pinch of cloth between her thumb and forefinger. "Did you make this dress?" she asked.

"Yes ma'am."

"Now I suppose you can see all these little stitches without glasses."

"Yes ma'am."

"I can't. This is homespun linen from Kingstree, isn't it?"

"Yes ma'am."

"Don't you ever get tired of saying yes ma'am?"

"Yes *ma'am!*" Celia exclaimed, and clapped her hand over her mouth. "Oh I'm sorry, Mrs. Lacy! I didn't mean to be rude."

"You're not rude," Vivian said. "You're scared. Now I'm going to ask you some questions and I want some intelligent answers. Marietta, bring Miss Garth a chair."

Marietta obeyed, and again Vivian leaned back. The questions were still not what Celia had expected—not about her, but about her dress. "How did you bleach the linen to that sand-color?" Vivian asked. "How did you measure those darts in the back?"

Celia answered as clearly as she could. After what seemed like a thousand questions Vivian raised her lorgnette once more, as if to make sure there was no stitch they had not discussed. Then she spoke.

"Your dress," she said, "is beautiful."

Celia gave a happy start. Vivian continued,

"That linen is good honest stuff, it's fine for men's hunting shirts and for children to climb trees in. But this is the first garment I ever saw made of it that had any more grace than a rice-barrel. My dear, if you started with a bolt of raw homespun and produced this, you're an artist."

For a moment Celia thought she was about to cry, which would have embarrassed her frightfully. Nobody had seen her cry since she was a little girl, and anyway she felt that Vivian would not like such goings-on. Vivian was saying,

"Miss Garth, you know your trade. You can begin here Monday. You'll come over every morning and work in my sewing room. I don't like going out for fittings. And now, please, what have you got in your pocket?"

With a blush, Celia drew out the rabbit's foot on its silver chain. Vivian took it, and began to laugh.

Celia thought how different Vivian was from Mrs. Thorley. This dress, for instance—she had worn it often in the shop, yet Mrs. Thorley had never noticed it. And yesterday during their interview she had rubbed the rabbit's foot many times, but Mrs. Thorley had not noticed that either. Such alertness undoubtedly made Vivian an exciting personality, but Celia saw that it would also make her a frightening one.

"Is this the rabbit's foot Jimmy Rand carries around?" asked Vivian. "First time I ever knew him to part with it." She gave it back, asking dryly, "I suppose you brought it because everybody told you I was an old crank?"

"Oh no, Mrs. Lacy!"

Vivian crossed her ankles. "You'll have to be a better liar than that," she said, "if you want to amount to anything in this world. I know I'm hard to work for. I want things done right, and mighty few people want to take the trouble to do things right."

Celia decided to be frank. "That's not the only reason I was nervous, Mrs. Lacy. You see, it was a week ago that Jimmy told me you were going to send for me. The waiting made me shaky."

"I did intend to send for you sooner," Vivian said smiling. "But a son of mine came home—he's been up the wagon track with supplies for General Washington. I've not done much this week but listen to his yarns."

Celia had never met any of the gentlemen adventurers of the wagon track. "Is that the one I wrote a letter to just now?" she asked eagerly.

"Oh no," said Vivian. "You wrote to Burton Dale—he's a rice planter. No lover of derring-do. The one on the track is Luke Ansell."

She examined the silver handle of her lorgnette. There was a pause. Somehow, it was a tense pause. Celia noticed that Vivian was turning the lorgnette over and over, her fingers working up and down the design on the handle. It was the first time during their conversation that Vivian had made a nervous gesture. Celia had heard of the perils of the wagon track, and the idea came to her now that Vivian knew all about these perils and was terribly afraid for her reckless son.

Celia began to feel awkward. It was time for her to go, but she could not properly do so until Vivian dismissed her. Since Vivian had spoken last, Celia decided it was her turn to say something and perhaps ease the atmosphere. She asked,

"Your son—is he planning to stay at home now?"

Vivian looked up. There was a bitter little smile on her lips. "Luke? No, he'll start back," she replied tersely, "as soon as he can load his wagons."

She shrugged, and twirled her lorgnette again. She was not going to shed any tears—Celia wondered if she ever did—but it was plain that Luke Ansell was going to take another blood-curdling journey in spite of all his mother could do to stop him. Celia could almost hear the clash of battle.

Jimmy had said Vivian always got her own way. But it seemed Jimmy was wrong. Evidently there was one person who could talk back to her. Celia thought Luke ought to stay home a while for his mother's sake, and she would have liked to tell him so; but she could not help feeling some respect for the fellow all the same.

Marietta stepped out from the shadow where she had been waiting.

"Miss Vivian, the sand has run out."

45

"Thank you," said Vivian. During the moment of silence she had recovered her poise, and when she spoke to Celia her voice was cool and clear again. "Then this is all, Miss Garth. I'm having some guests this evening and it's time I went to the parlor."

Celia stood up and curtsied. "Good night, Mrs. Lacy. I'll do my best."

"Please do," Vivian said crisply, but she added with a note of approval, "You have a good start. You like your work." She smiled a little. "Keep your weight down and your chin up— you'll get along. Good night."

## CHAPTER 5

MARIETTA let Celia out by a side door into the garden. The dark was gathering, cool and full of fragrance. Celia went along a brick walk through the flowerbeds, and pushing open the gate she stepped out on the sidewalk.

A block away the beacon shone in the spire of St. Michael's, and along both sides of the street the colored house-boys were lighting the lanterns over the front doors. In the better parts of town every house had its own light, and these streets were as safe by night as by day. Celia was used to doing her errands without being bothered, so now she was astonished to hear a man's voice exclaim,

"Good evening! I'm just in time to see you home."

With a start she looked around. In the glow of the nearest lantern she saw a big fellow who looked vaguely familiar. He was wearing a wine-colored coat, and he had pulled off his hat, showing his brown hair brushed back in thick ripples and tied behind. As he was facing the lantern she could see that he had a ruddy sunburnt face and bright blue eyes, the brightest and bluest she thought she had ever seen. With those brown cheeks and jewel-blue eyes, and his look of vigor and gay humor, without being handsome he was certainly attractive. And mighty sure of himself, thought Celia, who was not just now in a mood to flirt.

She replied coolly, "No, thank you. I know my way."

"Please don't be like that!" begged the fashionable stranger. He spoke with a boyish urgency. "You've no idea how your hair shines with that lantern behind you—it's a real moonlight gold. Even prettier than by daylight. Though it was mighty pretty when I saw you before, couple of hours back—remember?"

As he spoke she did remember—the brown young man who had doffed his hat to her when she was on her way here this afternoon. She had enjoyed his attention then, but now she thought of how Mrs. Lacy might react if somebody reported that her new dressmaker was hardly out of the house before she let herself be picked up by a strange man.

He was saying, "I saw you coming across the garden, so I waited for you. How do you happen to be here?"

"I was asked to call," Celia returned stiffly, "to discuss some dressmaking. And I don't—"

"Oh, then you must be Celia Garth."

Celia finished her sentence. "—and I don't walk on the street with just anybody!"

"But I'm not just anybody!" protested the unblushing cavalier. "I'm me. Me. Luke Ansell."

"Luke—?" Celia repeated. She was taken aback, and she had forgotten the surname of Vivian's hot-headed son. He took quick advantage of her hesitation.

"Ansell," he repeated firmly. He began to spell, counting off the letters on his fingers. "Not just anybody, Ansell. A for anybody, N for nobody, S for somebody, E for everybody, two L's for—" This time he was the one who hesitated.

Celia was laughing. "Yes?" she teased him. "Two L's for what?"

"Two L's for—" he pointed his finger at her and ended triumphantly—"for like-a-body, twice! I've seen you twice, I've liked you both times. So now won't you like me and let me walk with you to Mrs. Thorley's?"

He waited with enticing eagerness. A young man, with a look of rugged strength, evidently he was a son of one of Vivian's more recent marriages. "All right," agreed Celia.

"Good!" Luke exclaimed, and they fell into step. As they

walked along he said, "Are you going to sew for my mother?"

"Yes—I mean, she's going to let me try."

Luke chuckled softly. "Scared of her?"

"Yes!" Celia said, and felt better for saying it.

They were passing a house which had its driveway gate deeply recessed into the garden wall. Over the gate was a lantern. "Let's stop here," Luke suggested. "Maybe I can find a good sign for you."

While she watched him, puzzled, he drew a small thick book from his coat pocket. "What's that?" she asked.

"A Bible," said Luke, and began to turn the pages, evidently looking for some passage he had in mind. Celia was surprised. From what she had heard of the swashbucklers of the wagon track, a Bible seemed an unlikely piece of equipment. Luke was saying, "Fine print, but I've got good eyes and when you drive supply wagons you don't have much room for your own gear. What's your birthday?"

Still puzzled, she told him, "I was born the thirteenth of April, 1759."

"I didn't ask the year. I can see it wasn't very long ago." Luke was running his finger down the page. "Ah, here it is." By the light of the lantern above him he read, " 'She seeketh wool and flax, and worketh willingly with her hands.' " He looked up, and his blue eyes flashed on her through the dark. "There. That's your Bible verse. Sounds as if the Lord meant you to be a dress-maker."

"Where is that?" Celia asked eagerly. "And why is it mine?" Maybe it was the verse, or Luke's debonair ways, but she felt a springing confidence replacing the tremors of her day.

"It's the thirteenth verse of the last chapter of Proverbs," said Luke. "This chapter describes a woman. There are thirty-one verses, one for each day of the month, and the verse numbered to match your birthday is yours."

"Oh, I like that! Is there a man's chapter too?"

"Yes, the twenty-first chapter is for men. And my verse—" Turning back a few leaves he read it to her. " 'Whoso keepeth his mouth and his tongue, keepeth his soul from troubles.' "

49

The idea of Luke's being warned to keep his mouth shut struck Celia as so impossible that she could not help laughing. He asked,

"You think I don't pay enough attention to my verse?"

"Well—you don't seem like the quiet type."

Luke shook his head mournfully. "My mother says I talk too much. But on the wagon track I have to be so inhumanly silent, it's a relief to gabble when I'm at home." He put the book back into his pocket and they started walking again.

"It's very dangerous on the track, isn't it?" Celia asked.

"Why yes, it is," said Luke. He spoke in a matter-of-fact way.

But she wanted to know more, so he explained. For many years there had been a regular trade between Charleston and Philadelphia. The trading road went from Charleston to Camden, across the North Carolina line and through the towns of Charlotte and Salisbury, then across Virginia, Maryland, and Delaware, and into Pennsylvania. Today of course, though you followed the same route in general, you did not dare keep to the regular track. You never went the same way twice.

But any way you went, it was risky. The British attacked every wagon train they could catch up with. And besides the British, there were thieves in the woods looking for a chance to shoot the drivers, for the loads could be sold at enormous prices. But when Celia exclaimed at his courage, Luke shook his head.

"It just happens to be the sort of thing I can do," he told her.

They had reached the shop. Luke walked with her up the steps and into the parlor. The customers had gone and Agnes was about to lock up. Celia knew from experience that Agnes was dismayed at seeing a visitor walk in so late, but Agnes came forward, smiling with longsuffering sweetness, and asked the gentleman how she could serve him.

Luke bowed. He said he was not a customer, he had merely been seeing Miss Garth back from her interview with his mother. But now that he was here, he was glad he had come in. He flirted with Agnes and flattered her, and asked if she worked here every day.

Agnes was charmed. Celia, lingering in the background, thought she had never seen a skirt-chaser more expert. Remembering how adroitly he had won her favor a few minutes ago, she decided he was a man to beware of. Probably had a girl in every town between here and Philadelphia. And him toting a Bible, too.

The parlor was well lighted, and now she observed that with his wine-colored coat Luke wore blue knee-breeches and heavy gray stockings. She was surprised at the stockings. They were knitted of thick yarn such as a laboring man would wear, but the knitter had made them in an elaborate lacework pattern like the stockings of a gentleman dandy. Celia thought such a fancy design on such coarse stockings was silly. She wondered if Vivian had made them, and doubted it. She could not imagine Vivian's wasting her time like that.

Luke was asking Agnes how she kept herself so fresh and pretty after a day's work. She didn't look a bit tired, he said, but she must be. It was time she got some rest. He *would* like to take a look at the fashion dolls—that man-doll in the purple coat had given him an idea—but he did not want to detain her. Maybe Miss Garth would be willing to lock up after him.

As Celia was willing, and as Agnes really was tired (and looked it, in spite of Luke's honeyed fibs), he got his way and she went upstairs in a happy frame of mind.

Celia was sitting on the arm of a chair near the doll cabinet. Luke crossed the room and rested one hand on the cabinet, but he spoke to her without glancing at the dolls. "When I leave Charleston again, my mother and stepfather will go back to Sea Garden. Would you go along, and make her another dress or two?"

"I'd love to!" exclaimed Celia. "If—" She bit her lip.

"If what?" he asked smiling.

"Why, if your mother wants me—and if Mrs. Thorley will let me."

"Oh," Luke said. "If mother wants you she'll arrange it with Mrs. Thorley. As for whether or not she'll want you—" He grinned down at her. "I rather think she's going to like you. She was quite doubtful before you came over. Jimmy Rand made an eloquent speech, that's the only reason she said she'd see you at all. If she took you she must have been agreeably surprised."

Celia thought with a glow of triumph, This will show Mrs.

Thorley! But at the same time she remembered Vivian's troubled hands twisting the lorgnette. With a sharp glance at Luke she suggested, "You think your mother will worry less about you if she has clothes to keep her busy?"

"I think," Luke answered calmly, "that it's none of your business, but since you ask me, yes."

"Why don't you stay home this winter?" Celia asked.

Luke smiled at one side of his mouth. "I'm no parlor patriot," he said shortly.

"I suppose you'd call Jimmy Rand a parlor patriot!"

"Don't be absurd," said Luke. "Somebody has to guard Charleston harbor or I'd have no guns to load on my wagons. Remember what King David said about the men who stayed by the stuff?"

Celia shook her head.

"You'll find it in the Bible. He said the men who stand on guard are just as important as the men who go into battle."

She smiled, unwillingly. "You know a lot of smart answers out of the Bible."

"Lot of smart answers there," said Luke. He stuck his thumbs under his belt. "Now you stop bothering about my mother and me. You stick to your knitting."

The word "knitting" brought Celia's mind back to his stockings. There was a moment of silence. A chair stood by the wall, a dainty little chair without arms. Luke pulled it forward and perched on it like a large bird on a small twig, his heels hooked over the front rung, his elbows on his knees and his hands linked. "What are you staring at?" he asked.

"I didn't realize I was staring," she said with a touch of embarrassment. But since she did want to know, she took this chance to find out. "Mr. Ansell, who made your stockings?"

Luke went rigid as though with shock. His jaw dropped, his eyes were like two blue fires in his weatherbeaten face. For an instant he looked at her in amazement.

But only for an instant. Luke was used to shocks. He got himself in hand so fast that Celia almost thought she had made a mistake about his reaction. He relaxed, grinned, held out one leg and examined it. Finally, tucking his leg under the chair again, he hooked his heel over the rung as before. He replied serenely, "I did."

This time she was the startled one. "You!"

Luke nodded. "On the wagon track." Laughing at her surprise, he went on. "I'm no hero. As long as we're moving, the job isn't too fearsome. We're so busy with the teams we don't have time to think about how dangerous it is. But when we stop to rest—when the woods crunch, and every crunch may be redcoats or a gang of murdering robbers—then, dear lady, I'm scared. So I knit. With fancy patterns like this I have to count stitches. Eases my nerves."

For a moment Celia said nothing. She still could not guess why he had been so jolted at her query, but she was beginning to know something else about him. She looked him over—his thick rippling hair and his sunburn, his aggressive blue eyes, his whole air of strength and defiance and daredevil stubbornness. In a wondering voice she said, "Mr. Ansell, you—"

She stopped, hardly knowing how to say it. With a puzzled interest he prompted her. "Yes? Go on."

Celia said, "You *like* that, don't you?"

"Like what?" he asked mischievously. "Knitting?"

"You know what I mean," Celia retorted. "You like being scared."

Luke began to laugh, softly and almost proudly, as if he enjoyed her keenness. "Not exactly," he said, "but you understand it better than most people. What I like is the way I feel when I wake up in the morning, when I look around and say, 'Good Lord, I'm still here!' "

Celia nodded slowly. Luke got to his feet.

"Now," he said, "I'll ask you something."

She laughed a little. "All right."

"Do you always notice so much about other people?"

"Why yes," Celia said thoughtfully, "I think I do. I like to know about people."

"You're as sharp as my mother," Luke said. With a smile that was half amused and half admiring, he went to the door. Hand on the doorknob he gave her a parting glance, his eyes going up and down in a way that made her pleasantly conscious of her blond hair and brown eyes and slim waistline. "I've enjoyed meeting you," said Luke. "Good night." Turning, he grinned at her over his shoulder. "Good night," he repeated. "Sassyface."

The door banged and he was gone. But he had slammed it so hard that the latch had not caught and the door was swinging open again. She went to fasten it.

By the lantern over the doorway she could see him striding off into the dark. He was singing.

> "Now girls, why act so shy
> When provoking men come by?
> You know you're only wondering
> how you strike us—"

Celia stopped and listened. Luke's voice was dwindling, but the wind was blowing her way and it brought his song back to where she stood.

> "Oh forget the won'ts and can'ts!
> For since half the world wears pants,
> You might as well own up to it—
> you like us!"

## CHAPTER 6

*T*HE SAME WEEK that Celia began to work for Vivian, Roy was married to Sophie Torrance in the church of St. James Goose Creek, seventeen miles above Charleston. Vivian serenely stayed home, but her son Burton Dale and his wife attended, and so did Jimmy's mother. Jimmy told Celia they said the bride and groom and Aunt Louisa had all seemed healthy and happy, but Uncle William had looked wretchedly unwell. Celia was sorry about Uncle William. She had always been fond of him, though she had not respected him much. She could not respect people who never got their own way.

Jimmy said the Torrances were indigo planters, and Tories. Most of the indigo people were Tories. Some years ago the gentlemen in Parliament, wanting British sources of indigo that would compete with the crops raised by Frenchmen in the French West Indies, had voted to pay a bonus on every pound of indigo raised in the king's colonies. If the Americans should cut their ties with the king, of course his government would no longer pay them to raise indigo; therefore, Jimmy said to Celia, Mrs. Roy Garth would no doubt wear a green ribbon on her cap.

And from what Celia had said about Roy, Jimmy added with a wise twinkle, he wouldn't be surprised if Roy turned Tory also.

He told Celia all this one evening when he walked with her

back to the shop, and lingered in the little sitting room where the girls received callers. Celia agreed, laughing. For while Roy had never put himself to any trouble about the war, before she left home he had favored independence. Most of the rice planters favored independence because they were tired of British restrictions on the sale of their crop.

But though she was interested, after Jimmy had gone she hardly thought of Roy again. She did not have room in her head for anything but her work. Vivian was proving just as impossible a customer as they had warned her.

At first Celia had thought the situation ideal. Her workroom was on the third floor, overlooking the garden. Marietta brought her dinner at midday, and in the afternoon came in again to do any small services Celia might want. Everything was comfortable, everybody was pleasant. But there were times when Celia was in despair.

Vivian's dress was to be made of a printed silk imported by Godfrey Bernard. Celia measured, diagrammed, figured her cutting and seaming with exquisite care. But even so, she was not always good enough.

Every morning Vivian would come up to the workroom, in a bewitching wrapper and a cap of lawn and ribbons, always lovely, always the great lady who walked with pride. Celia admired her, envied her, and dreaded her visits. There were days when Vivian approved of what had been sewn yesterday, but just as often she did not, and Celia spent the next few hours taking out the stitches she had so carefully put in. Vivian was not bad-tempered, but she was merciless. She knew what she wanted, and what she wanted was perfection (or something so close to perfection that Celia often thought it was beyond human reach). And always, like a little demon sitting on Celia's shoulder and whispering into her ear, there was Mrs. Thorley's ultimatum. You will please Mrs. Lacy, or you will go.

With all these difficulties, Celia did think she had a right to peace and quiet in which to work. But there was no such thing as peace and quiet with Luke in the house.

She did not see Luke again. But she was constantly, and wrathfully, aware of him. Luke was all over the place, vital, noisy, always doing something, shouting to somebody to do something else, rattling up and down the stairs, warbling silly ditties at the top of his voice. Now and then she would have a respite while he was off collecting guns or gunpowder that had been smuggled into some secret cove, but in a day or two the racket of his presence would burst forth again. Celia wished he would make haste to load his stuff and be off to yell at mule-teams and George Washington.

Gradually she met the other members of the family. Marietta sketched their backgrounds for her.

Mr. Lacy was an urbane and scholarly gentleman of seventy. He had read as much Greek and Latin as Uncle William, but his head was not merely an attic of useless learning. Until he retired several years ago Mr. Lacy had been a successful rice planter. But he liked books better than people, and horses better still. Both in town and at Sea Garden he had fine stables and took regular horseback rides. He and Vivian had a quiet, friendly relationship that seemed agreeable to them both. Marietta said that Mr. Lacy and Luke, though so different, got along well. Luke called him "governor."

Burton Dale was Vivian's eldest son. In his forties, Burton was a big man, handsome in a thick, florid sort of way. Most of his clothes were too tight. Now in wartime the supply of good material was so limited that even rich men had to make their wardrobes last, and while the clothes stayed the same size the men sometimes put on extra inches.

Burton came to dinner now and then with his wife Elise. They were much alike—stiff-minded, very correct in their behavior, and a constant source of amusement to Vivian. They had two sons, but as Burton had married late his elder boy was only twelve years old.

Besides his plantation on Goose Creek, Burton had a town house in the lordly suburb of Ansonborough, at the north edge of Charleston. Favoring the rebel side in the war, he gave the army regular donations of both rice and money, and Celia supposed he would be happy to go on doing so as long as nobody asked him to make himself uncomfortable.

Marietta said Burton's father had died of fever brought on

when he went up to his rice-fields in the sickly season without taking any Peruvian bark with him. Burton had had four step-fathers. He addressed Mr. Lacy as "Sir."

Vivian's second son was Godfrey Bernard. His father was descended from one of the French Huguenots who fled to America when King Louis XIV forbade them to worship in France. Many of these Frenchmen had settled along the Santee River, where they had prospered so greatly that "rich as a Huguenot" became a proverb. Marietta said Vivian had had another son by this marriage, but he had died as a baby. Godfrey's father had lost his life not long afterward, drowned while on an exploring trip among the tributary creeks up the river.

Godfrey and his wife Ida—they had no children—lived around the corner from Vivian on Tradd Street. Their back yards touched in the middle of the block, and Godfrey, an energetic fellow who looked younger than his forty years, often ran down to the dividing wall to hand Vivian a box of ginger or some other hard-to-get delicacy that one of his ships had brought in.

Vivian's third husband had been Mr. Rand, a relative of Jimmy's family. By this marriage she had had two daughters. One of them had died; the other, Madge, now Mrs. Penfield, lived on Broad Street with her husband and three children. Mr. Penfield was a rice broker and an ardent patriot. As for Madge, she seemed to Celia one of those people who are just too normal to be interesting. Madge loved her family, enjoyed her life, and had a calmness that made her talkative sister-in-law Elise seem unfinished, like a half-iced cake.

Vivian's fourth husband, said Marietta, had been Mr. Ansell, father of Luke.

As she had told the family story in bits and pieces while she was helping in the sewing room, Marietta did not get to Luke's father until Celia had been working for Vivian about three weeks. Today Marietta had come up during the afternoon with a cup of coffee, for the time was now October and the weather had turned chilly. Celia remarked that she had not cared for coffee when the war began, but now she liked it as well as tea or maybe better. Marietta told her Mr. Luke had said the same thing the other day. She added that Miss Vivian had said she could hardly believe him, for Mr. Luke's father had been such a tea-drinker and it was strange to see Mr. Luke preferring something different because he was so much like his father.

While she spoke, Marietta had knelt to gather up some scraps from the floor. Celia said she did not know anything about Luke's father. She had not even heard that Luke was so much like him. Marietta said oh yes ma'am, Mr. Luke was the image of his father, that was what everybody said.

"Do you think so too?" Celia asked.

Marietta couldn't say personally, because she didn't remember Mr. Luke's father. He was killed in the Cherokee War when Mr. Luke was eight or nine years old. That must be nearly twenty years back.

Celia set her cup in the saucer. So Luke's father had been killed in a war. She thought of Vivian's hands twisting the silver lorgnette.

Marietta said the war had been a long way off, in the Carolina Upcountry. The Cherokee Indians had been raiding the frontier settlements, and American and British soldiers had gone together to put them down. Mr. Francis Marion—Colonel Marion he was now—had come riding through the country asking for volunteers. Mr. Ansell rode off with him. Marietta's sister had been a little girl then and she had told Marietta about this, and about the time when they brought word to Miss Vivian that Mr. Ansell had been killed.

It was dreadful. Miss Vivian was teaching a group of little colored girls to do mending, when her maid came in and said a soldier wanted to see her. When the soldier entered they sent the girls out, but the girls could see by his manner that he had come for something important. So they peeked around the edge of the window—they were just little girls, they didn't know any better —and they heard him tell Miss Vivian the news.

Miss Vivian didn't scream or faint or anything like that. She just sat there and turned green. That sounded funny, Marietta said, talking about a person turning green, but they all said this was just what she did. Then she got up and went into her bedroom and they didn't see her again for days and days.

People said she took it harder than any of the others. They said she hadn't cared for any of them the way she had for Mr. Ansell. Everybody was surprised when she married Mr. Lacy three years afterward. Some folk were shocked, for the fact was that while she didn't look it Miss Vivian was about fifty years old then, and anyway they thought four husbands were enough. Mr. Burton Dale, for instance, that's what he said. But Miss Vivian said she wanted a man around, to carve the roast and pour the wine and take her out in the evenings; and Mr. Lacy wanted to turn his plantation over to his son anyway, so why shouldn't they get married? She told Mr. Burton Dale to run along and tend to his business. You know Miss Vivian, she never paid any mind to anybody.

But when Celia was alone again she sat for several minutes, her needle poised over her work. She was thinking. She had begun to understand that there was a lot more courage in the world than she had realized, and a lot more need for it.

The house was quiet today. Faintly, from away below, Celia could hear the tinkle of the spinet as Vivian played a tune.

Evidently Luke was not at home. The place was never so quiet when he was around. Odd, Celia reflected as she resumed her sewing, that she had not seen Luke again since that first evening. Vivian's other children came by the house often, and spoke to her in friendly fashion if they happened to pass her in the hall. But though Luke lived in the house and the others did not, during the whole three weeks she had been working here he had never happened to pass her in the hall.

Yes, now that she thought of it, this was very odd. If it had not been such a foolish idea she might almost have thought he was avoiding her.

∙∾∙

She plodded away at Vivian's dress, sewing and ripping and sewing again. And at last, when she had been at the miserable thing six weeks, one day Vivian put on the dress and said it was right. In fact, said Vivian, this was the first dress she had had made since she came back from Paris that had *really* fitted her.

Celia held to the back of a chair, limp with relief. Still looking into the mirror, Vivian said, "Would you like to come to Sea Garden and sew for me this winter?"

Celia had been wondering if Luke was going to suggest this, and she had almost persuaded herself that she did not want to make any more clothes for Vivian, but as soon as she heard the invitation she knew she did. "I'd like to very much, Mrs. Lacy!" she exclaimed.

"Very well," said Vivian, "I'll tell Mrs. Thorley. We are planning to leave Charleston a week from next Monday."

Vivian had been out making calls. She had an elegant coiffure by her French hairdresser Mr. Hugo, and around her neck she wore a chain of thirteen little silver stars. This was a present from Luke: the stars represented the stars of liberty on the rebel flag, and it was the newest fashion.

Suddenly Celia realized that the house had been quiet for some days past. She could not recall how many, but she was sure it had been longer than usual. "If you're going to Sea Garden," she ventured, "does this mean Mr. Ansell is on his way again?"

"Yes, he's gone," said Vivian. "He left some time ago."

"And nobody knew!" Celia exclaimed.

"Why no," said Vivian. She held up her arm and examined the sleeve-ruffle of her new dress. "There are plenty of Tory informers in Charleston," she said, "who would be well paid if they could find out when the supply wagons started."

She was looking at the hem of the sleeve. But Celia knew she was not really looking at it, because she was not wearing glasses and she could not see such fine stitches without them. Celia said, "I hope he'll be all right, Mrs. Lacy."

"Thank you," Vivian returned in a low voice. Without looking up she added, "By this time, I suppose somebody has told you about his father."

"Yes ma'am."

There was a pause. It seemed to last a long time. Celia felt young and awkward. Suddenly Vivian looked up, her dark eyes bright under their black lashes.

"Celia, did you ever fall in love?"

"No ma'am," said Celia.

61

"Don't fall in love, Celia," said Vivian. "It's just asking for trouble. Make a nice cool-headed marriage—"

"Oh no!" Celia cried.

She spoke without thinking, as if the words came out by themselves. Vivian began to laugh.

"See what I mean? We can't help it, can we?" She turned around briskly. "Now get me out of this dress without wrecking my hair."

Celia unbuttoned the dress and slipped it down so Vivian could step out of it. She was thinking of how Vivian had covered up Luke's departure by going on with her own affairs—making calls, entertaining company, trying on her dress. And all that time she had known he was riding into deadly peril. She must have been sick with fear. Yet she had given no sign.

Celia held up the wrapper, and Vivian put it on. "Mrs. Lacy," Celia said earnestly, "since he left—I don't know how you did it."

Vivian was about to go out. Her hand on the door, she smiled over her shoulder. "Frankly, my dear, I don't either." She gave a graceful shrug. "But—one thing I've learned, Celia. You can do anything you *have* to do." As she went out, she touched the chain of stars Luke had given her.

Celia thought of Luke, his noise and his silly songs and his absurd stockings. She wondered why he had been so startled when she noticed his stockings. But he had seemed to like her that evening—he must have liked her or he would not have suggested that Vivian take her to Sea Garden. It really was strange that he had not let her see him again before he went away.

⌁

When Mrs. Thorley received Vivian's note, she made no apology for her earlier doubts. She merely said, "I am happy to inform you, Miss Garth . . ."

The next day Celia received a letter from Roy, telling her of the death of her Uncle William. After having heard of her uncle's look of ill-health at the time of Roy's wedding Celia was not surprised, but she felt saddened. Poor Uncle William, fumbling his way through life and now leaving it before he had ever had any fun.

Uncle William had left her five hundred dollars in South Carolina currency. Roy said this would be paid to her after he had come to town to sign some necessary papers. The details of the estate would be handled by Mr. Carter's assistant, Mr. Rand. *Mr.* Rand, Celia observed. Not *Captain* Rand. So Jimmy was right. Roy had decided to be a Tory. As she folded his letter she reflected that his father's death had occurred at an opportune time for Roy: after he had had an elaborate wedding—which the bride's family would have paid for—and before he had had time to give the usual balls and dinners for his new wife, which he would have had to pay for himself.

After supper she got some scraps of black crepe from Miss Perry and set about sewing a sleeve-band on the dress she was going to wear tomorrow. In ordinary times she would have been expected to go into full black, but the Continental Congress had urged the people not to discard their good clothes for mourning outfits. Even Tories, who flouted Congress as much as they dared, seldom wore full mourning these days because black crepe was scarce and expensive. As she stitched, Celia was thinking that this was something else Roy would find convenient. Undoubtedly he and Sophie had both bought a lot of clothes for their wedding, and Roy would have found it painful to let moths eat them while he bought others.

•~•

On Sunday, the day before she was to go to Sea Garden, Celia came to her room after dinner and packed her trunk. She had so few possessions that this did not take long, and she stretched on her bed for an afternoon of pleasant idleness.

All her roommates were out: Agnes spending the day with her aunt, Becky walking with two or three of her beaus, and Pearl entertaining a beau of her own downstairs. On the table Agnes had left a copy of *The Vicar of Wakefield,* and Celia was thinking she might like to read it. The day was raw and ugly, just the sort of day to get lost in a good book. But while she was thinking about it she heard tapping little footsteps in the hall and then a knock. Pulling a robe around her she opened the door.

Miss Perry was there, fluttering like a plump little bird, while from the doorway across the hall Miss Loring peered out to see what was disturbing her Sabbath rest. Miss Perry chattered in happy excitement. Celia had *callers*, she said. Such lovely people. Mr. and Mrs. Roy Garth.

Miss Perry was delightfully awed by people who wore fine raiment and fared sumptuously every day. She went on to say that Mr. and Mrs. Garth were waiting in the main parlor. Some of the girls were receiving gentlemen in the *little* parlor, and she was sure Mr. and Mrs. Garth would not like to talk to Celia in front of all those *strangers*. You could see they were used to *every* attention, such lovely people they were.

Behind Miss Perry, Miss Loring listened with patient endurance. Miss Perry's joyful disposition was one of the burdens heaven required Miss Loring to bear.

Celia wondered what Roy wanted to see her about. Something unpleasant, she was sure. She had an impulse to say she was sick, but she had too much curiosity. So she said, "Thank you, Miss Perry. I'll go down as soon as I can put on a dress."

"All right, my dear, all right!" Miss Perry trilled. She pattered off, while Miss Loring, relieved at the prospect of quiet, closed her own door.

Celia put on the dress she had worn to church this morning, a brown wool with a white kerchief. Slipping the rabbit's foot into her pocket she went downstairs.

The main parlor, not generally used on Sunday, looked dreary as she opened the door. There was no light except the dingy gray from outside; the cabinets were dull, the fashion dolls forlorn, as though they knew this was not their day. On the sofa between two windows sat Roy Garth and with him a woman in a long dark red cloak.

Hearing the door open Roy stood up. As she caught her first glimpse of him in all these months Celia noticed as she never had before, how much he looked like Aunt Louisa. It occurred to her that Louisa would have made a singularly handsome man.

Roy was tall and dark, with regular features and a generally imperious air like a man used to having people do what he told them. He wore a long cape of black broadcloth fastened at the neck with a dull gold buckle, and swinging back to show his dark blue coat and primrose-yellow breeches. He had a black band on his sleeve. Whatever else he might be, Roy was certainly a good-looking man.

And Sophie was a pretty thing, with gray-blue eyes and a fair skin and a face of harmless innocence. Celia knew her type because so many women like her came to the shop. Not really stupid, but she had never had to do anything for herself, so though Sophie was a woman in years she was still a little girl in her mind.

Sophie's garnet-red cloak had a hood trimmed with black fur. Celia thought the cloak would have looked much better on herself. That shade of dark red was one of her own best colors, that hood would have lain like a kiss on her golden hair. She detested Sophie for having it. Also she fancied that Sophie's eyes gave her a flick of condescending curiosity—so this is your poor relation, Roy? She did not like Sophie at all.

Roy was speaking urbanely. (No wonder Miss Perry had been so impressed.) "How do you do, Celia. I am glad to see you looking so well. May I present my wife?"

Sophie and Celia murmured politely. When he had set a chair for Celia, Roy sat down again on the sofa. For a minute or two they exchanged formal nothings. Yes, said Roy, her Aunt Louisa was well. Her cousin Harriet was also well; Harriet was now the happy mother of a little girl. Yes, his father's death had been a shock; he had been failing for some time, but no one had known the end was so near.

"I have been trying to settle my father's affairs as he wanted them," Roy said. "You can expect your legacy soon, from Mr. Rand."

He went on talking, but Celia, thinking enviously of Sophie's cloak, forgot to listen. As she realized that Roy had paused for an answer she jerked her thoughts back, and smiling to cover her lack of attention she said, "I don't quite understand you, Roy."

Roy uncrossed his legs and crossed them again. The light flashed up and down his black silk stockings.

"I thought I was making it clear," he replied courteously, "but I'll try to be simpler. In checking over the property, I find that my father made you a loan of one of the family heirlooms, an emerald necklace. Of course he—"

Celia caught her breath. "A *loan?*"

"Of course he had a right to lend you the necklace," Roy went on smoothly. "However—not that I want to be disrespectful to my father's memory, but—" he gave her a bland smile—"but I do think he made a mistake in letting you take it away from the family home."

Celia's mouth had popped open. She shut it hard. Roy was speaking in a voice like satin, as if he were a nursemaid trying to cajole a child into giving up the jam.

"And so," he continued, "since I'm head of the house now and responsible for the property, I prefer to have the necklace in my own care. If you'll get it, please, and give it to me—"

Celia cut in, "I think you're out of your mind."

Roy sat up stiff-backed.

"Uncle William didn't lend me that necklace!" Celia said angrily. "It's mine. It belonged to my father."

"Your father," Roy returned, "was the *younger* son, Celia. That necklace is an heirloom, entailed upon the eldest son in each generation. Therefore, it belonged to my father and now it belongs to me."

He was speaking precisely, as though he had rehearsed his lines. Chilly as the room was, Celia felt her skin get hot with rage. The necklace was upstairs in her trunk and she meant to keep it. Controlling her voice with an effort she said, "Uncle William told me the necklace belonged to my father."

Sophie gave a little sigh. Turning to Roy with pretty grace she murmured, "We're due at the Kirbys', dear."

"Yes, I know," Roy answered with a quick smile. He seemed to like being married to her. Addressing Celia again he said, "Let's not have any more fuss. I'm your guardian now." Celia felt a clutch at her stomach. She had forgotten this. "Anything you own is under my control," Roy reminded her. "So give me the necklace. I'll keep it safe, and when you are twenty-one we can consider your claim to it."

Celia sent up a wordless prayer that she was not showing how scared she felt. If only she had somebody to tell her what to do now! Her hand doubled itself into a fist, and to hide this betrayal of nerves she slipped the fist into her pocket. Her knuckles brushed the rabbit's foot.

Jimmy!

She replied carefully, "I can't give it to you now, Roy. My lawyer has it."

"Your lawyer?" repeated Roy. He was surprised, and also he seemed amused at hearing her say "my lawyer." Celia felt like poking her fist into his classic face. Roy went on, "Celia, don't act like a stubborn child! That necklace is part of the family estate."

Celia was so mad, and so scared, that she lost her temper. "The family estate!" she threw back at him. "You sound like you think you're the Duke of Doozenberry." She had sprung to her feet and was standing with her hands clenched at her sides. "Family estate! A lot of debts and rundown land—half of it nothing but a briar-patch—"

Roy was standing up too. With his dark hair and his anger-flushed face, and the black cape swinging around him, he looked dangerous. The thought flashed through Celia's head that she had hit him where it hurt most. Roy had married a rich girl, and maybe neither Sophie nor Sophie's family knew how much he needed what she brought him. But before he could say anything, Sophie's voice, sweet and smooth as cream, slid between Celia and him.

"Could I suggest something, Roy?"

Standing with her dark red cloak held around her, Sophie looked rich and spoilt and adoring. Roy turned toward her, his rage softening as their eyes met. "Certainly, my dear."

Sophie spoke to Celia. "Why don't you tell Roy the name of your lawyer and let them settle things between them?"

This was such sensible advice that Celia felt a grudging respect. She said, "My lawyer is Captain James de Courcey Rand, in Mr. Carter's office."

Roy spoke tersely. "This fellow Rand has the necklace?"

Celia hoped the Lord would forgive her for answering, "Yes, I gave it to Captain Rand to take care of."

"Odd," Roy said frowning. "He didn't tell me."

"Oh for goodness' sake, Roy," Sophie exclaimed in her sweet little-girl voice. "He probably thought you had told Celia she could keep it. He should have asked you, of course—I hope you'll speak to him quite sharply." Roy replied that he certainly would, and Sophie smiled. Eager not to be late at the Kirbys', she asked gently, "Shall we go now?"

This time Roy agreed. He opened the door for Sophie and she went out. But he paused a moment. "I'll see this man Rand in the morning," he said to Celia. "And by the way. The Garths have always been loyal subjects of the king. I was shocked to hear you give a military title to one of these rebel upstarts. Please don't do it again."

Celia said "Cat's foot!" But she was not sure Roy heard her, because without waiting for an answer he had gone out, shutting the door behind him.

## CHAPTER 7

*N*ow she had to see Jimmy and do it fast. She dashed upstairs. Panting, she unlocked her trunk and took out the time-rubbed case of purple velvet with the necklace inside.

The necklace was a really beautiful piece of jewelry, three heavy gold chains twisted together and set with seven emeralds. No wonder Roy wanted it. It would be lovely on Sophie's neck and would impress Sophie's family. The nerve of him, Celia thought as she put on her cloak and drew the hood over her hair. She'd show him.

Carrying the case under her cloak she went out into the damp gray afternoon. The Rands lived on Church Street near Broad. Celia knew the house, but she had never been there and as they attended St. Philip's Church she had glimpsed Jimmy's mother only once or twice, at the shop. She almost ran up Church Street, hoping Jimmy would be at home and that her visit would not be inconvenient.

A house-boy answered the door. Yes'm, he said to her, Mr. Jimmy was home. Yes'm, he'd tell Mr. Jimmy she was here, and would she step inside.

He went off. From down the hall Celia could hear the sound of men's laughter. Somebody was having a fine time.

Almost at once Jimmy appeared from the shadows beyond the

staircase. Hurrying to the front he grabbed her hands. "This is luck! You're just in time to meet my brother Miles. He's here from Bellwood. Come on in."

"Oh Jimmy!" Celia gasped. "Oh Jimmy!" She felt like shedding tears. Jimmy was so—oh, so *nice*. She squeezed back the tears, but even in the faint light of the hall Jimmy could see that she was troubled. He spoke in a lower voice.

"What's the matter, Celia? Can I do anything?"

"Could I talk to you, Jimmy?" she asked—"by yourself?"

"Why of course," said Jimmy. He opened a door. "In here. There's no fire, I'm afraid."

"That's all right." Celia sat down on the first chair she saw, and Jimmy perched on the edge of a table. Celia looked around. What a beautiful room. The furniture was mahogany, the rugs were woven in tapestry designs, there was a marble mantelpiece and a marble statue of a woman in Greek draperies. Jimmy was such an easy-mannered fellow that Celia generally forgot he had the background of a rich young ruler; now for a moment she felt abashed. But Jimmy was watching her with such warm interest that she forgot everything again, except that he wanted to help her.

She showed him the necklace and told him about her visit from Sophie and Roy. "Will you be my lawyer, Jimmy?" she asked.

"I sure will," he answered promptly.

"You'll lock up the necklace?"

"This very day."

"Jimmy, you're wonderful. But—"

"But what?"

"I'm still a minor, just as Roy said. Won't you have to give it to him if he insists?"

Jimmy chuckled wickedly. He linked his lean brown hands around his knee. "My dear, if there's one thing a lawyer knows, it is how to waste time. If I can't dawdle around till you're twenty-one, I ought to go back to school."

"But then?" she asked.

This time Jimmy spoke seriously. "If Roy can show me documentary proof that the necklace was entailed, I'll have to give it to him. But if your uncle told you it was yours he must have

70

known what he was talking about. I rather suspect he had lost the papers—that would have been like him—so there was no proof either way, and he gave it to you in a private interview because he knew Roy would raise cain and poor William just didn't feel equal to a battle."

Celia smiled. Jimmy was so clear-headed. "But you do feel equal to a battle?"

"Me?" Jimmy retorted with merry malice. "If it's a matter of Roy's word against yours—let me point him out to a jury. A strong man, a man of property, persecuting a helpless golden-haired orphan who is clinging to her mother's keepsake! Why, it almost moves me to tears."

Celia did feel moved to tears, and blinked hard so he would not notice.

Jimmy slid off the table. "Give me the necklace," he said, and dropped the case into his coat pocket. "Now come on in by the fire. We were just about to have a glass of wine and a biscuit."

Celia felt another touch of shyness. She did not know what sort of person Jimmy's mother might be, and she had never laid eyes on Miles. But Jimmy was already leading her down the hall. Near the back of the house he opened a door.

As soon as she stepped over the threshold Celia could feel the atmosphere of a pleasant and affectionate home. The room glowed with firelight. In her first glance she saw well-filled bookcases, and chairs that looked comfortably worn, and on a side table pink hyacinths blooming in a bright green bowl. In the room were Jimmy's mother, his brother Miles, his colored man Amos, and Jimmy's big handsome dog-of-no-breed Rosco, with a rabbit's foot on his collar. Mrs. Rand was half reclining on a sofa, Miles and Amos sat on the floor, while the dog lay in a warm corner looking on. He was a shaggy brown dog bigger than a collie, a splendid creature if you did not care who a dog's ancestors were.

Except that her hair was threaded with white, and years of good living had plumpened her figure, Mrs. Rand looked like Jimmy—the same quick black eyes and irregular features, the same air of mischief, the same utter lack of snobbery or pretense. Her maiden name had been Beatrice de Courcey. By descent she was pure French, but her husband's forebears had been English, and Miles Rand was like his father. Lighter in coloring than Mrs. Rand and Jimmy, Miles had a higher forehead and a more high-bridged nose, and he was not as lean and lanky as Jimmy was. But he was like Jimmy in his air of good-fellowship, and Celia felt at ease with him at once. Miles was in town on business. He had not brought his wife because her pregnancy made it dangerous for her to travel in this uncertain weather.

The colored man Amos had a skin the brown of coffee beans, and he looked like a fellow who enjoyed living. Jimmy had told Celia about him: when Amos and Jimmy were both just big enough to run around, Amos had been given to Jimmy as personal servant, and they had grown up together. As for the dog Rosco, Jimmy had found him in the woods on Bellwood Plantation, a stray half-starved puppy with a lame leg. That was eight years ago. Jimmy had brought him home and fed him and doctored his leg, and since then Rosco and Jimmy had never been far apart.

Jimmy took Celia's cloak, Miles poured her a glass of wine, and Amos passed the biscuits. "I've been wanting to know you better," Mrs. Rand said to her. "I've heard about you from Jimmy. Now I hear that Vivian likes your sewing so much she's taking you to Sea Garden."

Jimmy grinned. He was straddling a chair, resting his glass on the back of it. His mother continued,

"Amos, bring back the biscuits. Of course, child, you'll have two. With that waistline you can have a dozen." She laughed and patted her own plump sides. "Quite a bit of padding I've got. But oh, the fun I had getting it!"

Celia laughed too, and took another biscuit. They were flat little biscuits flavored with benne seed, which Miles had brought from Bellwood. Miles asked Celia how she liked this wine; he was proud of it, he had made it himself from grapes raised at Bellwood. Jimmy said she must forgive them, but the Rands all thought anything from Bellwood was better than anything raised anywhere else.

They were so happy and friendly that Celia would have liked to stay for hours. But Aunt Louisa had taught her that when you made an unexpected visit you should keep it short, so when she had finished her wine she stood up and said she must go. They urged her to stay longer, but she shook her head. Jimmy said he would walk with her back to the shop.

As he opened the front door Jimmy exclaimed that it was colder than he had thought, and asked her to wait while he got his cloak. When he had left her, Celia looked thoughtfully down the hall toward the sitting room. She had a puzzling sense of lonesomeness.

Celia was not used to feeling lonesome. Without thinking much about it, she got along with other people well enough. But Jimmy and his mother and brother, his servant and his dog—they had something she did not have. She had sensed it as soon as she went into that room. It was not merely that they got along; they had a warmth, an understanding, a—she could not define it, but she knew it was there.

Celia began to realize that she had never felt really close to anybody. As she stood between the warm sitting room and the chilly street, she felt that she was going out of Jimmy's kind of life into her own kind, and she did not like the change.

Jimmy came into the hall, wearing a long blue cape and three-cornered hat. "After I've seen you home," he said as they walked down Church Street, "I'll stop at the office and put your necklace in my strongbox."

They crossed Broad Street. Over at the east end where Broad Street met the Cooper River, they could see the great dark pile of the Exchange, and gray sea-gulls crossing the gray sky. Celia was remembering that ever since she had first met Jimmy she had thought there was something delightfully special about him, but she had not known what it was. Now she knew. Without being conscious of it, Jimmy showed the way he had been living all his life. That was what he had and she had not. But she still did not know what to call it.

They had fallen silent as they walked along. The street was nearly empty, for not many people took a Sunday stroll in such murky weather. Celia looked up at Jimmy. He smiled, and pushing his cape aside he drew her hand warmly into the bend of his elbow. As he did so, Celia knew what it was she had sensed when she went into that room. It was love. Not love for anybody in particular, just love. Jimmy was used to loving and being loved, and she was not. That was why she had felt lonesome.

They were nearing the shop. When the girls went out with their friends they were supposed to use the side door, so Jimmy and Celia walked along the side street and went up the steps to the door. The little hallway was empty, though they could hear the voices of the girls and their boy-friends from the back parlor. Closing the hall door behind him Jimmy spoke in an undertone.

"Now if anybody mentions the necklace, say you won't discuss it without advice of counsel."

"Counsel—that's you?"

"That's me."

"Jimmy, I—I don't know how to thank you."

"Don't try. I like doing it."

"You're grand. And Jimmy."

"Yes?"

"Since I'm leaving tomorrow, I'd better give this back." She took the rabbit's foot from her pocket.

Jimmy seemed surprised. "Why give it back?"

"I shouldn't take it out of town," said Celia. "Anyway, it's been a long time since you lent it to me."

"Lent it? I thought I gave it to you."

"Oh no you didn't!"

"Well, I'm giving it to you now."

"Oh but Jimmy—you've had it so long, and it matches the one on Rosco's collar—"

"That one will be luck enough for Rosco and me both." Taking her hand, he closed her fingers over the rabbit's foot and held them firm. "After all, weren't you born on a Friday the thirteenth?"

They smiled at each other intimately, as though the rabbit's foot was an important secret between them. Celia was glad he had given it to her. It would be like having Jimmy with her while she was away.

"Thank you so much, so very much," she said. Jimmy was still holding her hand with her fingers closed over the rabbit's foot, and looking down at her with that intimate smile. Celia added,

"I'm not sure how long Mrs. Lacy wants me to stay at Sea Garden. But for now, this is good-by."

"Good-by," said Jimmy, and then before she knew what he was doing, he had kissed her.

It was a kiss so light, so quick and yet so definite, that Celia started and caught her breath. In that same instant Jimmy put an arm around her and pulled her to him and kissed her again, and there was nothing quick or light about this one. In her amazement the bleak little hallway spun around her with the colors of paradise. She could not have told whether it was two seconds or ten minutes before she heard him say,

"Oh Celia, I know so many words—I can read Latin and I can speak French—but how does a man tell a girl in plain English that he loves her?"

Celia had wondered a thousand times what she would say in a moment like this, if she ever had one. And now that she had it, her throat closed up. Those tears that had been crowding her eyes all afternoon could be held back no longer and came tumbling down in the most idiotic fashion, but though she was crying she was laughing too, laughing softly and joyfully. She was astonished, she was speechless with the suddenness of what had happened. But it seemed that a thousand voices were singing in her heart, and what they told her was,

"This—this is what you've been missing!"

The thought lifted her on a warm cloud of happiness. She hid her face on Jimmy's blue-caped shoulder while he held his arms around her and she felt him kiss her hair. But at length—again she had no idea how long it had been—she managed to look up and answer him.

"I don't know how a man says it—I don't know how a girl says it either—I'm so amazed I'm dizzy—but I love you too."

And then, among all those words he knew, Jimmy found the right ones. Holding her head on his shoulder and stroking her hair, Jimmy made her understand that she was never going to be lonesome again. He had been trying for weeks to say this, he told her, but every time he tried he got scared. No, his mother didn't know about it, nor Miles—did she think he'd tell anybody before he told her?

"But I had to tell you now," he said, "because you're going away. Celia, Sea Garden isn't far—I'll come up there, we'll talk and make plans and do all the sensible things people have to do, but right now, I just wanted you to know."

Celia drew back a little so she could look up at him. The hallway had grown dark, but she felt as if all the light on earth was shining out of her eyes.

Then all of a sudden she and Jimmy were reminded that they were not alone in the world.

At the far end of the hall a door opened. They jerked apart. Through the doorway came the thin beshawled figure of Miss Loring, a candle in one hand and a bell in the other. She set the candle on the hall table, and ringing the bell as she walked she came toward the front and opened the parlor door.

"Six o'clock, ladies," she announced sharply. "Gentlemen, visiting hours are over." She spoke over her shoulder to Jimmy. "Sunday callers leave at six, young man."

Jimmy bowed. "Certainly, ma'am. I was just leaving."

He opened the outside door and stepped through. Since he was so obedient Miss Loring paid him no more attention, but went into the parlor to hurry out the young men lingering there. From beyond the door Jimmy reached his long arm into the hall and drew Celia out on the top step by him, in the dark.

"Good night," he whispered. "Darling."

He kissed her again, a kiss that had to be hardly more than a touch because Miss Loring was about to send everybody else out upon them. Then Jimmy was down the steps and gone. With a little sobbing catch in her throat Celia ran down the steps too, and along the side street to Lamboll Street, just in time to see Jimmy passing a lantern, and then the end of his cloak swinging around the next corner.

For a moment she stood still. She felt as if a wind full of stars had swept around her. It had all happened so suddenly that she could not think. She was only feeling that right this minute she was happier than she had ever been before, and why hadn't somebody told her it was like this to fall in love?

From high in the darkness she heard a musical whisper, the bells of St. Michael's marking the hour. How beautiful it was, this sound of the bells. It was as if the city had a voice of its own, and was saying "God bless you." The bells never seemed loud, yet you could hear them from end to end of town; when the wind was right you could even hear them out at sea.

And now within sound of the bells Jimmy had kissed her. Celia thought she would love the bells as long as she lived, and whenever she went away she would be homesick for them. She wished she were not going away tomorrow.

In the spire of St. Michael's the beacon flashed on and lit up the bonny town beneath. As she turned to go indoors Celia felt gay and warm. What was it Vivian had said the other day?—"Don't fall in love, Celia. It's just asking for trouble."

Now really, how stupid could an old woman get?

CHAPTER 8

*T*HEY WENT UP to Sea Garden on Herbert Lacy's trim little schooner. It was a beautiful trip through the soft autumn haze, among the chains of sea islands along the coast. With Herbert and Vivian, Celia sat on deck in a folding chair, a blanket over her knees and a book in her hand, but she did not read much. She had her own delicious thoughts.

Early this morning, when they were about to step on board the schooner, Jimmy had come down to the wharf to say good-by. He shook hands with Herbert, he wished Vivian a pleasant trip; and then he snatched a moment to whisper to Celia, "What I'm really here for is to tell you again, I love you."

Now Celia looked over the gray-blue water and the palmetto trees along the white beaches of the islands. She liked everything —the smart little boat and the salt air; the Negro crewmen, so expert that they never made a wrong turn in this tangle of water-paths; the lunch that the maids unpacked from hampers and served on deck. She had never dreamed how pleasant it could be to go from one place to another.

In the afternoon the men turned the boat into a little stream about ten miles south of the Santee River. They sailed between banks lined with moss-hung oaks and tall tupelo trees, till they came to a landing made of flat stones, from which a road led through the woods. Beside the landing, a bell hung from a cross-bar between two uprights. Vivian closed her novel and Herbert his volume of Plato as one of the men scrambled ashore and pulled the bellrope. This told the folk at Sea Garden that the master and mistress were home.

Standing on deck, waiting for the carts that would take them to the big house, Celia felt as if she was about to enter an enchanted forest.

•~•

Sea Garden was so near the coast that sometimes you could smell a salt tang in the air. This was why Vivian had called it Sea Garden.

She had owned the place since she was a girl in her teens. Vivian's family name was Pomeroy. From the earliest days of the colony the Pomeroys had been planters in the rich neighborhood of Goose Creek, where the family property still belonged to Vivian's brother Dan. Since Dan had been heir to the plantation, Vivian's father had provided that she should have an inheritance of her own: money, jewelry, and a building site in Charleston. Not many girls had such a dowry.

But Vivian had wanted land. Even then, before life had shown her how cruelly uncertain it could be, Vivian had sensed by some deep instinct that land was real, something you could count on. She begged her father to let her take part of her dowry and buy land.

As usual, Vivian got her way. This land was public property and she bought it cheap from the king's administrators. She told them she had chosen it because she liked the quietness and the sharp whiffs from the sea. This was true, but the real reason was that Vivian had seen the fine tupelo trees along the river banks and she knew that tupelos grew to that size only in the richest soil. The king's men did not know this. They were Britishers who had been given their fat jobs in America because they knew somebody at court, not because they knew anything about America.

Vivian loved Sea Garden. Whenever she married she would change her address to match her husband's, but this was her real home. Through all the changes of her life—while she married five men and was four times widowed, bore six children and watched two of them die, while she was sick or well, happy or heartbroken —Sea Garden had been her place of refuge. Since Herbert's retirement from charge of his own plantation they had lived here whenever they were not in town.

Set by a tiny stream, miles from the main road, Sea Garden was remote. You were not likely to come across it unless you knew it was there. Most of the property was still covered by forest, for the Lacys raised only what they used themselves. Thus they could leave the place in care of their Negro foreman, and go to Charleston—or in peaceful days to Europe—whenever they pleased.

Vivian had set the house on a little rise, in a grove of mighty oaks that had stood there for three hundred years. Because it was so far from everywhere she had built the house like a fortress, of cypress beams on a raised brick basement that had walls four feet thick. Like the town house, this one was not elaborate, but it had charm and comfort and security. Celia loved it at once.

Vivian kept her busy. In the mornings she sewed; in the afternoons she read aloud, or wrote letters, brief and arrow-sharp, at Vivian's dictation. "Mrs. Miles Rand, Bellwood Plantation, parish of St. Thomas. My dear Audrey, No wonder you are tired of waiting. I know these nine months seem endless. But Nature takes her own time. You cannot hurry a tree, or a baby, or a hard boiled egg."

When she had finished writing Celia went outdoors. As she walked under the trees, while the wind sent the leaves swirling around her and the sun fell on the ground like splashes of yellow wine, she wondered if anywhere on earth there was another such perfect place for a girl to be in love.

She did not keep her secret long. On Saturday of that same week Jimmy and Amos came riding up to Sea Garden, and while Marietta entertained Amos in the kitchen with cold ham and hot crackling-bread, Jimmy told Herbert and Vivian his news.

They were not surprised. Jimmy said his mother had not been surprised either. He had not realized he was so easy to see through, he added with a chuckle as he handed Celia a note his mother had written.

Celia felt a qualm. Mrs. Rand was a dear, but you never could tell how a man's mother was going to react to things like this. While Vivian showed Jimmy to a room—she always had rooms ready for guests—Celia slipped into the library. Sitting on the floor by the hearth she held the page to the firelight.

The note was short. "My dear Celia, Jimmy has told me the good news. I am delighted that you are going to be one of us. Affectionately, Beatrice Rand."

As she read it Celia had a sense of warmth and comfort that had nothing to do with the fire. She remembered the room she had been in last Sunday afternoon. And now she was going to belong there too. "One of us." It sounded so sweet, so welcoming, as if the atmosphere of that room was reaching out to enclose her.

When Jimmy came into the library they sat on the sofa by the fire and he told her about his conversation with his mother. Beatrice said she had heard good reports of Celia and she approved of the engagement, and she asked how soon he wanted to be married. But when Jimmy said right away, Beatrice burst out laughing and said getting married was not something you did at a week's notice. Besides, Miles and Audrey were expecting their baby in February. The first offspring of the head of the house—boy or girl, this would be an important baby, to be treated with respect. Everything else must stand aside till after the christening. That would be quite an affair, with uncles and aunts and cousins to be entertained—

Celia had never had any feeling of being part of a unit, belonging to other people and sharing their lives. "Oh Jimmy," she said softly, "it sounds so complicated—but so wonderful!"

Jimmy said it was wonderful and not complicated at all. Since the christening would be in March, if Celia approved he would like to set their wedding for April. And as she attended St. Michael's church, they would be married there by the rector, the Reverend Mr. Moreau. Celia agreed, and Jimmy said he would speak to Mr. Moreau as soon as he went back to town.

He turned so he could look squarely at her. His face had the happy glow that she knew and liked so well.

"Now," he said, "you're going to write a letter for me to take back to town, telling Mrs. Thorley you're giving up your job. You can finish whatever work you're doing for Vivian, but after that you're sewing for nobody. And until next April you're staying here with the Lacys."

Celia started. "Oh Jimmy, what makes you think they'll want me? Have you asked them?"

"Vivian suggested it herself," said Jimmy. "They both like you, and they like having people around. It keeps them from worrying. They've got plenty on their minds. Luke you know about, and Mr. Lacy has a grandson named Tom who's fighting with the Continentals somewhere around Philadelphia. What all this is leading up to—"

He paused for a tantalizing instant, then said,

"Vivian is going to give a ball for you, New Year's Eve."

Celia gasped. Nobody had ever given any sort of entertainment in her honor.

"She loves to give parties," Jimmy went on, "and she said this was a fine excuse. For your ball-gown she's going to give you a piece of stuff Godfrey brought her, I think she said garnet-red velvet—"

Garnet-red velvet. Quite suddenly, Celia burst into tears.

Jimmy took her in his arms and laughed at her. But Celia shook her head.

"It's too perfect," she said in a choking voice. Reaching into her pocket she grasped the rabbit's foot and held it tight as she insisted, "Nothing can be this perfect. Jimmy—I'm scared."

·~·

But after that day she had no time to be scared. She had too much to do.

She helped Vivian write invitations to the New Year's ball. She cut and stitched her dress of garnet velvet. She ran upstairs and down on Vivian's errands. Everybody in the household was running about—everybody but Herbert and Vivian. Herbert retired to his library or went for long horseback rides, blandly ignoring the fluster. As for Vivian, she reclined on the long chair in her boudoir and gave orders, and while the others bustled around her she remained calm as a cabbage.

New Year's Eve would come this year on a Friday. Most of the guests were expected to arrive the day before and stay over Sunday. Every bedroom in the house would be full, as well as the two guest-houses at the back, while the stables and servants' quarters would almost bulge. Audrey wrote Celia a pretty note, saying the state of her health prevented her attending the ball, but she did want to know Jimmy's bride-to-be. Wouldn't Celia come to Bellwood in March, and be her guest for the week of the christening?

Celia wrote back that she would be delighted. While she sewed on her ball-dress she thought of all she would do to make Jimmy's family like her. She would be always agreeable. She would carry on about the baby as if she had never seen one before. She would listen carefully to find out which relatives the baby was supposed to look like, so she could exclaim, "The very image of Uncle John!" All babies looked alike to her, but she would not say so, or make any other sassy remarks.

Even Roy was being amiable. Jimmy had written him about their engagement, and Roy had responded with joyful surprise. He said no more about the necklace. To Celia's relief, he said that since he and Sophie were in mourning they would not attend the ball.

She was planning to wear the necklace that evening, and a pair of bracelets Jimmy had given her. These were two garlands of gold roses, which Jimmy's grandfather had given his bride, mother of Jimmy's mother. "And now," Jimmy said to Celia, "they're yours."

•～•

At last it was the evening of December 31, 1779. The tall clock on the staircase landing at Sea Garden showed less than an hour before midnight. In an interval between dances Celia and Jimmy stood with a group by the punch-table in a corner of the ball-room, Celia in her dress of dark red velvet, Jimmy tall and dashing in his blue coat with silver buttons. As she looked over the assembly Celia thought she had never seen anything so magnificent.

The ballroom was two stories high and occupied a whole wing of the house. On three sides were long windows, and mirrors on the walls between them. On the fourth side was a marble fireplace with a leaping fire. The room was lit by two hundred candles. Pale green, made of the sweet wax of myrtleberries, the candles filled the air with fragrance. The candle-flames and firelight shone back and forth from the mirrors, and the beautiful people promenading the dance-floor moved as though in the radiance of a dream.

On a platform were the chairs of the Negro musicians, empty now while the men were outside around another punch-bowl. But the ballroom had a music of its own. Celia listened to it— voices and laughter, footsteps on the floor, the swish of skirts, now and then a clink as two friends touched their glasses. Outdoors, the night was black and sloshy, with gusts of icy rain. But here everything was bright, everybody was gay; between the window-curtains Celia saw raindrops sparkling on the panes like reflections of the women's jewels.

Her own reflection came back to her from a mirror on the wall. "I'm not really beautiful," she said to herself, "but tonight I feel beautiful. And I look like a girl who feels beautiful."

She had made the dark red velvet into a dress of splendid simplicity: low square neck, bodice that nipped her waistline to exquisite smallness, big skirt trailing behind her. Around her throat she wore the emerald necklace, on her arms Jimmy's bracelets of gold roses. In the candlelight her eyes were lustrous, dark brown, and her blond hair glowed like a moonbeam. Jimmy had said her hair was too pretty to be covered with powder. So Celia had brushed it to a shimmer, and Marietta had put it up into a fashionable coiffure with a decoration of little flowers made of the same dark red velvet as her dress.

She took a step to one side so she could see Jimmy in the mirror. He was handing a glass of punch to Vivian's daughter Madge Penfield. How debonair he looked—his blue coat, cascades of white lawn at his throat and wrists, his black hair in glistening ripples, his white silk stockings and silver-buckled shoes. She glanced from the mirror to Jimmy himself; for a moment their eyes met and they exchanged a quick smile. Then Jimmy, all grace, turned to Burton Dale's stout rosy wife Elise and asked if she would take a glass of punch.

Celia looked around again. She saw Herbert Lacy, in a pink

coat and white wig, chatting with Dan Pomeroy. Vivian was moving about with the poise of the perfect hostess, deft, gracious, beautiful. She was superbly dressed in white satin with an over-skirt of black lace. Her hair was a white tower, her jewelry silver with amethysts. Every man she passed, from ancient Simon Dale leaning on his gold-topped cane, to eighteen-year-old Paul de Courcey strutting in his brand new rebel uniform, paused as she went by and inclined his head in instinctive tribute. Vivian accepted their homage with the ease of long custom. She had been fascinating men for fifty years and it was no surprise to her that she was doing it still.

It seemed to Celia that everything had been perfect, from the very beginning of the ball when she and Jimmy had stepped forth to lead the minuet. She had been a miracle of grace—those were Jimmy's words, but even Vivian said she had done well. When Celia exclaimed, "Oh thank you, Mrs. Lacy!"—Vivian laughed and said, "I think now you may call me Vivian."

Celia liked this. Not only because it meant she had won Vivian's approval, but because it marked the change in her own status. She wondered if Jimmy would ever know how much he was giving her. These people—how different their attitude was now, from what it had been in her pre-Jimmy days!

Not all the guests had met her before, but a sizable number of them had come to the shop while she worked there. Celia observed these with amusement. When Vivian made the introductions, some of them greeted her as if they had never seen her until now, evidently thinking it tactful to ignore the fact that she had been a sewing-girl. But others were like Mrs. Baxter, who gushed, "Oh yes, I know Miss Garth, we are *quite* old friends." Or like Rena Fairbanks, who had been to school with Celia but had not called attention to it until tonight when she exclaimed, "We must get together soon and have a good long talk about the old days!" Celia smiled with cool politeness. It was fun to do a little snubbing herself.

But in general, they had been charming. She was the guest of honor and they treated her like it. She had danced and danced, and still had a list of gentlemen waiting their turns. She had even danced with Burton Dale, and though he had huffed and puffed through the measures he had danced with skill. But Burton's half-brother Godfrey Bernard, he was lean and light on his feet as a boy, and he had a suave elegance of manner that no boy could match.

Darren was not here. When she asked about him, Godfrey said he had sent Darren on a business trip. They had expected him back in time for the ball; probably the weather had delayed him. Celia was disappointed, but not too much. There were plenty of other men.

The next dance had been timed to end just before midnight. As it ended, the waiters would pass glasses of wine, and open the door to the hall so they could all hear the great clock strike twelve. Then when they had drunk to a happy New Year, Herbert and Vivian, followed by Jimmy and herself, would lead the way into the dining-room for supper.

And what a supper!—crab soup and scalloped oysters, wild duck cooked in wine, baked whiting with shrimp sauce, smoked ham, veal in coin-thin slices covered with cream; jellies and tarts and cream-puffs, and Madeira wine that had been aging for years in the cypress attic.

And after supper, more dancing. Celia set her glass on the table and exchanged another rapturous smile with Jimmy. The older folks might prefer to sit by the wall after supper and look on, but she and Jimmy were not tired. They felt like dancing till dawn.

It was time to primp for that next dance. As she crossed the hall toward the dressing room she could hear the clock, ponderously ticking toward midnight.

When Marietta had smoothed her hair and patted her temples with rosewater, Celia came back to the ballroom. She and Jimmy took their places. As they danced Celia looked around at the brilliant costumes and flashing jewels, and thought of a flower garden sparkling after a shower.

The dance ended, and the waiters began to pass the wine. The men of the family moved to stand in a group before the door to the hall—Herbert and his son Eugene, and Vivian's sons Burton and Godfrey. When she had beckoned Celia and Jimmy to the front so they would stand facing Herbert, Vivian took her place beside him.

One of the waiters placed a footstool in front of the doorway. Herbert stepped on the stool so they could all see him, and held up his glass. With his glistening white wig, his pink coat and lace ruffles, his face flushed with pleasure—for Herbert enjoyed a party as long as he had nothing to do but enjoy it—he looked gay and cordial, a man who had liked every one of his seventy years. The guests fell silent as he began to speak.

"Ladies and gentlemen, in a few minutes the year 1780 will begin. As you know, we are here to congratulate our fortunate friend Captain Rand on his engagement to Miss Celia Garth. So as our last act of the old year, let us drink to their happiness!"

As all the glasses were raised together it was like the sparkling of a thousand stars. There was a medley of words and laughter. Celia felt Jimmy's hand give her elbow a squeeze.

The waiters were refilling the glasses. Herbert raised his hand again to ask for silence.

"The clock is about to strike," he said. "Listen!"

They listened. Then it came, the deep solemn sound of the clock. Bong, bong—Celia felt her heart bounce like a ship in the wind. It was so beautiful, so thrilling—she looked at Jimmy. Soundlessly, his lips moved to say to her, "Happy New Year!"

—Bong, said the clock. Bong—

There was a noise outside. It was a noise made of many noises —horses' hoofs squelching in the mud, men shouting orders, a pounding on the front door and the sound of the door bursting open. In the hall, servants cried out in alarm and a dish dropped and broke on the floor. In the ballroom the whole company, as if pushed from behind, took a step toward the doorway. The room was suddenly full of voices as everybody asked everybody else what was going on.

Jimmy was holding Celia to him with an arm around her waist. A man strode into the ballroom, a burly creature who smelt like a wet dog. He had on a leather jacket and breeches, heavy riding-boots and a wide hat, and his face was covered with whiskers. His clothes were mud-spattered, dripping on the polished floor;

trickles ran off his sodden hat to his shoulders. The hat-brim was so limp that it hung forward and hid most of his face above the beard.

Just over the threshold he stopped. With a look of bewilderment he stared at the brilliant throng. A hundred shrill questions came at him, but he answered nothing because in that moment of shock he seemed to hear nothing. Three or four other bedraggled men came behind him, and like him they stopped as if blinded by the glitter within. And then—it was only an instant but it had seemed like a long time—they heard a cry from Vivian, a cry like music and laughter as she sprang forward.

"*Luke!*"

He turned and saw her, and swept her into his arms. They hugged each other, neither of them concerned that his miry clothes were wrecking her lace and satin, and the ardor of his embrace was sending her hair-powder up in a cloud that settled on his whiskers and made him look as if he had fallen into the flour barrel.

By this time a dozen mud-dripping men had come in. The guests were surging around them, and now there were more exclamations as this one and that recognized friends under the beards. Celia saw Herbert and Eugene Lacy grab the elbows of one fellow, and at the same time Jimmy cried, "Why there's Tom Lacy," and he let go of her as he hurried forward. Celia stood still, uncertain what to do now.

She was almost within touching distance of Luke and Vivian. "You crazy fool," Vivian was saying to him, "what have you been—"

Looking around at the dazzling room, Luke did not seem to hear her. "Mother, what is all this?" he asked. He spoke as if he had come upon some orgy in a strange land.

"A ball, silly—New Year's Eve!"

"Oh," Luke said. "New Year's Eve." He nodded vaguely, almost stupidly, like a man who had not for weeks past thought of what day it might be.

"Now tell me about you!" begged Vivian. She was so glad to see him that she was hardly aware of the others around her. Luke had pulled off his hat and was holding it crumpled in his hand, while dirty water dripped from the brim to the floor. All around the doorway were puddles and muddy footprints where the other men had come in. "You haven't been all the way to Philadelphia in this time!" Vivian exclaimed.

One of Luke's companions came hurrying over, elbowing fine gentlemen out of his way. He spoke to Luke.

Celia did not catch his words, but she heard Luke say, "Yes, yes, bring them in! Put them over there by the fire." He turned sharply. "Clear that door! Can't you hear me?—get out of the way."

Two men came in carrying a stretcher. Behind them in the hall Celia saw more stretchers approaching. On the stretchers were men with blood on their shirts, and clumsy bandages on their heads or arms or legs. As the carriers set down the first stretcher by the fireplace she gave a gasp of horror, for the man lying there was Darren, and on Darren's forehead was a tumble of golden-brown curls smeared with blood. Pushing through the crowd Celia rushed to the hearth and dropped on her knees beside him.

Darren seemed unconscious. Unlike Luke, he was shaved and he wore a good woolen suit, dripping now with the rain. Celia took his cold hand and rubbed it between her own. Leaning over the other side of the stretcher were Godfrey and Luke. "Darren will be all right," Luke was saying, "if this rain doesn't clog his lungs." As he glanced up toward the carriers bringing another wounded man, he saw Celia. With strained courtesy he said, "Will you please move out of the way, ma'am?"

Evidently he saw her only as a blur. Celia got to her feet, feeling about as important as a fly on the wall.

Except for Luke and the men with him—about thirty of them besides the five or six who had been wounded—nobody seemed to know what had happened. The whole ballroom was a-buzz. Servants had crowded in, and were fluttering about as if they wished somebody would tell them what to do. The guests were asking questions of each other, or of the air; or were staring around as if they expected to see handwriting on the wall. Several men were hurrying hither and yon, nervously telling other people to be calm, while two or three women stood sobbing in the middle of the floor.

Just as Celia had the impression that nobody was acting with any sense, the group around the hearth parted as if they had heard a command. Down the aisle thus made came Vivian, a bottle in each hand. Behind her was Jimmy carrying a tray with glasses and a pitcher.

In spite of the dirty streaks on her white satin, Vivian looked elegant and tranquil. "We'll have help for these men in a minute," she said to Luke. "In the meantime a swig of brandy won't hurt them, or you either."

Luke gave her a grateful smile. Jimmy was already kneeling by the stretchers, and Vivian handed him the bottles as she went on talking to Luke. The only surgeon on the place, she said, was the Negro who took care of the animals, but he knows a good deal about treating human wounds too. One of the house-boys had been sent to bring him in. "And now," Vivian ended crisply, "will you please tell me what's been going on!"

Luke stood with one elbow on the marble mantelpiece, his hand hanging limp. In his other hand he held the glass of brandy that Jimmy had passed up to him. Now that his men were safe Luke was letting himself relax. He was tired, almost too tired to talk. On the floor Godfrey was raising Darren's head and holding a drink to his lips; Jimmy was giving brandy and water to another man, and beside him, also giving aid, was the man he had addressed as Tom Lacy. A big fair young man, Tom had a bristly golden beard and a mane of straw-colored hair tied back with a leather cord.

Luke drained his glass. Still kneeling by the stretchers, Jimmy demanded, "Who did this, Luke?"

Luke drew a long tired breath. "Tories."

"Tories!" gasped Jimmy, and with him everybody else near enough to have heard the word. In the country below Charleston Tory bands had done a lot of raiding and looting, but here near the Santee the rebel sentiment was so strong that they had made little trouble.

Luke nodded, a grim expression around his vivid blue eyes. "They were after a cargo of salt," he said, "on one of Godfrey's ships from Bermuda."

Celia began to understand. There was no salt in South Carolina.

From the first settlement of the colony their salt had come from the salt-springs of Bermuda, and now smuggling it in was a vital business. Luke went on,

"There's a storehouse near the landing here, for bulky supplies that the Sea Garden boat brings up from Charleston. Godfrey had planned to store the salt there. Two or three days ago he got word that his ship was here, creeping among the islands, so he sent Darren and some others to get the salt into the storehouse. They were unloading the boat when a pack of Tories attacked. Thank God we came up in time."

There was another flurry of questions. Luke said they had saved the salt and left men to guard it. Jimmy asked,

"What makes the Tories so bold, all of a sudden?"

"I suppose," Luke said with a shrug, "they've heard the same news we have."

More questions. The group around him had been thickening with every word he spoke. Now Vivian's voice slipped like a thread of silk among the rougher voices of the men. "Tell us the news, Luke."

He spoke crisply. "The British are on their way to attack Charleston."

This time there was such a clatter of words that it was hard to make sense out of any of them. Celia moved closer, in time to hear Luke say,

"You'd better let Tom tell you. He's the one who told me. I was on my way north with my wagon party when we met Tom and his fellows riding south. I let the wagons go on to Philadelphia without me—if there's going to be trouble at home I want to be here." He held out the brandy bottle to Tom.

Tom sat back on the floor, his legs crossed in front of him. Above his beard his face was stung red by the wind and his eyes looked sunken. When he spoke, his voice had the dull monotone of weariness.

Tom said that when he learned the British were preparing for an attack on Charleston, he and various other Carolinians who had been in the northern army had received permission to come home. He and several of his friends had left Philadelphia eight weeks ago. At that time, the British—who had been occupying New

York for three years—had had a hundred ships in New York harbor ready to move south. Their leader was Sir Henry Clinton, commander-in-chief of the king's forces in America. Everybody in Charleston would recognize his name, for Sir Henry Clinton had been in command of the British land forces at the battle of Fort Moultrie. His second in command now was the Earl of Cornwallis.

Clinton had plenty of men—British, Hessians, and of course—here Tom's voice lost its tired dullness and he spoke the word venomously—*Tories*. Naturally the Tories had a British commander. Americans were good enough to fight for his fat majesty but not good enough to lead their own regiments. These Tories were led by a Britisher named Tarleton. They called themselves "Tarleton's Legion."

While he talked Celia saw Vivian in the background, watching Luke, so glad to have him at home that she did not care how frightening was the news he brought. Plainly she was fonder of him than of Burton or Madge or Godfrey, just as she had cared more for Luke's father than for any of her other husbands. Yet neither Luke nor his father would do what she wanted—and it occurred to Celia that maybe this was why she loved them best.

This was the first time Celia had seen Luke and Vivian together. She was surprised to notice how much alike they were. Luke was supposed to look like his father, and probably he did—for one thing, he had blue eyes while Vivian's were brown, and his features were more rugged than hers—but there was a resemblance: the humorous look about their eyes, their determined mouths and strong chins, the general expression of both their faces. Nobody would be surprised to hear that they were mother and son.

Celia realized that she had not been listening to Tom Lacy, and she pulled her attention back. Tom was saying the British had sworn to turn Charleston into a pile of trash. They had two good reasons for it. One was that they had never gotten over their licking at Fort Moultrie. The other reason was that they had to stop those supply trains. Traffic on the wagon track was so secret that few people realized how thick it was. But the British commanders knew.

Tom was interrupted by the arrival of the Negro surgeon and his helpers. The other men moved aside. They pressed around Luke and Tom, eager to hear more.

Celia drew back against the wall. She had thought she was not tired, but now her legs ached and her back hurt and she wanted to rest. Looking for a chair, she made her way along the wall; but every chair was occupied, and everybody was talking while nobody listened. She heard Madge Penfield say, "Bobby's only fifteen but he's been begging to get into it—now I'll never keep him at home."

At last Celia paused by the hall door where Luke had come in—how long ago? Hardly an hour, but in that little time how everything had changed!

She looked around at the wreckage of her betrothal ball. The floor was scratched, tracked with mud, smeared with dirty water. She could smell blood and a sharp odor of medicine. Jimmy and Godfrey were carrying Darren toward a bedroom. All around, women were weeping and shivering, men were pacing, shouting, slashing the air with their arms as if they were making speeches in Congress. Several of them were peering out of the windows as if they expected to see King George himself come riding through the rain. At the punch-table Paul de Courcey and some other young cavaliers were raising glasses in celebration of the glorious deeds they were going to do.

Somebody had thrown open the doors to the dining room. Now the men were gobbling the exquisite supper, going back and forth with bread and meat in their dirty hands, dripping gravy on their coats, spilling scraps all over the floor. Half of them, guzzling out of bottles, were already red in the face and talking too loud.

Her beautiful party had turned ugly and threatening and sad. The British were on their way to attack Charleston, to kill her friends—she felt a clutch of terror. By next New Year's Eve, some of the men in this room would be dead.

Celia prayed silently, "Please, Lord, don't let me think about that! I can't bear it."

She heard determined footsteps coming her way. Above the confusion these steps had a sound of purpose. Turning her head she saw Luke striding toward the door. By the hearth he had not seen her, but now he did, and he stopped short.

"Why—Sassyface!" he exclaimed. His blue eyes looked her up and down—her fashionable coiffure, the emerald necklace, the dress of dark red velvet with the close bodice and flaring skirt. On his bewhiskered face appeared a grin of admiration. "Wow!" Luke said earnestly.

Celia smiled at him. He made her feel so much better. Luke continued,

"How enchanting you are. I haven't seen anything like you since—since the last time I saw you."

She wondered how many girls he had said that to, since the last time he saw her. Not that it mattered. What mattered was that he had swept away her rising panic and made her feel again like a girl at a party. "Where are you going?" she asked him. "Not back outdoors in all this rain!"

"Why yes. I've got to take care of Jerry."

"Jerry?"

"My horse. I've put him under a shed, but I want to get him to the stable so he can have a rubdown and some corn. Though after seeing you," he added, "I think I'll let Jerry wait a few minutes longer." His eyes flashed over her again. "Is your figure really that good," he asked, "or do you do it with stuffing and whalebones?"

Celia began to laugh. "Do you think it's any of your business?"

"I'm afraid not," he answered sadly. "I wish it was. Maybe I've got no business right now but Jerry."

Jerry, she thought, Jeremiah the prophet. That was Luke for you, flirting like a heathen and choosing a Bible name for his horse. "And you, all the time quoting the Bible," she reproached him, "and even naming your horse out of it."

Luke replied mirthfully. "I'm glad you noticed his name. Because—" he spoke with a slow teasing drawl—"because an ordinary person, now, might think Jerry was short for Jeremiah. But of course, an intelligent young woman like you has already recognized that Jerry is short for Jeroboam-the-son-of-Nebat-who-caused-Israel-to-sin, as recorded in the Books of the Kings."

"I never heard of him in my life," Celia retorted, and before they could say anything else another voice exclaimed, "There you are!" Jimmy came hurrying toward them. "I've been looking for you," he said to Celia.

She smiled happily, and Jimmy said to Luke,

"Aren't you going to congratulate me?"

"Gladly," said Luke, "if you'll tell me what for."

"Didn't anybody tell you that this ball is to celebrate our engagement?"

"No!" Luke exclaimed, and his grin was like a burst of light. He could hardly have looked more pleased if Jimmy had brought him a pot of gold. "I do congratulate you, Jimmy," he said heartily. "And as for you, Celia, I wish you all the happiness there is."

Celia smiled and thanked him. But she felt a little bit puzzled and a little bit chagrined. It was not *quite* a compliment for a man to be so *very* glad to hear of a girl's engagement to somebody else.

Luke had put his hand on the doorknob. "I'll be around," he said joyfully, "to drink champagne on your golden wedding."

He went out to see to his horse. Jimmy asked Celia if she didn't want some supper—the tables, he said, were not completely demolished. They started toward the dining room. But without meaning to do so, Celia glanced back over her shoulder to the door where Luke had just gone out.

What an exasperating person. First he had spoilt her party and now he had given a slap to her self-esteem. Her radiant evening was tarnished, and it was even more Luke's fault than the fault of George the Third.

# CHAPTER 9

*I*N THE NEXT few days the guests scattered from Sea Garden like ashes from an explosion. Jimmy and Luke, with most of the other young men, set out for Charleston.

When she had waved Jimmy good-by Celia put on her cloak and went for a walk under the trees. She felt dazed, as if she had had a bump on the head. Though the war had been going on for nearly five years, always it had been something that was happening to other people. It was a shock to find that it could happen to her too.

"But I'm not going to let it muddle up my life!" she told herself, tramping hard on the wet leaves. "I'm going to marry Jimmy in April and be part of that wonderful family, just as I planned."

Putting her determination into words made her feel better. She went into the house and asked Vivian if there wasn't some work she could do. Always glad to put other people to work, Vivian gave her a bolt of homespun to make shirts for the men who would be pouring into Charleston for the British attack. She told Celia to take her sewing up to Darren's room and keep him pacified. Darren was in a fury of impatience. He had missed the glory of Fort Moultrie because he had been in Orangeburg on business for Godfrey, and now he was afraid that again the British would attack and be beaten off before he could get there.

For the next five weeks Celia made shirts and entertained Darren, while Vivian sent him up large meals, mostly slabs of meat. Darren had lost a lot of blood and Vivian said meat made blood. Her remedy proved a good one, for by the time Jimmy and Luke rode in again, early in February, Darren was able to come downstairs.

They all gathered in the sitting room, and while Herbert made hot rum toddies Jimmy and Luke described what was going on.

They told Darren his fears were groundless. The British could not attack for some time yet. Sir Henry Clinton had reached Savannah, a hundred miles south of Charleston, but his ships and his men were alike in bad shape. They had had a hard voyage, and now the men had to rest and mend the ships. Meanwhile the rebels in Charleston were preparing for defense.

Luke and Jimmy looked jaunty in their rebel blue uniforms. Luke had not worn a uniform until now, though Jimmy told Celia he had volunteered for duty on the wagon track early in the war, during a recruiting tour of his father's old commander, Francis Marion. "I bet Vivian doesn't like that fellow," Celia said to herself as she watched Luke standing by the mantelpiece. Still, it was probably not Marion's fault that either Luke or Luke's father had gone to war. The sort of men they were, they would have had no need of Marion's beguiling words. For the truth was —she had suspected it, and now as she watched him she was sure of it—Luke was enjoying every bit of this. He was telling them about the wall of hornwork they were building to protect Charleston, from river to river across the peninsula. His voice was rich with enthusiasm, his whole personality had the fire of a man doing what he was born for.

Jimmy was different. Leaner and more sinewy than ever, Jimmy was sprawled in an armchair with his drink, as usual looking as if he had nothing on earth to do. When he talked of the Charleston defenses he spoke with knowledge and efficiency. But Jimmy made her think of a man who had a job to do and was doing it well, not because he enjoyed it but because it had to be done.

When they had a chance to be alone, Jimmy said he wanted to talk about their plans for getting married. They sat on the sofa before the library fire, and with an intent grimness unlike his customary casual manner, Jimmy said he wanted to keep the April date. "Will you, Celia?"

"Of course!" she returned. "That's exactly what I'd planned myself."

He took her hands in his hard bony grip. "Bless you!" Then, still serious, he went on. "I asked Mr. Moreau if he would marry us right now—this is war, I said, who cares about proprieties?" As he paused Jimmy gave her a wry smile. "Mr. Moreau said he cared. He said he would not marry a girl under age without the written consent of her guardian. I thought of getting in touch with Roy, but then I thought it might not be a good idea just now, considering his principles—"

"Roy hasn't got any more principles than a fried egg," said Celia. "He was glad to have me making a good match, but now if he thinks the king's men are going to come out on top he's likely to say he doesn't want me to marry a rebel. You're right not to bother with Roy. In April, I'll be of age and can do as I please."

Jimmy said he and Mr. Moreau had talked it over. Mr. Moreau would read the banns ahead of time, and then any day they chose after Celia's birthday he would perform the ceremony.

Jimmy went on to tell her that Herbert and Vivian would be going down to Charleston soon, to pack the silver and other valuables in the town house and bring them to Sea Garden for safekeeping. Celia could go with them. When the Lacys returned to Sea Garden, she could continue to live in their house on Meeting Street for the brief time remaining before her marriage. She would be the guest of Burton Dale and Elise, who had moved into Vivian's house because their own home in the Ansonborough suburb was so close to the defense lines. Some people were running out of Charleston like scared chickens, but Burton had declared that he was going to stay. He did not believe the British would get in and he had a lot of property to take care of.

When times were right again, Jimmy said, he and Celia would have a house of their own. At first they would live in the house on Church Street. His mother was at Bellwood with Audrey, who had no mother of her own, but they would have the colored housekeeper and several women servants. The menservants were busy on the defense works.

Miles would be there part of the time, for he was in Charleston working on the defenses. And they might have to give quarters to one or two other soldiers, friends of theirs. The military barracks, at the northwestern edge of town behind the hornwork, was so crowded that as many men as possible were living in private homes.

"It won't be the way I'd meant it to be," Jimmy said smiling.

"I don't care," said Celia, "as long as you're there."

He kissed her happily.

Jimmy and Luke could stay at Sea Garden only overnight. The mission for which they had been sent from Charleston was to gather laborers from the country and arrange to have them come to town for work on the defenses. Luke chose the men he wanted from Sea Garden, and Herbert said he would bring them down on the schooner.

Vivian made no protest when Jimmy told her the plan for Celia to stay in Charleston. She gave the two of them an understanding smile.

"All right, dear," she said to Celia. "Stay where your heart is. I would too."

•~•

Jimmy and Luke rode off the next morning. Several days later the schooner followed. Darren went along on the boat, well enough now for military service.

As the weather had grown milder the four of them sat on deck: Herbert reading, Celia finishing another shirt, and Vivian doing nothing in her own graceful fashion, while Darren told Celia how they were going to flatten the redcoats. Celia sewed diligently, for the shirt was nearly done and she wanted to get it off her hands. Jimmy had given her the legacy from Uncle William, and she intended to buy some fine lawn in town and make him a cravat, as a wedding present.

After lunch Vivian gave Darren a novel and told him to quit jabbering, for she and Herbert were going to stretch out in their deck-chairs for naps. Amiable as always, Darren turned his chair away from the sun and opened the book. Celia went on sewing until finally, with a sigh of pleasurable virtue, she snipped the last thread. Stuffing the shirt into her workbag she stood up for a stretch.

Herbert and Vivian were asleep, with scarfs over their faces to shut out the light. Darren's book could not have been very exciting, for he too had drifted into a nap. The sun was slanting westward, close to the tops of the palmetto trees on the islands, and the long shadows of the palmettos were pointing out to sea.

When she had taken several turns around the deck Celia sat down again, drawing her blanket over her knees. The air smelt salty and clean. She could hear the swish of the sea, and the creaking ropes, and the voices of the boatmen; the sounds all blended into harmony.

Not used to daytime naps, she had not expected to fall asleep, but as she lay back in her chair she slipped into a pleasant doze. She did not know how long it lasted; however, after a while, through the rhythm of the sea-sounds the wind brought her a strain of music.

The bells of St. Michael's were chiming the hour. Celia opened her eyes. The schooner was coming into harbor, and Charleston was saying, "Welcome home."

Everybody else was awake. Darren was helping Herbert direct the men as they brought up the trunks. Marietta held a looking-glass in front of Vivian, who was tying a blue veil about her hair.

Celia stood up and looked around. The harbor was crowded with ships—men-of-war flying the rebel flag, private boats from the plantations, supply ships of all sorts, rowboats full of soldiers. Celia felt a thrill skip over her nerves, shocking and at the same time invigorating, as she saw all this preparation for war. She looked across to the town, pink and gold in the sunset as she had seen it so often, and seeing it again she smiled. But even as she did so the smile froze on her face.

Standing there in the middle of town was something she had never seen before. It looked like a great black finger pointing upward among the roofs. Much taller than any of the buildings around, the black thing stood stark against the bright sky.

Celia stared. Then all of a sudden she heard a gasp in her own throat as she recognized the things for what it was. This was the steeple of St. Michael's, painted black.

Now that she saw it she could understand why they had done it. St. Michael's was the tallest structure in town. That dazzling white spire could be seen for miles. It would have made a perfect target for the king's guns, guiding them to the corner of Broad and Meeting Streets, the most important corner in town. And of course, these nights they would not light the beacon that used to shine so far over the water. This was war, and St. Michael's was dark.

Celia turned her head to look at the others. They were all on deck now—Vivian and Herbert and Darren, Vivian's maids, the boatmen and the laborers who had come to work on the defense lines; they were staring at the steeple, and on all their faces was the same shock that she had felt herself. And now for the first time since she had heard of the British plan to wreck Charleston, Celia felt a cold creeping fear. The soldiers and men-of-war had not scared her. But that black steeple made her think of a buzzard, waiting.

•⌣•

That evening Miles and Jimmy called, and before he was past the front door Miles was shouting that he had a son.

He said Beatrice had sent the news, and since Bellwood was only twenty miles from Charleston he had received permission to go up and see the baby. He had come back to town yesterday. Audrey was recovering well, and the boy was fine and kicking. "The fourth Miles Rand of Bellwood!" he said, and Celia felt a little glow of shared pride. His words had such a sound of strength and permanence. They made her more than ever glad that she was going to be one of the Rands.

Miles had taken Jimmy's dog Rosco to Bellwood and left him there. Jimmy had sent him reluctantly, but Rosco's appetite for meat was great, too great to be met in a town where provisions had to be stored for thousands of men. Celia liked hearing about Jimmy's affection for his dog; it reminded her that Rosco too was part of the family block, all strong and safe together.

The next morning Luke banged in, full of reckless well-being. Celia and several maids, directed by Vivian, were in the dining room packing silver into crates. Elise was there too, but she was no help. Used to plenty of servants, Elise rarely did anything for herself, and now after Vivian had sent her on one errand upstairs Elise was worn out for the rest of the day.

Luke was fairly booming with news about the war. The defenses were going up fast, he told them—the wall and earthworks across the peninsula, the gun emplacements around the three sides that faced the water, and much more that he could not discuss. He said Colonel Francis Marion, who had been drilling recruits near Dorchester, had been summoned back to town and would probably be put in command of Fort Moultrie.

Luke and Vivian walked off for a chat, leaving Celia wrapping a silver tea-service. After a while Luke poked his head around the dining-room door. He had to leave in a few minutes, he said, but first he wanted to go out to the stable and see Jeroboam-the-son-of-Nebat. Wouldn't Celia walk out with him, and catch a breath of air?

Celia joined him, and they walked along the brick path that led past the vegetable garden to the stable, where the horse was standing with his head out of the open half-door. He was a handsome creature, of a reddish chestnut color. Luke said, "Hi, Jerry!" Stroking the horse between the ears he spoke to Celia. "You're going to stay in town and get married, come what may?"

"Why yes!" she exclaimed, with surprise and a touch of defiance. "You didn't bring me out here to tell me you think I ought to go back to Sea Garden!"

"Certainly not," Luke returned, laughing shortly. "I think Elise will drive you daft, but that's none of my business. What I did want to say—"

"Yes?" she asked, smiling contritely.

"If things should get tough," said Luke, "you can always go to Bellwood and wait for Jimmy there. Bellwood is on the Cooper River, and that river is going to stay open."

"I won't go to Bellwood," Celia said firmly.

With a grin and a sigh, Luke reminded her that in wartime it was never wise to be sure. You had better make up your mind to do whatever you had to do.

He went on to explain about the Cooper River. Nearly all the men and supplies from the interior had to come down this river to Charleston. The army had based a strong cavalry guard at Moncks Corner, the town on the river at the head of navigation. This was the most dangerous post in the state. The British would do all they could to capture such a vital waterway, but these men were a picked group. They would be commanded by Colonel William Washington, a young cousin of the general and one of the most brilliant cavalry leaders in the army.

"I just wanted you to know," said Luke.

Celia thanked him, but she insisted, "I'm not going to leave."

"As you please," he said. He held out a lump of sugar to Jerry.

Celia thanked him for his interest, and said she had better get back to work. As she walked toward the house she heard Luke's voice raised in song.

"Oh I'm not a knight in armor and I'm not a
          serpent-charmer,
     I'm a plain old cotton farmer and I think
When King George's war is finished then his crown
          will be diminished,
     For his royal head is sure a-gonta shrink."

·~·

With the colored girls, Celia worked until Vivian told them to stop and get ready for dinner. She said they could have the afternoon to themselves.

Vivian's daughter Madge came to dinner. Madge had the I'll-be-cheerful-if-it-kills-me look that so many women were acquiring these days. Her husband and her young son Bobby were on the defense lines. Madge, with her younger boy and her little girl, expected to go to Sea Garden with Vivian and Herbert. It was clear that she dreaded the separation and equally clear that she was not going to make a fuss about it. Celia admired her courage.

With grim humor, Madge told them a good deal of news. She said Tory families were scrambling out of town. If you had clothes of any shade of green you had better not wear them, lest somebody throw a brick at you. She told Celia that Mrs. Thorley had sent the sewing-girls to their homes, and her shop was closed.

Godfrey was planning to give a supper-dance one evening

soon, and they were all to be invited. "That means you too," Madge said to Celia, smiling across the table, "and Jimmy, if he can get away."

She went on to say that everybody was giving parties. The whole town had a frantic gaiety. Vivian told Celia to take out her red velvet dress. "Wear it now," said Vivian. "You don't know when you'll have another chance."

Herbert said he would bring down the oldest Madeira from the cypress attic. "We might as well drink it now," he agreed.

Burton assured them again that the British were not going to get in. But all the same Celia felt a shiver. Her hand hidden by the napkin in her lap, she reached into her pocket and rubbed the rabbit's foot.

After dinner Vivian retired for her afternoon rest. Celia put on her cloak and went out to buy the lawn for Jimmy's cravat, thinking how fortunate it was that she had Uncle William's five hundred dollars just now. Nobody would expect her to have much of a trousseau in these times, but when she had finished the cravat she could get material to make a few pretty things for herself.

The best stores were at the east side of town, near where Broad and Tradd Streets met the Cooper River. It was a bright windy February day, and Celia walked briskly. But before she had gone far, she began to feel dismayed. Though she had been away from Charleston only about three months, it seemed to her that everything had changed.

In ordinary times this was a quiet neighborhood where you met nice people, where storekeepers bowed and said, "How do you do, ma'am, may I serve you?" But not today.

Everything was in a noisy jumble. She had never seen these streets so crowded, soldiers and sailors and non-military folk, some of them well dressed and others in clothes that looked— and smelt—as if they had never been washed. The road was jammed with wagons and wheelbarrows and handcarts, each one loaded with all it would hold: military crates as the soldiers moved food and guns, or trunks and piles of furniture as civilians moved their property out of town. On the sidewalk people kept bumping into her, most of them in such a hurry that they did not appear even to notice that they did so.

She had not dreamed it was going to be so hard to buy anything. Half the stores were locked up, with boards nailed across the doors and windows. Those that were open had little to sell, and the prices were outrageous. She saw a pair of cotton stockings, of not very good quality, for fifty dollars, and a pair of men's shoes for seven hundred. The clerks were nearly all elderly men or cripples leaning on canes. Their manners were surly. When she asked for lawn they said if she didn't see what she wanted they didn't have it, and implied that they were doing her a favor to let her buy anything at all with American money.

There was nothing in plenty except rice, and cubes of indigo for home dyeing, and coffee and sugar and molasses, which had been brought so abundantly from the West Indies. How I hate King George, Celia thought as she pushed her way from one store to another. Turnip-head. Giving me all this trouble.

But at last she found some good white lawn. There were three yards and a quarter in the piece and the man refused to cut it. Take it all or none, he said, and he charged her three hundred dollars. When she had paid another ten dollars for sewing-thread, Celia came out into the street again.

She felt tired and windblown and dusty and disagreeable. How much noise there was!—people shouting, wagons rattling, hammers banging as men boarded up the houses they were about to leave. Somewhere toward the hornwork, soldiers were drilling, for she could hear a military march. Toward the west she saw the spire of St. Michael's black on the red sunset sky.

She had come back into the residential section of Broad Street and was about to pass a white house with iron-railed steps coming down to the sidewalk. As she came close to it, a ball of mud shot past her and struck the house, throwing a splash on her cloak. Stopping in alarm, Celia thrust her package under her cloak just as another mudball went by, and at the same time a piece of brick smashed into the lamp over the doorstep. The lamp shattered. With a gasp, Celia put her free arm over her eyes to shield them from the flying glass.

In the street she heard angry yells. Close beside her a woman screamed and a child began to cry. As Celia cautiously lowered her arm from her eyes, more mud struck the house, along with sticks and handfuls of garbage. She saw now that by the curb in front of the house was a carriage with a skinny little horse—the good horses had been taken by the army—and on the curb were bags and boxes, as though someone was about to leave home. Turning her head again toward the crying child, Celia saw what was happening.

The house-door was open, and on the steps stood a man and a woman, both in long traveling cloaks. He had his arm around her shoulders, and between them they were sheltering a boy three or four years old, while behind them were two terrified colored maids. Apparently they had been about to leave the house when a gang of riffraff, black and white, had caught sight of them and had begun pelting them with trash gathered up in the street. Pressed against the wall, afraid to move, Celia could hear the boys yelling.

"Tories! Bootlickers! King-lovers! *Tories!*" Among these epithets were others that she had never heard before, but by the way the words were snarled out she could tell that they were dirty words.

The man on the doorstep, about thirty years old, looked as if he might be quite a handsome fellow in normal times, though now he was ugly with rage. Saying something to the woman, he bent to take up the little boy in his arms. As he did so the wind blew back the hood of the woman's cloak. In the late sunshine Celia saw a flash of red hair, and with a start she recognized Mrs. Kirby, the pretty Tory whose little boy was named for the king. The thought skipped through her head, This is the first time I've ever seen Mrs. Kirby when she wasn't talking.

Evidently following a direction her husband had given her, Mrs. Kirby crossed her arms over her face for protection and started toward the carriage. Her husband went beside her carrying little George, and the two colored women followed. A shower of sticks and refuse came at them. The wind blew back Mrs. Kirby's long cloak, and Celia saw her figure. Mrs. Kirby was going to have another baby. But if her tormentors noticed this it made no difference. They went on hissing their nasty words and throwing dirt on her dress as she scrambled with trembling haste into the carriage. Her husband gave her the little boy, and as Mrs. Kirby took the child in her arms Mr. Kirby threw in the baggage. Banging the carriage door, he leaped into the driver's seat and shouted to the horse. Under a new shower of mud and garbage the carriage rattled off toward the Cooper River wharfs.

People on the sidewalk stared after it. Some of them looked frightened, some disgusted, and several laughed as though it was a good joke. Nobody had moved to rebuke the mud-slingers or to give the Kirbys any help. Now that they were gone, the onlookers shrugged and started again about their business.

Celia drew her cloak around her and pulled the hood close about her face, fearful lest they start throwing things at her too as she hurried past the Kirbys' house. But the loafers were scattering in search of fresh amusement. As fast as she could, Celia made her way home. Little as she liked Tories right now, she felt sick.

◆~◆

When she told Jimmy about this episode he felt sick too. He told Celia not to go out alone again.

Herbert and Vivian arranged to leave Charleston in March, the morning after Godfrey's supper-dance. Besides Madge and her children they would take Burton's two boys, who would stop a few days at Sea Garden and then go on to stay with Elise's brother, Gilbert Arvin, at his home across the Santee River.

As she took out her velvet dress for the dance, Celia thought how wise Herbert and Vivian were, and what courage they had. She knew they did not want to leave Charleston any more than she did. Vivian would be leaving her three sons, and Herbert his much-loved grandson Tom, and there was no way to know when letters could be sent to Sea Garden. But they were going so these people they loved would have no reason to worry about them; and they had planned it so they would attend a dance on their last night at home, and say good-by gaily, in party clothes.

It was about five in the afternoon. Celia laid her dress on the bed, and beside it her emerald necklace and the bracelets of gold roses. Marietta was taking out the hairbrush and comb and the curling-irons. Marietta was in fine spirits. Vivian was going to let her stay here to wait on Celia, an arrangement that suited Marietta exactly since Amos was with Jimmy on the defense lines.

Mr. Hugo was expected about now, to do Vivian's hair. Once in his hands Vivian would not be able to move until he had finished, so Celia went down to ask if Vivian had any instructions for her.

As she came down the stairs into the hall she heard a whistled tune from outside the front door. A man stamped up the steps and banged the knocker. Since it did not require much imagination to guess who came calling with such impatient fire, Celia opened the door and was not surprised when Luke strode in and whammed it shut behind him. On his arm he carried a basket piled with snowdrops.

"Morning!" Luke greeted her. "Afternoon!—which is it?"

"It's afternoon," Celia said in astonishment, "and what's the matter with you?"

"Nothing's the matter with me, only I'm so busy with this war that I sleep in snatches and never know what time it is." He held out the basket of snowdrops. "These are for mother—will you give them to her?"

"Luke!" said Vivian's voice from the back of the hall. She came toward them, a rose-colored boudoir robe trailing behind her and a rose-colored scarf about her hair. Brushing past Celia she stood in front of Luke and demanded, "What's this about your volunteering for duty at Moncks Corner?"

Celia caught her breath. She remembered that Luke himself had said this was the most dangerous post in the state.

"Who told you that?" Luke asked Vivian sharply.

"Paul de Courcey. He came by here looking for you, had some orders. Oh Luke, you fool!"

Luke stood just inside the door, holding his hat in both hands. His hands were so big they nearly hid the hat between them.

In front of him Vivian looked as delicate as one of the china figurines Celia had been packing. Celia thought how strange it was that Luke had once been curled up inside Vivian's small slim body. He said, "I'm sorry Paul told you. I thought you wouldn't have to know."

"When did you offer to go?" asked Vivian. Her voice was not loud. But it made Celia think of a cry of pain.

"Yesterday," said Luke. He looked like a small boy caught in a piece of mischief. "It wasn't until yesterday," he went on, "that I knew they needed more men for Moncks Corner. But Colonel Marion told me, and he never exaggerates."

"Oh, Marion!" said Vivian. "Has that man *no* faults?"

Luke smiled a little. "Not many, anyway."

Vivian waited a moment to calm herself. Watching the two of them so close together, Celia thought again how much they looked alike, and how much alike they really were. In a resolutely quiet voice Vivian asked, "Luke, why are you doing this?"

He shrugged. "Somebody has to do it."

"But why you?"

"Why not me?" he asked.

Reaching to the basket on Celia's arm, Vivian took out a spray of snowdrops and held it to her nose. She smiled bitterly at Celia through the flowers. "I have three sons," she said, "and no matter what happens I know in advance how they're going to behave. Burton will do what's socially proper, Godfrey will make money out of it, and Luke will try to break his neck."

There was a tap at the front door.

"That's Hugo," said Vivian. "Let him in, Luke."

Plainly glad to have the conversation interrupted, Luke opened the door. Hugo was a dapper little white-wigged Frenchman about fifty years old, with a turned-up nose and darting black eyes. He spent his days in the dressing-rooms of great ladies, and people said of him that he knew more scandals than anybody else in town. Vivian enjoyed his visits. Now as Hugo came in, carrying the leather case that held the tools of his trade, Vivian smiled upon him, let him kiss her hand, and said,

"Go right in, Hugo. I'll be there in a minute."

Hugo bowed to her and to Celia, murmured an obsequious greeting to Captain Ansell, and went high-stepping down the hall. Vivian looked up at Luke again. She spoke tersely.

"Your neck is unbroken, Luke, but it's not unbreakable."

Luke did not answer. There was nothing he could answer, and no argument she could give him, and they both knew it. Vivian went after Hugo toward her dressing-room.

Luke threw his hat toward the hall table. The hat struck the basket Celia was holding, and fell to the floor. "Sorry," Luke murmured, and bent to pick it up. As he put the hat on the table Celia asked abruptly,

"Why don't you stay with the troops in Charleston?"

Luke stuck his thumbs into his pockets. His blue eyes stroked her as he returned, with a note of patient exasperation, "Why don't you mind your own business, Sassyface?"

"Are you trying to prove that you're braver than other men?" she insisted.

Luke smiled faintly. "Celia, I'm not braver than other men, or less brave. I'm just me. I can't sit out a siege. If I tried, I'd be no good to my country or myself. Understand?"

Celia bit her lip. Almost against her will she said, "Yes—and I think Vivian understands. She enjoys taking risks as much as you do. A woman wouldn't marry five times if she didn't. If you're like your father then your father was like Vivian—maybe that's why she was so crazy about him."

Luke's smile had widened as she talked. He nodded slowly. "You make good sense, Sassyface," he said, and he too started toward the back. "I'm going out to the kitchen to get something to eat. See you tonight—dance with me?"

"Why yes," she said, "I'd like to."

He thanked her and went off down the hall. Celia looked after him. Funny, she thought. Since he came home this time he was not avoiding her any more.

## CHAPTER 10

As GODFREY LIVED just around the corner on Tradd Street, that night they walked to his party. The house was full of lights and music. Godfrey loved to entertain and he did it well. His wife Ida stood with him to receive the guests: a quiet sort of woman in a quiet gray dress. Celia wondered what a gay fellow like Godfrey had ever seen in her.

As for herself, she looked well and knew she did, and she danced until she was breathless. Except that so many of the men were in uniform she might almost have forgotten the war.

But once she was forcibly reminded, when Godfrey paused between dances to pour wine—his oldest Madeira, for like his stepfather Godfrey had said, "We might as well drink it now." Jimmy went to bring her a glass. While she waited Celia drew back a window-curtain and looked out. In spite of the lanterns over the house-doors the street seemed dark, for she was used to seeing it lit by the beacon in the steeple of St. Michael's. But now the steeple stood dark against the stars. In the very top, a watchman was keeping a lookout.

Hearing a footstep Celia turned and saw Luke, carrying wine to his partner. Luke paused a moment beside her and he too looked out of the window. "Lighten our darkness, oh Lord," he said softly. For an instant their eyes met, and Luke gave her a smile before going on. But Celia felt a chill, as though the dark steeple loomed above them with a menace of wrath. She was glad to see Jimmy returning, and his merry, intimate smile that she loved.

The dancing began again. As on the night of New Year's Eve Celia felt like dancing till the sun came up, but the party ended shortly after midnight because the men in uniform had to get back to quarters. Vivian and Herbert lingered for a last word with Godfrey, and Jimmy walked with Celia around the corner. They stood on the front steps of the Lacys' house, glad to have a few minutes alone. The air was fragrant around them, the west wind soft on their cheeks. From Vivian's garden two mocking-birds called to each other. A carriage clattered by, full of people going home from another party. A moment later came two uniformed men on horseback, military patrols.

As the hoofbeats dwindled off, a commotion burst out from Tradd Street. They heard sudden loud voices; somebody screamed, several men began shouting orders.

"What on earth—" Celia began, and Jimmy said, "Let's go see." They started down the steps but as they reached the side-walk they saw Vivian hurrying toward them, followed by Miles.

"Oh you silly creatures!" Vivian was calling. "Running off—you're missing the excitement!"

"What's happened?" they demanded, and Miles started to tell them, but Vivian was already telling them.

"My darlings, we were standing in front of Godfrey's house, saying good night, when a fellow came running down the street —just a boy and scared out of his wits—he was jabbering and pointing toward a house all lit up for a party, and he said there was a man about to jump out of the window—"

They listened breathlessly. Vivian chattered on.

"Well, we'd never seen a man jump out of a window, so we were charmed. We ran as fast as we could, wondering if there really was a man and hoping he wouldn't jump till we got there—and we came to the house and the boy pointed up to the second story, and my dears, there *was* a man about to jump out of the window, and just in that instant while we looked up at him—he *jumped!*"

"Was he killed?" Celia demanded.

Vivian shook her head, and now at last Miles got in a few words.

"Not killed," said Miles, "but hurt—we heard him groan after he fell." Miles was more serious than Vivian about the whole matter. "That's why I came for you," he said to Jimmy. "We need help to keep the sidewalk clear till we can get a stretcher."

Jimmy said he would be glad to help. They all started back toward the corner, and he asked, "Does anybody know why the man jumped?"

Miles shrugged. "Drunk, I suppose. They were having a bachelor party."

"I see," Jimmy said good-naturedly. "He tippled, and he toppled. Could happen to anybody. Know who he is?"

Miles said he had not waited to find out. There was a lot of confusion, he said—the injured man's fellow-tipplers had rushed out, eager to aid him but so hazy-headed that they were merely in the way; and also in the way was a bunch of gawkers, the sort who seemed to spring up from the ground whenever an accident took place.

"Like you and me," Vivian whispered to Celia, and they both giggled. They had reached the corner, and a little way along Tradd Street they saw the crowd. Light streamed out of the open doorway of the house from which the man had fallen, so the people were clearly visible: several of Godfrey's guests, the gawking strangers Miles had spoken of, and members of the bachelor party. The last-named gentlemen had been having a fine time. Their noses were red and their wigs crooked, and they toddled like children just learning to walk.

Celia heard Luke's voice shouting to them to stand back and not try to lift the injured man—let the stretcher-bearers take him up when they get here. Herbert, catching sight of her and Vivian, came to meet them, and Jimmy went with Miles. Vivian asked Herbert, "Is he much hurt?"

"They say he's broken his ankle," Herbert told her. "Luke sent those two mounted patrolmen to bring a surgeon."

"Really?" said Vivian. "I didn't know military patrols could go on errands for ordinary folks."

"Ordinary folks?" Herbert repeated. "Didn't anybody tell you who he was?"

"Why? Somebody we know?"

Herbert said, "It's Colonel Francis Marion."

Celia gave a start. No wonder they were all in such a flurry. She looked again toward the group in the shaft of light. Marion lay on the pavement, while Jimmy, Luke, and several other men in uniform had constituted themselves a military guard. Nearer at hand, Burton was exclaiming that this was the worst, the very worst thing that could have happened, and Godfrey was saying, "Marion, of the whole Continental Army! Why couldn't it have been somebody else?"

Then, just beside her, Celia heard a funny little sound. Turning, she saw Vivian biting her handkerchief in an effort to keep quiet. Vivian was choking with laughter.

As her eye caught Celia's, Vivian beckoned her a step nearer. "Isn't it wonderful?" she whispered. "That speckless hero!"

At this, Celia began to laugh too. She laughed and laughed. She thought she knew just how Vivian felt.

Vivian was exulting. "He's not perfect. He got a fuzz on. He doesn't know how happy he's made me."

Two soldiers came up carrying a stretcher, followed by a surgeon with a bagful of instruments. At Luke's command the group parted to let them through. They picked up Marion and carried him back into the house.

As they disappeared through the doorway Vivian kissed her hand and waved.

"Francis Marion," she murmured, "for that sinful skinful, I almost like you."

❦

The next morning the schooner left for Sea Garden. Elise sobbed loudly at parting with her boys; she made considerably more noise about sending them to stay with her brother than either Madge or Vivian made about leaving their sons to face British bullets.

When Burton had gone out to consult with Godfrey about storing meat for the garrison, and Elise had retired to her room with smelling salts, Celia roamed about the house. The rooms looked cold and empty. The essential furniture was still here, but with the loss of Vivian and Vivian's pretty trifles the place had lost its charm. Celia had a frightening sense of being alone.

To keep from brooding she set to work on the cravat she was making for Jimmy. This calmed her nerves and she went down to dinner in a better mood. As only Burton, Elise, and herself were at table, she expected a tiresome meal; but having been out for some hours Burton had plenty to tell them.

He said everybody was talking about Marion's accident. The break in his ankle was a bad one and he would be helpless for weeks to come. He was being moved to his own home, a plantation near Eutaw Springs in the parish of St. John's Berkeley. And, Burton told them solemnly, the tale that Marion had been tipsy last night was nothing but gossip. Wicked, malicious gossip, no doubt started by Tories.

He said he would give them the facts.

Certainly there had been a party, and some of the guests had had too much to drink. But not Marion. Marion was a temperate man, a very temperate man. When the party got too gay, Marion decided to leave.

He slipped away unobserved and went to the front door, but found it locked. The host had locked it to make sure the company continued to drink until they were all under the table— that was some men's idea of hospitality. So Marion went upstairs and opened a window, intending to climb out and leave the party that way. But he slipped and fell. Simplest thing in the world, said Burton.

"Why of course," said Elise. She usually echoed Burton's opinions, not because she really considered him a fount of wisdom but because it saved her the trouble of doing any thinking of her own.

Celia said nothing. As she was going to be their guest for the next six weeks she had no wish to start an argument. But she had her own thoughts and they were sassy thoughts. She thought this was the silliest yarn she had ever heard.

That afternoon Miles dropped in. Last night Miles had taken it for granted that the man on the pavement was there because he had been too merry, but now that he had learned the man's name he had changed his mind. Tory talk, Miles said indignantly.

With an effort, Celia kept her mouth shut.

The next day Elise had guests to dinner. This was not like the dinners Vivian gave, where the people were gay and the talk was light and everything had an air of frivolity. Elise and Burton's friends were solid folk, serious about life.

Celia thought the food was good. But Elise apologized for each dish as it was passed, explaining either that this was a substitute for something she would rather have served, or that this was not made as she would have liked because she could not get the proper ingredients. Both Elise and Burton said they did not know how people in town were going to live, with the army taking all the food that came in. The company sighed and said they did not know either. They talked darkly about their future meals; you would have thought they expected to be reduced to such a state that they would be glad to eat the cheese out of a mouse-trap.

Celia watched the waitress pass a dish of chicken stewed with little sausage balls. She did not know what these others might have, but she did know that Vivian had left the storerooms of this household stocked with hams and spiced beef and sides of bacon, grits and cornmeal, syrup and sugar and rice. Also they had vegetables coming up in the garden. She wondered if these people ever laughed at anything.

The talk turned to Francis Marion, and they certainly did no laughing here. Everybody agreed that Marion had tried to leave the party because he did not care to get drunk. But this was not all. No longer was it enough to say that Marion was a temperate man. Now they were saying he had never had a drink in his life. He had never taken an eggnog on Christmas Day. He would not touch a pudding flavored with brandy. If you doubted this you were a disloyal American, a friend of the king, you might even be a spy who ought to be locked up in the dungeon under the Exchange.

That evening after the company had left, Jimmy dropped by. He and Celia went into the little reception parlor. It was the first time she had seen Jimmy since the night of Marion's accident, so she asked him to tell her: was the great man drunk that night or wasn't he?

Jimmy groaned. "Oh, my grandpa's Sunday wig! You too, Celia?"

"I just thought you might know!" she retorted. "You were there, guarding him."

"I didn't bend over to smell his breath," said Jimmy. He smiled contritely. "I'm sorry, Celia, but I'm exasperated. This thing has even held up work on the defenses—men throw down their tools to argue about it. But I'm not exasperated with you. Go on with what you started to say."

She told him about the talk at dinner. As he listened, Jimmy's lips had a quiver of mirth. When she paused he said,

"Now tell me what you think."

This was the first time she had been asked for her opinion. It was a pleasure to give it.

"I never heard such a silly tale," she said. "The man who gave the party had locked his door, he'd be a fool not to lock it in the middle of the night with the town jammed the way it is. And if Colonel Marion wanted to leave by a window I don't know why he chose one on the second floor. There were plenty of windows downstairs. I think he was tipsy."

Jimmy, laughing, did not answer at once.

"Wasn't he?" Celia demanded.

"Celia darling," said Jimmy, "I don't know. I saw Luke this afternoon and he doesn't know either. Frankly, we both think the same thing you do, but we're sick of the argument. Losing Colonel Marion right now is a calamity. That's what matters, not what he drinks for supper."

His voice was grave now. But he grinned at her again as he asked,

"You haven't spoken your mind about this to anybody else, have you?"

"Oh no."

"Don't talk about it," said Jimmy. "Somebody will say you ought to be deported and I can't do without you."

Celia promised. When he left her, she stood a moment on the front steps, looking after him. Jimmy had said "calamity," and Jimmy was a man who meant what he said.

She looked toward the dark steeple of St. Michael's. "Lighten our darkness," she whispered. "Lighten our darkness."

．～．

The next morning was cool and diamond-clear. When she was dressed Celia opened her window and rested her elbows on the sill, enjoying the early spring freshness. Her room was on the north side of the house, overlooking the carriage drive and the brick wall dividing this property from that of the people next door. From where she stood she could see over the wall into their garden, gay with hyacinths and daffodils and a peach tree with bursting pink buds. The air was full of birdsongs. Close by her Celia heard a thrasher pouring out such happy melody that she smiled as she listened.

An upstairs window of the other house opened, and over the sill leaned an elderly man whom she recognized as Mr. Simon Dale, a relative of Burton's father. At Mr. Dale's elbow she saw his grandson, a boy about twelve years old, handing him something.

Mr. Dale held up the object, which she saw now was a long thin spyglass. For an instant Celia thought the old wretch was trying to peek into her bedroom, but at once she knew she was wrong. Mr. Dale was not looking toward this house at all. He had turned his spyglass southwest, toward the point where the Ashley River flowed around the tip of the Charleston peninsula into the sea. He must be looking at a boat. Celia smiled a silent apology to the old gentleman as she turned from her own window and started to go down for breakfast.

As she opened the door her nose caught a whiff of sausage. At the same time she saw Burton standing at a window here in the upstairs hall, and he too held a spyglass to his eye and was looking toward the Ashley River. Celia wondered what was going on over there. Maybe he would let her see too. She had never looked through a telescope. Eagerly, she went toward the window.

Intent on what he was looking at, Burton did not hear her footsteps until she had reached his side, then with a start he turned. "Why good morning, Celia," he said.

His manner was so abstracted that she was afraid her interruption was not welcome. "Excuse me, sir," she returned hastily, "I didn't mean to trouble you."

She started to back away, but he held out the spyglass as if glad to share something of interest. "Do you want to take a look?" he asked her.

"Oh yes!" Celia exclaimed. She touched the thing carefully. It was like a tube in several sections, the smallest section toward the eyepiece and the largest at the other end. "Will you tell me what to do?" she asked.

"Of course," said Burton. He shrugged. "You'll have to see them sooner or later, might as well be now."

"But what are you looking at?" she asked.

Again he was startled, then he smiled as he answered, "I forgot you were just awake. Tom Lacy came by early to ask for some breakfast—he'd been on duty all night—and he told us. The British are there on the west bank."

"The British!" she gasped. Forgetting the spyglass she leaned over the sill and looked. Her eyes, younger than his, could see them even without the glass—a number of small boats in the river, and tiny figures moving on the other side.

But she wanted to see more. Burton showed her how to put the eyepiece to one eye, and turn the lenses to adjust them to her vision. As her view cleared, the trees across the Ashley River seemed to spring closer. She moved the glass to get something more than trees into her range, and at last she saw what she was looking for, men in red coats and tan breeches and high black boots. It was hard to see what they were doing, but they were scrambling about as though very busy, and more of them were wading ashore from rowboats in the river.

Celia had a queer feeling as if there was a lump of something cold under her ribs. Until this minute, the soldiers of King George had been a vague mass in her thoughts, abstract like the problems in a book of arithmetic. But now that she saw them they became men, men who wanted to destroy the town she lived in and everything she had to live for. The lump under her ribs began to get hot. It was like a burning pain.

Slowly she lowered the glass. Her thoughts must have shown in her face, for Burton gave her a reassuring smile.

"They're not going to get in," he said. "They've tried before—remember?"

"Why yes!" said Celia. She spoke with a sense of lightness. Of course they had tried before, they had tried twice—at Fort Moultrie, and again just before she came to work at Mrs. Thorley's, when a British force under General Prévost had marched up from Florida. Prévost's men had done a lot of looting around Beaufort, but they had not set foot in Charleston. The hot lump under her ribs began to dissolve as Burton said heartily,

"So don't you be scared. You keep your pretty face pretty, for Jimmy. Now we'd better get some breakfast. I've got to go out soon."

As they turned from the window they heard little pattering steps, and Elise came hurrying toward them followed by her maid Tessie.

"If you're going down, Burton," Elise urged him, "let me have the glass—I'll take it up to the attic, we can see much better from there. Tessie, do bring me some more coffee. I declare, I'm so excited I can't eat a thing. I'm going to ask Susan Dale to come over here, and Patsy Baxter, I don't believe the Baxters can see from their house, I'll send a note to Patsy—"

Celia tried to look demure. Mrs. Baxter's name was not Patsy. It was Charlotte. But the wife of George the Third was also named Charlotte, and when the war began Mrs. Baxter had announced that no good rebel woman should bear the name of the British queen. So she asked her friends to call her Patsy, because somebody had told her that this was George Washington's pet name for Martha.

Burton gave Elise the spyglass. "Oh dear, there are more and more of them!" exclaimed Elise, all a-flutter with pleasurable tremors. "Isn't this amazing? I do think we were wise to stay in town. Everybody is going to be asking us about this for years to come. Tessie, maybe I could eat just a little sausage, and some

hominy, be sure it's hot—Celia come up to the attic after breakfast and get a really good look—"

Celia said, "Yes ma'am," and fled downstairs.

All day long the king's men were plainly to be seen, but they
gave no trouble. Directed by Sir Henry Clinton, they minded
their business. This business was the bridging of Wappoo Creek,
a stream that flowed into the Ashley River on the side away from
town. The high windows were crowded with women and children and old men, watching. Every man strong enough to be useful had work to do on the defenses. Burton, in charge of sandbagging some buildings on King Street, was out all day.

He was out all day every day, while the redcoats slowly moved
their wagons across the bridge they had built. They kept moving
up the far bank of the Ashley, and as they went, here and there
they built a platform and dragged a cannon to stand on it. On
the Charleston side of the river the rebels threw up earthworks
and placed cannon of their own. With Elise and Elise's friends,
Celia watched from the attic windows. It was gruesome, it made
her flesh creep, and yet it was fascinating and she could not make
herself stop watching.

The redcoats had appeared first on Tuesday, the seventh of
March. The following Sunday morning while Celia was dressing
for church she heard a boom that shook the air. She had just put
on her petticoat and was about to tie the strings at the waistband;
at the sound she stopped and stood poker-stiff, listening. After
the boom came a rumble, and in the midst of the rumble she heard
another boom. The noise was like thunder and yet different. It
was not, in fact, like any other noise Celia had ever heard. The
boom came a third time, and the rumble behind it, and this time
she knew what it must be. They were firing those guns on the
river. The battle for Charleston had begun.

Snatching up her dressing-gown she rushed out into the hall.
Three or four housemaids had dropped their tasks and were
there too, squealing and shaking with fright, while a small colored
boy clung to his mother and begged her not to let the British
eat him up.

Celia went to the attic. Burton had left the house early and
she did not know where Elise was, probably looking through the

spyglass at her own bedroom window. But Celia did not need the spyglass to see that during the night the British had set up cannon on the far bank of the river just across from the end of Tradd Street. These were the guns they were firing, while the rebels on the earthwork at that end of Tradd Street were shooting back. Between the guns the river was half hidden by puffs of smoke, but after peering through squinted eyes Celia observed that most of the British cannonballs were splashing into the water. Not one of them had come past the great earthwork into town. Most of the population of Charleston seemed to be running about the streets, but nobody was getting hurt. And while she stood and watched, the firing slackened.

The smoke began to clear. It seemed that the British were not really trying to hit anything. They just wanted to announce that they were here. And the rebel guns, rumbling in reply, were merely answering, "We're here too."

Now it seemed that the guns had stopped for good. As she watched the smoke blowing away Celia spoke aloud to herself. "That was a battle. That will be something to tell my grandchildren." But she had a sense of disappointment. She had thought a battle would be more impressive than this.

# CHAPTER 11

*A*FTER THAT SUNDAY there was more firing every day. The cannon would boom for an hour or two, then get quiet, then after a while they would start again. On both sides it had a sound of bravado. The British went on setting up guns on their bank of the river, the Americans on theirs. Neither side was strong enough yet to make a real attack; Celia wondered why they fired at all.

After four or five days she asked Jimmy how much longer they were going on like this. Jimmy had come by the house not long after breakfast, dusty and unshaven and hungry, saying he had a few minutes to spare and would Celia scrape up some leftovers in the kitchen? She brought him a snack of cheese and cornbread, and he gobbled gratefully.

In answer to her questions he said the firing was not useless. The watchman in the top of St. Michael's had reported that the Americans were doing considerable damage to the British positions but because of the great earthworks they were receiving very little harm to their own. In the meantime they went on strengthening their defenses. The chief watchman in the steeple was Mr. Peter Timothy, who had been for years editor of the *Gazette*. He was a trained observer and you could trust what he said.

Celia nodded impatiently. "Yes, Jimmy, yes. But they won't keep firing like this, off and on! What's going to *happen?*"

Jimmy rubbed his fist over his stubbly chin. "Sweetheart, I can't talk about that."

A few minutes later he hurried away. When she had taken the tray out to the kitchen Celia paused at the foot of the back staircase. From above her she could hear the voices of Elise and half a dozen others, chattering as they passed around the spy-glass. The attic here, standing as it did on top of a three-story house, provided one of the best vantage points in the neighborhood, and women were always dropping in to look at the red-coats. Celia was welcome to join them, but just now she did not want to. She felt uneasy. Not because Jimmy could not answer her questions, this she could understand. But though Jimmy spoke cheerfully he did not look well. He was not merely tired, he was tense—Jimmy who was usually so loose-jointed that it was restful to look at him.

Celia went up to the sewing room and took out the cravat. This cravat occupied not only her hands but her mind, for she was edging it with double-antique drawnwork and this meant she had to count threads every time she put in her needle.

The wind blew in from the garden. It was a west wind, satiny on her cheeks, and now the flowers were blooming so thickly that even here on the third floor she thought she could smell them. When she was tired sewing she intended to go down and pull up some weeds. Unlike Elise she could not bear to sit in the house all day.

She heard the garden gate bang, and the wind brought in a mighty tune.

> "Plant on my grave a weeping willow tree,
>     A tree that sobs by night and day
>         (Sad stuff),
> And that weeping willow tree will be weeping over me
>     When you've dried up and blown away
>         (Puff, puff)."

It was Luke's voice and Luke's brand of nonsense and it brought her a sense of refreshment. He was going around toward the back. Leaving her workbasket on the table Celia ran downstairs and out by the back door. Luke was striding past the vegetable garden, toward the stable. As he stopped to pull up some carrots he saw her, and waited.

"Good morning, Sassyface!" he shouted. "Am I lucky enough to have you looking for me?"

She laughed and nodded. Luke rubbed the carrots on the grass to get off the dirt, and they walked together toward the stable.

"Did you have something to tell me?" he asked.

"Nothing special," said Celia. "I just thought it would be more interesting to talk to you than—" As she spoke she had glanced around toward the attic window, and now she stopped, realizing that she was not being very polite about her hostess. Luke grinned.

"I told you she'd drive you daft. Ida's planning to go up the river to stay with her folks, and Godfrey asked Elise if she wanted to go along, but not Elise. She's having a fine time here."

They had reached the stable. Jerry put his head out of the half-door and nibbled the carrot Luke held out to him. After a moment Luke spoke again, this time more seriously.

"Sassyface, I've come to take Jerry. I won't be around for a while."

"Oh!" Celia stepped back so she could look up at him more directly. "You mean—you're leaving for Moncks Corner?"

"Not today. But soon. I want to have Jerry ready to go. Where's Burton?"

"Still sandbagging."

"I'll probably see him. I'm not going to say good-by to Elise, she'd burst out bawling—not because she cares what becomes of me but she thinks that's the proper way to send a hero off to the wars."

He paused, and stood stroking Jerry. Celia waited for him to speak again. When he did speak, it was with a smile of appreciation.

"You're easy to be with, Sassyface. You don't talk all the time."

Celia made herself smile back at him, hoping there was nothing in her face or manner to show that she was feeling tremors of fear, as if somebody were brushing her skin with small cold feathers. She liked him and she dreaded his going into danger. She asked, "When are you leaving town, Luke?"

He answered with a look of amusement. "Honeychild, even if I knew, I wouldn't tell."

"Oh, I'm sorry!" she cried. "I forgot—you don't ask a soldier things like that."

"Right, you don't. But if you do, he doesn't answer so no harm's done." Luke waved a greeting to a small black boy who had been sent from the kitchen to gather parsley in the garden. Turning back to Celia he said, "Now you'll do something for me, Sassyface."

She nodded.

"You'll go back into the house and get on with whatever you were doing before I came, and if anybody asks you what I was here for you'll say I needed Jerry. I've taken him before. You'll say nothing about this being the last time. Do that?"

"Yes," said Celia. She managed to look steadily into his blue eyes. "Yes, I'll do that."

"Thanks," said Luke. He took her hand. "I like you, Celia. Jimmy's a lucky man. Remember what I promised—I'll be around for your golden wedding."

He lifted her hand and kissed it quickly. Celia was thinking, You'll be around for my golden wedding if the British don't kill you before I'm even a bride. She felt such a pain in her throat that she could barely push her voice out.

"Thank you," she said, "and good-by." This was the first time she had ever said good-by to a soldier. It was harder than she had thought. "God bless you, Luke," she said softly, and she turned and hurried back toward the house. But she reminded herself that she must not run; they would suspect something if she seemed agitated. Slowing her pace she went on, past the garden and the kitchen-house, to the back porch, and then up the back staircase and into the room she had left.

But her hands were not steady enough for her to take up her drawnwork. She walked up and down. From far across the Ashley River she heard the cannon start again. The sound sent goose-bumps over her skin. She wondered when she would see Luke again.

•◥•

She did not know when Luke left town. She did know that during the next two weeks the British kept moving up the far bank of the Ashley, setting gun emplacements as they went. But they seemed in no hurry about it. Through the spyglass she could frequently see the men sitting around, not doing anything at all. It made her nervous. She thought it would be easier—on herself at least—if they would really start their attack.

She saw Jimmy only in snatches. He was always good-humored, always ready to eat with relish whatever she brought him from the kitchen, but his face was lined and he was getting thin. Jimmy had always been lean, but now he was almost gaunt. When she spoke of this he said it was because he had never worked so hard in his life. The militiamen coming in from the country had had only the sketchiest training, and the officers were on duty day and night getting them into shape. "But how they can shoot!" Jimmy exulted. "Those boys can hit anything they can see."

"Speaking of shooting," said Celia—"oh Jimmy, I don't want to ask a lot of questions I shouldn't, but—"

Jimmy was eating muffins and cold ham. As she left her question unfinished he wiped his lips, and his black eyes glinted at her merrily over the napkin. "You want to know why Sir Henry Clinton doesn't attack?" he asked. "That's no secret." Laying the napkin on the table he gestured toward a window that stood open near by. "The west wind," he said.

Celia frowned, puzzled.

Jimmy explained that Clinton could not attack without his full force of troops, and ships to block the harbor. Those men she saw across the river had come up from Savannah in small boats by the inland waterways, but the men-of-war and troop transports had to come by sea. "And the wind is blowing from the west," said Jimmy—"out of the harbor, not in."

"Where are the ships now?" she asked.

Jimmy's long arm made a sweep toward the sea. "Out there. They've left Savannah, but they can't get to Charleston. And the longer the wind holds," he added smiling, "the more time we have to get ready for them."

A day or two later, Celia had just waked up in the morning and was still stretching when she heard a knock on the door. Raising herself on her elbow she called an answer and Marietta came in, full of excitement.

"Miss Celia, we can see the king's ships!"

Celia sat up in bed. "Where? Not in the harbor!"

"Oh no, no ma'am, they can't get in. They're away out to sea, out beyond Fort Moultrie. Mr. Burton is up in the attic right now, looking at them. He let Tessie and me look too, through the spyglass."

Celia was already up. She grabbed the pitcher and poured water into her washbasin. "Tell Mr. Burton I'll be up there in no time at all. Is the coffee made? Would you bring me a cup?"

She dressed as fast as she could and dashed up to the attic. Burton and Elise were there, and Tessie with Elise's smelling salts. Burton had the glass. But today for the first time he was not looking out of a west window toward the Ashley River, but out an east window facing the harbor. When they heard Celia's footsteps he and Elise turned, and Elise exclaimed, "Come see!" Burton offered her the spyglass.

Celia looked. And there they were, ships with the British flag, scattered along the eastern horizon out beyond the harbor entrance. There were twenty ships or maybe fifty; she could not tell how many because they kept moving, disappearing below the horizon and coming into sight again, as if they were trying to find a place where the wind did not blow. Burton pointed out the different types—men-of-war and troop transports and supply ships, while Celia felt flickers of excitement all over. Oh, she was glad Jimmy had wanted her to stay in town. She would not have missed this, not for a pair of gold shoe-buckles. But as she watched the ships in front of her and remembered that line of British guns behind her, she had a curious choky feeling in her throat and a tightness around her middle. It was as if she was being squeezed. For a moment she could not get her breath properly; when she could, she heard her own voice saying—more to herself than to the others—

"The wind can't blow from the west forever."

"Oh now, don't talk like that!" Elise begged her, and Burton smiled encouragingly, as on the morning when he first showed her the redcoats. "Don't worry," he said. "They won't get into town. They've tried before."

With this Celia had to be content. To tell the truth it was not difficult, for the same spyglass that showed her the men-of-war showed her also that Charleston was now enclosed by a ring of protective guns. On the west side of town these guns fired steadily at the king's men across the Ashley River. On the east side the Americans sank several ships of their own at the mouth of the Cooper River, and stretched a great chain below the surface, so that even when the wind should change, the king's ships would not be able to come in close.

American boats were swarming down the Cooper River bringing supplies to town. The streets were thumpy under the tread of marching men. Many of these had no uniforms, but it did not matter, because the people of South Carolina raised so much indigo that nearly every man in the state had at least one blue coat. Those who had no blue coat—or no coat at all—wore a bit of blue ribbon on their hats, or on their shirts if they had no hats, to mark them as rebel soldiers.

The major headquarters of the Continental officers was a residence on Tradd Street. Every day Celia could see important-looking men going in and out. They wore splendid uniforms, with swords and epaulettes and fine white wigs, and their faces were grave and stern, the faces of men busy with destiny. It made her feel confident just to watch them.

Now toward the end of March the roses fell over the garden walls in sheets of red and white, and the smell of jasmine overpowered the smell of gunpowder. In spite of the bristle of cannon around town Charleston was utterly lovely. And day and night Celia could feel the west wind.

She finished Jimmy's cravat. It was an exquisite piece of work; she had never made anything finer. When she gave it a last pressing and spread it on the table in the sewing room for Marietta to see, Celia smiled proudly.

Marietta smiled too, in admiration. "He'll love it, Miss Celia."

"I'll give it to him," said Celia, "next time he—"

From the downstairs hall came a burst of voices. One of Elise's friends must have brought a great piece of news. "Oh my goodness," said Celia. "Bring me a clean towel to wrap this in, then we'll find out what's happened."

Marietta obeyed. As Celia began to wrap the cravat they heard footsteps on the stairs. The ladies were hurrying up to the attic, for while Elise had been tired out by one trip upstairs when they were packing the silver, she could run up six times a day to watch the redcoats. Celia went to the door, and caught a glimpse of Elise and Mrs. Baxter, with Tessie and Mrs. Baxter's maid, but they were crossing the landing so fast that they did not see her. She finished wrapping the cravat and slipped it into a drawer.

"Now then," she said to Marietta, "come on."

In the attic they found Elise and Mrs. Baxter at a window, leaning out over the roof with the maids behind them, all four giving little screeches of enjoyable terror like people hearing ghost stories. Mrs. Baxter held the spyglass. She was a pretty little person about twenty-eight years old, and she still had girlish dimples in her cheeks.

"I can't see a *thing!*" she was lamenting.

"Let me try," said Elise.

She took the spyglass and leaned out so far that Celia thought it was a good thing the roof projected beyond the window, to catch her if she fell. With a mental picture of Elise tumbling over the sill and bouncing on her plump bottom, Celia smothered a giggle as she touched Mrs. Baxter's elbow and asked, "Please, what's happening?"

"Oh my dear—don't you *know?*" Mrs. Baxter exclaimed. She drew back from the window, beaming with the joy of a news-monger who finds a fresh audience. "You haven't heard?" she asked, prolonging the suspense. "Nobody *told* you? Well, I can't say I'm surprised. I just heard it myself and came to tell Elise. Why my dear," she said with exasperating slowness, "the British have landed! They're fighting!"

"Landed?" Celia repeated. "Where?" For she knew the wind had not changed. The ships still could not get into the harbor. But Mrs. Baxter gestured northward, toward the neck of land that joined the Charleston peninsula to the mainland.

"Up there. They've crossed the Ashley—they went up the river in rowboats in the middle of the night, away up above

*130*

town, miles above, and crossed. And this morning our men went up the highway out of town to meet them, and now they're having a battle—haven't you heard the guns?"

Celia had been hearing guns every day for three weeks. She could not tell whether or not she had heard any extra ones this morning. She stood still, listening. She heard the babble of Elise and the colored women, and something else Mrs. Baxter was saying, and also she heard a distant sound of firing. But now that she was noticing, she could tell that the sound did not come from the Ashley River; it came from the north, toward the hornwork wall, and the guns did not roar like cannon. This noise was a series of pops with a long, low thrumming behind them—rifles maybe, or muskets. Celia knew rifles and muskets were different but she did not know what the difference was.

Elise, cross with disappointment, was wailing, "We *can't* see from here!"

Celia wet her lips. She spoke with determined steadiness. "What—regiment—has gone up to—meet the British?"

Elise turned around. She smiled comfortingly. Silly Elise might be, but she had a kind heart. Also she had some respect for Celia, because Celia did not talk much and was calm in her manner and competent with her hands, and most of all because Celia was engaged to Jimmy and he was such a good catch. "Continental troops," said Elise. "Not the militia—not Jimmy."

Celia felt a marvelous lightness. Until she felt it, she had not known how frightened she had been. But now she had as much curiosity as they had. "Maybe I can see the battle," she offered eagerly. "Could I try?"

"But if I can't see," said Elise, loath to give up the spyglass, "you can't either."

"I can climb out on the roof."

"You'll get hurt!" they cried.

"Oh no I won't. I'll be careful."

They moved aside and Celia scrambled out, with no worse result than blackening her dress. The slope of the roof here was gentle, and Celia supported herself against the gable that held the attic window. Elise handed her the glass.

"What do you see?" they begged as she put it to her eye.

"Smoke," said Celia. "Big thick puffs of smoke. It's a long way off, above town."

Now that she was out here, with a view in all directions, she turned her head to see what else the glass would show her. On the Ashley River the cannon were not firing. With no smoke there to hide her view she had a good clear look at the redcoats, and she could see men among them who were not redcoats.

These men's coats were blue with red facings, and they wore helmets of fantastic height. The helmeted men appeared to be officers, directing their troops. For a moment Celia was puzzled, then she realized who they were. Hessians. The German soldiers hired by King George to kill his subjects in America. As she looked at them a shiver started at the back of her neck and went right down to the bottom of her spine.

A little farther up, working on the gun emplacements, were more men who were not redcoats, and neither were they Hessians. Many of these wore no coats, but the men directing them were in uniform, and as she looked Celia had glimpses of green. Americans. Tories.

She had a sick feeling all over. Jimmy had told her, with his characteristic fairness, that some Tories honestly believed in the side of the king. But Celia knew, and Jimmy knew, and so did everybody else, that many men had joined the Tory regiments because there they got regular pay in hard British coin, while the patriots were paid in paper that bought less every week. Celia looked at the Tories across the river and felt her lips curl with anger.

In the window, Elise and Mrs. Baxter wanted to know what she was seeing. "Troops everywhere," said Celia. "And that battle up yonder. Here, take the glass, I'll come in."

She climbed back through the window, and leaving the spyglass with Elise she went to a trunk by the wall and sat down. All those men, she thought, all those ships, closing in like a drawstring. Again she had that feeling of being squeezed.

Tessie had burst into sobs of fright. Elise said, "Oh, do hush, they're nowhere near us," but as she drew back from the window she said to Mrs. Baxter, "You know, Patsy, maybe we shouldn't stay in Charleston. Maybe we *ought* to leave."

Mrs. Baxter nodded. "I've been thinking so too. Have you heard there's smallpox in town?"

"Oh good heavens!" said Elise.

"We can leave by the Cooper River," said Mrs. Baxter.

"Burton and I could go to our country place at Gaylawn," said Elise, "or to my brother's plantation on the Santee. That's where our sons are, you know—we should have gone with them, our place is really with our children, don't you think so? And Burton isn't as young as he was, he's a good deal older than I am, you know, I was nothing but a *child* when I married, all this work is hard on him."

Celia was sitting up stiffly on the trunk. They had said so firmly that they were going to stay in town! If they left, would they make her go with them?

Marietta, who had been soothing Tessie's fears, came over to the trunk. With an understanding smile she said, "Miss Celia, don't you think it would be nice if you and I went down and made some coffee?"

Celia sprang to her feet. "Wonderful. You go on to the kitchen. I'm black from being on the roof, but I'll wash and change my dress and I'll be there in a minute."

They were pouring the coffee when another maid came to say that Captain Rand had dropped in. Celia ran indoors. Jimmy was in the parlor, dustier, leaner, tireder than ever. He gripped her till it hurt. Hot coffee? he repeated when she asked him. Yes, yes, heaven must have inspired her to make it now. Celia went out to the kitchen to tell Marietta to bring him a cup, then went upstairs to get the cravat.

When she came down Jimmy sat by the dining room table, sipping coffee and sighing with pleasure. As she unfolded the towel, she heard him gasp.

"Celia! Why that—that's a work of art!"

She smiled joyfully. "Then you do like it?"

"Like it? I never had such a cravat in my life." He reached toward it, but drew back. "I don't dare touch it."

"Why not?"

Jimmy held out his hands. Celia had been so glad to see him

that she had not noticed how grimy they were. He looked again at the beautiful cravat. He looked at it for a long time. When he spoke to her again his voice was almost reverent. "Celia, I can't tell you how I feel about this. I'm so tired, I've got so much on my mind—I never was any good at words and now I seem to be worse than ever. But you'll never know how beautiful this looks to me. And you'll never know how much I love you." He took her soft clean hands in his hard dirty ones and kissed them.

She said softly, "You don't like this war, do you, Jimmy?"

"No," he answered. He looked at her straight and spoke without hesitation. "I don't think I'm a coward, Celia. But I wasn't meant for killing. I'll do whatever I have to do, and do it the best I can, but I can't make myself *want* to do it. I can't hate the British, I can't hate Hessians, I can't even hate Tories."

"I can," said Celia. "I do."

Jimmy shrugged a lean shoulder. "Well, it won't last forever. And in the meantime—Celia, I'm so glad you're here. Just seeing you at odd times like this, it means such a lot." He looked at the cravat again, a smile lighting his tired face. "Put that away till I can wear it."

She nodded, and waited while he finished his coffee. Then he had to leave. As she closed the front door after him she knew that no matter what Elise and Burton might do, nobody was going to get her away from Charleston.

*A*BOUT SUNSET the firing died down. But in the morning the cannon on the Ashley River started again.

Now Elise was really frightened. The king's men across the river were cannonading, the king's men above Charleston were digging a trench across the neck of the peninsula, the king's ships were in sight and might get in any day. She clung to Burton and told him they had to leave town.

He put her off, saying he could not go today. They had a boat and could leave any time, but first he had work to do. He had moved much valuable property, including all the furnishings of their suburban home, into a city warehouse. This warehouse was a stout brick building, but it had to be barred and sandbagged, to make it safe from thieves in town as well as guns outside. When he had done this, said Burton, he would talk about leaving. Only he still did not think there was any reason for it, he added as he went out after breakfast.

During the morning Mrs. Baxter came in. She said she and Mr. Baxter had decided to go up the Cooper River to her father's plantation. It wasn't right to keep poor little George here where he might get hurt.

"Don't you think we should leave too?" Elise demanded of Celia.

Celia shook her head.

"But my dear," cried Mrs. Baxter, "haven't you heard what those British under General Prévost did last year along the Edisto River? They raided people's homes—"

"They stole *everything*," said Elise. "They even ripped up the mattresses with bayonets to see if people had hidden money inside—"

"They shot the cows and chickens," said Mrs. Baxter, "and left them to rot on the ground."

"They rounded up all the Negroes," said Elise, "and shipped them to the British West Indies to be sold in the canefields—"

"And what they did to women—" began Mrs. Baxter, but Elise cut in shrilly,

"Oh Patsy! Not before a young girl—that's not *nice!*"

At last Mrs. Baxter went home to pack. Dinner was a sketchy meal, for Elise had scared the wits out of the maids. However, when Burton came in he managed to restore some order by assuring them that though they could hear the guns, no shells were coming into town. Also he brought some encouraging news. For two years now, the king of France had been sending men and ships to aid the Americans, and several months ago the Marquis de Lafayette had gone back to France to urge that he send still more. Now the word was that King Louis had agreed, and a French fleet was on the way to Charleston.

Elise spent most of the next day in the attic with the spyglass, looking for the French ships. But they did not arrive, and when they still had not arrived by the following morning she was in despair again. This was Sunday, but Elise said she simply did not feel strong enough to go to church.

Leaving Tessie to pat Elise's head with rosewater, Burton and Celia and Marietta walked to St. Michael's. Above the faroff rumble of guns, Celia listened as the banns were read. ". . . James de Courcey Rand, bachelor, of the parish of St. Philip, and Celia Garth, spinster of this parish." She counted happily. Today was the second of April. Her birthday was eleven days ahead. After that, she and Jimmy could be married.

Two days later Elise said the Baxters had left town. And so, according to Elise, had practically everybody else, though Celia could still see plenty of people in the streets. But it was certainly true that whenever she turned the spyglass eastward she saw boats hurrying off by way of the Cooper River. That river was safe, guarded by Luke and the rest of Colonel Washington's cavalry.

The military men were glad to have these people go. Civilians got in the way. There had even been talk of ordering all non-combatants out of town. But the fact was that many people had nowhere to go. Leaving town was simple enough for those who had country homes, or whose out-of-town friends could give them accommodation. But ordinary folk—clerks and tailors and women who taught school—they had no country homes. Few of them even had boats, and the army had no boats to spare. So they stayed.

There were also a good many men like Burton, who wanted to stand by their property. But much as Burton wanted to stay, he was fond of Elise, and her terrors were wearing him down.

That night, not long after they had gone to bed, they were wakened by loud gunfire from the neck of the Charleston peninsula. Everybody jumped out of bed. While the kitchen servants huddled around the cook-fire to pray and sing hymns, Elise wandered through the house in a white robe that floated around her and made her look like a chubby ghost. After her came Tessie and the housemaids and their children, in various states of wailing fright. They roamed up to the attic, where if you looked toward the Neck you could see the shells flaring and bursting in a mighty display. When Elise had borne as much of this as she could, she and her train rambled down to the cellar, and here among the bins and storage kegs they crouched and covered their heads. After a while, tired of not seeing what was going on, Elise would lead them up to the attic again.

Hurrying into his clothes, Burton went out to make inquiries. He came in and told Elise that she had nothing to fear. All this gunfire was coming from American guns. The British, busy digging their trench from river to river across the Neck, were not shooting back. If she would go to the attic again, and look, she would see that the shells were all going outward toward the British lines.

Elise merely shook her head and trembled. "But I want to be with my children, Burton! My precious boys, why did I send them away and not go with them? What do you suppose is happening to them now?"

Burton told her the boys were undoubtedly in bed asleep. There were no British north of the Santee River.

"How do you know where the British are? That dreadful man Tarleton is all over the country, raiding and looting and killing people—oh, nobody knows *what's* going to happen!"

Burton sighed helplessly.

Burton had never had many decisions to make. He had been born into a good family, he had been to the right school and lived in the right neighborhood and had always tried to do the right thing. But until now, he had always known what the right thing was. Now he really did not know. Burton was confused. He had learned the rules so carefully, and now they were of no use to him. He felt that somehow, somebody had not played fair.

At last Elise climbed back to the attic. She sat on a trunk. The cannon rumbled. Elise turned to Celia, who stood at a window watching the faroff exploding shells.

"Have you heard what the officers have decided to do?" moaned Elise. "They're going to take the army out of town and let the redcoats march in without a fight. They're going to leave us to be murdered and have our houses burned over our heads."

Celia did not answer. It would not have mattered if she had, for Elise was starting down to the cellar again.

Celia and Marietta stayed in the attic, watching the shells. Celia thought if Elise had not been here this would have been an exciting adventure. But as the hours passed she found that a battle, especially a battle in which you are not yourself being shot at, gets monotonous. It was like an endless display of fireworks.

She and Marietta wore cloaks over their nightgowns, but as the pre-dawn mist crept in they began to shiver. Marietta smothered a yawn.

"Let's go back to bed," Celia said to her.

Marietta agreed gladly and they went down the staircase. In the second-floor hall they met Elise, taking whiffs of her smelling-salts.

"I've sent Tessie out to make coffee," said Elise. "Where **are** you going?"

"To bed," said Celia.

"What! You can't sleep now! They're still firing! Nobody knows what's going to—"

"I can't stay awake till the end of the war!" Celia retorted, and before Elise could answer she went into her own room and shut the door. When she had pulled the curtains together to keep out the daylight she got into bed, and she knew no more till she woke up at noon.

The cannonade was still going on. By this time the British were returning the rebel fire, and a few shells had even reached the earthworks in front of the city. But the firing was slow, with long spaces between shots. Late that afternoon the maids managed a pick-up supper, after which Burton and Elise went to their room. They both looked worn out, and Celia hoped that now they would get some rest.

After her long sleep this morning she felt wide awake. She went into the library and stood by a side window looking over the garden. How peaceful it seemed in the evening glow—the sweet yellow jessamine, the roses scrambling over the walls, the magnolia tree full of buds. Under the roar of the guns she could hear the silver sound of crickets. She wished she could know what was really going on. She had no idea what Jimmy was doing, or Darren, or Miles. She wondered if it was true that Tarleton's Legion was galloping about the country, and what part of the country they were in. She wondered how Luke was, and Vivian and Herbert, and Beatrice and Audrey and the baby. She wondered if Francis Marion had reached his plantation safely, and if his ankle still hurt him very much. How long since he fell? About a month—it seemed like a hundred years.

Now I'm getting mopey, she thought. I'd better do something.

She glanced toward the bookcases. There was plenty to read, for Herbert had taken only the valuable books to Sea Garden. Celia brought a candle, and chose *Robinson Crusoe*, which she had heard about all her life but had never read. Going to a big cushioned chair by the window, she curled up comfortably and opened the book.

After a few pages she was absorbed. The guns made an undertone like distant thunder. The evening grew dark, the candle burned steadily, the damp fragrances of the garden came in by the window. Celia read on and on. And then all of a sudden she heard a noise as if the world had exploded.

She sprang up. The book fell sprawling at her feet. The noise went on like the roar of a thousand volcanoes; the windowpanes shook, the poker fell clattering on the hearth; at her side the candlestick quivered on the table, and she snatched it up and set it on the hearth close to the grate so if the candle fell it would not set anything on fire. She heard screams of fright as Elise and the maids woke up, and more screams from the street. Flashes of light were splitting the dark over the garden.

Grabbing the candle seemed to have used up her own power of movement. Her hands clasped in front of her, she stood still, listening.

At first the noise had seemed to be everywhere, on all sides of her and in the sky and under the earth. But now she could tell that the roars were coming, not from the lines across the Neck, but from the southwest, somewhere close to the spot where she had seen the first redcoats across the Ashley River. She had never heard so much noise in her life. Slowly, she raised one hand and stroked her ear. It seemed strange that she could also hear the little brushing sound of her fingertips.

Now that she had moved she kept on moving, doing things with little jerky motions like a doll. She bent and picked up her book, smoothed a crumpled page, and placed the book on the table. She saw that the glass holder on the mantelpiece, which contained the rolled paper lamplighters, was trembling under the force of the guns; she took it carefully and set it on the floor so it would not fall and break. Kneeling by the hearth she took the tongs and fire-shovel and laid them beside the poker so they would not fall either. Still kneeling there, she burst into tears and began to sob with fright.

The first sound of the bombardment had nearly stunned her. But now that this first shock had passed, her senses were awake again and what she realized made her shake with terror.

This was no token firing to remind you that the British were here. These guns meant business. She remembered what Tom Lacy had said—that Sir Henry Clinton had not forgiven Charleston for his defeat at Fort Moultrie. This time he had vowed to turn the place into a pile of dust and corpses. And tonight he had started.

Burying her face in the seat of the chair Celia pressed her arms against her ears and clasped her hands behind her head. This shut out some of the noise but it did not make her stop shaking, long violent shakes that went through her whole body and made her neck jerk and her teeth chatter. Nobody came in to ask how she was, maybe because they did not know she was in the library, maybe because they were all too scared to think of her. She was not thinking of them either. All she could think was that any minute one of those shells might land in here and blow her to pieces.

But after a long time the shakes in her body began to lessen. The noise was still as great as ever, but somehow it was no longer so terrifying. Celia felt herself relaxing. Her hands untangled themselves. The fingers were stiff and her elbows were painful with tension. As she slowly raised her head, and sat back on her heels, she moved her arms and hands to get them feeling natural again.

The guns crashed. The room was full of great fluttering shadows thrown by the candle on the hearth. Suddenly it was lit for an instant by another flash from outside, as if the sky had cracked with great lightning.

Celia felt a sense of astonishment. She wet her lips. She heard another crash of cannon. She said in an awed voice,

"I haven't been killed."

She wet her lips again. The noise hit on her ears. She said,

"Maybe I'm not going to be killed."

She got to her feet. Her legs were stiff, and she walked around the room in the noise, to ease them. As she walked she had a feeling that there was something familiar about all this.

At first she did not know what she was thinking of, but as the firing went on she remembered—the first time she had talked to Luke, in the parlor at Mrs. Thorley's, when she had said to him, "You like being scared," and he had answered, "What I like is the way I feel when I wake up in the morning, when I look around and say, 'Good Lord, I'm still here!' "

This was how she felt right now. She was still alive and it gave her a sense of triumph. Standing there in the bombardment, still trembling, Celia nodded slowly. This was what he had meant.

.~.

The firing lasted all night. Toward morning it lessened, but it went on at intervals all day.

Before daybreak Burton had promised Elise that they would leave. They would take their maidservants—the men he would have to leave on the earthworks—and Celia and Marietta too if they wanted to go. Celia said no.

When they had had a few hours' sleep Marietta put on some hominy grits to cook, along with a pan of bacon. As soon as he had finished his breakfast Burton went out to arrange for sharing his boat with some friends who would help with the sailing.

Elise went to her room and began frantically opening her bureau drawers and throwing her clothes around and calling for somebody to pack them. Celia said she would do it—not that she loved Elise, but she wanted to keep occupied. The maids were bringing all sorts of tales about people who had been hurt last night, and Jimmy might have been among them. She did not want to think about it.

But while she was packing, a maid came to say that Mr. Darren Bernard was here to see her. Her heart jumping at the thought of the news he might have brought, Celia dashed downstairs and out to the front steps where Darren was waiting.

"How's Jimmy, Darren?" she gasped as she reached him. "And you?"

"Fine, both of us. That's what I came to tell you, and to ask how you are—all right?"

She nodded, nearly sobbing with relief. Darren drew her against the side of the open doorway and waited for her to get calm. Celia blinked, and looked up with great thankfulness. She noticed that it was a beautiful day, cool and clear, and an acacia tree across the street was blooming in a great big fluff of gold. How strange Darren looked, soiled and unshaven, with a long jagged tear in his stocking—Darren who had always been so well dressed. "Can you come in?" she asked. "A glass of wine, something to eat—"

He shook his head. "Too much to do. I had to pass here, and Jimmy told me to take five minutes, no more, to stop by and give you a note." He drew the note from his pocket.

She thanked him. "Tell me what happened last night, Darren."

Darren said a few men had been struck, and two small houses had been knocked flat, but altogether the bombardment had done remarkably little harm. He had no time to say more.

Celia went indoors and up to her room. Jimmy had written his note on a scrap of paper torn from some account book. He had scribbled hurriedly.

"My dearest,
I asked you to stay, now I am asking you to go. If Burton leaves town, or anyone else you know, go with them. Go to my mother at Bellwood. If you cannot get to her go to Vivian or any friends you have in the country. When this is over I'll find you. Jimmy."

Celia crumpled the note in her fist. From her open window she heard the chirp of a sparrow above the grumble of cannon. She said aloud,
"I am not going."

She tore Jimmy's note in half and then in half again.

"I am going to stay here," she said, "because I love Jimmy."

But even as she spoke she knew this was not the reason. She was going to stay with Jimmy not because she loved him but because he loved her. Until that gray Sunday afternoon last fall she had never had any feeling that anybody loved her. She had not known how precious it was, this knowledge of being loved. No, she was not going anywhere.

She gathered up the scraps of Jimmy's note. There was no fire in the house, so she went downstairs and across the back porch and along the covered brick walk to the kitchen. Here the cook-fire smoldered in the fireplace, watched by a small black girl on a stool. Celia dropped the scraps on the fire and watched them burn.

# CHAPTER 13

*N*OW AT LAST they were gone. Celia and Marietta were alone. At the last minute Burton had had an attack of propriety. It disturbed him that Celia should be here with her only companion a maid no older than herself. For a moment Celia was afraid she was going to be carried off, but she reminded him that her twenty-first birthday was only a week ahead and after this Mr. Moreau would marry her to Jimmy. And so, glad not to have any more women on his hands, Burton let her have her way.

They left Friday, the seventh of April. It was surprising how peaceful the house was. The cannon were firing, but no shells were coming into town and by now Celia was so used to the distant grunts and grumblings that she hardly noticed them.

She planned that while Marietta did the cooking she would take care of the garden. They had plenty of rice and meat, but they would need vegetables too. That afternoon they went to the storeroom and cut off a slab of spiced beef, and put it in water to soak out the salt overnight so it could be roasted for tomorrow's dinner. "We'll have it with rice and gravy," said Celia, "and some green peas. I'll pick the peas in the morning."

It was like playing house. In the evening when they had locked up, Celia took *Robinson Crusoe* to her room and read until she was sleepy. The guns were almost quiet as she blew out her candle.

She woke in the night with a feeling of having had an uncomfortable dream. The room was dark, and she could hear the guns in the distance. Moving restlessly, she realized that she was uncomfortable because she was too warm. She threw back the blankets but she was still too warm. Getting out of bed she pushed back the window-curtains and opened both windows as far as they would go. But the room still felt stuffy, and she had a hard time going back to sleep.

When she woke again it was morning. Before she opened her eyes she knew it was going to be a hot day. After breakfast she went out to the courtyard. Clouds were gathering over the sun and even here among the trees and flowerbeds the air seemed heavy. The birds were silent, as if they had no energy to sing, and the guns were silent too, as if the men had no energy to shoot. Celia felt her chemise clinging damply to her skin.

She wet her forefinger and held it up. After a moment one side of her finger began to be cold, the side toward the south.

Now she understood. In the night the wind had changed. No longer was it blowing from the west, from the high ground and the clean pine woods; it was coming over the swampy sea islands. As she lowered her hand Celia looked at a blue-jay pecking at the grass. In spite of the heat a shiver went over her as she said to him,

"Now those ships can get in."

She went indoors and up the stairs to the attic. From oversight or consideration, Burton had left his spyglass, and Celia looked out to sea. The British ships were no closer to town than they had been yesterday—the tide was out, she noticed—but no longer were they just sitting there waiting. Alongside the sails, from masts to decks, the seamen had run lines of ropes; along the ropes they had strung small flags of different colors, and they were moving the flags to make changing designs. This was how ships talked to each other and to their friends on shore. Celia had no idea how to read the signals, but she did not need nautical language to guess that the admiral on his flagship was saying to Sir Henry Clinton on shore, "We are coming in! When the tide turns, we'll be on our way!"

She was not the only one who guessed this. The Cooper River

was crowded with fleeing boats—schooners, little fishing craft, even open rowboats where children crouched among bundles of food and clothing while their mothers sweated at the oars. Celia wondered where they were all going to sleep tonight.

As the day went on the south wind grew stronger, blowing clouds thick over the sky. Celia and Marietta had not much appetite for the spiced beef. They told each other it would taste better this evening when they could slice it cold, but they both knew they were not hungry because they were tense about the British ships.

As the afternoon advanced, they waited. They climbed out of the attic window to the roof and turned the spyglass in all directions. Around them the roofs and high windows were crowded with people. Not a gun sounded. All the soldiers—Americans, British, Tories, Hessians—were watching the ships. The men had mounted the earthworks, they stood on the gun platforms or were precariously balanced on the guns themselves, craning their necks. In the top of the black steeple of St. Michael's stood Peter Timothy, a spyglass in one hand and a pen in the other, watching and making notes of what he saw, while messengers waited to take his reports to headquarters. The clock in the steeple showed that the time was close to four.

The day was tropic-hot, fifteen or twenty degrees hotter than yesterday. Celia could feel the sweat trickling down her face. She lowered the spyglass. Out there in the distance the men-of-war looked no bigger than butterflies. But even so far away she could see that they were tall ships, splendid and terrible. The tide was mounting toward its flood. As she watched, the men-of-war formed into a line, one behind another with long spaces between them and a pilot boat leading the line. They began to move.

The flags held stiff and jaunty in the wind, the white sails billowed high against the gray sky and the gray sea and the gray horizon line. Celia hardly breathed as the first ship came near the island seven miles away from her, where Fort Moultrie guarded the sea-gate of Charleston.

Out of the corner of her eye she saw Marietta's hand tensely holding the edge of the gable beside her. Celia's own hands were stiff with excitement. Then it happened, what she and Marietta and everybody else had been waiting for. It was as if Fort Moultrie blew up into a thousand lights as the American guns opened fire.

They saw it, and then they heard it. Even at this distance the crash was so fierce that they ducked backward and put up their arms to shield their eyes. After an instant they looked again. Above the island and the men-of-war were pillars of smoke, sparkling with the exploding shells. At the head of the line the admiral's flagship roared and flashed as her guns returned the fire. She looked as if she was sending out bolts of lightning.

The flagship passed the island and came on. Celia could not tell whether the ship had been damaged or not.

The guns of the fort roared away as other ships sailed into the smoke. And now Celia could see that one ship was gravely damaged—a mast was broken and dangling down, dragging part of the sails down with it—but the ship struggled crookedly on. Then in the midst of the black clouds she saw another ship catch fire. The fire leaped across the deck, catching the great sails like sheets of paper, and Celia stood with her lips parted, her whole body tingling with triumph, and Marietta cried out.

"Oh I can't bear it—men on that ship—"

Slowly Celia turned her head. Marietta leaned against the gable, her eyes covered. Celia looked back at the ship. She had forgotten there were men on it. But even so, they were the king's men, trying to kill her friends. She did not care if they got killed first.

"Miss Celia," Marietta said brokenly, "I'd like to go in."

Celia said, "All right," and Marietta climbed back through the window. Celia stayed where she was, watching and listening, now looking at some detail through the glass, now lowering the glass to get a view of the whole. It all had a dreadful glory: the roars and lightnings, the blazing vessel, the other ships fighting their way through the smoke; on shore the thousands of soldiers in their many-colored uniforms, the people crowding roofs and windows, the other people fleeing by the boats in the river. Celia stood there spellbound.

The ships came in. Not all of them, for besides the one set afire from the fort another ran aground and was burned by her own crew so the Americans could not take her, and the men in the fort did serious damage to several others. Those that passed the fort came as close as they could to Charleston, though this was not very close because of the ships the Americans had sunk across the front of town. But they were near enough for Celia to see them clearly through her glass: the guns on deck pointing toward her, the sailors in wide flapping breeches and tarry pigtails, ready to shoot.

By St. Michael's clock the time was nearly six. Celia's legs, her back, her head and neck, were stiff and aching. Her hands were black from the dust of the roof, and there were black streaks on her skirt. She wondered if she was wicked, to have been so exhilirated by a battle. Well, not exactly wicked. But she might as well own up to it—she did not have Marietta's gentleness, or Jimmy's. She thought of Luke. He would not have shuddered when that ship caught fire, any more than she had. Luke would have shouted with glee.

What she needed now was to get washed. Climbing back through the attic window she went down to her room. In the mirror she looked even worse than she had thought—her hair was like last year's bird-nest, her cap was all on one side, there was a black mark down her cheek, and her kerchief looked as if she had used it to dust the furniture. As she unpinned her cap she heard a knock on her door, and Marietta looked in.

"Miss Celia, Mr. Jimmy's here. He says he can't stay but a few minutes so please hurry—"

Celia was already hurrying. Jimmy waited at the foot of the staircase, and she almost tumbled into his arms.

He kissed her long and hard. At length he drew back a little and stood looking down at her as if his eyes would eat her up. He seemed not to notice that her hair was tousled and her face dirty; he gazed at her as if he had never seen a woman so beautiful.

"I was afraid you'd get away before I could say good-by," he said. He spoke softly, almost in a whisper. "Godfrey told me Burton had definitely decided to leave town. Will he take you to Bellwood or to—"

Celia stiffened her courage to answer. "Burton left yesterday."

She felt Jimmy give a start. He began to reply. She did not

listen, but rushed on, explaining why she had stayed behind, why she could *not* go.

"I want us to be together, Jimmy!" she finished. "Whatever happens to you, I want it to happen to me."

For a moment Jimmy said nothing. His black eyes were intense in his gaunt face. She felt his arms tighten around her. He kissed her again, this time less with passion than with a deep understanding. His lips against hers, he said, "I did think you ought to go. I still think you should have gone. But now that you've made a fool of yourself, I'm glad of it."

Celia felt a thrill of joy. She did not care what might happen. This was worth it.

But Jimmy stepped abruptly back from her. He held her hands, but now he spoke not like a lover but like a soldier giving commands. "Take every pitcher and bucket in the house," he ordered, "and fill them, some with water and some with sand. Put them all over the house—close to the walls so you can get at them but won't stumble over them in the dark."

Celia remembered the burning ship. "You mean we may have fires in town?"

Jimmy had no time to answer questions. He went on with his orders. "Take some blankets and drinking-water down to the cellar. When the firing starts, you and Marietta stay there. Start filling those buckets now, before dark—keep one by you tonight when you go to bed." He demanded, almost roughly, "You'll do this?"

Celia's throat felt thick, but she managed to say, "Yes, Jimmy."

"I don't know when I can see you again. But—" he smiled, and the smile was like a sudden light on his face—"I'll get word to Mr. Moreau that we're to be married as planned. Next week. I've been counting. The thirteenth of April is Thursday."

As if I hadn't been counting too, thought Celia. Aloud she said, "And we won't have to live at your house with Miles and those strange officers. I can stay right here, and when you get leave we can be alone together, with Marietta and Amos to take care of us."

"And I love you," Jimmy said softly, "more than—"

149

There was a pounding at the front door and a man shouted Jimmy's name.

"Time's up," said Jimmy. He kissed her again quickly, and opened the door. Before she could say good-by he had whisked down the steps and away.

Celia called Marietta. They went out to the back yard, and using garden-spades they filled four buckets with loose earth. Each of them took a bucket to her room and they put the others on the staircase landings. Celia was not at all sure this was necessary. Not only was this house built of brick with a slate roof, but so were the houses on both sides and most of the others near by. In its early days Charleston had had several disastrous fires, so now most people built with brick, using as little wood as possible. But she wanted to do everything Jimmy had ordered. If he had scolded her for staying in town she would have been hurt and defiant, but after what he had said she was glowing with happiness. Now she knew she was necessary to him. Nobody had ever really needed her before.

That night the town was as quiet as if the British were back on the other side of the ocean where they belonged. The next day was Sunday, but Celia did not try to go to church. About mid-morning she heard the guns, but the firing was off-and-on and when she looked from the roof she saw that only a few shells were coming over the earthworks into town. Most of them were just burying themselves in the earthworks, sending up great explosions of dirt. But now she saw that not all the British missiles were exploding shells. Some of them were real balls of fire. She could see them blazing their way through the air. So this was what Jimmy had foreseen. Brick walls or not, if those things hit wooden posts and shutters they could make plenty of trouble. Celia went in and began to look for more buckets.

Again that night the guns were fairly quiet, but at dawn Monday they started again. All morning they boomed. The air was sultry, and acrid with smoke. Celia and Marietta carried blankets down to the cellar. Built with heavy brick walls and iron air-gratings at sidewalk level, the cellar was dim and dismal. It was not dirty, for Vivian kept house the way she did everything else, by demanding perfection of other people; but it was not inviting.

Celia and Marietta agreed that they would not spend any time here unless things got really dangerous. When they had also brought down two chairs, and a covered jar of water and two cups, they went up to get their dinner.

While Marietta put on the rice to cook Celia went out to the garden to cut mustard greens. To her surprise, the guns had fallen silent. The smell of smoke had nearly all blown away, and she could hear birds twittering. From over the wall where Godfrey's Bernard's back yard touched this one, she heard him call to her, and she went to the gate.

Godfrey, who was out most of the time directing the storage of food supplies for the garrison, had been surprised to see that she had not left town with Burton. He made no protest, however; Celia got the impression that he had too much on his mind to care what anybody did. She asked him why the guns had stopped. He told her Sir Henry Clinton had sent a formal demand for surrender, and the guns would stay quiet until an answer was received.

"Surrender!" Celia exclaimed. "We're not going to surrender, are we?"

"Of course not," said Godfrey. "It's just a formality." He smiled a little, but it was a wry smile, almost mocking. Godfrey's face was lined with fatigue. He pushed his handkerchief across his forehead. "This crazy weather!" he burst out. "We haven't had an April heat-wave like this in twenty years."

As he walked off Celia looked after him with a frown. Usually so jaunty, today Godfrey was troubled. His comment on the weather had been spoken with a fury hardly justified by a few days of merely uncomfortable heat. There was such a lot she did not understand.

Monday night was silent, hot, and sticky. When she came down Tuesday morning Celia told Marietta they could do very well with a cold dinner. Just cornbread and cheese, and a salad. After breakfast she went out to gather salad greens.

The lettuces grew in neat crisp rows. Celia stooped to pull up one of the heads. As her hand touched it she heard a long screaming whistle in the air. An object flashed by her and struck the ground between her and the stable, with such force that it shook the ground in ripples like those made by a stone thrown into water.

It had happened so suddenly that Celia had hardly moved. Now she heard the air full of screaming whistles, and thuds of things falling, and cries of panic. There was a tremendous noise as the thing in the garden exploded. The earth around it rose up like water from a fountain; the earth under Celia's feet seemed to rise and strike her, and her face went down into the lettuce bed.

Her fall was so violent that the breath was knocked clean out of her chest. Struggling for air, she breathed in nothing much but grains of dirt. Choking and coughing, she managed to push herself up with her hands. For a moment the stable and trees and garden walls swung around her. Gradually as her head cleared she wiped her eyes on her sleeve and spit out the dirt in her mouth. She heard more whistling noises, and more sounds of people screaming and running in the street, and she saw more things flying in the air above her. She heard guns roaring from every direction, and now she knew what had happened. The rebels had refused to surrender and the attack had really begun.

The shell had made a hole five or six feet across, but falling in the grassy space between garden and stable it had done no harm. The near edge of the hole was about twenty feet ahead of her. Celia felt herself tremble as she thought, "If I had been standing there instead of here, I would be dead now."

But she was not dead. Again, as on the night of that other bombardment, she had a sense of triumph. She rubbed her arm, grimy with garden soil, and the feel of her fingers on her healthy skin gave her a delicious pleasure. The guns were yelling and smashing as if they would split her ears. And she had thought the other attack was noisy! It seemed to her that until this minute she had never heard a real noise in her life.

But she was not as panicky as she had been that night. Jimmy had told her to take refuge in the cellar. As she turned toward the house she saw Marietta, just getting her own wits in order, running toward the back steps. Celia went to join her and they fled together down the cellar stairs.

Here in the musty dark they could hear the guns crashing, and through the street-gratings they could see running feet and hear screams—whether of pain or fright they could not tell. Before long Celia felt that her nerves were being torn to strings. For all she knew, half the town might be blown to pieces by now. Staying in the cellar was like being buried alive.

"Marietta!" she said sharply.

Marietta stood peering out of a sidewalk grating. She wheeled around. "Yes ma'am?"

"Let's go up in the house," said Celia. "I'm sick of this."

"You and me both, Miss Celia!" Marietta exclaimed, and they ran up the cellar steps. After all, Celia was thinking, that shell this morning had landed in this yard by pure chance. The British might fire a thousand more before another one came close.

Up in the light again she found that her idea was reasonable. The bombardment was as fierce as ever, but no more shells had fallen on this lot. With Marietta she went up to the attic. From here they could see that a brick sidewalk not far away had been torn up, and over near the harbor-front threads of smoke showed them that some buildings were on fire. Marietta shivered, and wondered if many people had been hurt. Celia hoped not. But again she found that there was a dark fascination about it all.

The guns fired all that day and all that night. At dark Celia and Marietta dragged the mattresses off their beds and carried them down to the cellar, but they could not sleep. It all seemed more frightening at night. The explosions were so hideously brilliant; the fireballs, which were merely pink glimmers in the daylight, now in the dark looked like imps flying across the sky. When they had stayed in the cellar till they could bear it no longer Celia and Marietta went upstairs and looked out of the windows till they could bear that no longer, and they fled to the cellar again.

At last it was morning. The bombardment still went on, but the daylight was friendlier than the dark. They made their way to the kitchen, where they ate a breakfast of cold cornbread, then they went back to the cellar. And finally that night, after forty hours of battle the men on both sides were exhausted and the firing died down to a few irregular shots.

How wonderful to sleep all night and wake up to a quiet morning! To have hot coffee and bacon for breakfast, to look out with the spyglass and see what surprisingly little damage the bombardment had done.

For Charleston was not only a city of brick, but a city of gardens. In colder climates people placed their houses close together, with little or no space between them, so that a town was an almost solid target and any shell fired at random was likely to hit something. But here, even in the poor neighborhoods, the houses stood wide apart for air and coolness. There were abundant green trees, and every family had its own well. The British had made a few direct hits, but most of their missiles, like the one Celia had seen, had fallen into damp garden earth and fizzled out.

While Marietta put rice and salt beef on the fire, Celia went out to the garden and pulled up the lettuce she had meant to pull up day before yesterday. Here among the vegetables she found a burnt-out fireball. Taking it in her hand she examined it with loathing curiosity: an iron shell six or eight inches long pierced all over with holes. They had packed it with some sort of inflammable stuff—maybe rags or cotton soaked in oil—and set it alight, then they had shot it into town to start a fire. A fragment of the stuffing, still in the shell, had a nasty smell of burnt grease.

Celia threw the thing down. Jimmy had said he did not hate the British. Well, she hated them enough for two.

In St. Michael's steeple the clock pointed to nine. It was starting out to be another hot day.

Her basket on her arm, she went toward the kitchen-house. She always remembered exactly how it happened. Her foot was just touching the brick walk that led to the kitchen; through the open doorway she saw Marietta steaming the rice; Celia called, "I've brought the—"

Then it came.

Every British battery started at once. The guns on the Neck, on the sea islands, on the men-of-war, all burst into action. For a moment Celia stood where she was, stupid with shock. She saw bombs, and red-hot round shot, and fireballs blazing across the sky. They came from every direction, so many of them that above her she saw two shells meet in mid-air and blow up. Marietta had dropped on her knees by the kitchen fireplace. With clasped hand she was rocking back and forth, pleading, "Jesus, have mercy. Jesus, have mercy."

The basket slid off Celia's arm to the ground. The whole world seemed to be reeling and cracking around her. She couldn't just stand here. They had to get down to the cellar. Turning her back to the kitchen she looked along the walk to the main house. The walk was covered, so dishes could be brought in conveniently on rainy days, but it had wide arched openings on both sides. As Celia turned, a fireball flashed through one of these arches. She heard herself scream.

"Marietta! The house is on fire!"

The fireball had struck the edge of the back porch. As it struck, it broke open as it was meant to do. The blazing stuff inside fell on the wooden boards of the porch floor and sent out tongues of oily flame. The boards caught and crackled.

There was a bucket of water by the back door, and a bucket of earth somewhere near—where had they put it? She could not remember, but she ran to the house and snatched up the water. How heavy it was. When they set it here it had not seemed so heavy. She managed to carry it to the fire, spilling a good deal of water in her haste, and dumped what was left on the burning boards. It was not nearly enough. Looking around wildly she saw Marietta, half carrying and half dragging the bucket of earth, which Celia remembered now had been placed by the porch steps. As she reached the fire Marietta gasped, "Get a rug, Miss Celia."

A rug—of course. Celia dragged out the first one she saw, a thick doormat lying by the hall door. While Marietta looked for more earth Celia beat at the fire. The rough fibers of the mat hurt her hands. She thought angrily of how hard it often was to make a fire burn when you needed it.

At last it was out. The porch looked as if a giant had taken a bite out of the edge, leaving a crescent-shaped indentation. The white posts on either side of the crescent were blackened with smoke.

Celia felt tenderly of her chafed hands. Marietta held to a post, dizzily. Her white apron was scorched and her white cap was pushed over one ear. "Miss Celia," she murmured, "where do you reckon they are? Mr. Jimmy, Amos—"

"Hush!" Celia exclaimed. "I don't want to think about—" A shell whistled above the garden. She grabbed Marietta's hand and they ran to the cellar.

About eleven o'clock the firing slackened, and they filled the buckets again. But at noon it all started over.

A shell struck a corner of the stable and sent bricks flying, another shell tore a limb off the magnolia tree, and more fireballs fizzled in the garden. After dark a fireball struck the stable door. While they beat out the fire Celia remembered Jerry's handsome head looking out of this door, and she wondered what Luke and Jerry were doing tonight.

At last, she and Marietta were simply too tired to feel frightened any more. While the shells went on howling they dragged themselves into the kitchen and ate rice and beef. The food was a help, but they still ached in every joint and the shells were still screaming threats of fire and death. Celia dropped her head on her arm and listened. What a day it had been! The most dreadful day she had ever lived through. Somehow she had an impression that there was something special about this day. At first she was too tired to think what it was, then she remembered. Today was Thursday. It was the thirteenth of April, 1780. Her twenty-first birthday.

She gave a harsh little laugh. How she had looked forward to this day! The golden day when she would be her own boss, free to get married, free of Roy—she wondered where Roy was. Probably on the indigo plantation of Sophie's family, safely wrapped in their riches and their Toryism. While she, in Charleston, was free to celebrate her birthday.

Was it always like this, she wondered, when you got the things you waited for?

# CHAPTER 14

*A*T MIDNIGHT the guns quieted. Celia and Marietta stumbled down the cellar stairs and fell on their mattresses and went to sleep. In the morning there was firing, but it was so much less intense than yesterday's that they hardly noticed it.

It was nearly noon when Celia carried a bucket of water through the flower garden and set it by the brick wall that divided the garden from the street, to be ready in case a fireball struck one of the house-shutters on this side. Through the wrought-iron gate she could see the street, agog with people. Taking her bunch of keys from her pocket she went to the gate. As she put a key into the padlock she remembered the evening when she had pushed open this gate and met Luke under the street lamp. He had said, "You've no idea how your hair shines with that lantern behind you—it's a real moonlight gold." Celia put up her hand to her hair. It seemed a long time since she had thought of what color it was.

Two militiamen came by, pulling a handcart holding a crate of rifles. Their tired whiskery faces lit with smiles as they were refreshed by the sight of a pretty girl. But one of them warned, "You better go down cellar, miss."

Celia smiled back and said she would. But no shells were falling in this part of town, so she stayed in the gateway, looking out.

Men were moving guns, powder, barrels of meat and cornmeal, all the varied supplies that came in every day by the Cooper River. On the house across the street Celia saw an ornamental white cornice above a window, charred by a fireball.

A man's voice shouted from down the street. "Miss Celia! Miss Celia!"

Celia ran to the curb and peered around. Rattling toward her was a cart, drawn by Amos in place of a horse.

Usually dressed with the care of a prideful house-man, today Amos was tattered and dirty and soaked with sweat. His shirt was so torn that it was hardly a shirt any more; his breeches, made of good blue homespun, were torn too, and flapped about his knees. He wore no stockings, and his shoes were furry with dust. Panting, he stopped his cart by the curb.

"What is it, Amos?" she cried.

Amos raised his arm to push back the sweat that was about to drip over his eyes. "Miss Celia—it's Mr. Jimmy. I've got him here. He's bad hurt."

For an instant it seemed to Celia that the sun turned black. Steadying herself with a great effort, she put her hand on the side of the cart and looked.

Jimmy lay on the bare boards, not even a blanket under him to cushion the jolts. But he did not know this. He did not know anything. In one leg of his rebel blue breeches there was a bloody rip, and under the rip a gash in his thigh, oozing blood. The blood was creeping out to make a puddle beside him.

Celia felt something solid come up into her throat. By some instinct she knew that she was about to let out a hysterical scream, and she knew also that this was what she must not do. She must keep her head now if she never did another sensible thing as long as she lived.

Swallowing hard, she looked up at Amos. "We've got to stop this bleeding."

"I've done all I know how, Miss Celia," he told her earnestly, "but it keeps breaking open. You see—he's got a bullet still in him."

Celia gasped in horror. "You—why didn't you have a surgeon take it out?"

"I tried to, ma'am," said Amos. There was a sound of desperation in his voice. "But so many men are hurt, I couldn't find a surgeon that didn't have them lying in rows waiting for him. That's why I brought Mr. Jimmy here. I thought maybe you—" Amos looked at the cart, took a step away from it, dropped his voice. "Miss Celia, if we don't get that bullet out he'll bleed to death."

"I'll get a surgeon," Celia said. She spoke vehemently, to hide from herself as well as from Amos the fact that she did not know where she was going to get one. "He can't lie here in the street," she went on briskly. "Bring him in—not this gate, it's not wide enough, I'll open the gate to the driveway."

Snatching the keys from her pocket she ran past the house to the carriage drive on the other side. She heard a shrill grating sound—in her confusion she could not tell whether it was the whine of a shell or the screak of her key in the lock—but anyway she got the gate open and Amos dragged in the cart.

He brought it to the edge of the back porch. Vivian's bedroom was on the first floor, next to her boudoir, but when Celia said she would make up the bed in there for Jimmy, Amos shook his head.

"Miss Celia, excuse me ma'am, I don't believe that'll do. I could tote him, I'm right stout, but I'm scared to move him that far. He's not bleeding much now, but if it really got started again—"

"I see." Celia looked at the blood oozing out of Jimmy's wound. With a shudder, she pulled off the kerchief around her neck. "Here, Amos, tie this around his leg, and maybe you can make the blood stop."

While Amos obeyed, she ran to find Marietta. With frantic haste they pulled the mattress off Vivian's bed and dragged it to the back porch. Standing each on one side of the cart they held it as steady as they could while Amos lifted Jimmy and let him slip gently down to the mattress. The pain of movement roused him; Celia heard him groan faintly, and murmur something about water. Marietta went for a cup. Celia dropped on her knees by the mattress and put her hand on Jimmy's forehead. The skin was dry and blazing hot. Jimmy's eyes opened. She was about to bend and kiss him when a stern dark hand closed on her wrist and Amos spoke with dreadful urgency. "Miss Celia, *that surgeon.*"

Celia sprang to her feet. Of course, this was no time to be a sentimental fool. While Marietta brought the cup of water and Amos lifted Jimmy's head, helping him to swallow, Celia glanced toward the gate that led into Godfrey's back yard. Godfrey knew everybody.

"I'll be right back," she said to Amos.

She ran across the yard and through the gateway. The guns seemed louder, the shells closer, or maybe it was only her imagination. Godfrey's back door, like all doors these days, was locked. Celia pounded with her fists, shouting his name.

After what seemed an endless time—though it was really only a minute or two—a startled Negro woman's voice demanded, "Who's that? What you want?"

"It's me!" Celia cried. "Celia Garth. I want Mr. Godfrey Bernard—open the door!"

With exasperating slowness, a key turned and the door swung open. In the doorway stood a fat colored woman with gilt rings in her ears and a blue kerchief on her head. "What's the matter, honey? You scared?"

"I want Mr. Bernard. I need a surgeon. Captain Rand has been hurt—Captain Jimmy Rand—"

"Oh Lawsy mussy!" The woman threw her apron over her head and rocked back and forth, wailing. Two other colored women came up the stairs from the cellar where they had taken refuge, shrilly demanding a share in the new trouble. Celia caught the arm of the nearest one in a savage grip.

"Oh hush, can't you?" she exclaimed. "Where is Mr. Bernard?"

"He's not home, honey."

"Where is he?"

They didn't know. He was all over town these days. Was Mr. Jimmy bad hurt?

Farther down the hall a door burst open and a man's voice demanded, "What's going on? Don't you know I've got work to do?"

Celia cried out in relief. The man was Darren, holding a ledger in one hand and in the other a quill that was just dropping a blot on his shirt. Not long ago a blot on Darren's shirt would have been a calamity, now he hardly noticed it. He gave Celia a tired smile.

"Sorry, I didn't know it was you. But Godfrey's feeding half the army and I have to keep these records for the quartermaster."

"Mr. Jimmy done been hurt!" cried the fat woman, eager to be first with the bad news. The other women burst out wailing again. A shell whistled close and they all ducked.

"Can I speak to you, Darren?" Celia begged.

"Come in here." He showed her into the room where he had been working. Papers lay helterskelter over tables and chairs, and account-books were stacked on the floor. Darren set down his ledger and quill. "What's this about Jimmy?"

She told him as fast as she could. "Please get a surgeon, Darren! Please, before—" She could not add "—before he bleeds to death." The words stuck in her throat.

But Darren understood. With his ink-stained hand he pushed back his hair. His face, usually so merry, was grim as he said, "Every surgeon in town is on the lines, worked half to death." He stood thinking, while Celia twisted her hands in a torture of suspense. "Maybe—" Darren said slowly, "maybe—taking out a bullet isn't such a job, you know. Painful, but—" He smiled suddenly. "I've got an idea. You go on back to Jimmy."

"Oh Darren! God bless you." She seized his inky hand and kissed it. "Hurry!"

◦~◦

The day was hot and grew hotter. Jimmy lay on the mattress on the back porch. Amos had managed to stop the bleeding but they were in terror lest it start again. Already Jimmy had lost so much blood that he was weak as a baby. Celia could only hope that this was blurring his consciousness of the pain. She sat on the floor by him, waving a fan to blow away flies, while Amos brought water from the well and gave him frequent drinks, for Jimmy was burning up with thirst. Celia brought some rice, but though he tried, Jimmy could swallow only a few grains. Remembering the trays Vivian had sent up to Darren at Sea Garden, Celia told Marietta to cut a slice of the spiced beef and make some broth. "He can eat it this afternoon," she said, "after the surgeon has been here and he feels easier. Meat makes blood."

Marietta went to the kitchen. Amos held up Jimmy's head to give him more water. Jimmy's head dropped back on the mattress, close to where Celia's hand was resting. He turned his head and his lips touched her wrist. She bent to kiss him, and felt his skin fiery under her lips.

"Oh God," she prayed silently, *"please!"*

She heard a mosquito whang past her ear. Good heavens, one more torment—wouldn't this heat-wave ever blow over? She moved the fan harder, to keep the mosquitoes away from Jimmy.

Maybe she should have tried to find Miles. If he knew Jimmy was wounded he might be able to do something. But Amos said Miles was on duty somewhere along the Neck, while Jimmy had been at the south end of town. That was why Amos had brought him here, it was so close.

Oh God in heaven, please send that surgeon!

The shells rang through the sweltering air. But there were not very many of them, as if the men on the lines were too hot to do much real fighting. Celia sent Amos to look at St. Michael's clock. Not yet one. They had been waiting less than an hour.

She told Amos to go to the kitchen and have Marietta give him something to eat. While he had his dinner Celia stayed where she was. Jimmy lay with his eyes nearly shut, his breathing shallow and slow. He hardly moved except when a wince of pain went over his face. Under the sunburn his skin had a greenish cast. Celia looked at the palm of her own hand, healthy pink, and hated herself for it.

And then—oh blessed sound!—under the roar of guns she heard the bang of the driveway gate, and Darren's voice shouting,

"Celia! Here we are!"

Dropping her fan, Celia sprang up and ran down the back steps and around the house to meet him. "Yes, Darren! You've brought the—"

She stopped in dismay. For with Darren was no surgeon, but the little monkeyfaced French hairdresser, Hugo.

Hugo was all dressed up in his powdered wig and spanking-fresh clothes, as if he had come to do Vivian's hair, and he held the leather bag in which he was used to carrying his pomades and curling-tongs. As he saw Celia he gave a snappy little bow like a dancing-master.

"It is an honor to be of assistance, miss," he purred. "And where is the poor brave gentleman?"

Celia could have burst into tears, but she managed to answer, "On the back porch."

"I will see him," announced Hugo, and he went prancing off. Darren caught Celia's elbow, and bent his head to speak in a low voice.

"He can do it, Celia. Hugo wasn't always a fancy hairdresser. He used to be a plain barber-surgeon."

"Come on then!" she cried. "He'll need things—hot water, bandages—"

"Wait," said Darren, and while she burned with impatience he pressed a coin into her hand. Celia started as she recognized a gold Spanish doubloon. These were handled only by the richest West Indian traders; a gold doubloon would have fed an ordinary man for a month.

"Darren! Where on earth—"

"Borrowed two of these from Godfrey. Just took 'em, I know where he keeps everything. Tell Jimmy to pay them back when he gets well—I'd be glad to, only I don't expect ever to have that much money all at once." Darren chuckled shrewdly as he explained, "Hugo didn't want to come outdoors while the guns were going. But he changed his mind when I offered him one doubloon on the spot and promised him another when the job was done. So when he's finished, give him that."

"Aren't you going to stay?" she asked in alarm.

"Can't," said Darren. He spoke seriously. "I've got to get these reports to the quartermaster. There'd be trouble if they knew I'd left my work even this long. Now good-by, and good luck."

He hurried off. Celia went around to the back porch. Hugo, bending over the pallet where Jimmy lay, had turned back the sheet and was examining the wound. As he heard her footsteps he looked up.

"Ah, Miss Garth. You have servants here?"

"Yes, two. I'll bring them—in the meantime can I help you any?"

She tried not to look at Jimmy. She did not want to see that blood-caked gash and think about what horrible things Hugo was going to do to him.

"You can take my coat, if you please," said Hugo, "and my cravat—" he took them off as he spoke and gave them to her—"and my wig, and may I ask you most particularly to put them in a place that is not dusty? Especially the wig, it is fresh-cleaned and powdered."

"Yes, yes," she said. Her hands shook with impatience. Hugo was quite bald, she noticed. His head looked like a round brown onion.

"And if you will be kind enough to bring me some large towels to protect my garments, and a basin of hot water. Have you bandages?"

"We'll tear up a sheet," said Celia, wondering why she had not had sense enough to do this before. "I'll be right back."

She rushed into Vivian's boudoir and threw his coat and wig across the damask upholstery of the long chair. In the bedroom there was a cabinet holding sheets and towels. Celia caught up an armful, and on the porch again she flung them to Hugo before running out to the kitchen to tell Amos and Marietta he was here.

Marietta had dropped into a chair by the kitchen table and was crying. As long as she had been around Celia and Jimmy, Marietta had managed to keep up a show of courage, but now with Amos she had let herself go, and was sobbing from fright and weariness and sheer nerves. Amos stood by her, patting her shoulder and trying to give her comfort. Under other circumstances Celia would have let her alone to have her cry out, but now she had no concern for anybody but Jimmy. She crossed the room and took Marietta's arm.

"Please stop crying! Mr. Hugo is here and he needs— Amos, make her stop crying!"

"Mr. Hugo?" Amos repeated in astonishment. "What's he—"

"He's going to take out the bullet," Celia said shortly. To Amos' gasp of shock she burst out. "Maybe he'll do it with a pair of curling-tongs! But he's all we've got. Now you bring some hot water and tell Marietta she's got to tear up a sheet for bandages. And *hurry!*"

By this time Marietta was standing up, dabbing at her eyes. "There's water in the pot, Amos," she said shakily. "Miss Celia, I'll come with you."

On the porch, Hugo had tied one towel around his neck like a bib and had laid another over his knees. With careful fingers he felt around the wound. Jimmy shuddered with pain and a groan came through his clenched teeth. Marietta hid her face.

"I can't look, Miss Celia!"

"Then don't look," Celia snapped. She could not look either; she was quaking from head to foot and she had to speak roughly lest her voice break. She snatched up one of Vivian's sheets and shook out the folds. "Here. Tear this into strips. About two inches wide—is that right, Mr. Hugo?"

A shell crashed somewhere near them, and the porch trembled. Hugo trembled too, but recovered himself and said he would need a pair of scissors to cut the cloth away from the wound. While Celia brought the scissors from her workbasket Marietta sat down on the back steps and began tearing up the sheet. Celia knelt by Jimmy and put her hand into his. He managed to turn his head and smile at her, trying to say something. She put her ear close to his lips.

"It's—not so tragic," Jimmy murmured. "Lots of men—have had it done. If I yell—sorry. I love you."

"I love you too," she whispered back.

Behind her she heard Amos' footsteps as he came from the kitchen, bringing a basin and a bucket of hot water. He filled the basin, and Hugo said,

"Miss, if you please?"

His English had just enough of a French accent to spice the scandal he brought to the boudoirs. Celia raised her head. Hugo was holding out the fan she had been using before.

"You will kindly sit here on the floor by the basin," said Hugo, "and hold this fan. You will keep the fan moving so that no flies or mosquitoes will disturb me."

Celia took the fan and began to wave. She thought, "The United States is fighting a revolution and so I have to sit fanning this little fop." But she could see the reason for it. A mosquito-stab might make Hugo start, and jerk his hand, and tear the wound— she shuddered, and tried to control her nerves so as to wave the fan in long slow strokes that would send a steady breeze. Hugo spoke to Amos.

Celia tried not to hear what he was saying. But she could not help hearing. He was telling Amos to put his knee on Jimmy's chest and hold Jimmy's body above and below the wound to prevent any starts of pain while Hugo was probing for the bullet. When Amos was in position Hugo reached into his case and took out a small block of wood. He spoke to Jimmy.

"Captain Rand, sir, you will clamp your teeth on this. Then you will not by accident bite your tongue."

Still waving the fan, Celia looked down. She looked at the steaming water in the basin. She heard the guns thundering, and the sheet tearing in Marietta's hands, and the chirp of a bird that had hopped up on the porch. She saw Hugo's hands dipping a cloth into the hot water, and then some instruments—she was not seeing very clearly, but one of them looked like a razor and another like a big pair of tweezers. Maybe it really was a pair of curling-tongs. She heard the scissors snipping; she heard the heavy breathing of Amos close by her, and she was reminded that he loved Jimmy too and his part of the task was not easy, and she felt less alone. She wondered how many men were having surgeons dig into their living bodies for bullets right this minute, and she thought she could not possibly have stood this if she had not known it was being done to a lot of redcoats too and it hurt them as much as it hurt Jimmy.

She heard noises coming out of Jimmy's throat. Not screams. Choking lumps of sound, wrenched out by crazy blind agony. Celia began to pray.

She asked God why He let things like this happen. She asked Him to give her strength to keep the fan moving. She begged Him to punish the British. She heard Jimmy's gasps of pain, and pleaded, "Oh Lord in heaven, let Hugo find the bullet soon!"

She saw a line of blood trickle across the mattress and stain her skirt. A drop of sweat rolled off her cheekbone and fell into the basin with a clink. Hugo cried, "Voilà! I've got it!"

Celia let the fan slip out of her hand. She brought the bandages, and she went to the edge of the porch to throw out the bloody water in the basin; and there was Amos, bless his heart, ready to rinse the basin and fill it again. There was sweat of tension on his dark face too, and they exchanged a glance of sympathy for each other.

At last the job was done. The gash in Jimmy's leg was bound up, and he lay in limp exhaustion. Celia looked at the bloodstains on the mattress, and her skirt, and the towels, and she thought of all he had lost before and wondered that he had any blood left in him.

Hugo was washing his hands. Celia drew a clean sheet over Jimmy, and gave Marietta the fan to keep flies away. She got to her feet again, with difficulty, for she had been so rigid that her knees were stiff. Hugo untied the towel around his neck and stood up too.

He was as dapper as if he had been crimping a lady's hair, his little monkey face beaming with satisfaction at a piece of work well done. Smiling at Celia, he asked, "You will be so kind, miss, as to show me where you put my coat and wig?"

She led him into the house. When he had put on his cravat and his coat, and adjusted his wig before Vivian's looking-glass, Celia put her hand into her pocket and took out the gold doubloon.

"This is for you, Mr. Hugo," she said. "Thank you for your kindness."

Hugo took the doubloon daintily between his thumb and forefinger, turned it to catch the light, and put it affectionately into his purse. One foot back of him, he made a bow as if he were starting a minuet. He kissed her hand. "It was a pleasure to be of service, dear lady."

He picked up his leather bag, turned toward the door, and winced as he heard the zing of a shell. For a moment he stood looking up, as though he could see the shells through the ceiling, and listened nervously. But as he did not hear another zing close by, he strutted off, his coattails flapping behind him.

Celia stood where she was, her hand on the back of one of Vivian's pretty damask chairs. She heard Hugo's little mincing steps patter down the hall toward the door. Now that this was over, the strength seemed to have gone out of her. The room did not look steady. She saw a window swing back and forth like a locket on a chain, and she saw that one pane had cracked from the vibrations of the firing. Everything turned black around her as if a giant had blown out the sun, and the floor rose up and hit her on the head.

## CHAPTER 15

ELIA was ashamed of herself. She had never fainted before and she told Marietta vehemently that she never would again. But Marietta said everybody was entitled to an occasional weakness. Marietta herself had finally had that good cry, and she felt better for it.

Celia had come back to her senses with a skinned elbow and a lump on her head, and such a queer dizzy feeling that she was still huddled on the floor when Marietta came to look for her. Marietta said Mr. Jimmy was dozing. As soon as Hugo had gone Amos had told her to bring Mr. Lacy's best West Indies rum, and he had made Mr. Jimmy take a big drink, big enough to give him some rest. Then Amos had left to see if he couldn't get a message to Mr. Miles Rand. And now, Miss Celia had better eat some dinner.

Celia had forgotten that she had not eaten anything since early this morning, eight or nine hours ago. Maybe that was one reason she had keeled over. She had a plate of rice and beef and snap-beans, and it did her good.

When Jimmy woke, blazing with fever and thirst, Marietta held his head while Celia gave him spoonfuls of the beef broth Marietta had made. It was a long hard meal. Over and over Celia had to sit helplessly with the bowl in her hands, while Jimmy trembled under a wave of pain and she tried not to let her tears drip into the broth. All afternoon the guns rumbled in the sultry air, the mosquitoes whined, and Celia waved her fan over Jimmy and prayed that Miles would get here soon and bring a real surgeon with him.

It was after dark when Miles finally arrived, but he did bring a surgeon. While Amos held a candle the surgeon bent over Jimmy's pallet, and Miles put an arm around Celia and whispered, "Thanks for all you've done." She was surprised to be thanked. But she found Miles' arm around her a comfort. It made her feel like what Miles' mother had said, one of them.

The surgeon said Hugo had done a good job. Jimmy's main trouble was that he had nearly bled to death. Given a rest and plenty of good red meat, he would be all right. Miles had managed to borrow an army litter, so when Celia and Marietta had made up the bed in Vivian's room he and Amos carried Jimmy indoors. Marietta brought a mosquito net from a closet and made a pavilion over his bed. This done, Miles said he had leave to stay till morning, so the others could get some sleep.

Celia felt her way down the cellar stairs. She had not brought a candle, as their supply was limited and they had no way to get more. In the darkness she found her mattress and sank down. Too tired to undress, she took off her shoes and buried her face in the pillow and tried to shut out the noise of the guns. She thought of Jimmy helpless in the room above her, as she gripped the pillow and whispered the evening prayer. "Lighten our darkness, we beseech thee, oh Lord, and by thy great mercy defend us from all perils and dangers of this night—"

·~·

She fell asleep, and in spite of the noise she slept till morning. When she came to the door of Jimmy's room Amos was giving him spoonfuls of beef broth. Amos said Mr. Miles had had to go back on duty, but Mr. Jimmy had slept some, off and on, and now he was taking his broth just fine.

Celia drew a bucket of water at the well and went up to her room. When she had washed and put on clean clothes, she felt well. Rest and red meat, that was all Jimmy needed. She would manage.

She started out to the kitchen to see about her own breakfast. On the back porch she stopped with a sense of pleasure. No wonder she felt so well. It must have rained during the night, for the trees were sparkling as though every leaf held a jewel. The temperature had fallen, and even with the smell of smoke and gunpowder there was a luscious April tang in the air. Celia gave a happy little skip as she went into the kitchen, where Marietta served her a dish of hominy grits with slices of grilled ham.

Later, Celia remembered how light-heartedly she had eaten that ham. She had even tossed scraps to a jaybird that was hopping on the window sill. She told Marietta—still light-hearted, never dreaming of what was about to happen—not to make any more beef broth for Jimmy until tomorrow, as they had enough for today.

About ten o'clock, the disaster came.

Celia was standing on the back steps, reflecting that since all the shooting seemed to be up on the Neck this would be a good time for her to gather vegetables. Just then Amos appeared on the porch.

"Miss Celia," he said to her, "there are some soldiers at the front door."

Celia turned in alarm. "Soldiers? What kind of soldiers, Amos?"

"Oh, they're our kind, Miss Celia, they're rebels, but they want to see the lady of the house. They say it's orders."

Puzzled and somewhat frightened, Celia went in. Just inside the front door stood an officer of militia and two privates, and through the doorway, still open behind them, she saw a handcart by the front steps. The officer, a smallish young man with a shock of light hair, stood straight, heels together and hat in hand. He spoke politely.

"Good morning, ma'am, how do you do. I'm Lieutenant Boyce. You're Mrs.—Miss—?"

"Miss Garth," said Celia.

"Yes ma'am. Will you show us the way to your kitchen storeroom, please ma'am?"

Celia started. "But what—"

"Orders, ma'am," said Lieutenant Boyce. "And we're kind of in a hurry, please."

Though very polite, he evidently meant what he said. Bewildered, Celia made a gesture toward the back door. "Through here."

"Thank you ma'am. And you'll please have somebody unlock the gate to your driveway, so we can bring in the cart. Now we'll follow you."

She led them through the hall, past Jimmy's bedroom to the back door, where Amos stood watching with wide questioning eyes. Celia gave him the key and told him to unlock the gate. The lieutenant sent one of his men to bring the cart, while he and the other man went on with Celia. Still perplexed, she led them through the kitchen and into the storeroom beyond.

The storeroom was kept cool by heavy brick walls and a high ceiling. Against the walls were barrels, above the barrels were shelves lined with jars and canisters and boxes of many sizes. The air had a tempting spicy smell. The private soldier sniffed with enjoyment; Lieutenant Boyce gave him a look, and spoke to Celia.

"Now ma'am, we'll be grateful if you don't make any fuss. We want all the meat you've got, and all the salt."

Celia gasped. The other private who had been sent for the handcart came into the room, and without looking at Celia again Lieutenant Boyce gave the men quick orders. They began taking the lids off the barrels to see what was inside.

Standing in the middle of the room, Celia watched in a rising panic. The men were opening every box and smelling the contents of every jar. One of them brought a chair from the kitchen and climbed on it to reach a side of bacon that hung from the ceiling. Lieutenant Boyce began rolling the barrel of spiced beef toward the door. Celia went to him.

"Please!" she begged. "There's a wounded soldier in the house —Captain Rand—he's nearly bled to death—he's got to have meat!"

The lieutenant spoke with strained patience. "Sorry, ma'am. We need this for the ones that can still fight."

*The ones that can still fight.* Celia thought of Jimmy, drained of blood, his face green on the white sheet. He could not fight, it would be many weeks before he could fight again. So they did not care what became of him. She cried out in anger.

"What have you done with all those boatloads of stuff that I saw coming down the Cooper River? You've got food enough to—"

"Please step out of the way, ma'am," said Lieutenant Boyce, giving the barrel another turn. It was plain that Lieutenant Boyce had been given strict orders to be courteous, and equally plain that he thought it was easier to face British guns.

Celia tried once more. "What can I give Captain Rand to eat?"

"I reckon he can eat rice, ma'am," Boyce answered wearily.

"Without salt?"

"I'm afraid so, ma'am. What's in that jar, Perkins?"

The man addressed as Perkins took his nose out of the jar he held, shook his head, and reached the jar toward Celia questioningly. She took a whiff and looked up.

"Cloves."

"We've got no use for 'em," said Lieutenant Boyce. "Put 'em back. What've you got there, Kane?"

"Rice, sir."

"We don't need rice. Leave it. What's that now, Perkins?"

"Cheese, sir."

"Bring that."

Amos and Marietta stood in the doorway watching with dismay. The lieutenant spoke to Amos. "Give me a hand with this barrel." Amos glanced at Celia. She said despairingly, "I guess you'll have to." As they rolled the barrel out to the cart she thought of Jimmy. Didn't these men know they were killing him? She felt a sob come up into her throat, and swallowed fiercely. They were not going to see her cry.

When they had filled the cart the two privates pushed it out to the street, transferred its load to a mule-drawn wagon standing by the steps, and trundled the cart back to be filled again. Celia, who had followed them outside, stood looking up and down the sidewalk at other groups of soldiers bringing food from other homes. Here and there women stood by the doorways, some of them weeping or screaming threats, others like herself simply looking on. Far up on the Neck the guns sounded. In the doorway of the house next door old Simon Dale leaned on his cane. His son was on the earthworks, but his son's wife and her children stood by the front steps, watching dumbly. Young Harry Dale, about twelve years old, had his arms around his two little sisters.

When the men were gone Celia and Marietta left Amos with Jimmy while they went to see what was left. The men had taken all the hams and bacon, all the beef, all the salt and cheese. They had left the rice and grits, cornmeal, coffee and sugar and molasses. And of course, Celia recalled, there would be vegetables, if the shells didn't tear up the garden and if she could keep the weeds down. She could live, and Marietta—she had never tried to eat unsalted food but she supposed they could if they had to—but what about Jimmy?

A shell whistled, closer than they had been coming today, and another shell screeched across the path of the first. Marietta cried out and Celia covered her face. But as the sounds dwindled they relaxed again.

"One thing I keep thinking about, Miss Celia," Marietta said stoutly, "we're shooting at them just as hard as they're shooting at us."

Celia had started for the door, intending to go in and see how Jimmy was. "I hope," she said savagely, "we're killing them by *swarms*."

In Jimmy's room Amos sat on the bed, under the mosquito net, holding Jimmy's head so he could swallow water from a cup. When Jimmy had had all he could take, Amos stood up. The effort of swallowing had used all Jimmy's strength. He lay exhausted, his eyes closed.

Celia waited. After a while she raised the net, saying softly, "Jimmy. Jimmy dear."

He half opened his eyes, murmuring her name. This was all he could do. Moving back, Celia let the net fall, and as her eyes met the black velvet eyes of Amos she knew they were both thinking the same thing. "If we can't get him some meat to make blood, he's going to die."

She ordered herself, Whatever you do, don't act scared! Beckoning Amos outside the hall door, she spoke in a low voice.

"Give him the rest of the beef broth whenever he's able to take it. And don't worry. I'll find something else for him by tomorrow."

"Yes *ma'am!*" said Amos. He was so eager to believe her that his voice was enthusiastic.

Celia had an inspiration. "I'll speak to Mr. Godfrey Bernard," she said. "I'll go right now."

She turned and ran toward the back door. How stupid of her not to have thought of Godfrey before. One of the chief heads of supply, he would surely know where she could get meat for a wounded soldier.

The shells were wheezing as usual, but none seemed close. Catching up her skirts Celia ran across the back yard, through the gate and into Godfrey's property.

On Godfrey's back porch three Negro maids were wandering up and down in a state of near-hysterics, while on the steps a small black boy sat bawling. The women rushed toward her with the dreadful news. The soldier-men had been here and had taken all the meat they had, and what was worse Mr. Godfrey himself had helped carry it out, and now they were all going to starve.

Thanking heaven that Marietta did not carry on like this, Celia asked if Mr. Godfrey was at home. They said yes, he was in his study.

She went down the hall toward the room where she had seen Darren yesterday. Godfrey would help her, he *must* help her; the colored women had said the soldiers had taken all the meat, but how did they know what supplies Godfrey had access to? She knocked on the study door.

Godfrey's voice answered. As she pushed open the door he stood up in surprise.

"Why Celia!—how's Jimmy?"

She ran to him and caught his hand in both of hers. "Oh Godfrey, Jimmy's desperately hurt! Please help him!"

Moving a ledger from a chair Godfrey told her to sit down. He returned to the chair by the desk where he had been sitting before she came in. He told her he had heard of Jimmy's wound but had not been able to come over and inquire. He had been out since before daybreak helping organize the search, which had to be unexpected lest people hide their supplies.

While he talked, Godfrey sat with his head on his hand, as though too tired to look up. She had never before seen Godfrey when he looked the least tired. He was saying,

"I'll be free for the rest of the day, so if there's anything I can do for Jimmy—"

"Oh yes, yes," Celia cried. She went on to tell him about Jimmy's loss of blood. "He's got to have meat, Godfrey! Tell me where I can get some."

Godfrey did not look up. His voice had a weary sound as he said, "You can't get any meat, Celia."

She started, unbelieving. "But haven't you got—"

He shook his head. "No more than you have."

He sounded strange, and he looked strange. Godfrey had always looked like what he was: a rich man, a successful man, a man who knew how to get along in the world. But now his face was lined, his body slack, his whole attitude that of defeat. Celia felt a creeping dread.

"But all those tons of beef that came down the river!" she exclaimed. "Oh Godfrey—" she held out her hands to him, pleading—"Godfrey, what's *happened?*"

Still without looking up, Godfrey smiled the same wry, mocking smile he had given her the last time she talked to him at the back gate. "I told you the other day," he said. "The weather. The crazy heat."

It had been hours since Celia had thought of the weather, but now she remembered how delightful the morning had been after last night's rain. The windows of this room overlooked Godfrey's flower garden, and the air coming in was fresh and cool. "But the heat-wave's broken," she protested.

"Too late," said Godfrey. Now at last he raised his head. "There's no reason why I shouldn't tell you," he went on, as if it gave him some relief to talk. "Everybody will know it by night. Remember when that west wind kept blowing and the king's fleet couldn't get in? That gave us time. We brought in meat enough to last the garrison for months. Then all of a sudden, that heat. Nothing like it for years. The meat started to spoil. Not enough salt."

"But you brought in so much salt!"

"Not enough," said Godfrey. He shrugged.

Celia thought of the black steeple where Peter Timothy watched for the French fleet. She asked, "How long can we hold out?"

"I don't know. The military men aren't talking."

"Aren't we still getting supplies by the Cooper River?" she asked.

"Oh yes. That cavalry band is doing a great job. But everything that comes in by the river now will have to go to the men on active duty. There won't be enough for the rest of us."

Celia could hear the shells whining like great mosquitoes. She wondered if they were doing much damage. Godfrey stood up and restlessly arranged a pile of ledgers on his desk. Celia looked out of the window, where two yellow butterflies were doing a love-dance above the roses. "Godfrey," she pleaded, "haven't you *any* meat? Did you give them all you had?"

"What else could I do? They were searching every other pantry in town."

"Yes, I see," she answered. She stood up too. A point of honor, she thought resentfully. Maybe I'd feel the same way if it wasn't for Jimmy. But if Luke were here instead of Godfrey I bet he'd get meat for Jimmy somehow.

She said she would go back. Godfrey picked up his coat, which hung over the back of a chair.

"I'll come with you," he offered. "Maybe we can think of something. The meat is all under army control now, but I'll do anything I can."

She was grateful for his sympathy. After all, he could hardly be blamed if sympathy was all he could give her. He was like a man dizzy from a blow. Godfrey was used to doing what he set out to do, and this wreckage of the meat supply had hurt his pride as much as it hurt the prospects of the army. Usually so resourceful, just now he was too stunned to have an idea in his head.

They walked together across the two back yards, and Celia

led him to Jimmy's bedside. Jimmy had fallen into a troubled sleep.

As Godfrey raised the net Celia saw the shock on his face. He had thought she exaggerated Jimmy's danger; well, he thought so no longer. Celia said, "I'll find Amos," and went out to the kitchen.

Amos had come out to heat the last of the beef broth while Jimmy dozed. Celia told him Godfrey was here, and when he had gone in she tried to eat some rice Marietta had cooked. Without salt the stuff tasted awful. After a few forkfuls she gave up.

Too nervous to keep still, she went up to the attic and opened the window that looked eastward over the harbor and the Cooper River. Along the streets she could see windows twinkling as they reflected the sun. She could hear the guns, and here and there she saw a puff of smoke, but the firing was not violent.

Out there in the harbor she saw the British fleet. No supplies would come to Charleston that way. Celia picked up the spyglass and turned it toward the Cooper River.

Now in the bright sun the river looked empty, for the supply boats waited until after dark to slip past those British guns on the Neck. It made her almost sick to think that only twenty miles up the river was Bellwood Plantation, stocked with red meat and milk and eggs and salt—everything Jimmy needed.

Celia spoke aloud. "If I could get a rowboat, Amos could take Jimmy up to Bellwood."

She felt a stirring of hope. Maybe it was not a good idea, but any idea was better than none. How long would it take to row those twenty miles? She did not know, and she did not know if Jimmy could stand the trip. But Amos was a strong man and devoted to Jimmy; he could do it if it could be done.

Another thought struck her with cold discouragement. Even now, Amos should have been working on the defenses. He had managed to bring Jimmy here and stay with him so far, but as soon as somebody in authority learned that he was here, he would be sent back on the lines. Every strong young man, white or colored, was required to be at some post of duty. Burton, who had finished his job of sandbagging and was well past military age, had had no trouble leaving town, but a husky young fellow like Amos could not possibly get a pass through the lines, unless on a mission useful to the army.

*A mission useful to the army.*

Celia lowered the spyglass to the floor. She closed the window and stood up. Her thoughts were dancing.

Now she knew what to do. She ran across the attic and down the stairs so fast that she tripped and had to catch the banister to keep from tumbling headlong. At the door of Jimmy's room she stopped to catch her breath. The door stood ajar, and she saw Godfrey supporting Jimmy's head while Amos gave him the last of the broth.

Her hand in her pocket rubbing the rabbit's foot, she waited till they had finished. When Godfrey stood up she beckoned him into the hall.

She spoke eagerly. "Godfrey, you said you'd do anything you could to help Jimmy. And you can help him. You can get him to Bellwood."

He frowned, puzzled. She hurried on.

"The men gathering supplies—they have authority to take anything they need from any plantation, I know that. But I bet it's hard work sometimes. Some people are Tories and some are just mean—they hide their cattle in the woods and their hams under the hay in the barn—don't they?"

Godfrey smiled and nodded. "We've had a good deal of trouble that way. But what about Jimmy?"

"Well, it's a lot simpler if our men know that on a certain plantation the people are on their side. So just for one trip, have Amos assigned to the supply service. There must be some boat starting upriver tonight. Put Jimmy on it. With Amos. Give Amos a letter to Mrs. Rand telling her that in return for the boatmen's bringing Jimmy home, she's to give them whatever they want. He's her son, Godfrey! I don't know how much she has already given, but for the chance to nurse Jimmy and feed him decently—she'll tell the men to take anything the boat will carry!"

Godfrey gave a slow, thoughtful nod. "Yes—I believe—it could be done." Unlike Celia, who had been talking as fast as her tongue would move, he spoke deliberately, thinking of ways and means. "I can get a pass for Amos to guide them to the plantation landing. He'll have to come back with the boat, of course, to work on the—"

A shell whanged overhead. Celia started, and Godfrey put a firm hand on her shoulder.

"You go down cellar," he said in a voice of command. He sounded like himself again. "I'll manage this."

Celia did not want to go to the cellar, but neither did she want to waste time arguing, so she obeyed. Godfrey sprang to action. Sitting on the cellar stairs, her arms wrapped around her knees, she heard him calling Amos and giving orders. She smiled confidently. Godfrey could not control the weather, but that was about the only thing in Charleston that he could not control when he put his mind to it. He would get Jimmy out.

◆～◆

And he did. Godfrey had yearned for a new challenge. He grasped at Jimmy's need as a lesser man might have reached for a bottle, to dull his thoughts of his own defeat.

With boundless energy, he got all preparations made by nightfall. He found Miles; he found a surgeon, a stretcher, a mule and wagon; he found a boat and crew about to go on a supply trip. He did all this though the British had increased their firing and a shell knocked a hole in one corner of his own stable. He took this lightly, saying, "No matter—no horses there now."

When Jimmy learned what they were planning, he rallied all his shreds of force to protest against going to safety while Celia stayed behind. Miles reminded him of the reason. A few of those men on the supply boats were patriots who worked for love of their country, but most of them were hard-fisted sailors who made these dangerous journeys because they got paid for it. They would carry a wounded man for more pay, but a girl would be practically torn to pieces before morning. Jimmy knew this, and he did not want Celia to make the trip, but he did not want to leave her. Jimmy had never been seriously sick in his life before. This whole experience of helplessness insulted his manhood. He was not a baby, he said, and he did not want to be treated like one;

and even as he said it, the effort of talking brought a cold mist of sweat to his forehead, and his words died off from sheer lack of strength to continue. He had to yield.

Miles told him good-by and went back on duty. The surgeon dressed Jimmy's wound, and he left too, and Godfrey went out to attend to some last details. The day was declining in a pinkish twilight. Celia went to Jimmy's room to say good-by.

The surgeon's examination of his wound had been agonizing, and now Jimmy was lying in strained exhaustion. But when she pushed back the net and put her hand on his and bent over him, he opened his eyes and smiled at her, murmuring, "My dearest."

His voice was so weak and low that it brought a sob into her throat. Jimmy, dear Jimmy, she thought, who hated this war because he could not hate his enemies. She kissed him softly, and Jimmy said,

"Celia, lie down by me."

She lay on the bed and put her head on the pillow close to his. With a great effort Jimmy turned and put his arms around her. They did not say anything. Celia thought how cruel it was that Jimmy should have been hurt the day after her birthday. If only that shell had not struck him, Mr. Moreau would have married them and they would have been together like this all night, their heads on one pillow and Jimmy's arms around her. And she would not have been afraid of anything because for the first time she would have felt that she really belonged to somebody.

The pink evening faded to purple. The front door banged, and Godfrey's energetic voice sounded in the hall. Celia slipped off the bed and knelt beside it.

"Good-by, darling," she whispered.

Her throat choked up and she could say no more. She walked away and stood in a corner of the room, smothering her tears. The boom of the guns rose, and dwindled again. There was a knock on the door and she called an answer. Godfrey came in.

With him was Marietta, holding a candle. She had been saying good-by to Amos and there were tears on her cheeks too. Godfrey told Celia briskly that the wagon was waiting at the door, and he and Amos would put Jimmy on the stretcher and carry him out.

"He'll be all right," Godfrey said encouragingly. "It's going to be a dark night—the moon goes down at ten, and the men won't start till after that. They'll slide past the guns without a whisper."

Celia said "Yes." She squeezed the rabbit's foot. She did not know which she hated more, the king's men firing the guns or those other men who had made it all happen by signing the Declaration of Independence.

# CHAPTER 16

*T*HAT NIGHT—Saturday—the firing was slow, but at dawn Sunday the guns began to make pandemonium. Unwashed and unbreakfasted, Celia and Marietta cowered in the cellar. By the sounds, they could tell that the shells were coming from all directions—from the trenches north of town, from the Ashley River on the west and the harbor on the east, from James Island a mile to the south.

The cellar had a damp chill. By the light from the sidewalk gratings, Celia could vaguely measure the passage of time. The sun was shining, but she thought hopefully that it would probably rain this afternoon. In late spring and summer they had thunderstorms several times a week, and these would dampen the king's gunpowder and quench his fireballs. And oh, what a joy to know Jimmy was out of this!

The thought cheered her so that it even lessened her fear of the shells. She went up and made coffee—the kitchen-house, brick and very solid, was fairly safe—and Marietta found some cornbread left over from several days ago. It was stale and hard, but at least it had salt in it and tasted better than that unsalted rice.

While they were in the kitchen a shell came whistling up

Meeting Street, and Godfrey's fat cook rushed to call over the fence that it had struck the steeple of St. Michael's. With Marietta, Celia ran out to the sidewalk to look. To her relief she saw that the shell had glanced off, doing no damage except to make a white mark like a blaze on the black steeple. But as it fell into the street the shell had struck the statue of William Pitt, breaking off his left arm at the shoulder.

Celia gave a shrug as she turned to take refuge in the cellar again. The Americans had put that statue there because William Pitt had been their friend. Maybe it was fitting that the British should break it now.

Sunday night and Monday, and again Tuesday, the firing was steady. But now after a month of battle, Celia and Marietta had learned that the guns on the neck of the peninsula sent shells mainly into the north side of town. The shells falling here in the south side came from the men-of-war or from the islands. So they would listen, and if they heard firing from the north only, they knew it would be fairly safe to leave the cellar.

The garden was getting weedy, but the vegetables were still growing, a godsend to enliven their meatless and saltless meals. Monday, Marietta cooked rice with chopped onions. Tuesday, she mixed cakes of cornmeal and water, and served them hot with mustard greens.

It was midday when they ate the cakes, but the kitchen fire felt welcome, for after the heat of last week the weather had turned freakishly cold. The guns on the Neck were keeping up a deep thud-thud, but those on the ships were quiet. Marietta, washing the dishes, remarked, "I wonder what Amos and Mr. Jimmy are doing now."

"Right this minute," said Celia, "I bet they're having dinner at Bellwood. Beefsteaks, hot baked sweet potatoes with chunks of butter—"

"Oh Miss Celia!" Marietta sighed. "Don't tease me with such talk."

"I won't," Celia said laughing. "I can't stand it either." She heard a sound of thunder, heralding the afternoon rain. "I'll bring in some water," she said, "before the shower starts."

She went out, a bucket in each hand. Standing by the well, she listened. The growling of the guns still came from the Neck, but when she saw Marietta go into the garden for vegetables, Celia called that they did not know when things would get rough so she'd better hurry. Marietta called back grimly that she certainly would.

Celia filled her buckets, lugged them into the kitchen, and came out again carrying two more. As she set the empty buckets beside the well she heard Marietta scream.

She wheeled around. Marietta was standing by the gate to Godfrey's yard. Her basket had dropped from her arm, scattering radishes and onions around her. On the other side of the gate Godfrey's cook was lamenting, patting Marietta's shoulder, wiping her eyes on her apron, and calling upon heaven. Celia ran to them.

"What's happened?" she cried.

Marietta, sobbing into her apron, spoke in gasps. "Oh Miss Celia—Annie says—that man Tarleton—"

"That devil-man Tarleton!" Annie stormed, and between her sobs Marietta said something else. Now they were both talking at once and Celia could not understand either of them. She shook Marietta's arm.

"Stop crying, can't you? What's wrong?"

Half choking, Marietta tried to make her words plain. "Oh God help us—Annie says—that man Tarleton and his Tories—" Another sob broke her voice but she struggled on. "They've taken Moncks Corner, Miss Celia—they've killed nearly all the men with Colonel Washington—*they've got the Cooper River!*"

Celia felt little fires run along her nerves. She heard Annie exclaiming,

"It happened last Friday, Miss Celia, but Mr. Godfrey he just got the news—"

And Marietta cried out, "Miss Celia, if Amos and Mr. Jimmy went up the Cooper River Saturday night they're sure dead now."

She and Annie went on talking but Celia did not hear what they said. The guns went on firing but she did not hear that either. She seemed to be standing in a world where time was suspended and nothing happened at all. Then as things began to clear she found that her hands were holding the gate in such a grip that it was hard to move them. She heard the guns again, and the voices of Annie and Marietta, but nothing made sense.

Her swirling thoughts could toss up but one idea. Tarleton and his Tories—they held the Cooper River. And she had sent Jimmy straight into their hands so they could finish killing him. A Charleston supply boat, going up to get food for the rebels, would be a prime target for their guns.

Her knees gave way. She sat down on the ground among the fallen radishes, she put her head down on her knees and burst into tears. Sobs shook her and ripped through her till she felt as if she was being torn to pieces, and she could not stop. A shell screamed close overhead but she did not notice.

Another shell whizzed above her. She did not look up. But she felt a man's hands on her shoulders, and heard Darren's voice say, "Come with me, Celia."

The words roused her. Darren helped her to her feet, and she leaned against him, still too shaken to stand alone.

"I was on my way over here," said Darren. "I'm sorry you had to hear it like this."

Celia wet her dry lips. "Darren—Jimmy?"

"I'll tell you all I know. But let's go in. These shells now are coming from the ships."

He led her toward the house. She walked mechanically, stumbling over the soft earth.

"The boat may have gotten through to Bellwood," he said. "Or maybe the men have tied it up behind some bushes, and are hiding."

Celia blurted, "And maybe they're all dead."

Darren's arm jerked her to a standstill. A fireball had fallen on the ground in front of them. When it had sputtered out, leaving a black ring in the weeds, he led her indoors to where the stairs went from the back hall down to the cellar. They sat on the steps, and he told her all he could.

A courier had slipped through with the news. Before daybreak last Friday—the same morning that Jimmy was wounded—Tarleton's Legion had attacked the cavalry base at Moncks Corner. The cavalry had withstood many attacks, but this time Tarleton was too strong for them and they had scattered. The

Tories had then crossed the river by a bridge and had routed another band of rebels camped at the church of St. John's Berkeley.

"This means," said Celia, "that since last Friday, there's been no way out of Charleston at all."

"No *sure* way," said Darren. "But the boat might have made it. Moncks Corner is a long way above Bellwood."

"And suppose Tarleton raids Bellwood?"

Darren sighed. His tired, handsome face was stern with warning. "Celia, if you turn your imagination loose you'll go insane."

She tried to speak calmly. "Do you know anything about Luke?"

Darren said no, but Annie's tale that most of the rebels at Moncks Corners had been killed, was exaggerated. The official report was that a good many of them had escaped into the swamp.

He went on talking, to ease his own nerves as well as hers. He said the church of St. John's Berkeley was near Colonel Marion's plantation. He hoped Tarleton's greenjackets had not captured Marion, as they would certainly have liked to do.

Celia sat on the cellar steps twisting her hands in her lap, hearing the shells and not hearing them, telling herself to be brave and quaking with cowardice. Marietta came and sat on the stairs too, crying quietly. They heard a thunderclap, and the rain began.

At length Darren said he had to go. He promised that if he had any news of Jimmy or Amos he would bring it. But he had to say—for Darren was not sophisticated enough to make up pretty stories—that his chance of getting any such news was small.

In the cellar Celia and Marietta crouched in corners like two scared animals while the guns roared and the shells crackled around them. Hand in her pocket, Celia felt the rabbit's foot. She thought of Jimmy as he had given it to her, tall and strong in his rebel blue uniform, his black eyes twinkling warmly.

She thought of Vivian's fear at Luke's going up to that post of danger. And Vivian now, hearing of this defeat, pacing the floor at Sea Garden as she wondered if Luke had gone like his father.

She thought that any knowledge, anything, would be easier than living like this, not knowing.

•~•

After Tarleton cut off the Cooper River, living in Charleston was like living in a jail. The city was enclosed in a double ring of guns, British guns pointing inward and rebel guns pointing out, and now they were firing all the time.

Time itself became a crazy uncertainty. Often Celia did not know whether it was morning or afternoon, or how long it had been since she had eaten or slept or changed her clothes. She and Marietta hunched in the cellar, while the earth trembled and shook, and shells screamed in the air, and smoke rolled through the sidewalk gratings. Sometimes she tried to remember what silence was like, but she could not.

At last, exhausted, in spite of the noise she would fall asleep on her mattress. She never knew how long she slept but it was never long enough. A shell would wake her; she and Marietta would sit up, their nostrils full of smoke, sure that this time the shell had fallen on this property, and they would run up the cellar stairs to look.

Sometimes they would be right—there was a new hole in the garden, or a fireball had struck and they had to beat out the fire. They would do what had to be done, and scurry back to the cellar. Like rats, thought Celia.

In the respites when the firing was mostly on the Neck, she went to the attic and looked through the spyglass. She could see ships coming in with fresh troops and supplies for Sir Henry Clinton. Darren told her these ships came from the Bahama Islands, or from Florida, where the British had a large force at St. Augustine. "Clinton must have lots more men than we have!" Celia exclaimed.

Darren said, "Oh yes, that's no secret."

But sometimes what she saw through the spyglass cheered her. She was not only cheered, she was amazed, to see how little damage had been done. In spite of weeks of bombardment and thousands of shells, Charleston was still almost intact—saved by the trees, and the gardens, and the rain.

Charleston was not, as the king's men had promised, being pounded into a pile of trash. But another enemy was here, more menacing than Clinton and Cornwallis and all their guns. Hunger.

A few days after she had news of Tarleton—demoralized with fear, she did not know just how long—Celia was called again to greet soldiers at the front door.

This time their leader was not as polite as Lieutenant Boyce had been. He did not introduce himself and he did not say "please" or "thank you." He gave her orders and told her to hurry up. The men went through the storeroom like wind. They took the cornmeal, the molasses, the grits, the coffee; they left her nothing but one barrel part-filled with rice.

Some days later more soldiers called. This group did not stay in the storeroom. They searched the house from cellar to attic. They made her unlock every door and they poked into every corner, lest she had hidden something to eat. They dumped the bureau drawers, emptied the linen shelves, pushed the books off the bookshelves to the floor. Marietta wept at the mess they made. They carried off a lot of Herbert's liquor, but they found no food because there was none to find.

After this, Celia and Marietta sparingly ate rice. When they could come up to the kitchen they would boil a pot and bring it down to the cellar with plates and spoons. They ate it whenever they were hungry enough to get it down. Cold and unsalted, it was a clammy diet.

When she dared go out Celia searched the garden. The shells had torn up half the plants and the rest were almost lost in weeds, but creeping about on hands and knees she did here and there find carrots or a few radishes and onions, a parsley plant half blackened by a fireball, or a vine still bearing beans. She gathered whatever she could. The beans Marietta cooked with the rice, the others they gobbled raw, tops and all.

Celia dreamed about food—ham and hot buttered biscuits, frizzling fried chicken, the honey-rich creaminess of sweet potato pone. When she looked out of the attic windows she was less aware of the men-of-war than of all the fish in those waters. She thought of sea bass and shad roe, flounder stuffed with shrimp, fried oysters and hush-puppies. When she went down to eat scanty cold rice, she found that she was crying and her tears were dripping into the plate, and even her tears were not salty any more.

As often as they could—which was not often—Godfrey or Darren or Miles would come in to ask how she was. What little they could tell her was scary. So many reinforcements had come to Sir Henry Clinton that he had sent Cornwallis up the country with three thousand men to raid the plantations for food supplies. Had they raided Bellwood or Sea Garden? There was no way of knowing.

Godfrey told her this across the back fence. His face, unshaven, had a drawn look, and his eyes were dull. In spite of his gold doubloons Godfrey was not getting any more to eat than she was.

Celia walked back across her own yard. As she neared the kitchen-house she stopped short, looking down at the mangled remains of a dog. A spaniel with a glossy brown coat, he had run in here as he tried to get away from the guns. He had been a fine little fellow, well cared for, somebody's pet. Celia thought of Rosco and wondered if the owner of this dog had been as fond of him as Jimmy was of Rosco.

Half sick, she brought a spade and buried the poor little body in the garden. She wondered if dogs went to heaven, and rather thought they did; certainly they deserved it more than some people. And Jimmy would hardly be happy in heaven without Rosco—she wiped her eyes on her sleeve, wondering if Jimmy was still alive.

She never remembered when she realized that the city could not hold out. It was just that one day she knew, and it seemed that she had known it for a long time.

They were starving. The British had captured Fort Moultrie; the troops on the Neck were moving closer to town; and inside the town the patriots were being driven to desperate risks. Celia did not know how desperate until the afternoon Miles and Darren came by, hot and dusty and streaked with sweat, asking for water.

They had almost nothing to say. They drank greedily, and hurried on.

Later she learned that they had hurried on because they had volunteered for a dangerous job that night. They were part of a detail who moved ten thousand pounds of gunpowder out of the magazine on Cumberland Street, because the king's troops had moved so close that they might any day hit this magazine and blow up the whole neighborhood. Working in the dark while shells crashed around them, Miles and Darren and their companions trundled the powder along Cumberland Street to State Street, and down State Street to the Exchange, where they stored it in an underground vault out of reach of the guns. Celia learned about the moving of the powder because that night Darren and Miles were both wounded.

Darren got only a minor nip in the leg. But as they went down State Street a shell exploded near by and a splinter struck Miles' right shoulder. When the powder was safely stored Godfrey had both Miles and Darren brought to his house, where the surgeon said Darren would be walking before long and had nothing to worry about. But Miles was not so lucky. His wound festered and sent him into a fever, and the next day he was out of his head. Godfrey sent one of the maids to ask Celia if she would help take care of him.

While Celia sat by his bed giving him sips of wine-and-water, Miles babbled deliriously about storing the gunpowder under the Exchange. Darren, who sat in the same room, his bad leg propped on a chair and a writing-board on his good knee so he could go on with his records for the quartermaster, heard what Miles was saying. He beckoned to Celia, and told her not to repeat it.

"If the Tories don't know where we put the powder," said Darren, "there's no sense in telling them."

"I won't say anything," she answered.

Darren shrugged. "Though as a matter of fact," he said, "there must be dozens of people who know. Anybody who happened to look out of a window on State Street last night could have gotten a pretty good idea of what we were doing. It was dark, but not that dark."

"I won't say anything," Celia repeated.

She spoke dully. She felt dull. She was so tired—tired of fear, of worry, of broken sleep, and the sheer breaking effect of not having enough to eat. She hoped it would not last much longer.

•~•

It did not last much longer. Clinton sent another demand for surrender. He knew they were starving—before he offered his terms, his men fired some shells that did not explode; the shells proved to be stuffed with rice, a taunting reminder.

There came a day and a night and a day of silence, then another night of thundering fire. Then the guns were quiet again while the couriers went back and forth.

Sitting on the back steps, Celia tried to remember how long all this had been going on. The weather had the usual warmth of late spring. She saw that the buds were opening on the magnolias, and the dogwood trees were in full bloom. It must be, she thought, about the middle of May.

So the siege had lasted two months. It seemed like years.

•~•

There was nothing to do but wait. When night came Celia and Marietta went to the cellar and tried to sleep. It was not easy, for after weeks of wild racket the silence made them nervous. Even when they fell asleep they kept waking up, startled by the lack of noise.

But at last sheer exhaustion gave them rest. When they woke up it was mid-morning. The guns were quiet. The city was waiting. It seemed to Celia that the very air ached with waiting.

To occupy the time she heated a pot of water at the cook-fire and washed some clothes. Every garment she owned was soiled, but when she had hung out a few stockings and chemises she was so tired she gave up.

Strange to remember the energy she used to have. She went into Vivian's boudoir and looked at herself in the mirror. She had grown so thin that she could gather her dress into folds at the waistline. Her skin had a greenish cast, like Jimmy's when he had lost so much blood; her hair, once such a rich bright gold, was drab as old hay. "I look just the way I feel," she said, and turned as she heard Marietta at the door.

Marietta too showed the ugliness of hunger. Her golden-brown skin had a moldy look, and her eyes, which used to be bright as black jewels, were lusterless. She said she would warm over some rice if Celia felt like eating it. Celia shook her head. She knew she needed food, but she was sick of unsalted rice.

She dragged herself up the stairs to the attic. With the spyglass she looked around at Charleston. What a *mess*.

Less than a hundred buildings had been destroyed and not many others showed serious damage, but the place certainly needed a good sweeping up. Charleston had always been a well-kept town: the steps scrubbed, the brick sidewalks brushed, the litter carted off. Now the streets were choked with rubbish—bricks, branches of trees, pieces of woodwork knocked off by the shells, and all sorts of garbage, for since people had had no way to dispose of trash they had simply thrown it out. The gardens had gone wild. Weeds gobbled the flowerbeds, and grass was springing in untidy clumps where it was not wanted.

Lowering the spyglass Celia sat down on a goods-box by the window. The redcoats had taken Charleston, and she found that she did not feel much of anything. She was too tired. Later, she supposed, it would all come to her—the bravery and tragedy of it, the steeple dark as though in mourning for the men who had died in this lost fight for liberty. But right now, though she knew it with her mind, she did not feel it with her heart. All that seemed really important was that now she could find out what had happened to Jimmy, and at Bellwood they would have plenty to eat.

That afternoon Miles sent to ask if she would come to see him. She found him sitting up in bed, his right arm in a sling. Miles said he felt pretty well, except that it was a nuisance to be crippled. A man didn't know how much he needed his right arm until he couldn't use it.

He told her the American and British commanders had agreed on terms of surrender. The rebel soldiers would march out of the city tomorrow and give up their arms, the Continentals first and then the militia. The terms were fair. The Continentals would be held prisoners until they were exchanged, each American for a British prisoner of the same rank. This meant Tom Lacy and Paul de Courcey, and technically it also meant Luke—though Miles added with a chuckle that if Luke were free now they would probably have a hard time catching him.

But the militia—which included himself and Jimmy, Darren and Godfrey, Lewis Penfield and young Bobby—would be enrolled, then allowed to go home and earn their living at any peaceful occupation. As long as they did not fight the king again they would be regarded as prisoners on parole, and their property would be let alone.

These terms, signed by Henry Clinton and the British Admiral Arbuthnot, were being printed and would be posted around town tomorrow morning. "Now," said Miles, "I want to talk about you."

He said he wanted her out of Charleston as fast as possible. The king's troops would march in when the rebels marched out, and a town newly taken by a siege-crazy army was no place for an attractive young woman. Miles was not strong enough to manage either a boat or a horse, but Godfrey intended going to Sea Garden as soon as they would let him. Miles wanted Celia to go along.

As for Miles, as soon as he was able to move he would go to Bellwood to see how his family had fared. "Then," said Miles, "if Jimmy still isn't strong enough to come for you himself, I will."

He spoke as if he knew Jimmy was alive and getting well. Maybe he could not bear to speak any other way. Thank heaven, thought Celia, their suspense had not much longer to last. She said, "All right, I'll go to Sea Garden with Godfrey," and after a moment's pause she exclaimed, "I'm glad it's over."

His eyes meeting hers, Miles smiled grimly. "Now that I can be frank," he said—"so am I."

At her start of surprise he shrugged his good shoulder.

"Luke and Jimmy and I had a lot of arguments," he went on. "They believed in independence. I didn't. I stayed home till the redcoats attacked Charleston. I'm no Tory and I'll not shoot my own people. But now, if I can go home and live as I did before, I'll be glad of it."

Looking at the lump of bandage on his shoulder, Celia could not decide if Miles was brave or foolish. It was bad enough to get hurt fighting for a cause you believed in, like Jimmy. But to suffer for a cause you did not even understand—that was something else she would have to figure out later. All she really knew now was that the siege was over and she was glad of it.

*A*T ELEVEN O'CLOCK the next morning the American army began to march out of town and stack their guns by the hornwork wall. Celia watched from the roof with her spyglass.

From roofs and attics of other houses she saw other women, with girls of all ages and here and there a small boy. There was not a male human being left at home except small boys. Clinton had announced that the words "American army" meant every male in Charleston above early childhood. Earlier this morning Celia had watched while old Simon Dale, too lame to walk across a room without his stick, was wheeled up Meeting Street in an invalid chair pushed by his twelve-year-old grandson Harry. After them came a blind man, trusting their eyes to help guide him. They were all three on their way to be listed as captured soldiers.

With cool wisdom, Godfrey had told her the reason for this decree. It was no credit to Clinton that with three times as many men, and the whole countryside to draw upon for food, he had taken so long to beat the hungry little garrison of Charleston. He was ashamed to send home so small a list of prisoners as he would have had if he had recorded only the names of the men who had actually borne arms. So he was enrolling the old, sick, blind, crippled, the boys, the Tories, even his own paid spies, as his captives. Their names and addresses would be real, and his clerks were not adding anything else about them.

Sir Henry Clinton, continued Godfrey, was hoping to get a peerage out of this war. Clinton was the cousin of an earl. All his life he had stood in the shadow of rank and wealth, just close enough to be snubbed as a poor relation. More than anything else on earth Clinton wanted to hear himself called "my lord," and have the prestige and income that went with a title. If he could bring home enough glory from America, surely George the Third would reward him with his heart's desire.

After watching a while, Celia went indoors and helped Marietta close the blinds and draw the shades. Miles had told them to lock up the house before the king's men marched in, and keep it dark.

Since she had to live like a mushroom, during the next few days Celia could not observe much. She learned that the men of the king's army were quartered in the American barracks, while the principal officers had moved into the finest residences in town, requiring the owners to receive them as guests. Fortunately Vivian's house was not splendid enough to attract attention.

The militiamen from the country were going home as fast as they could. Some of them were depressed, others were glad it was over and said it never should have started. Whatever their feelings, they had given their word not to fight the king any more and now they wanted to get back to their families, to their farms and sawmills and blacksmith shops. They went on any sort of raft that could be pushed up a river, on any mule not too decrepit to be ridden, and many a man simply stowed his parole paper inside his shirt (if he still had a shirt) and started to walk home.

Godfrey put Darren in charge of his affairs and made ready for his trip out of town. He wanted to see Vivian at Sea Garden and find out what had happened to Luke, then go on to the home of Ida's parents and bring her back to Charleston.

Besides Celia and Marietta, Godfrey planned to take Lewis and Bobby Penfield with him to Sea Garden, and he offered to take Miles as well. But Miles declined. His heart was at Bellwood. Now strong enough to stand and take a few shaky steps, Miles smiled at Celia and promised her she would not have long to wait.

For a day or two it looked as if they might not get away. The British had taken possession of all the shipping in the harbor, including the private boats by which the plantation owners had expected to go home. But by dint of influence, sweet-talk, and just plain bribery, Godfrey managed to get the use of a schooner. It was not a comfortable ship nor even entirely seaworthy, but it did get them to Sea Garden.

To their great relief they found that Sea Garden had not been visited by any of the foraging troops led by the Earl of Cornwallis. Off the main routes of travel and enclosed by miles of forest, Sea Garden had been what Vivian had meant it to be, a place of refuge. But the folk there—Herbert and Vivian, Madge and her two younger children, and the servants—had lived in a torture of suspense. When Godfrey rang the landing bell and Celia watched the reunions, she stood aside in wistful envy.

"That's how it would be for me," she said to herself, "if this were Bellwood. Oh, I want to go home." She had never seen Bellwood, but whenever she thought of it, she thought of it this way. Home.

One happy item Vivian did have to tell: Luke was all right. With a group of his comrades, Luke had escaped Moncks Corner and vanished into the swamps.

She told them this while they were eating the supper Godfrey had begged for as soon as they landed, for food was still scarce in Charleston and they were all famished. Godfrey listened eagerly to her story. "You're sure of this, mother?" he demanded.

"Certainly," said Vivian. "Luke came by here to see me."

"When was that?" he asked.

Vivian's dark eyes snapped a look at him as though at an impertinent child. "Recently," she said.

She would say no more. Luke was well and at liberty, and she thought his brother had a right to know this much; but if she had seen him again, if she knew what he was doing now or what his plans were, she would not tell.

The next morning Godfrey borrowed a horse from Herbert and

set out for the home of Ida's parents on the near bank of the Santee. He planned to visit there a few days, then bring Ida back to Sea Garden so they and the Penfields could return to Charleston together. While he was gone, Herbert's workmen would repair the creaky old schooner. Herbert's schooner was safely tied up in his boathouse, but Godfrey had warned him to keep it there—if they took it to town the British would certainly confiscate it. To be sure the surrender terms had guaranteed property rights, but Godfrey was too wise in the ways of men to think the leaders of a conquering army meant every word they said.

For two weeks Celia heard nothing from the outside world. But the days were beautiful, the nights were quiet, and she had all she wanted to eat. She could feel her vigor returning, and her glass showed her how much better she looked. Everybody treated her like a welcome guest. If she had not been so anxious about Jimmy these two weeks would have been delightful.

The others did find them so. Lewis Penfield remarked at breakfast one morning that it was so pleasant at Sea Garden he wished he could idle here all summer. It was going to be a lot of work and trouble getting things organized again in Charleston. However, he added, it had to be done and as soon as Godfrey returned they would go home and set about their share of it.

Celia had observed that Lewis seemed to agree with Miles about the future. Lewis had offered his life to defend Charleston, but he felt that the rebellion—in South Carolina at least—had failed, and now they would be wise to return peacefully to their status as colonial subjects of the king. Celia thought this was sensible. However, she had not said so because she had observed also that Herbert and Vivian did not feel that way. They had not surrendered.

Later that day Burton and Elise and their sons reached Sea Garden on their way home. After dinner they all gathered in the big front parlor and talked. Burton had a good deal to say.

He was sorry the rebellion had failed. But he agreed with Lewis that Clinton's terms were fair—peace and protection for everyone who would stay at home and mind his own business. However, Burton said he was concerned about Luke. Clinton had announced in plain words that every man still bearing arms against the king was now regarded not as a soldier, but a traitor. He turned to Vivian.

"Mother, if you would use your influence with Luke—"

Vivian shrugged. "Nobody has any influence with Luke."

"You'll be seeing him sooner or later," Burton urged. "Tell him Tarleton has set out with a good-sized force, to hunt up any armed rebels still in South Carolina. If Luke should be captured—"

"Burton dear," said Vivian, "if you can make Luke do anything he doesn't want to do, you're smarter than I am." She turned her head toward the window, as if glad to get off the subject. "Now what's that?"

They heard the sound of horses' hoofs in the driveway. Celia, who sat nearest the window, sprang up, and with a joyful cry she scrambled over the sill to the porch.

The late sun was sending golden spears through the oak trees. Through the shafts of light Miles and Amos were riding toward the house.

Celia ran across the lawn. Catching sight of her, Miles leaped from his horse and ran to meet her.

"Jimmy's all right!" he shouted as he ran. As they met he caught her to him in a big joyful hug, and Celia sobbed with relief on his shoulder. "He's still lame," said Miles, "but he's getting well. Everybody at Bellwood is well. I've come to take you home."

◆～◆

"To take you home." Oh, what beautiful words. Mrs. James de Courcey Rand, one of the Rands of Bellwood.

For Miles told her he wanted her to think of herself this way. "You'll live in Charleston because of Jimmy's law practice," he said, "but Jimmy's old room will be kept ready, and you'll both be welcome at Bellwood any time. It's the *family* place, remember."

Already, though he was not thirty years old, Miles was thinking of himself as a patriarch. Celia hoped he would have a lot of children and grandchildren, he would enjoy them so. And while she had never been interested in babies, she thought now that it would be nice to have some, all part of this big warm household.

Miles brought her a letter from Jimmy, glowing in every line with love and impatience for her. Jimmy said he was hobbling on a cane, but his leg was getting stronger every day and he felt fine.

Miles told them the supply boat had reached Bellwood safely, and when they heard of the loss of Moncks Corner the crew had scattered, leaving the boat behind them. Tarleton's raiders had gone down the other bank of the river and had not come near; however, some days later, Bellwood had been visited by a British foraging party led by Cornwallis himself. They had come to the big house and stated that they wanted food.

Of course the colored folks had been scared stiff, and after the tales they had heard the white folks were pretty scared too. But Cornwallis and his men had done everything in good order. They had taken a great deal of meat and corn, and some tons of feed for their horses, but there had been no insults to the women, no rough behavior of any sort. And they had left plenty of food— rice and grits, poultry and meat animals, besides the garden greens. The people at Bellwood had not suffered. Certainly, Miles said laughing, not nearly as much as he and Celia had suffered worrying about them.

Herbert urged him to stay for a visit, but Miles said he had promised Jimmy to delay at Sea Garden no more than three or four days. Celia was glad of this. Much as she liked the Lacys, she was tired of being a guest. She wanted to go home.

•~•

So now it was a fragrant June morning and they were ready to leave right after breakfast. Everything was arranged. Madge and Lewis were to go along as chaperons. They would take Marietta and Madge's maid, and a colored boy named Elby to help Amos take care of the horses. From Sea Garden to Bellwood was a ride of nearly thirty miles, too far for horses cumbered by saddlebags to go in one day. They planned to rest overnight at a hunting lodge that belonged to Herbert, and ride on to Bellwood tomorrow.

Celia gave a little skip as she went into the dining room for breakfast. Vivian never came to breakfast, but everybody else was there. The maids brought in hominy grits and butter and fresh broiled flounder. Everybody was in high spirits—or nearly everybody. Celia had finished her fish when it occurred to her that Herbert had said almost nothing, and his usually genial face looked grave. She wondered if he thought something might happen to them on the way to Bellwood. She did not know why he should worry, for while Clinton had taken their army weapons the men were all well armed from Herbert's own gun-room.

Miles remarked that they had better get going as soon as they could. Herbert pushed back his chair and stood up. Before they left, he said, he would like to speak to them in the library.

Puzzled and a little apprehensive, they followed him. Though she rarely left her room so early, Vivian was in the library, her coffee tray beside her.

Closing the door, Herbert spoke to them without preliminary. "I'm sure you have all guessed," he said in a low, quiet voice, "that Luke has kept in touch with his mother. Last night he sent a piece of news that I think I should tell you." Herbert paused a moment. Vivian sipped her coffee. "Among the men Luke has met in the swamps," said Herbert, "there's talk that Clinton has revoked the paroles."

There was a buzz of amazement. Celia said nothing because she did not know what Herbert was talking about. She was annoyed at this delay; she wanted to start for Bellwood and Jimmy and her wedding, she wanted to forget about the war.

But the men in the group had understood. Lewis was saying, "I don't believe it."

"I don't either," said Miles. "If you believe all the talk you hear these days you'll get wheels in your head."

"It would be utterly dishonorable," said Burton.

Vivian set down her cup. "Dishonorable," she said dryly. "But not impossible."

There was another outburst of talk. They insisted it could not be true. Everybody knew how excitable Luke was.

Celia remembered her betrothal ball, and how Luke had exploded into the ballroom. She thought crossly that it seemed to be Luke's mission in life to wreck her big moments.

But if she couldn't stop their gabble she might as well understand it. Herbert had sat down in a chair near hers. She plucked at his sleeve.

"Please sir," she said as he turned, "what does it mean?—'revoke the paroles'?"

Herbert answered bluntly. "It means," he said, "that Sir Henry Clinton is a liar."

Celia was astonished. Herbert did not often speak like this.

He went on. "You'll remember, when Clinton offered terms of surrender he guaranteed that if the militiamen would give up their arms, they and all the citizens of Charleston would be regarded as prisoners of war on parole. As long as they did not fight the king, they could go home and live in peace."

Of course she remembered. She had heard it often enough. Celia nodded.

"Well, now that he has taken their guns," said Herbert, "Luke hears that Clinton has posted notices in Charleston saying he didn't really mean that. Clinton says now that they must all take an oath as subjects of the king. This would mean that they could be called up for regiments to fight on the king's side."

Celia sat up straight. "You mean—he says that Miles and Godfrey—and Jimmy—must turn Tory and shoot the Americans like Luke who haven't surrendered?"

"That's right."

"But they won't!"

Herbert smiled. "No, they won't."

"What will he do to them?"

"I don't know."

"But he promised—Miles told me—"

Herbert nodded.

"That's not honest!"

"Of course it's not," said Herbert, "and I hope it's not true." He smiled again at her shocked face. "Actually, my dear, I don't think it can be true. But I did think Miles and Lewis should hear it, because both of them—and Jimmy—are militiamen on parole."

The voices of the other men were rough with disbelief. Celia bit her lip thoughtfully. There *was* that childish business of Clinton's enrolling boys and Tories and old men as his prisoners of war. That wasn't honest either. She remembered what Godfrey had said about Clinton's wanting to be an earl. Burton was exclaiming that no British officer would stoop to such a trick. Hadn't Miles been telling them about the courteous behavior of Cornwallis when he came to Bellwood? Yes, of course, Celia reflected. But then Cornwallis was already an earl.

Anyway, she wished they would quit talking about it and get started toward her wedding. Watching Burton, excited and red-faced, she hoped that now he would get himself some new clothes. He was fairly oozing out of the clothes he had.

In his reasonable way, Miles was saying that since they could not verify the rumor no matter how long they sat here talking, wouldn't they be wise to follow their plan to start for Bellwood early so they could rest in the heat of the day? Madge, who had kept quiet until now, said yes, she thought so too. Celia stood up gratefully.

So they said good-by, and started.

They followed a track through the woods around Sea Garden, came out into open country, went into more woods. Now sometimes the road widened as it passed a trapper's cabin, sometimes dwindled till it disappeared among the trees. But Miles and Amos led the way without hesitation. They had played here as children, had hunted and fished and boated here as grown men, and they knew every wood-sign, every sound and scent, almost every tree.

They reached Herbert's hunting-lodge well before dark, and set out early the next morning. "How soon can we get to Bellwood?" Celia asked Miles as they rode.

He grinned at her. "Before noon."

He began to describe the place for her. A big white house with broad piazzas. A lot of outbuildings, and quarters for the servants and fieldhands. He said the main buildings were near the river, in a grove of oaks left from the original forest. Around the grove were the fields. However—Miles smiled an apology—she must not expect much of the fields this year. When he should have been directing the spring planting he had been in Charleston, so nothing much had been put in but the necessary food crops. He had plenty of work ahead of him, getting the place in order.

After a while she dropped back. She was so happy, riding through the woodland and knowing that every step of her horse was bringing her nearer to Jimmy. Now in June the woods were glorious, the tall long-needled pines and the oaks hung with moss, the great banks of yellow jessamine making the air sweet, and such a profusion of birds and butterflies—Celia drew a long breath of the fragrant air and sighed with pleasure. Though the sun was bright, here under the great trees she was not uncomfortably warm. A wild grapevine had been clinging to a tree at the side of the trail, but it was broken, and its branches lay on the ground. She heard Miles call Amos.

"Look at this," Miles said as Amos rode up. He was indicating a bush of jessamine ahead. It too had been broken and trampled on. Miles asked, "What do you think, Amos?"

Amos answered without hesitation. "Somebody's been along here, Mr. Miles."

Lewis and Madge had been riding behind Celia. Now, noticing that something was amiss, Lewis hastened his horse and drew nearer to Miles. "What's wrong?" he called.

Miles showed him the broken bushes, which now could be seen on both sides of the road.

"Not fresh-broken," Lewis said after a moment's examination. "Couldn't you and Amos have done it when you rode to Sea Garden last week?"

"Not so much. This was a good-sized party."

Celia stopped her horse and looked around her. The ground, thickly covered with leaves and pine-needles, showed no tracks, but she saw horse-droppings two or three days old. Miles and Amos were examining the bushes with the expert eyes of men who had learned woodlore from boyhood. Miles said,

"These fellows were not headed Sea Garden way. They were riding toward Bellwood. I don't like this, Lewis."

Behind her, Celia heard Madge telling the colored girls not to be alarmed. Celia made herself glance around with an encouraging smile, but she too felt uneasy. The bushes, pressing on the road, were damaged as far ahead as she could see. Ahead of her she heard Lewis say,

"I wouldn't be too concerned, Miles. We're facing toward

Charleston, and a lot of people are riding to Charleston these days."

"This isn't the main road to Charleston," Miles returned shortly.

"Couldn't a party go to Charleston this way?"

"Could. Kind of roundabout, though."

"A good many people who left town are on their way home now," Lewis suggested. "This might be the easiest way for some of them."

"Yes," said Miles, "and foraging parties are still out getting supplies for the British garrison—" He shrugged, shook his head, and tried to laugh. "Oh, it's a public road, anybody could have used it. I guess I'm still on edge. Takes time to get over what we went through during the siege."

Lewis agreed heartily that it certainly did.

They rode on. Amos stayed by Miles, while Lewis dropped back again to talk to Madge. Celia was thinking. It was easy for Lewis to be cheerful. Lewis' wife was here with him, his children were at Sea Garden. But all the people Miles loved best were at Bellwood.

After a while Miles called her to catch up with him, and told her they had almost reached Bellwood. A few more miles of woods, then they would come into the clear, and could see ahead of them the Bellwood fields and the grove that shaded the buildings. He said nothing more about the signs of other horsemen on the road. As in Charleston he was trying to keep her cheerful, pretending to be sure everything was all right. But Celia was still worried. Again she fell back. Marietta asked if she felt all right. Celia said, "Oh yes, fine," and told Marietta to go ahead and ride with Amos.

Behind her, she heard Madge exclaim how beautiful the wild flowers were this year. Madge was so happy to have Lewis and Bobby safe from the Charleston siege that she was living in a rainbow world. Celia reflected that probably it was foolish of herself to be worried. As Miles had said, this was a public road; anybody could have used it. The woods softly enclosed her again. It was like an enchantment—the chirps and rustling leaves, the swaying gray streamers of moss, the sweetness of jessamine. Celia loved flower scents and the fresh clean smells of outdoors.

But as she rode along her nostrils caught a whiff that was not clean. Faint but foul, something else was mingling with the scents of the woods.

The smell blew away, but in a minute or two she caught it again. This time it reminded her of the smell in a smoky room that had been shut up all night. But not exactly like that—besides the smoke smell there was something else befouling the air, a nasty smell, like—it was hard to define it, then she thought—like what people meant when they said they smelt a dead rat.

# CHAPTER 18

HEAD OF HER, Miles was riding in silence. But the others were merry—Amos and Marietta laughing about something, the horse-boy Elby flirting with Madge's maid, and Lewis telling Madge anecdotes of the siege.

". . . no roosters crowed in the mornings, all eaten. People had even eaten their pet birds. On the lines we still had coffee—"

Suddenly Miles turned his head. "What's that smell?" he exclaimed.

Lewis and Madge did not hear him, but Amos did. Amos raised his head and sniffed, scowled, sniffed again. "I don't know what it is, Mr. Miles. Sure is nasty."

Miles dug his heels into his horse's flanks. "Come on!" he cried. "We're just loafing along! Celia—"

But Celia had already caught up with him. "How much farther, Miles?" she called as they hurried their horses.

"Nearly there!" he shouted back.

She heard Lewis calling to them both. He caught up with them and urged them not to hurry so. The horses would stumble over one of these fallen branches, and then where would they be?

Reluctantly admitting the sense of this advice, they slowed to a more reasonable pace. As they rode along the smell grew heavier. It filled the air with a rank staleness. Whatever the source, they were riding toward it, and they were riding toward Bellwood. Celia clamped her teeth on her lip, afraid lest sheer nervousness would make her cry out.

The woods were less dense. The track widened. They were coming to the edge of the clearing where the fields of Bellwood lay. The smell thickened to a stench. Celia and Miles were side by side, ahead of the others. She gave him a sidelong glance. Miles' lips were turned in toward his teeth and set in a hard thin line. Between his eyebrows were two ridges of strain. His hand holding the bridle was stiff. At Bellwood were his wife and child, his mother and brother, the household servants who like Amos had been his friends and playmates from childhood. Miles was holding himself sternly in check, but he was in torture.

Celia felt creepy all over, as if things were crawling on her skin. The back of her neck hurt.

Now the air was so foul as to be almost unbearable. They came out of the woods. Below them lay the fields, hundreds of acres broken here and there by orchards and vineyards; beyond, the Cooper River was like a silver ribbon in the sun; and by the river, less than a mile from the edge of the clearing, was the grove of mighty oaks left from the forest to shelter the plantation buildings.

With a groan of horror Miles jerked back on his bridle and stopped his horse. Celia stopped too, rigid with shock.

The others rode up. She heard them exclaiming but she did not understand the words.

She did not need words. She was there. Before her lay Bellwood. And all over Bellwood was the sight and silence and smell of death.

·~·

From the edge of the woods the ground sloped gently to the river-bank, so that she was looking downward over the fields. The grove was a mass of burnt tree-trunks standing like tall black sticks. Among them she saw chimneys, gaunt and dark against the bright river; piles of ashes, charred pieces of wall standing crookedly, half-burnt timbers lying as they had fallen in the fire that had burned the great house at Bellwood and the smaller buildings around it.

Around the black ruin the fields were strewn with the dead bodies of animals. There were hundreds of them, pigs and sheep and cattle, flocks of poultry, colts and a few old horses. The bodies lay bloated and stinking in the sun. Some of the animals had been slaughtered for food, the meaty parts cut off and the rest left to rot; others had simply been killed with bullets or bayonets to complete the work of destruction. Of these last, most had swollen twice their size and rolled over on their backs. Their legs stood up stiff in the air.

From where Celia and the rest had stopped their horses, to the trees across the river, they could not see a moving creature except the buzzards circling above the corpses. The air was putrid with the stink of rotting flesh.

Celia did not know how long she sat there in her saddle, not moving because she was nearly stunned. She had more impressions of voices. Vaguely, as if through a twilight, she saw Marietta on her knees vomiting. She felt a movement of her horse, and saw the dark hand of Amos grasping the bridle. She realized then that her horse had sensed the horror ahead and needed a controlling hand.

Just as she saw Madge riding closer she heard a yelp of rage at her side and pounding of hoofs. Miles, who like herself had been paralyzed with shock, had come to his senses and had started at a gallop toward what used to be his home. That roused her in earnest. Striking her horse savagely with her heel she went after him. She heard Amos cry out "Miss Celia!"—then she heard more hoofbeats behind her, but she did not look around.

She was making a wild journey. It was a journey of filth and stench, dried blood on the ground and rotting entrails swarming with flies, carcasses scorched by scraps of fire blown from the big house. Her horse was scared and hard to manage. Celia was hardly aware of the horse. She had grown up on a plantation and was a good rider, and this was useful now; with her heel and knee and hands she gave directions without thinking of what she was doing. All she could think of was getting to the black place where the house had been and finding out what had happened, and it seemed that it was taking her hours to get there.

Ahead of her she heard Miles shouting, and behind her Amos.

Miles was calling Jimmy, Audrey, his mother. Amos called Jimmy, and people she had not heard of before, the colored folk who had grown up at Bellwood with him, his friends.

Nobody answered. Overhead the buzzards squawked, angry to be thus annoyed at their feast.

Now she was there. She sprang to the ground, and Amos yelled for Elby to come help him tie the horses. Celia looked at the black destruction.

It covered even more ground than she had realized. Bellwood had been a spacious establishment. She could see the foundations of the great house, with the wide brick steps and marble carriage-block still there. Behind the house she saw the kitchen—such solid brick that it was damaged less than the rest—and beyond that, burnt remnants of storehouses, stables, servants' quarters, and she did not know what else, reaching away till she lost sight of them among the scorched tree-trunks.

She was standing in what had been the driveway. This had curved away between two lines of trees, and those farthest from the house were still there, lacing their branches overhead. In front of the house there had been a lawn—she could see patches of trampled grass that had escaped the burning, and charred clumps of shrubbery. Scattered about the lawn she saw pieces of silver and china, broken furniture, a crystal decanter cracked and trodden into the earth. On one side a path led through what might have been a garden, and beyond that were more trees. On the other side she saw a big oblong enclosure bordered with fancy brick coping, like a flowerbed. Inside the coping the soft garden earth had been thrown up in a pile about four feet wide and seven or eight feet long.

Celia had stood in a dazed silence as she stared at the rest of it. But when she saw that pile of earth it seemed that every nerve in her body trembled. She put her hand over her mouth and found that her mouth was open as if to scream, but she was not scream-ing. Her throat was stiff, and all that came out was a little croak-ing noise like the sound of an animal in a faroff swamp. That mound was fresh, and it bore no marks of trampling hoofs. It was a new-made grave.

She felt a hand gently taking hers. Madge Penfield was trying to give her support. But it meant nothing. She could not respond, she simply could not. She stood rigid as a gatepost, staring.

She saw Miles stumbling around among the ruins like a man not quite sane. He picked up the fragments of things that had been in his home, looked at them, put them back on the ground. Lewis was with him, trying to give sympathy as Madge was trying to give it to her, and getting no more response.

A little way off Amos stood in the shadow of a scorched tree, shaking his head as if he knew it could not possibly be true and he would wake up in a minute. Beside him Marietta stood holding his hand. Farther off, Madge's maid was sobbing a prayer, and Elby sat on the fallen branch of a tree murmuring, "Lord help us. Lord help us."

Then all at once they heard something else. Celia started, and Miles stopped short, holding a silver soup-ladle that he had picked up from the ground. He raised his head and listened. There was no mistake. From the far end of the grove beyond the garden, where the fire had not reached, they heard a dog barking.

It was Amos who first recognized the bark. Amos leaped, he shouted. "Praise the Lord! Mr. Miles—it's Rosco!" Before the words were well spoken he and Miles had started on a run toward the trees.

They had gone only a few yards when Rosco came running out of the thicket toward them, barking his welcome. They met him halfway and dropped on their knees, then as Miles hugged the dog Amos sprang up and shouted again. A big sturdy Negro man was coming out of the grove behind Rosco. Amos ran toward him.

"Big Buck!" he cried. "Oh, Big Buck—I never was so glad to see anybody in my life—shake hands—"

Then Amos stopped. For at the sight of him, Big Buck had sat down on the ground and started bawling like a baby.

Followed by Rosco, Miles sprang up and crossed to where Big Buck sat sobbing. He grabbed the colored man's shoulder and shook it, while Amos shook his other shoulder and the rest of them gathered round. Except for Celia they all knew Big Buck, and all of them together were demanding to know what had happened.

"Where's everybody?" Miles exclaimed, and Amos, giving Big Buck another shake, ordered him, "Talk up, you! Where's the folks?"

As though he had understood the question, Rosco howled.

Lewis put a hand on the dog's head to quiet him. Still sitting on the ground, Big Buck struggled to say what he had to say.

"The white folks is dead."

Nobody said anything. They stared at him blankly, like idiots. Overhead a buzzard squawked. Big Buck spoke again.

"The colored folks all but me is carried off."

Still nobody answered. It was as though every one of them had received a separate knock on the head. Big Buck added,

"It was them green Tories and Tarleton."

He stopped again. He put his head down on his fist and shook with sobs.

• ∾ •

But at last Big Buck told his story.

"It's two days, maybe three days after Amos and Mr. Miles went to get Miss Celia. It's in the morning, ten-eleven o'clock. We're all busy because Mr. Jimmy he say, shine up everything before Miss Celia gets here. I'm spadin' up the flowerbed over yonder and Miss Beatrice is tellin' me to make it real pretty for Miss Celia. The baby is upstairs fast asleep and Mr. Jimmy he's on the porch tellin' Miss Audrey what Miss Celia looks like. He's got his cane by him because he can't walk by hisself. Then we see these men in green jackets come ridin' out of the woods.

"They just come ridin', and when they see the house they start yellin' and hollerin' and shootin' and they ride right across the fields. Miss Audrey she screams out and Mr. Jimmy he come hobblin' down the front steps. He can't walk fast and by the time he gets out to the front the green men are all over the place. I don't know how many but it sure seems like a lot, and the colored folks are runnin' up and it seems like everybody is hollerin' all at the same time and it's hard to know what's goin' on.

"But a fellow on a horse he rides straight to Mr. Jimmy and I hear him ask if he's the man that owns the place. Mr. Jimmy he says no, the man that owns the place is his brother and he's not home. And the fellow on the horse and two-three others with him, they bawl out yes, that's what they thought, Mr. Miles is gone to North Carolina to join the rebel troops like that man Sumter.

"Mr. Jimmy say he don't know any man name Sumter. He say anyway his brother ain't gone to join no rebel troops, his brother give parole in Charleston. And the men on the horses they holler back and say there ain't no more paroles. They say everybody got to join them now and they say Miles Rand is gone like Sumter. They say they'll do to him what they did to Sumter and this will teach Miles Rand he better fight for the king.

"And I hear Mr. Jimmy talkin' back to them. Shoutin' mad he is. Mr. Jimmy say not he nor his brother will ever fight for the king. And then there's a gunshot and he falls down.

"I try to run help Mr. Jimmy but all the folks is screamin' and yellin' and runnin' around so I can't get nowhere. The green men is ropin' the colored folks and tyin' them together, and one of them grabs me but I've got my spade and I bang him on the head. Miss Beatrice is kneelin' on the ground by Mr. Jimmy and I hear her moanin'.

"Then I see more green men comin' out of the house loaded up with things, mirrors and bottles and forks and spoons and all like that. They stuff their shirts full of things and carry all they can hold besides, and a lot of them are uncorkin' bottles and takin' drinks. Some of 'em try to catch me again and I run around and hide in a cabin. But there's a lot of the colored folks hidin' in the cabins and the green men set the cabins on fire so the folks would have to run out and they could catch 'em and tie 'em up.

"When I run out I see the stables are on fire too, and the trees and the big house. I run around to the front and there's a green man draggin' Miss Audrey out of the house and her screamin' and fightin'. He hollers at her that she must not go back in because everything in there is on fire and she'll catch fire too. But she screams back that her baby is in there and he can't keep her out. And he can't. All of a sudden she breaks away from the man and runs indoors and everybody is scared to go after her because now the fire is comin' out of the windows. All around they's shootin' the animals and ropin' the folks, and there's howlin' and screamin' and I hear one green man say these folks will bring good prices in the West Indies and make them all rich.

"I'm so scared I can't hardly move but I know I got to move and I knock down another green man, maybe more than one, and I run around and around so they can't catch me. And all of a sudden I hear Miss Audrey scream again and I look up and there she is at a window upstairs with the baby, and the whole house is burnin' and crackin' and she can't get down. And then she jumps out of the window and she sort of turns over in the air and her head hits the ground and there she lies, not movin', and the baby underneath her. And some green man runs over to her and hollers out this is a crime. But I don't know what else he says because just then another green man he grabs me and I see he's got a rope and I knock him over and I start to run.

"I just run. I ain't lookin' to see where I'm goin'. I don't see anything, I just run. I get to the trees and I run and run and somewhere in there I run right into a tree and I fall down on my face. I hear all kinds of noise and I see smoke but I just lie on the ground because it seems like I can't breathe no more and I can't get up.

"I reckon I fainted or somp'n because after a while I come to. I know it's been a long time but I don't know how long, only now everything is quiet. The fire is burnt down but I'm still scared. I'm scared to go back and scared to stay where I am. Then I hear a dog and after a while Rosco comes sniffin' up and he finds me. I don't know why they ain't killed Rosco, maybe they figure can't nobody ride him or eat him so he ain't no use, or maybe he run away like me. Rosco howls and hollers and grabs my clothes and tries to drag me back. At first I'm scared to go but then I figure that if there was any of them green men still here they could have found me by now with all the racket Rosco is makin'. So I let him bring me back.

"And there I see the house all smokin' and everything is like you see it now. The green men have took all the horses except a few they didn't want, and them they killed. They took all the meat they could carry and what they didn't take they killed just like you see. And everything is quiet like a graveyard except

Rosco whimperin'. And then I see Miss Beatrice comin' to meet me.

"Miss Beatrice looks like crazy. Her clothes are all torn and dirty and her hair is come down and her hands are cut and bloody. But she's glad to see me. All the other colored folks is took away and she didn't know even one was left.

"Miss Beatrice can't hardly talk but she wants to talk. She say the man that shot Mr. Jimmy killed him right there. And Miss Audrey and the baby died from jumpin' out of the window. And Miss Beatrice done dragged them all three yonder to the flowerbed. She had picked up my spade and she was tryin' all by herself to dig a grave.

"But Miss Beatrice ain't strong enough to dig a grave and I say let me do it. She stands up there and watches me. Mr. Jimmy is lyin' on the ground by us, and the baby and Miss Audrey. I think Miss Audrey's neck is broke and the baby's head got broke when he hit the ground. Miss Beatrice just stands there like a stick only she keeps talkin'. Not talkin' like somebody that's got somp'n to say but just talkin'. Same words over and over. This will teach Miles Rand he better fight for the king. This will teach Miles Rand he better fight for the king. Over and over like that.

"I get the grave dug and put in Miss Audrey and the baby and then I pick up Mr. Jimmy. And Miss Beatrice she falls over on the ground. I try to help her but there ain't a thing to do. Her heart is stopped beatin'. Just like that. So I have to put her in the grave too and I cover them up and then I'm scared to stay around any more and I take Rosco and go off and hide in the trees yonder, and I keep wonderin' if the green men will come back but they don't. Ain't nobody been here till you folks come today.

"And that's what happened, Mr. Miles. And I wish somebody had to tell it to you besides me."

◦~◦

Somewhere near by the other Negroes had begun a chant. It was a low musical keening, every other line a plea of "Lord have mercy, Lord have mercy."

Celia heard them. She was sitting on the ground. She still sat there. Lord have mercy, Lord have mercy.

Miles stood up. He took his pistol out of the holster at his side. Madge gave a cry of alarm and Lewis sprang to his feet. Without pausing Miles strode across to Rosco and shot him in the head.

He spoke over his shoulder. "Why make him live without Jimmy?" he asked.

# CHAPTER 19

ELIA never had a clear recollection of her journey back to Sea Garden or of the next few days. She did not remember that she talked at all about what she had seen at Bellwood. She had never been a great talker, and now she seemed to have been stricken almost dumb. She went about quietly, ate what they set in front of her, lived somehow.

Vivian asked if she did not want a cot moved into her bedroom so she could have Marietta with her at night. Celia shook her head. She slept in snatches, and when she was tired of tossing in bed she would get up and sit by a window, where she could watch the patterns of moonlight or listen to the fall of summer rain. She did not want anybody there, urging her to sleep when she could not sleep.

But the nights were long and cruel. She would dream about the awfulness at Bellwood and wake up shaking with sobs. Or she would dream about Jimmy, and wake up to the black knowledge that Jimmy was dead. She thought what fools they had been to let that prig of a parson keep them apart. Suppose he did refuse to say the holy words till after she came of age? Why had they waited? At least she could have had something to remember.

The first thing she noticed—she did not recall how many days had passed before she noticed it—was that neither Miles nor

Amos was anywhere to be seen. She could not remember anything about Miles since the moment when he had snatched out his pistol in half-blind fury and shot Rosco. She had thought he was going to shoot himself, and had wondered why Lewis had sprung forward to stop him, since after what he had heard Miles must be already dead inside.

She thought of this one morning when she came out on the piazza and saw Madge cutting a bouquet of sweet peas. Celia went out and asked her what had become of Miles.

Madge was too wise to be evasive. She said that after Miles had fired the shot he stood there staring at the smoking pistol. Then all of a sudden, like a man pursued by things nobody else could see, he turned and plunged into the woods. Just as suddenly, Amos and Big Buck went after him. Lewis told the others to let all three of them go. Among the Negroes carried off by Tarleton had been the people Amos and Big Buck loved best. They and Miles would understand one another now.

Celia pulled a handful of sweet peas from the trellis and walked away, tearing them to pieces and letting the petals scatter on the ground. She wished she could go into the woods too, and hide, like a sick animal.

That afternoon Godfrey and Ida rode in. They had not heard of the holocaust at Bellwood, but when Lewis told them about it they exchanged meaningful glances, and Godfrey commented harshly, "So, that butcher meant just what he said."

Celia, sitting on the piazza, heard these words through a window. The others asked Godfrey what he meant, and he said, "You haven't heard about Colonel Sumter?"

At this, Celia came in. Vivian held out her hand, and Celia sat on the floor by Vivian's chair. Vivian did not forbid her to listen. She knew a forced sheltering was not kind. "Go on, Godfrey," Vivian said.

Godfrey said that since the home of Ida's family was near a main crossing of the Santee, they had frequent visitors. While there, Godfrey had heard a lot of news.

He said that after revoking the paroles Clinton had taken ship for New York, leaving Cornwallis in command of the king's men in the south. When he had set up a supply post at Camden in the northern part of South Carolina, Cornwallis sent Tarleton out to get equipment and Tory recruits. He told him also to clear up any "nests of treason" he might find.

This Major Tarleton was twenty-six years old. He came of a well-to-do family in Liverpool, but already before the start of the American war he had run through the fortune his father had left him. When the war began he decided to enter the army, that refuge of debt-ridden aristocrats. His mother bought him a commission. Tarleton set out for New York, announcing that it was his purpose to kill more men and bed more women than any other hero of his majesty's troops.

So far his success in both his aims had been so great that he was generally referred to as Beast, or Butcher, or Barbarian, or uglier words. His own first name was Banastre, which nobody could pronounce anyway, and Americans said the other names were more fitting.

Colonel Thomas Sumter was an officer of Continental troops. He had taken part in the battle of Fort Moultrie in 1776, but in the quiet years following that victory he had retired to his plantation. He had not aided in the defense of Charleston because he had been prostrated by tragedies of his own. Father of a large family, he had in the space of a few weeks seen an epidemic kill all his children but one small boy; and about the same time his wife was stricken with paralysis and left unable to walk. Sumter had hardly known when the British attacked Charleston, or cared. But when he learned that the city was taken he roused himself to fight again. Leaving his wife and child in care of a niece and the family servants, Sumter rode off to organize rebel troops in North Carolina.

Tarleton had hoped to catch up with him. But failing in this, he destroyed Sumter's plantation with the same terrible thoroughness he had used a few days later at Bellwood. Sumter's little son scrambled up a tree, where he clung out of sight and watched the havoc. But Mrs. Sumter, in her chair in a room upstairs, could not move.

Tarleton ordered the house set afire. Busy supervising the destruction outside, he paid no attention to Mrs. Sumter's screams. But two of his men, more decent than their leader, made their way back into the burning house and carried her out before the walls fell in. They left her there among the ruins of her home, and as they rode away Tarleton spread the word that this was how he intended dealing with any other traitors who continued to fight their lawful king.

As Godfrey told his story Celia sat where she was, on the floor by Vivian's chair. She was not crying. She felt tortured with a helpless hate.

Godfrey urged Herbert and Vivian not to stay any longer at Sea Garden. He begged them to come to Charleston with him.

But all that evening, all the next day, Herbert and Vivian said no.

Herbert said, "We have no big fields, no army of Negroes to be carried off. We're not worth the trouble of a raid."

Vivian said, "Our schooner is in the boathouse. If we get scared we can come to Charleston any time."

At last, the afternoon of the second day, they said they were tired arguing and wanted to rest. Herbert went to his library, Vivian started for her bedroom. As she stood up, Godfrey made one more exasperated effort.

"Mother, I know it's because of Luke that you want to stay here. But what *good* are you doing?"

Vivian smiled serenely. "Godfrey dear, wouldn't you just love to know?"

Celia had kept in the background. But now she slipped out and spoke to Vivian in the hall.

"Please, may I say something? I won't take long."

"Come in here," said Vivian. She opened the door of the room where she kept her household records, and sat down by the desk. Celia stood before the desk, twisting her hands. "What's the trouble?" Vivian asked.

How calm she was, how sure of herself. How Celia envied her. Celia herself was as tense as a fiddle-string. She spoke in jerks. "Vivian—you're going to stay here all summer?"

"Why yes," said Vivian, like any lady asked about her summer plans. "Why?"

"Then," Celia said—"then may I stay too?" She stopped, wet her lips, made herself go on. "You see—it wasn't until just now—

when they begged you to leave Sea Garden—that I realized—I haven't anywhere to go."

She thought she had never spoken words that were so hard to say. Crying for shelter like a stray cat.

Vivian smiled a little. "Why yes, Celia, you can stay here."

"I won't stay forever!" Celia promised hastily. "I'll go somewhere—I'll do something. But right now—I'm all mixed up."

Vivian was looking straight at her. "You'll have to make your own life, Celia," she said. "We all do. Nobody can help us much."

Vivian must know what she was talking about. She had lived deeply, had had experience of loss. Celia blurted,

"Vivian, you—so many—what *do* you do?"

"You live through it, Celia," said Vivian. Her voice was firm. "You find out—and sometimes it's very surprising—that no matter what you lose, there's always something else. Life can still be good."

Celia stood with her hands still clenched, angry with herself for asking. "Life can still be good." Oh, it was easy for Vivian to say that. Her world was full of blessings—riches and high position and so many people who loved her. Vivian could not know what it meant to be alone, and desolate.

Celia brought herself back to her purpose. "Thank you for letting me stay. But I don't want to be a burden. Haven't you some work I can do?"

"Plenty," Vivian answered tersely. She opened a drawer. Expecting a sewing-basket, Celia was surprised to see her take out shears and garden gloves. "The flowers need looking after," said Vivian. "You can start in the morning."

Later Celia thought, whatever Vivian does it's not what you expect her to do. But somehow it's usually right.

The Bernards and the Penfields left for Charleston. As Burton and his family had left already, there was nobody at Sea Garden now but Herbert and Vivian and Celia, and about twenty Negroes. The summer tasks went along. Marietta said it was almost like old times.

Celia's work began as soon as she had had breakfast. Directed by Vivian, she raked and spaded, pulled up weeds and trimmed the bushes, thinned the spring bulbs and put in new ones for autumn blooming. By the time she stopped to get ready for dinner she was dirty and aching and dripping with sweat. But when she came to table she was hungry, and at night her muscles relaxed, so that she went to sleep with peace in her body even if it had not yet reached her heart.

There were still times when she dreamed of Bellwood and woke up shuddering, and other times when she lay awake wondering what was going to become of her. One night she woke to such hot stillness that she could hardly breathe. When she went to the window she could not feel a stirring of wind. Outside, the trees looked weird in the faint greenish glow of the moon. The long gray moss hung motionless. Celia could hear the croaking of frogs, and now and then the chirp of a night-bird.

The air was like a burden. Wide awake and restless, she thought it might ease her nerves if she walked around. She was not in the habit of roaming about the house at night, but it would not matter if she was very quiet. She put on her dressing-gown and slippers. They were soft quilted cloth slippers, and would make no sound. Opening the door carefully she went into the hall.

Through a front window came the glow of the moon. It did not give much light, just that greenish radiance, ghostly on the long gray moss and ghostly here as it threw the shadows of the windowpanes in rectangles on the floor.

How quiet it was, how lonesome. This was a house built for a large family and many guests, but now there was nobody on the second floor but herself. On a front corner was the master suite of rooms. Herbert and Vivian used to have these for their own, but in late years, since they had found it tiresome to climb stairs, they had changed to rooms on the first floor. The servants slept in their own wing at the back of the house. The closed doors along the hall, and the empty rooms behind them, seemed grim, unfriendly.

Celia went to the railing of the staircase and looked down. The stair-well was black. Below her, on the landing halfway down, she could hear the deep slow ticks of the great clock. She thought of how they had raised their glasses New Year's Eve, and how Jimmy had given her that gay loving smile as he whispered "Happy New Year!"

How loud the clock sounded in the silent house. The slow tick-tocks seemed to draw her downstairs, toward the ballroom. She gathered her robe around her and felt her way down the stairs, guiding herself with a hand on the rail.

The lower hall was dark but not completely black. Over the front door were panes of heavy glass, through which the moon shone dimly. As Celia paused at the foot of the stairs to see her way, above her the clock gave a low stern whirr. It was about to strike. Remembering the ballroom, she shivered and put her hand over her eyes. The clock struck two.

Moving soundlessly, she made her way toward the ballroom. In these days the ballroom looked very little like the gorgeous place where they had danced last New Year's Eve. With no prospect of entertaining company any time soon, Vivian had protected the floor with heavy canvas, and had moved in some pieces of furniture that she wanted out of the way for the summer. Celia stood a moment on the threshold.

The curtains were closed. At the front windows she could see a shimmer of moonlight around the edges. The furniture, shrouded in dust-covers, looked like lumps of thicker darkness in the dark.

She went inside. The place had the musty smell of a room little used. Moving along the wall, she put out her hand and found the marble mantelpiece. The hard cold feel of it was refreshing on her damp skin. She thought of the room as it had been that night, the candles glancing back and forth from the mirrors, the music and laughter, the tinkle of glasses and the swish of silk. And how happy she had been.

Over by a corner window was a black lump that might be a chair. She went toward it, and held back the window-curtain long enough to see. The window was locked top and bottom, and had a heavy oak beam across it. At night every window in the house was locked except those of the occupied bedrooms; Herbert went around to make sure of it, and the locks were of a complex design. It would do nobody any good to break a pane and reach in from outside.

Under the dust-cover was a deep cushioned chair such as Herbert liked to draw up by the fire in winter, but for which he had no use in sticky weather like this. Celia let the curtain fall, and curled up in the chair. Right over there on the wall, so near that she could almost have touched it, was the mirror where she had seen herself when she stood by the punch-table thinking, I'm not really beautiful but I feel beautiful, and I look like a girl who feels beautiful.

She did not know how long she sat there, remembering, telling herself she ought to go back to her room because the pain of remembering was so great, but staying here anyway, remembering more. Suddenly in the silence she heard a sound.

She stiffened. Her skin prickled as she thought, *Tarleton.*

But maybe she had not heard anything. Or maybe Herbert and Vivian could not sleep either, and were up, moving around. She hadn't heard anything and if she had it wasn't important.

She heard it again.

Footsteps. Soft, careful footsteps. Somebody was in the house. It could not be Tarleton, or sneak-thieves—nobody could force a way into this house without a banging and battering that could be heard a mile. It was Herbert or Vivian, no doubt about it.

But the steps did not come from the direction of the rooms occupied by Herbert and Vivian. They came from the back of the house and they were coming this way.

It had been only a second or two since she had heard the first sound, but it seemed an hour. With no conscious direction of her own her head had turned toward the door, but otherwise she had not moved. She could not. She sat deep in the chair, tense with fright.

Somebody was standing in the doorway. A man—she could barely make out his figure in the dark. As she had done, he stood a moment on the threshold to get his eyes adjusted to what glimmer of light there was, then with the sureness of a man who knew his way around, he went to the nearest window. His footsteps were almost soundless on the covered floor.

He moved the curtains a little way apart. Through the window came a faint light. The light was so dim, and Celia so frightened, that it took her an instant to recognize Luke.

Luke wore neither hat nor coat, and the moon shone around the hard lines of his body. He turned from the window and started back toward the door. She saw that he had on heavy boots that would have clumped noisily if the floor had been bare. So it was to protect Luke, and not the dance-floor, that Vivian had laid that canvas.

Celia had nearly exclaimed when she saw him, and almost instinctively she had pressed her fist over her mouth. Luke was a fugitive, maybe even now he was being pursued. If she spoke and startled him she might betray him. She sat still, barely breathing.

Luke was at the doorway. In a low voice he said, "Come in, sir. You can see your way now."

He stepped aside. His voice, his manner, his every movement, showed a deep deference. Celia stared through the dark. Somebody important was about to come in.

Two men came through the doorway. One of them was a Negro, and leaning on his arm was a white man, smaller in build, who walked with a bad limp.

With the colored man's aid, the little cripple took a few halting steps toward Luke. The three men exchanged whispers. Though Celia could not make out the words, she could tell that Luke was still addressing the lame man with the greatest respect.

Luke walked toward the fireplace. Against the dark wood paneling of the wall by the mantel, Celia could barely make out his figure. He said,

"Ready, Colonel Marion."

Marion!

Celia felt a shock. She had thought Marion would be a *personage*. Not a shriveled-up shrimp. He might improve when he could walk—that fall last March must have been a bad one, since he was still limping in midsummer—but even standing up straight he would not look as if he amounted to much.

Supported by the Negro, Marion hobbled toward the fireplace. Then, while Luke stood there, Marion and the colored man went through the wall.

Celia felt pins and needles in her hair.

There was no door next to the fireplace. On both sides there was that dark wood paneling, against which the white marble stood out in beautiful contrast. But Marion and the Negro had gone through the wall. Luke stood there alone. Now as he turned around she could see that the wall was still there—she saw a faint reflection of moonlight on the paneling.

Luke had started again toward the door. In her amazement Celia forgot her caution. She said, "Luke!"

He wheeled on one foot and stared around. She had stood up, and he saw her, a white figure in the dark. She said, "It's me—Celia."

"Oh," said Luke, and coming quickly toward her he caught her hand in his. His hand was rough and hard, and felt enormously strong. "What are you doing here?" he demanded.

"Why, nothing," she returned. "I couldn't sleep. Luke, where did Colonel Marion go just now?"

Luke's hand closed on hers. She felt that he could have snapped her fingers like toothpicks. When he spoke his voice was low but it had a force like cannon.

"You never saw Colonel Marion in your life," he said, "except once when he fell out of a window on Tradd Street."

"Oh, all right!" Celia retorted. "What do you think I am, a Tory spy? I won't say anything if I should run into Cornwallis, or Tarleton—Tarleton—" Her voice cracked. With her free hand she covered her eyes. "I'm sorry, Luke. But I'm so torn up. Maybe you haven't heard—" Her throat closed and she could say no more.

"Yes I have," said Luke. He was suddenly very gentle. His grip on her hand relaxed. He drew her to sit again in the big chair, and he sat on the chair-arm beside her. Celia spoke again.

"I didn't mean to cry. I thought I was through with crying. I'm all right now."

Luke stroked her hair softly. "Celia, Jimmy is in God's hands. And so are you, and so am I. That's all I can tell you."

There was a pause. In the close dusty air Luke had a smell of the woods about him, redolent of earth and leaves and grass, what she had always thought of as a "green smell." Celia turned in the chair so she could speak to him directly. "Luke," she said, "I didn't see anybody tonight. Not you, not anybody. I won't tell."

"I know you won't," he said.

Again there was a silence. Celia liked sitting here with him.

After a while she ventured, "Luke—Colonel Marion—" She hesitated.

"What about him?"

"He's very important, isn't he?"

"He sure is," said Luke. Celia could not see the expression of Luke's face, but she could hear the smile in his voice. "I guess," added Luke, "Colonel Marion's about the most important man within a thousand miles."

Celia exclaimed, "But—he's so puny!"

Luke laughed softly in the dark. "Honeychild," he said to her, "when that man's leading a charge, he looks nine feet tall."

She supposed he was right. The men who had served with Marion all seemed to think of him that way. Luke went on,

"The British are combing the country for him. As long as he's at liberty we're not licked and they know it. He has to slip around like a puff of smoke. Always moving."

"Who's the colored man?" she asked.

"That's Buddy. His name is Oscar, but Colonel Marion calls him Buddy so the rest of us do too. They grew up together."

Like Jimmy and Amos, thought Celia, and the memory gave her a twinge of pain. She was glad when Luke spoke again.

"Celia, how long have you been sitting here? How much have you heard?"

She told him. He ignored her mention of the wall, but when she said their footsteps had approached from the back he said,

"That's right. Good ears. Mother always leaves me something to eat—I won't say where—so whenever I'm in the neighborhood I can creep in and get a meal."

"Do you want me to call Vivian?" she asked.

"No. I've left her a message. And I'll be grateful if you don't tell her you've seen me. It might worry her that I didn't have sense enough to explore this room before I let Colonel Marion come in."

"I won't tell," Celia said again.

But she wondered how long he could go on like this, he and Marion and their friends. Hiding, whispering, moving by night like spooks.

"Luke, tell me really," she begged, "is there any chance for the rebels now?"

"Yes, plenty," said Luke. He spoke with conviction. "Some things I can't tell you. But this much I can: there's a rumor—I don't know if it's a fact, we're trying now to find out—there's a rumor that General Washington has sent us a force from his main army. They're supposed to be on their way."

Celia could almost feel hear heart leap. Luke went on.

"If it's true, of course Colonel Marion will offer his services to the officer in command. So will I. I'm tired of running."

Celia thought what it would mean to know the British were gone, the country safe from more horrors like Bellwood. With a hopeful sigh she leaned back. Her head brushed Luke's arm, which lay across the back of the chair, and she felt him wince. She sat forward. "Are you hurt, Luke?"

"Scratched up a little. Moncks Corner, and another scrap at Lenud's Ferry. Almost well now. Mother has been bandaging me up."

Celia wondered where they had been seeing each other. No doubt in that space behind the wall, whatever it was. But Luke was not going to talk about that and it was no use asking him. She thought of Marion's lameness, and asked, "How are you getting around?—he can hardly walk."

"Horses. Back in the woods."

"You still have Jerry?"

"Not since Moncks Corner. I shot him myself before we ducked into the swamp. No man of Tarleton's was going to have Jerry. The governor gave me another."

She felt herself smiling as she asked, "And I suppose you gave him some crazy name out of the Bible?"

"Sure. His name is Bill."

"Bill? There's nobody in the Bible," exclaimed Celia, "named William!"

Luke chuckled. "Bill, short for Bildad the Shuhite."

"Who?"

"Bildad. In the Book of Job."

Celia began to laugh. It did not occur to her until later that this was the first time she had laughed since Jimmy died. Luke stood up, saying he had to leave now.

She stood up too. "I'm glad I had a chance to talk to you, Luke," she said. "It's done me good."

"If that's so, I'm glad too. And I want to tell you one thing more." Taking her hand in his again, he spoke with low-voiced assurance. "Celia, you haven't lost everything. You have plenty left."

She shook her head. "Like what, for instance?"

"Yourself," said Luke. Again she shook her head. He went on, "Jimmy used to talk about you a lot. He was proud of you. He said you had gumption."

"I haven't got any gumption," she said wearily.

"If you hadn't," said Luke, "I don't think Jimmy would have liked you. And if you had gumption before, you've got it still. All you need is to use it."

His words had a bracing effect. "Thank you, Luke," she said. "I'll try."

"And now," he said, "go upstairs, as softly as you came down. Go to your room. Don't try to see me leave."

Celia promised. She went out, up the stairs, and into her room. She shut the door silently.

In the closed room downstairs she had not noticed it, but here the air was fresher than it had been before. A breeze had started. Beyond the window the moss was swinging, the leaves were fluttering with a sound like the clapping of little hands. Celia took a deep breath, and stretched, and yawned. She went back to bed and to sleep.

The next day was clear and windy. Celia worked the flowers, but all morning she looked for a chance to go into the ballroom. After a while, when Herbert and Vivian set out for a walk, she thrust her trowel into the earth and hurried in, to examine the wall by the fireplace.

The paneling was oak, each panel about eight feet high and two feet wide and carved in a rectangular design. The structure was ingenious: every alternate panel stood out about an inch farther than the one on either side of it. Evidently one of the panels was made so it would slide across its neighbor, thus making a door. And this must lead to some exit from the house, letting Luke and Marion come and go in secret. How it was done she could not discover. But Vivian and Herbert were providing them with food, and maybe they were also acting as a center of information—Luke had said he had left a message. No wonder they had refused to go to Charleston.

Celia pressed her lips together tight. There was not much she could do to help get rid of the redcoats, but she could keep her mouth shut. She went back to the flowers.

## CHAPTER 20

*T*HAT AFTERNOON, Roy and Sophie made a call at Sea Garden. They came in a rowboat with a maid and manservant, and two other Negroes who helped with the rowing. Roy announced their arrival in the usual way by ringing the bell at the boat-landing, and waited until Herbert and one of his men rode to the landing to see who the visitors might be.

Gracious and charming, Roy begged that Mr. Lacy would forgive the trouble he was causing. Nothing but necessity would have made him intrude this way. But Sophie was expecting a baby, and she needed special consideration.

Roy explained that he had been serving as clerk and guide to a British officer, Major Edmore. They had been in Charleston, but recently Major Edmore had been put in command of a force that was now on its way by ship to a post on the north bank of the Santee. As Roy had to go along, he had obtained permission for Sophie to go too.

They had started early this morning and had hoped to finish their journey by dark. But the British sailors, not familiar with the sea islands, had not moved as fast as they expected, and now they had been forced to tie up for the night. Sophie and her maid were the only women on board, and the ship had no place fit for them to sleep. So, as they had tied up in the mouth of the little stream that led to Sea Garden, Roy had borrowed one of the ship's boats, hoping the Lacys would be kind enough to give his party a night's lodging.

His request could hardly be refused. Herbert ordered that a cart be brought to carry Mr. and Mrs. Garth and their servants to the house.

When she heard the names of the guests Celia fled to her room. But she had not been there long when she heard a knock, and Vivian came in. Closing the door behind her Vivian said, "I expect you to come to supper, Celia."

Celia shook her head.

"You're going to have to get used to facing people," said Vivian. "You might as well start."

Celia felt a wondering respect. Last night she had learned that Sea Garden was a refuge for Francis Marion. Roy was a Tory fawning for British favors. Vivian must be terrified, but she gave no sign of it. Celia thought, She doesn't know I know about Marion. Maybe that's better. We have to put on a brave front for each other. "Did you," she began—"did anybody tell Roy about—Jimmy?"

"No details," Vivian said kindly. "I suppose our servants will tell his, but I hope Roy and Sophie don't hear it until they've left." She went on to explain. Learning that Celia was a guest of the Lacys, Roy had asked assiduously about her welfare. Herbert had told him briefly that her fiancé had been killed in the war. Roy had said he was sorry to hear it.

"I bet he's sorry," Celia snapped. "He's sorry he's lost a chance to get a connection with a prominent family. Vivian, do I *have* to—"

"Yes," said Vivian. Celia thought of what Luke had said last night about Marion. Right now, Vivian too had an air of being nine feet tall.

A little later Marietta came to call her to supper. Marietta said, "Your kinfolks sure are nice, Miss Celia. Mr. Roy, he said he was sorry to be making extra trouble, and he slipped all the house-folk silver money."

She held out her hand to show an English shilling. It had been a long time since Celia had seen one, and she felt angry to see it now and be reminded that American dollars were no good any more.

But the evening was easier than she had expected. Roy was, as Herbert had described him, gracious and charming. Sophie, though her figure was clumsy, had as pretty a face as ever and was evidently doing her best to be agreeable. When Celia came downstairs they gave her a few words of sympathy about her loss, then tactfully dropped the subject.

Celia was glad to observe that Vivian had not fancied up her supper. The table was attractive, with its fresh cloth and bowl of flowers, but no more so than usual; and the meal was what Vivian had planned to serve, cold meats and hot cornbread, pitchers of buttermilk and platters of summer fruit. Vivian asked Sophie what it was like in Charleston now.

Sophie said it was very gay. There were so many British officers in town, and delightful men they were. Some of them were sons of *noblemen*, Sophie exclaimed with joyful awe. Everybody was having picnics, dinners, balls—in fact, there were so many entertainments, and so many extra men, that some girls went to several parties every evening, staying just long enough at each for a dance or two.

Listening, Celia felt sick. That brave defense forgotten. The defenders locked up on prison-ships while the girls danced with the enemies. The whole town gone Tory. Everybody licking the boots of the conquerors.

She wondered how Herbert liked hearing all this, with his beloved Tom on a prison-ship in Charleston harbor. Glancing at him, she saw only a courteous host attending to the wants of his guests. She marveled at his self-possession and Vivian's, and did her best to seem as poised as they were. But she was glad she had never been a chatterbox, so if she could not talk now they would think nothing of it.

Roy and Sophie seemed to be enjoying their supper. Roy was just asking Herbert if these delicious figs and peaches came from his own trees.

Herbert said yes, and went on to ask Roy more about how things were in Charleston.

Roy said the town had never been more prosperous. Any man

who wanted a job could get one at good pay. The stores were open and you could buy anything you wanted. When the British came in, a number of British wholesale merchants had come too, bringing every sort of goods, which they had sold to Charleston storekeepers.

Sophie said that after the half-empty stores of wartime it was such a joy to have plenty of nice things again. While they were in Charleston she had had some lovely clothes made for her expected baby. At Mrs. Thorley's, of course. Oh yes, Mrs. Thorley's shop was open and everybody was so glad of it. Celia felt a pinch at her heart. Last summer it had been Audrey who ordered baby-clothes from Mrs. Thorley's.

When they finished supper Herbert asked Roy if he would care for a glass of brandy. Celia went with Vivian and Sophie into the parlor.

The summer sun was a long time setting. Sophie chattered, telling Vivian how grateful she was for this hospitality. "You've given us a beautiful room," she exclaimed.

Vivian replied that she hoped they would be comfortable. It was a shock, she knew, to be unexpectedly benighted on a journey.

"It's really Roy's fault," Sophie said with a giggle. "He told Major Edmore we could make the whole trip in a day, and he should have known better. I *told* him we couldn't, I *said* we ought to make some provision for spending the night on board. But you know how men are, they won't take advice from a woman. So now we have to inconvenience you."

Vivian assured her that it was no inconvenience. They had plenty of room, and they enjoyed hearing the news from Charleston.

With the skill of a practiced hostess she encouraged Sophie to go on talking. Celia did her best to keep her face blank, but her thoughts were almost shouting. *Roy meant to get delayed here. What does he want?*

Roy and Herbert came in. Roy asked if he might take Sophie for a stroll. She needed regular walks and she had had no chance for one today.

They went out. A moment later they could be seen in the sunset afterglow, sauntering under the trees.

Herbert took the place Sophie had left. There was a brief silence. Now that Herbert and Vivian were letting themselves relax, both their faces showed lines of strain.

Celia spoke abruptly. "Vivian—I want you to know, I heard what she said."

Herbert glanced questioningly at Vivian, who told him, "You were right. Sophie is too simple-minded to guess it, but it looks as if Roy got stranded here on purpose."

"You were right?" Celia repeated. "How did you know?"

"Well, it *is* a long trip, too long for one day," Herbert returned, "and also—" he smiled shrewdly—"dear child, no honest man needs to be *that* charming."

Vivian had dropped her head on her hand. Celia thought a lesser woman would have been having hysterics about now. She herself could guess how important the secrecy about Luke and Marion must be, since Vivian had not taken even Godfrey into her confidence. And they could not have gone very far since last night.

The dusk was gathering. Roy and Sophie came indoors, and to Celia's relief Roy said that as they had to start early in the morning they would go early to bed.

When Celia had undressed and blown out her candle, she opened her bedroom door carefully. The hall was even darker than it had been last night, for the moon had not yet risen. Vivian had given Roy and Sophie a room across the hall. Under their door Celia could see a line of light. While she watched, the light disappeared.

She waited and waited. Everything was quiet. They must have gone to bed and to sleep. At last she went back into her room, leaving the door ajar so she could hear if Roy started spooking around outside. She lay down in bed, but she did not feel sleepy.

All of a sudden it was morning. Celia blinked, and raised herself on her elbow. She had been so certain she was going to stay awake, at least until the small hours after midnight. But after her long wakefulness of the night before she had been more tired than she had realized. Her door still stood ajar as she had left it. Maybe Roy had not stirred from his room in the night, but he was certainly stirring now. This was what had waked her. It was early, the sun just appearing, but Roy was making ready to leave. She heard him in the hall, telling Sophie's maid to carry something, and his manservant to carry something else. Celia sprang out of bed and hurried to get dressed. She wanted to see them go.

As he had been yesterday, Roy was smooth and charming. Sophie prattled—she was so very grateful, they must come to see her sometime, where on earth had she put her scarf, dear dear she hardly knew what she was doing, she wasn't used to being up at this hour and she was only half awake.

Vivian said she quite understood, she wasn't used to being up so early either. Vivian was calm as always, but she did not look well. Her face was drawn, and there were shadows under her eyes. Celia guessed that she had spent last night guarding that secret entrance to the ballroom.

Roy and Sophie and their servants took Herbert's cart to the landing. Herbert rode alongside on horseback, and the driver brought the cart back alone, saying Mr. Lacy had gone for a ride.

Vivian went to her room. Celia set about working the flowers. She thought Vivian was catching up on her sleep, but when the first sound of hoofs told her Herbert was returning, Vivian came hurrying across the porch. She fairly ran to meet him as he dismounted.

"The ship is gone," said Herbert. "They're aboard."

Vivian let out a sigh of relief that was like a sob. "You're sure?"

"Sure. It's an ordinary small troopship. Headed north toward the Santee, just as he said."

Vivian pressed her hands to her temples. Celia was pretty sure she was pressing a wild headache between them. Dropping her garden shears Celia hurried to where Vivian and Herbert stood. "Can I help?" she asked.

"Yes," said Herbert. "Go make her a milk punch. And if you make it double strong it won't hurt her a bit."

Celia ran to obey. It was good to do something. But how much longer, she wondered, could they keep this up? And what, oh what did Roy want here? Oh General Washington, *please* send that army!

•◞•

He was sending it—early in August Darren brought news that he had, in fact, sent it. The troops were now crossing North Carolina, and Darren was on his way to join them.

Darren rode up to Sea Garden on an afternoon of pouring rain. Tired, hungry, drenched with mud, mounted on a skinny little mare, Darren was nevertheless in his usual happy frame of mind. He told them it was a hard matter these days to get out of Charleston. When Cornwallis heard the Americans were coming, he had locked up the town. Nobody could leave without a pass signed by Colonel Balfour, city commandant. No ship-captain could take out anybody but the crew he had brought with him, and roads on the land side were heavily guarded.

However, since people must eat, passes had to be given to fishermen and to farmers driving produce wagons. Darren had slipped out in a wagon on its way back home, hidden under the sacking that the driver had laid over his fruit-baskets that morning to keep off flies. Darren had chosen a steamy day of clouds and mosquitoes, when the guards in their woolen uniforms were so miserable that they were nearly out of their minds, and not too careful about inspecting. Once past the guards, the driver was enriched with money supplied by Godfrey, and Darren went looking for a horse.

Darren told them Godfrey was eager to aid the new army, but it was not so simple for Godfrey to get out of town as for an obscure fellow like himself. Godfrey and Ida had two British officers billeted in their home, and his absence from the dinner-table would be noticed at once. They would probably find him and bring him back before he had even tried to pass the guards.

However, said Darren, Godfrey and Ida were mighty fortunate in their billets. Some of the men quartered in private homes were behaving like pigs. But others were gentlemen, and the Bernards had two of these.

Celia heard this unwillingly. She did not want to hear anything good about any man on the same side as Tarleton.

237

"What about Tarleton?" she asked.

Darren gave a shrug. Tarleton, he said, was behaving just as might be expected. He had established himself in the home of a woman whose husband was a prisoner of war. Tarleton had made his hostess and her children—four children, of both sexes—all eat and sleep in one room, while he used the rest of the house to give parties for his officer friends and an assortment of harlots. When the poor woman pleaded that she be allowed to use two rooms, if only for the sake of decency, Tarleton replied that rebels deserved no consideration. It had been a matter of great pleasure to the patriots of Charleston when Tarleton came down with malaria. Unfortunately he did not die of it, but they were glad he was miserable for a few weeks.

Darren spent the night at Sea Garden and left the next day. After this, for three weeks they heard nothing at all.

Wretched weeks they were, hot and full of rain. The creeks overflowed, the woodland turned to a bog. They might as well have been in prison. Neither friends nor enemies could reach them. Vivian told Celia that Luke and Marion, with some others, had gone to join the army, and Celia, remembering Luke's request, did not say she had heard this already. They did not know how many men Marion had with him, but they did know the men were ready to fight like fiends.

But this was all they knew.

Herbert sought refuge in his books. Vivian read too, and played the spinet by the hour. They both devised tasks to keep the servants busy, for the Negroes found it as hard as the white folks to bear this dragging isolation. Celia thought she had never felt so restless. As she could work outdoors only now and then, she begged for something else to do, and was glad when Vivian gave her the household mending. Day after day they prayed for the new army, and peered through the streaming window-panes for a messenger who might bring them news.

At last the rain stopped. The sun appeared, and with it came a wind from the sea. On a bright morning at the end of August they heard the clang of the landing-bell.

The folk at Sea Garden were so thirsty for news that they all, black and white, dropped whatever they were doing and ran toward the landing. Those who got there first stopped and stared. Those coming up behind, who could not see yet, heard a long deep groan of despair. They ran on, calling "What's the news?" But the folk on the landing had not needed to ask the news. They saw it.

They saw a ramshackle rowboat, such a wretched thing that they wondered how it had made any journey at all. In the boat were seven beaten men, and by the landing-bell an eighth. Their clothes were caked with blood, and every man of them had an arm or leg tied up with rags. It was Darren who had rung the bell. He had barely managed to ring it, because he had only one arm he could use. The other arm hung in a sling made of cloth torn from his shirt.

Darren was saying thickly, "Please help us." He leaned on the upright that held the bell, too tired to stand up any longer. There were a hundred questions, but all Darren could answer was, "This time it's *really* over."

Herbert ordered the cart, and brought the men to the house. While he worked with the Negro horse-doctor, Vivian tore up cloth for bandages, and Celia helped the maids bring food and pitchers of milk. At last they got the men cared for. That afternoon, Darren told them the story.

He said Washington had sent down a force of Maryland and Delaware Continentals. The men were well-trained, well-equipped, veterans of many battles. There were no better fighters in the army. On their way they had been joined by militia from Virginia and North Carolina. Cornwallis was to be attacked by a first-class force.

Congress had agreed with Washington when he chose this army from among his finest troops. But Congress had overruled his choice of a general. Washington wanted to send Nathanael Greene, the fighting Quaker who had won distinction at the battles of Trenton and Brandywine, and even more distinction in the thankless job of quartermaster-general. But Congress said no. They gave the command to Horatio Gates.

Gates was popularly called "the hero of Saratoga." But Washington was not the only military man who thought he did not deserve to be called a hero. True, the battle of Saratoga had been a great American victory and Gates had been there. But the soldiers said Gates had merely been there. They said the victory had been won by other officers who did not have Gates' talent for talking about themselves.

However, Congress chose Gates.

The army left Washington's camp in New Jersey under the leadership of the Baron de Kalb, a brilliant German who had come to America early in the war to aid the rebels. De Kalb led them as far as North Carolina, where Gates joined them and took command. Here, too, Francis Marion and about twenty of his friends rode in. Luke was among them.

Marion's men did not look pretty. Fugitives in the swamps for months past, they had broken their shoes and torn their clothes, and they were gaunt from scanty fare. They had good horses, but the horses, too, were hungry. Half the men had no guns, and those who did had no powder or shot to put into them.

Their leader did not look pretty either. In his months of eluding the British, slipping from swamp to cabin to plantation house, hiding under haystacks and horse-blankets, Marion's broken ankle had had small chance to heal. He limped grotesquely. His own clothes had fallen apart, and he now wore a pair of somebody's breeches, much too large, and a red coat somebody else had taken from a British soldier. He had neither comb nor razor, and no soap.

Baron de Kalb welcomed him. General Gates did not.

Gates had a self-assurance that amounted to self-worship. He had come to beat Cornwallis and he had no doubt that he was going to do it. He was not familiar with this part of the country, but that bothered him not at all.

Marion had been born in the region now held by the British under Cornwallis. He knew the roads and rivers, the best places to get food, the temper of the people. He had come to tell Gates what he knew. Gates was not interested.

As Marion was a fellow-officer of the Continental Army, Gates could not refuse to see him. But Gates had already made up his mind. Cornwallis was marching toward the British post at Camden. Gates had decided to go at once to meet him, give him a beating, and then march in triumph to Charleston.

Marion urged him not to be in such a hurry. The men had already marched four hundred miles in summer heat. Marion advised him to let them rest, and to give the militia more training before he made them face the British regulars. Gates was bored.

Choosing a bad road—and ignoring Marion and everybody else who told him there were better ones—he led his men through North Carolina, and made camp just about the South Carolina line. Here, by a stroke of luck, he had a chance to get rid of Marion.

Into camp came a messenger from Kingstree. He brought word that the men of the Kingstree neighborhood were organizing to fight, and they wanted an experienced leader. They had sent him to ask for Marion.

Fine, fine, said General Gates. Let Marion go right on and take charge of those men, and he had just the job for them. When he had won his victory—which he would do in a few days now— the British would naturally try to escape to the coast. Let Marion lead his men to the rivers and destroy all the boats he could find. With the boats gone, the British could not get away. They would be rounded up and made prisoners.

Marion did not say what he thought of this order. Gates was the commander and Marion had to obey. With his ragamuffin band Marion rode out of camp.

Thus it came about that Marion was not present at the battle of Camden, where Gates led his troops into the worst defeat an American army had taken since the war began.

Gates was so eager for his triumph that he would not wait to drill the militia. He would not wait to collect decent food supplies, nor even give his men time for proper cooking of the food they had. On the morning of the battle half his splendid veterans were so sick they could hardly stand. As for the militiamen, besides being queasy with bellyaches, many of them had never been in battle before, and they were so ill-trained that when they met the British they did not know what to do.

The battle did not last two hours. The men were cut to pieces, the ground strewn horribly with their dead and dying bodies. Those who lived to run away were chased for twenty miles by Tarleton and his cavalry.

Baron de Kalb fought until he fell with eleven wounds. He lived three days more, humanely tended by British surgeons under orders of Cornwallis, who knew a great soldier when he saw one, and gave him honor. As for Gates, he galloped away in blue panic. Mounted on a racehorse, he did not stop till he had gone seventy miles. As soon as he could find a fresh horse he started again, and he kept running until in three days he had gone two hundred miles from Camden. He never came back.

◦⤙•

"And now?" asked Herbert.

"God knows," said Darren.

The four of them—Herbert and Vivian, Darren and Celia— sat by a front window in the glow of late aftenoon. Two men who had come with Darren had been put to bed; the others, whose wounds were less severe, sat on the lawn planning how they were going to get home.

Darren had fought with the militia. As they staggered away from Camden this chance group had found the ramshackle boat tied up at a landing not yet reached by Marion's men. They took it and fled. In pain and nearly starved, sometimes they rowed, sometimes drifted, sometimes hid in the bushes while British horsemen galloped past. Often they saw smoke rising from some country house that was being looted and destroyed, for the British were dealing terrible punishment. Darren thought of Sea Garden, so out of the way that the redcoats had probably bypassed it. He led the others on, by crooked streams, through the pouring rain, till they got here.

Darren leaned back in his chair, his left arm in a sling, his handsome face sunken with weariness. He added that he might as well tell them all the bad news—here was a bit brought by the Continentals from Washington's headquarters. Remember the French fleet, which they had so yearningly awaited in Charleston? Well, it had finally reached America. Heading for Charleston, the fleet met an outgoing ship which brought word that the British had already taken the city. The French commander turned north and put in at Newport, Rhode Island, to wait for orders. Three days later a British fleet reached Newport. Finding the French in the harbor the British had to anchor outside the entrance. So now there they were. The king's men could not get in, the Frenchmen could not get out. The two fleets just sat there, making each other useless.

Celia looked around at the others. Darren, though slumped with defeat, was saying he was lucky to have only a trivial wound. Vivian and Herbert, though sick at the story of Camden, were glad that Luke had gone with Marion and that Tom was a prisoner, so neither of them had been there. Everybody, thought Celia, has something to be happy about. Everybody but me.

She remembered how glad she had been to hear that Gates' army was on the way. They could not have given her back Jimmy, but if they had chased out the British they would have given her a sense of being free again. But they had failed. She had nothing.

She turned to Herbert. "Mr. Lacy, have we lost the war?"

Herbert spoke gravely. "Washington sent us the best he had. And pretty nearly *all* he had."

Celia did not want to hear any more. She left them and went to the side porch, out of sight of the soldiers on the lawn.

In front of her she saw the gold and copper sky. The air was rich with the scent of honeysuckle, and she could hear birds chirping their evening songs. Such a beautiful world and such horrible things happened in it.

She knew now what she had to do. She had to go back to work at Mrs. Thorley's. Sophie had said the shop was open. There was plenty of trade, and Mrs. Thorley would be glad to have her. And she needed work—she had no money but a few American bills, good for nothing now but to start the kitchen fire.

How she dreaded going back. She could just imagine what it would be like with the other girls. Dutiful sympathy, and under it smirks of triumph. Oh, she thought she was going to marry a rich man. Yes, and once she got in with those people she forgot about her old friends. She didn't invite any sewing-girls to that ball New Year's Eve. Well, it just goes to show you. Doesn't do to put on airs too soon.

But that would not be all. They would talk like this for a while, then they would find something else to smirk about. That would not last forever. But the job in the shop—that would last, and last, and last. She thought of Miss Loring and Miss Perry, old maids who weren't ever going to have any fun. Now she would be like them. In a few years more, the younger girls would be whispering, I hear that once she had a beau, but he died. They would giggle. You mean Miss Garth? I don't believe any man was ever in love with that scrawny fussbudget.

And she would wither away. One of our old and valued employees.

Oh Miss Loring, was it like this for you?

# CHAPTER 21

*V*IVIAN APPROVED of Celia's decision to go back to Charleston. "There's no solace like work," she said. Celia smiled politely, but she was not impressed. She envied Vivian, who was so rich she did not need to work.

Herbert's son Eugene rode over one day to see how they were, and Vivian asked if he knew anybody who could take Celia to Charleston. Eugene said two neighbors of his, Mr. and Mrs. Kirby, were planning to go to town shortly. Eugene and Mr. Kirby were old friends, and still liked each other in spite of the fact that Mr. Kirby favored the king.

Those Tories, Celia thought angrily. It did seem that Fate was making every circumstance as unpleasant for her as possible. She envied Darren, who was a man and could ride to town by himself.

She packed her belongings. There was one box that she had not opened since she went to Bellwood to be married. It held her emerald necklace and the bracelets of gold roses Jimmy had given her; and also, folded in a covering of heavy muslin, the cravat she had made for him. The necklace she looked at sadly. Probably Roy really would get his hands on it now and give it to Sophie. She glanced at the bracelets, and quickly shut the case. If she ever saw Miles again she would give them back. They were family treasures and she was not part of the family.

But when she foolishly opened the muslin covering and saw the cravat, and remembered how many hours of her life she had put into it and what happy hours they had been—then it was as if an animal was clawing into her bosom and tearing her heart out. She took the cravat between her hands and ripped it to pieces. As she yanked at the cloth it seemed to her that in destroying her beautiful creation she was also destroying her girlhood and her young dreams. She took the shreds out to the kitchen and burned them in the cook-fire.

Before she left she gave the rabbit's foot to Marietta. "Keep it for Amos," she said, "to remember Mr. Jimmy by."

Marietta wrapped the silver chain around the rabbit's foot and put it into her pocket. When she looked up there were tears in her eyes. "Miss Celia, if you should hear anything about Amos—"

"Yes, of course," Celia promised. "I'll get word to you." She envied Marietta, who still had somebody to live for.

Eugene sent a note to Mr. Kirby, who wrote back that their schooner would stop for Miss Garth on the way to town. When they came to Sea Garden they made only a brief pause, and Mr. Kirby avoided mention of politics. Mrs. Kirby, pretty as ever with her green eyes and red hair, chattered about her clothes and her children. She now had two children, her little boy George, named for the king, and her new baby Freddie. She explained that Freddie also was named for the king, as "George William Frederick" was the full name of George the Third.

Herbert told Celia goodby with grave pleasantness, and gave her a volume of Shakespeare's comedies to amuse her leisure. Vivian said, "I've handed Mr. Kirby a note for Burton. You can stay with Burton and Elise until you're established at Mrs. Thorley's. Goodby, dear."

On the boat, Celia spent her time helping Mrs. Kirby's maids wait on her. Mrs. Kirby was not a deliberate snob; it merely would not have occurred to her that a working girl had any mission in life but to wait on her betters. At the Charleston wharf two redcoats came on board and asked Mr. Kirby to identify himself.

Mr. Kirby showed them a document signed by the British

commandant of the district where his plantation was located. This certified that Mr. and Mrs. Kirby were loyal subjects who during the late insurrection had given aid and comfort to his majesty's troops and who had permission to return to their town house. One of the redcoats scribbled a paper allowing them to land.

The harbor was busy with British ships. Ahead of her Celia saw Charleston, glowing like an opal in the evening sun. It would have been beautiful except for the black steeple of St. Michael's with the white scar where the shell had struck.

They went in a hired coach to the Kirbys' home on Broad Street. Before dark Burton called for Celia, and they walked to Vivian's house on Meeting Street. He told her his own house had been damaged by the firing, and so far—ahem, he cleared his throat—he had not been able to manage the repairs. She noticed that Burton still wore clothes too tight for him. Evidently he was not as prosperous as he used to be.

It seemed to Celia that they passed dozens of British flags and hundreds of men in red coats. I'll have to get used to it, she told herself. At the corner of Broad and Meeting Streets they passed the statue of William Pitt, with his left arm gone and the broken place at his shoulder like an open wound.

Elise told her it was so nice to see her again and she did hope Celia wouldn't mind sleeping in a little room on the third floor. It was all they had empty. The boys were with them, and also two officers were billeted here. British, yes, but really quite nice. The officers had gone to a party this evening. Really it was lucky that they were staying here, because Burton had not taken the oath of allegiance to the king, Godfrey had but not Burton, and sometimes things were made quite unpleasant for men who had not taken the oath. But with two officers in the house things were so much simpler. The maid would show Celia to her room and would she please hurry down again because supper was nearly ready.

Celia was washing up when suddenly she stopped, the cake of soap between her hands. Elise had said Godfrey had taken an oath of allegiance to the king. Celia thought of Godfrey's patriotism during the siege. But now he had given in. And from the way Elise spoke, probably a lot of other patriots had too. I'll have to get used to it, Celia told herself again.

The next morning she wrote to Mrs. Thorley, saying that her fiancé had been killed in the war and she would like to come back to work. A servant of Burton's took the note to the shop and brought back a reply. Mrs. Thorley said she was distressed by the news, but would be glad to have Celia's services again. She asked Celia to call this afternoon. Godfrey and Ida had come in to see her, and Godfrey said he would tell Darren to come over and walk with her to the shop.

Not long after dinner a maid came to tell Celia that Darren was in the reception room. She hurried down. Darren was well dressed and looked as merry as ever, but as he crossed the room to meet her she noticed that he limped and carried a cane. When she asked why, he said he was still having a little trouble from the leg-wound he had received during the siege.

"Oh!" she said, surprised, for she had not noticed Darren limping when she saw him at Sea Garden. "You mean the night you moved the—"

"Shh!" Darren said quickly. He beckoned her nearer, and gave her a smile of conspiracy as he whispered, "It's still there. Walled up. No sense in telling them."

Celia smiled back. It was a pleasure to know there were ten thousand pounds of gunpowder in the Exchange, which the king's soldiers would like to use to shoot rebels but which they had not found. It was even more of a pleasure to observe that Darren was still loyal to the patriot side. But her bright thoughts were darkened at once, for Darren said briskly,

"First we'll go to the office on Queen Street so you can swear in as a British subject."

"What?" she exclaimed. "Me?"

"Didn't they tell you?"

Celia shook her head.

Darren made her sit down by him on the sofa. He told her that if you did not declare yourself a good subject of King George you could not hold a job or engage in business. He pushed aside the curtain so she could see carpenters repairing a house damaged during the siege. Those men might have principles, said Darren, but they had taken the king's oath because without a paper in your pocket saying you had done this, you could not earn a living.

"Have you done it?" she asked shortly.

"Oh yes. Everybody has, except a few men so rich they don't need to work."

"Like Burton," Celia said with astonished respect. So this was why he had not repaired his suburban home and had not bought new clothes. He was holding out.

"Yes," said Darren, but he added seriously, "I'm afraid even men like him are going to have to give in. Colonel Balfour—the city commandant—arrested about forty rich men the other day and shipped them to the British fort at St. Augustine, because they hadn't taken the oath. Since then every man who hasn't taken it is afraid of being exiled, and a lot of them have been swearing in so they can stay with their families."

There was a silence. Celia wondered if he was trying to justify Godfrey. She thought Godfrey was rich enough to live without working, but she could not imagine his doing so. Activity was his life.

She was amazed at Darren's attitude. He had slipped out of town in a farm cart so he could fight for his country, and now he talked about taking the king's oath as though it was like signing a receipt for goods. Maybe he did have to take the oath, because he had his living to earn, but he might have shown some anger at the British for making him do it.

Then she asked herself, Why am I finding fault with Darren? He says I've got to take the oath too. I suppose if I had a really noble character I'd proudly refuse. Yes, and then what? I can't ask Burton to support me, he's got all he can do taking care of his family. And Godfrey, he'd tell me to go ahead and take the oath same as he did. So what could I do? Beg my bread from door to door and sleep in an alley and get arrested for vagrancy? Well, I'm not *that* noble. I'll swear in. They've killed Jimmy and wrecked Bellwood and ruined my life and now they're making me kneel down and kiss their boots. Oh, I hate them for making me do it and I hate myself for doing it.

Darren had limped to the door and was waiting for her. Celia stood up. "All right," she said. "I'll go with you."

A building on Queen Street had been partitioned into small

offices for the king's troops. Darren showed Celia into a room where two bored-looking redcoats lounged at desks. Darren spoke to one of them, showed his own paper, and said that Miss Garth wanted to take the king's protection and resume her former employment.

The redcoat yawned, asked her name and age and wrote them in a ledger, yawned again, asked where she wanted to work, and wrote that too. Then he said, "Raise your right hand do you solemnly swear bumble bumble bumble bumblebumblebumble." Celia put her left hand into her pocket and crossed her fingers, held up her right hand and answered "Yes." The redcoat took a printed form out of a drawer, filled in the information she had given him, put on an official stamp, and handed her the paper. As she took it he rubbed his eyes sleepily and asked the other redcoat what time it was. Celia and Darren started for Mrs. Thorley's shop.

Celia was shocked at the look of the town. The streets had been cleared, but at the corners were piles of bricks and broken glass and other trash, not even yet carried away though the siege was four months past. Some stores were open and doing good business, but others still had boards nailed across the doors and windows. Repairs on damaged buildings were makeshift: windowpanes had been replaced by oiled paper or sheets of tin, chimneys mended with pieces of brick stuck unevenly together, woodwork painted badly or not at all. The whole place looked tired and sick. Just the way I feel, she thought.

It was late afternoon, the fashionable hour for shopping and driving, and the streets were full of people. Here and there Celia saw redcoated soldiers on guard. Others, off duty, idled along the sidewalk or leaned on the walls, watching the people go past. They eyed her with such meaningful glances that she understood why Godfrey had sent Darren to be her escort. She saw officers accompanied by well-dressed ladies and gentlemen. Several of these she recognized as customers of the shop, and she thought, Now I'll be making their clothes and I'm no better patriot than they are.

At the shop she went to the side door, trying not to remember the gray Sunday afternoon when she and Jimmy had come to this door together and he had kissed her in the little hallway. Darren said he would leave her now.

He limped down the steps and away. Celia looked after him. It was really odd about that limp. She was sure he had not had it when she saw him at Sea Garden.

•~•

In Mrs. Thorley's office you would not have thought anything had happened. Mrs. Thorley sat at her desk, large, calm, starched. The room was in perfect order. The windows even had all their panes. Either this building had been mighty fortunate or Mrs. Thorley had managed to get some glass from somewhere; knowing Mrs. Thorley, Celia rather imagined it was the latter.

Mrs. Thorley greeted her as if Celia were reporting for duty after a holiday. "Come in, Miss Garth. I hope you are well?"

"Yes, Mrs. Thorley, thank you."

Celia stood respectfully before the desk. It had seemed the same. But it was not the same. Mrs. Thorley was saying, "I trust you have taken the king's protection, Miss Garth?"

Celia felt a twitch of shame as she answered, "Yes, Mrs. Thorley."

"May I see your paper, please?"

Celia handed it over.

"This seems in order," Mrs. Thorley said crisply, and returned it. She folded her large hands on the desk. "Take a chair, Miss Garth."

Celia sat down. She crossed her ankles and laced her fingers on her lap. It was like that other afternoon a year ago when Mrs. Thorley had summoned her to say she had received a letter from Mrs. Lacy.

But again, it was different.

This time the difference was in Mrs. Thorley herself. She had not spoken twenty words when Celia realized that Mrs. Thorley no longer looked upon her as a beginner fit only for buttons and bastings, but as a dressmaker who knew her trade. Mrs. Thorley was actually asking her what sort of work she would like to do. She said there was now a plentiful supply of good materials, and they had more orders than they could fill—orders for dresses, and

*251*

fancy caps and kerchiefs, and the delicate little gauze aprons so fashionable just now, and gentlemen's fine shirts and sleeve-ruffles—

And as Mrs. Thorley talked, offering her the sort of work she had yearned for, Celia felt nothing at all.

She remembered with wonder, almost with disbelief, how she used to enjoy working in the shop. She remembered how she had sent up prayers that Mrs. Thorley would keep her here, how she had schemed to prove that she was worth keeping. How she had dreamed of the day when they would give her the fine sewing she could do so well. And now she did not care. Embroidery or bastings, it did not matter. She remembered a proverb. "When you get what you want, you don't want it."

Mrs. Thorley was still talking.

However, she said, last year Miss Garth had been very good at minding the parlor. Not every young lady could receive the visitors with just the right manner, gracious and yet distant. And at present, circumstances were perhaps more difficult than usual. Of course, in the parlor, with its frequent interruptions, Miss Garth would not be able to do the sort of work that required close attention. Mrs. Thorley asked Celia which she preferred.

Celia did not hesitate. In the parlor something was happening all day long. She would have no time to sit and remember. She chose the parlor.

Mrs. Thorley nodded gravely. She said Celia's trunk had been brought over by a servant of Mr. Dale's, and had been put into her old room. Miss Todd and Miss Duren were there, and Miss Kennedy was expected back. Mrs. Thorley made a note in a ledger. "Then this is all, Miss Garth."

Celia stood up. "Thank you, Mrs. Thorley." She curtsied and went to the door. As she reached her hand toward the doorknob Mrs. Thorley said, "Miss Garth."

Celia turned toward her again. "Yes ma'am?"

Mrs. Thorley's face was large and calm like the rest of her. She said, "You have my sympathy, Miss Garth."

"Thank you ma'am," said Celia. She supposed people felt they had to say something, yet she wished they would not; every word of commiseration was like a finger touching the wound. Mrs. Thorley's deep voice was speaking again.

"It is hard to lose the person one loves."

"Yes ma'am," said Celia. She thought, Oh hush! You'll make me cry and I don't want to cry any more.

Mrs. Thorley said, "I remember well." Her voice had softened strangely. "So many years, and sometimes it still seems like yesterday."

Celia's eyes had stretched wide, but there were no tears in them; she was gazing at Mrs. Thorley in astonishment. The woman meant what she said. Mrs. Thorley had been kissed often, and with love.

Mrs. Thorley said, "I wish I could make it easier for you, Miss Garth. But I cannot. I can only say again, you have my sympathy."

In a low voice Celia answered, "Thank you, Mrs. Thorley." Somehow she knew those words had been hard for Mrs. Thorley to speak. Mrs. Thorley never showed any weakness. She could not afford to. For the first time it occurred to Celia that maybe Mrs. Thorley was not naturally made like a man-of-war, she had had to make herself that way. Celia spoke again. She said, "You have my sympathy too, Mrs. Thorley. I think you're mighty brave."

Mrs. Thorley ran the tip of her tongue over her lips. Her hands moved a trifle. It struck Celia that Mrs. Thorley was embarrassed and did not like the feeling. Celia thought she had better get out of here. She curtsied again, and Mrs. Thorley gave her a nod of dismissal.

Celia went out, closing the door softly. She felt certain that they were not going to talk about this subject again.

After this, she half expected Miss Loring to make some confidence, and maybe Miss Perry too. But they did not. They spoke brief words of sympathy and no more, and Celia never found out if either of them had ever had a lover. She reflected that they probably felt it was none of her business, and they were right.

And so in those bright blue days of September, 1780, Celia went back to her job of minding the parlor.

It was not quite the same job nor the same parlor. Charleston was a town held by troops. They were a conquering army, they were a long way from home, and many of them considered that they were privileged to do exactly as they pleased. Mrs. Thorley had changed the parlor accordingly.

Across the room from wall to wall there was now a balustrade nearly as high as Celia's chest, standing between the front door and the doors that led into the rest of the building. In front of the balustrade—so as not to dismay her legitimate customers—Mrs. Thorley had placed attractive furniture: comfortable chairs, a table with a bowl of flowers, the cabinets with their tempting displays. But the balustrade itself was broad and sturdy, and to get past it you had to go through a gate that could be opened only from inside. Across this barrier, Celia greeted all visitors with a smile. But within call was always Miss Loring or one of the older seamstresses, who could provide, when necessary, an atmosphere of ice and vinegar.

Celia never went to the front side of the gate during business hours. If someone wanted a closer look at a sample in one of the cabinets, she took a duplicate from a case on her side of the rail and handed it across. This custom had been in effect since a day when a couple of smart-alecky British lieutenants had asked Miss Loring to show them samples of linen shirting. Miss Loring went around to open the cabinet indicated, and when she bent over the lock one of the smarties thought it a fine joke to pinch her skinny bottom.

But there was not much of this sort of thing. Most of the redcoats who came in were escorts of Tory ladies, and behaved well enough. They sat in front of the balustrade swapping stories, or they mopped their foreheads and complained about the weather, or asked Celia for the *Gazette* to pass the time. The newspaper these days was edited by a Tory, and he had changed its name to *The Royal South Carolina Gazette*. He printed official announcements, news of parties attended by British officers, and reports of great British victories in parts of the country where the king's men were still fighting the troops of "Mr." Washington.

In the shop itself, life had not changed much. Mrs. Thorley still served milk. She still forbade discussion of the war. Several of the girls had not returned since the siege and new ones had replaced them, but this could have happened any time. The longer

Agnes Kennedy stayed away the better Celia liked it. She was in no mood to put up with Agnes Kennedy's sweet disposition, not now when she herself felt nothing but a black helpless hate.

She hated Charleston and everybody in it.

The city commandant, Lieutenant-Colonel Nisbet Balfour, was a fattish offensive man with a nasty reputation. People said of him that he had won his laurels while the British occupied Philadelphia. At that time Balfour had served as procurer of women for his commander, Sir William Howe, as well as for other leaders of the king's troops. He did this duty so well that they promised him he would not be forgotten when the plums were passed around. So now Balfour was lord of Charleston.

Under such a ruler, the town had lost its old decency. The streets were dirty. There were more taverns than ever before. Near the southeastern docks there had been a bad fire two years ago, and because of wartime shortage of materials much of the burnt area had not been rebuilt; now this was a community of shacks where women both white and colored received the soldiers. Even the better parts of town swarmed with trollops.

From her window on the third floor, Celia could look over Charleston and see what was going on. The Lutheran Church on Archdale Street, and the lovely little Unitarian Church next door, were both being used as stables. The White Meeting House, for which Meeting Street had been named, was now a storehouse for army supplies. Horses were trampling on the graves in the churchyards. They kicked at the tombstones, and cracked them or knocked them over, and the stones lay broken among the weeds. Celia heard that the British army chaplains had protested to Balfour about this desecration, but if they had, he paid no attention.

St. Philip's and St. Michael's, as representing the established Church of England, had not been disturbed, but services were now conducted by clergymen who favored the king. People who did not want to join in prayer for the king's army, stayed home.

Celia stayed home. Looking out of her high window on Sunday mornings, she was disgusted at how many people she saw going into the churches. She knew, she just knew, there had not been that many Tories in Charleston before the British marched in.

But this sight was not the only one that disgusted her. Day after day she felt nauseated as she watched people in Charleston, in spite of all that was being done to them, toadying to their conquerors.

Of course there were some who had been on the king's side all the time. The Kirbys, the Torrances—if they welcomed the British now you could not be surprised. But the Baxters were inviting redcoat officers to dinner, and so were dozens of other families who used to be patriots. Even Godfrey Bernard was meeting the British with smiles, Ida was dancing at their balls— when she thought of it, and remembered Bellwood, Celia could almost feel her heart shrivel.

It seemed to her that nobody had any self-respect any more. Except maybe those men who had been sent to St. Augustine.

There were others who had tried to hold out. But a messenger brought a proclamation from the headquarters of Cornwallis at Camden. Cornwallis said that certain wealthy persons in South Carolina were persisting in their treasonable efforts. He therefore ordered that if you had not sworn allegiance to the king, and still refused to do so, your property would be confiscated and turned over to somebody who deserved it. A loyal subject of the king named John Cruden was put in charge of the confiscation, with the title Commissioner of Sequestrated Estates.

On the twenty-first of September, the *Royal Gazette* proudly published the names of one hundred and sixty-three men who had held to their principles as long as they could, but now had given in and taken the oath to save their property. The paper came while Celia was at dinner. When she returned to the parlor that afternoon she saw the announcement and the list. She did not read the names. She could not. She threw the paper on her worktable and walked over to a side window, where she stood pretending to adjust the curtain.

There were no customers in the parlor just now. Through the open window Celia could see redcoats walking and driving with well-dressed women whose husbands and fathers had taken the oath so they would not have to be poor. She heard a street-peddler calling that he had fine fresh grapes to sell.

Everybody, she thought, has something to sell. And the British and Tories and bootlickers have money to buy it. So we've quit. And I'm no better than anybody else. I'm working in a fashionable shop, smiling at the people who have money to spend, forgetting that I ever believed in anything.

She felt sick with contempt, contempt for herself and for her country.

Americans, she thought, are no good. We don't deserve to be free.

# CHAPTER 22

*S*HE HEARD the front door open. As she turned she saw Mrs. Kirby, crisp and pretty in flowered muslin, followed by a nursemaid carrying baby Freddie. Celia put on her pleasant professional smile and went to the balustrade. "How do you do, Mrs. Kirby."

Mrs. Kirby said how do you do, and didn't Celia think it was remarkable how Freddie had grown since they came to town, really he was so advanced that most people wouldn't believe he was only four months old, and today's *Gazette* had carried an announcement by Mrs. Thorley that a shipment of striped and printed silks had arrived and she would like to see them only she didn't have much time because they were going to have supper tonight with Mr. Kirby's parents and she had to get there early and arrange the flowers because Major Brace and Captain Woodley were going to be there and her mother-in-law wanted everything especially nice and she did hope the silks were ready to be seen because if they weren't ready she just couldn't wait.

Smiling graciously, Celia said the silks were ready. Before she had finished her sentence Mrs. Kirby's words were tumbling out again, this time addressed to the nurse.

"Then you can take Freddie on over to his grandma's. Mamma's 'ittle precious wanna go to danma's? Mamma's 'ittle precious be good? Mamma's 'ittle—" The door opened again and she broke off, "Why Emily, *darling!*"

The lady addressed as Emily was Mrs. Leon Torrance, wife of Sophie's brother. The Torrances had just come to town from their plantation, and Celia had seen Mrs. Torrance only once before, last week when she came in to order a dress. A pretty brunette, wearing white lawn with red stitching and a hat with a red plume, today Mrs. Torrance was accompanied by two British officers.

She introduced the officers to Mrs. Kirby, who showed off her baby while they murmured polite admiration. At length Mrs. Torrance said she simply must get upstairs for her fitting. The two officers, fanning themselves with their hats, said they would go over to that new tea-shop on Cumberland Street. It was so near the waterfront, maybe they would find a sea-breeze there to cool them off. This weather was murderous. They bowed themselves out, promising to call for Mrs. Torrance in an hour.

As the door closed, Mrs. Kirby looked after them petulantly. "They make me tired, always carrying on about the weather. Everybody knows *any* weather is better than what they get in England!"

"It's not the weather," said Mrs. Torrance, "it's those heavy woolen uniforms. They say the men at Camden are miserable, with all the outdoor patrolling they—"

"Oh for pity's sake," exclaimed Mrs. Kirby. "The supply officers are doing the best they can! They've got a shipment of lightweight clothes ready for Camden right now—I know because my husband arranged the purchase—the wagons were held up because they had to wait for some shoes but they're leaving here for Camden the first of October and that's *definite*. Shall we go up, darling? You know I'm in a *tearing* hurry—"

Celia opened the gate. Mrs. Kirby went through, then Mrs. Torrance, who smiled and said, "Thank you, Miss—why, I don't believe I know your name."

Before Celia could say anything Mrs. Kirby was saying it for her. "Why this is Celia Garth, she came to work here after you went to the country last year—"

"Garth?" repeated Mrs. Torrance, and Celia thought her face

showed a flicker of displeasure. But Mrs. Torrance said politely, "How do you do, Miss Garth," and Celia curtsied and said, "How do you do, Mrs. Torrance." She went to the staircase door and opened it, and they went through, Mrs. Kirby still rattling on.

"—have it made with a skirt of gray and green stripes and a plain green overskirt looped rather high—"

Celia returned to her table and took out the ruffle she was hemming. She was glad the British soldiers were suffering in their woolens. The temperature this afternoon was about eighty, not too hot if you wore summer clothes. But it must be awful in those heavy red coats and tight belts. She hoped the shipment destined for Camden would get lost, so the men there would have to go on suffering.

Oh, how she hated everybody. She hated Mrs. Kirby and Mrs. Torrance. She hated Mrs. Baxter, who came in and ordered some kerchiefs embroidered with her initial. C for Charlotte, said Mrs. Baxter, and Celia wondered if she thought they had forgotten how she used to dislike being called by the name of the British queen. Or maybe, as long as she was being socially accepted by the winning side, Mrs. Baxter just did not care.

She hated her old schoolmate Rena Fairbanks, who came in with three handsome young Britishers, red coats and high shiny boots and hair glistening white with powder. Rena said she wouldn't be a minute, so the men sat down in front of the balustrade to wait for her. Celia opened the gate. At the ball New Year's Eve Rena had been cordial, but today she acknowledged Celia's service with a cool smile. She did not want to be too friendly with a sewing-girl before these elegant aristocrats. All the British officers were aristocrats. They had to be. Even the most broadminded of them were astonished at the American army, where tailors and ironworkers held commissions and gave orders to the sons of gentlemen.

Celia returned to her sewing. She heard one of the redcoats saying the rebel soldiers on the prison-ship in the harbor were deserting by scores to join the Tory troops. Celia wondered if this was true. She knew the British were offering them all sorts of inducements to do so. Well, if it was true she wouldn't be surprised. Why expect the prisoners to be any better than their friends on shore?

The door opened again and three persons came in, a middle-aged couple and a young girl. The man and woman were stout and red-faced and elaborately dressed; the girl, about seventeen years old, was rather pretty, or would have been if she too had not been so overdressed in ruffles and silk flowers and gilt-buckled shoes. At sight of the British officers she giggled, her mother inclined her head as though in awe, and her father slapped the counter loudly, like a man in a tavern summoning the barmaid.

Celia set aside her workbasket and came in answer. The man announced that his name was Hendrix and he came from down Beaufort way. He said this was his wife Mrs. Hendrix and this was his daughter Miss Dolly, and the ladyfolks wanted to see some of them imported silks.

Celia said she would go upstairs and report their wants. Mr. Hendrix told her to step lively. And remember, he called after her, they wanted to see only the best. Don't waste their time showing them nothing but the best.

Celia went upstairs and told Miss Perry. Miss Perry exclaimed, "Dear dear, we do get such astonishing people in here nowadays," and asked Ruth Elbert to wait on the Hendrixes. Ruth went into the big display room, where the walls were lined with shelves piled with bolts of material. Putting several bolts of silk on the table she said acidly to Celia, "All right, bring them in here." Celia went down and told Mrs. Hendrix and Miss Dolly that the silks could be seen now.

Pulling out a fat purse Mr. Hendrix gave his wife a handful of money—"these working women always want at least half on account, you know." He went to the door, saying he had some business on Queen Street and he'd meet them later.

Miss Dolly had been trying to flirt with the British officers, who did not want to flirt with her and were making a desperate show of interest in the *Royal Gazette*. Celia opened the gate. Out of the corner of her eye she observed the men's relief as Miss Dolly and her mother went through.

At another time she might have been amused. Today she was

not. The Hendrixes were the sort of people she hated worse than redcoats. She had seen these newly rich Tories before, and she knew how they made their money. Mr. Hendrix had said he had business on Queen Street, which meant the British military office on Queen Street. And it made her sick.

It had come about because the more level-headed of the king's men had been trying to stop the looting of barns and smoke-houses. They knew the king's soldiers could not eat unless the people of the country raised food, and people would not raise food unless they had a fair chance to profit from their efforts. So officers in the country districts had received commands that when their men took supplies, they must pay for what they took.

To encourage food-growing, they paid rebels as well as Tories. But the payment was made by promissory notes, which could be exchanged for money only at the army office on Queen Street in Charleston.

This was all right for Tory planters. But hundreds of these notes were given to people who could not come to town to cash them. There were women whose husbands were dead or prisoners of war, who could not travel alone through a war-riddled country; there were men who had served with the rebel troops and could not get passes to travel at all. So their Tory neighbors, who did have passes, bought the notes for a fraction of their value, came to town, and redeemed them in full. Then they came into Mrs. Thorley's shop demanding nothing but the best. As Celia led the Hendrix women upstairs she wished she could push them back down the staircase and break their necks.

But she could not. She led them into the display room, curtsied respectfully, and went back to the parlor.

All afternoon she smiled and answered questions and went upstairs on errands. At last it was time for people to go home to supper. Mrs. Hendrix and Miss Dolly came down; Celia opened the gate, and curtsied as they swept grandly past her and away. Gradually the other customers left. Celia began to lock up.

She walked over to the side window and looked out. Oh, what a stately town it used to be, and how ugly it was now. She closed the window and locked it, and as she drew the curtain she heard the front door open.

She turned with annoyance. Nobody had any business coming in so late. But the caller was Darren, saying he had purposely called at the last minute because he had hoped to find her alone.

Still limping, he met her at the balustrade. "How are you?" he asked.

"All right," said Celia.

Darren looked at her keenly. Except for his limp he seemed like his old self: happy-faced, well dressed in brown linen coat and breeches, his hair brushed smooth and tied behind. As he looked her over he shook his head. "You don't look all right," he said.

"I'm tired," she returned, "and cross."

"Any special trouble?" he asked in his pleasant sympathetic way.

"No. Just everything."

"Maybe this will cheer you up," said Darren. "I've come to bring you an invitation. Godfrey and Ida want you to come to dinner Sunday. They're also having the Penfields, and me, if you're interested—"

"And Major Brace," she asked, "and Captain Woodley?" These were the two Britishers billeted in Godfrey's home. "And a few more redcoats? No I won't."

The room was getting dark, but she could see Darren frown with surprise. "Brace and Woodley are good fellows, Celia," he said. "You'll like them."

"No!" Celia said harshly. She had been keeping her feelings inside too long; now she let herself go. "I took their miserable oath. I'll be polite to the British and Tories who come into this shop because I've got to hold my job. But I won't sit at table with them when I don't have to, and I won't walk or ride or dance with them. I know everybody else has given in but I'm sick of everybody else."

Darren's face was grave now. As she paused he said in a low voice, "We didn't want to take that oath either, Celia. We had to."

Celia rested her elbows on the ledge that topped the balustrade. She dropped her forehead on her hands and pushed her fingers up through her hair. Without looking up she said,

"Oh, I know that. And I know we have to put up with the king's men. But we don't have to do what everybody's doing! Bowing and smirking—you'd think the king did us a favor by sending them over here to put us back in our place. Oh, I hate every man in a red coat or a green coat—but even worse I hate all these people who are groveling in front of them." She raised her head. "I feel so helpless, Darren! Like a worm being stepped on."

Darren picked up his cane, which he had leaned against the balustrade. Looking down, he moved the point of the cane on the floor as if drawing imaginary pictures. After a moment he looked up and spoke briskly.

"Look. I don't really want to go to Godfrey's Sunday. I'd rather be with you. Suppose I pick up some dinner somewhere, then come by here for you and we take a walk."

She smiled. It was her first genuine smile of the day. "Oh Darren, you're so nice! But your leg—won't that be hard on you?"

"We can rest in the corner park on Broad Street. Will you?"

"I'd love to."

"Good. And we can drop in for tea at that new place on Cumberland Street. They serve luscious buns with the tea. I'll call for you about three—right?"

She nodded and thanked him again, and Darren limped away. Celia went around to the front of the counter and locked the door. She felt better. But she was not sure she wanted to go to that new place on Cumberland Street. It would be full of redcoats drinking their everlasting tea, and Americans who had been patriots last year but who were now swilling tea by the quart to prove how much they loved the king. She did not want to drink tea with them. In fact, now that she thought of it, she did not want to drink tea at all.

Sunday was a gleaming day, a day for flowers and pretty clothes. Again Celia did not go to church. She washed her hair, and while it was drying she took out her prayer book and read the Bible lesson for the day.

Darren called for her, and they walked out among the other Sunday strollers. Darren had very little to say. Celia spoke of what nice weather it was, and how delicious the sweet-olive blooms smelt across the garden walls. But though Darren answered, he seemed to be thinking of something else. She was surprised. It was not like him to take a girl out and then not pay attention to her.

On Broad Street, at the corner in front of the great market, stood some fine old trees with benches under them, a favorite spot for people to rest and chat on pleasant days. Because of his stiff leg, Celia expected Darren to want to rest on the first empty bench they came to. But he did not; they roamed under the trees for several minutes before he suggested that they sit down.

He had chosen a bench under an oak heavily hung with moss. The tree cast a deep shadow, and the ground before them was slightly damp. When they sat down Darren still had almost nothing to say. He began drawing designs on the ground with the point of his cane, as if he had purposely chosen a seat where the ground was soft enough for this.

Celia tried to make conversation. "I wonder how Vivian's flowers are doing. If I were at Sea Garden now, I'd be planting stock and carnations."

"I don't know much about gardening," Darren said. "Is this the time to plant those?"

"Yes. September. You start in the week of the new moon."

"Why the new moon?"

"I don't know. Probably silly, but that's when it's done."

There was another pause. With his cane Darren made more curlicues on the ground, and then rubbed them out with his foot. Another couple on a bench near them got up and walked on. With a glance around him Darren stood up, saying, "Stay where you are, I just want to stretch my bad leg." He walked all the way around the tree, and as she turned to watch him she observed that nobody was sitting near them now.

Evidently this was what he had been waiting for. As he sat down again he said in a low voice, "Celia, I've got something to tell you."

She answered eagerly. "Yes, Darren?"

Again he was scratching absently on the ground. Watching his cane, he said in a careful undertone, "Keep your voice down— just loud enough for me to hear you."

"Oh," she said faintly. "All right."

Still watching the nonsense design he was drawing, Darren nodded. "That's it. And don't act surprised. Understand?"

Celia felt excited. She had no idea what she was about to hear, but it sounded important—in fact, Darren made it sound almost creepy. "I understand," she said.

"I've got a message for you," said Darren. He was still watching the ground.

"A message," she repeated breathlessly. "You mean a letter?"

"No, no, not a letter. A message."

"Who sent it?"

"Friend of yours. And *please*," Darren said through his teeth, "don't ask me who. Don't mention any names at all."

"All right," she said, just above a whisper. She added, "I'm listening."

With his foot, again Darren began smoothing out the curlicues on the ground. He asked, "You've got a Bible, haven't you?"

Celia caught her breath. This sounded like Luke. Darren was a dear, but he was no deep student of Scripture or anything else. No wonder he did not want her to speak Luke's name. Luke had been a fugitive with Marion, and if the British had not captured Marion after their victory at Camden they were certainly looking for him. If they should hear that Darren had been in touch with a friend of Marion's, they might throw him into jail and say he would stay there until he told them what he knew. Remembering that he had warned her not to show surprise, Celia smiled and said as quietly as she could, "Why yes, of course I've got a Bible."

Darren had leveled the ground in front of him till it was as smooth as a sheet of paper. "This friend of yours," he said, "told me to tell you to read a verse in the Bible. Look here, on the ground."

Again he began to make marks with his cane. But this time the marks were not squiggles; they were letters, firm and clear. He wrote, "I Kings." Celia understood. He wanted her to read something in the First Book of the Kings.

"Got that?" asked Darren.

"Yes," said Celia.

He rubbed it out. In its place he wrote, "19–18."

She understood that too. Nineteenth chapter, eighteenth verse. "All right," she said.

"Sure you won't forget?"

"I won't forget."

"And you won't speak of it?"

"Not to a living soul."

Darren rubbed out the figures, and drew more zigzags on the ground where they had been. Celia said in her mind, First Kings 19–18. Darren stood up. "Shall we go over to Mr. Westcott's tea-shop?" he asked.

"I'd rather go home," said Celia, "and—read the Bible."

"Anything you want," Darren agreed smiling. They started back toward Mrs. Thorley's.

Again they did not talk much, but this time Celia was glad of it. At the side door she said, "Thanks, Darren, it was a nice walk," and he answered, "I'll see you again soon."

Celia ran past the parlor and upstairs. On the third floor she ran to her room, praying that Pearl and Becky would be out, and they were. She snatched up her Bible from the table where she had left it this morning.

She had run up the stairs so fast that her chest hurt from lack of breath and her hands were shaking. Pausing a moment she breathed deeply, and tried to be calm as she turned the leaves. Here it was. First Kings. Nineteenth chapter. Eighteenth verse. Her eyes darted over the lines.

"Yet I have left me seven thousand in Israel, all the knees which have not bowed unto Baal, and every mouth which hath not kissed him."

Celia read it twice. With a puzzled shake of her head she sat down to read it again.

This time she told herself not to be in such a hurry. She went back to the start of the chapter, and slowly and carefully, she began.

She read how the people of Israel had turned away from the God of their fathers, to worship the false god Baal. How the prophet Elijah had cried out to the Lord in despair. All the people, he said, had yielded to the false god.

But an answer came to Elijah. He was wrong.

Celia sat up straight. She remembered her own words to Darren the other day. She had talked about "everybody." Now he had brought her an answer.

"Yet I have left me seven thousand in Israel, all the knees which have not bowed unto Baal—"

As she closed the Bible Celia felt a thrill of certainty. Everybody had not yielded. Something was going to happen.

## CHAPTER 23

$\mathscr{S}$OMETHING DID HAPPEN, and sooner than she had dared to expect.

Two days later, on Tuesday, Celia was summoned to Mrs. Thorley's office. Mrs. Thorley said she had received a note from Mrs. Godfrey Bernard, asking that Miss Garth be allowed to take supper with her this evening. The girls' evening engagements were carefully supervised, but Mrs. Thorley said Mrs. Bernard understood the rules. The note said her husband's cousin Darren Bernard would call for Celia and escort her back to the shop by nine o'clock. So permission was granted.

After her curt refusal of Sunday dinner, Celia was surprised that Ida should invite her again. But Darren must have softened what she had said, or maybe—the thought burst like light upon her—maybe this was no ordinary invitation to supper. She said, "Oh thank you, Mrs. Thorley." When Darren called, she was dressed and waiting.

The maid told her the young gentleman had said the evening was chilly and Miss Garth would please wear her cloak. Celia did not relish the idea. The evening was cool, but not that cool. Her cloak was an ash-gray cape with a hood, which Aunt Louisa had bought for her three years ago. It was the sort of thing you would expect Louisa to buy, so heavy and sensible that it was likely to last ten years more. Celia compromised by throwing it over her arm.

When she went down she saw Darren glance at the cloak as if to make sure she had brought it, and also she noticed that he too was carrying one. As they went down the side street toward the corner he asked, in a low voice such as he had used last Sunday, "Can you hear me now?"

So she had been right—this was no ordinary invitation. "Yes," she said breathlessly.

"There's a carriage waiting for us at the next corner," said Darren. "Not Godfrey's, but don't say anything."

Celia nodded. She felt quivery. Something was happening and she wished she knew what it was.

The sun had gone down and a lavender twilight was closing in. Darren led her to a carriage. It looked like a cheap coach-for-hire, the sort you could see any day on almost any street. The paint was peeling, the horse was scrubby, and the coachman was no beauty either. He was shabbily dressed and looked half asleep, his hat pulled over his eyes and his chin sunk into his collar. Darren opened the door and Celia got in.

The inside of the coach was no prettier than the outside. The floor was covered with straw instead of a carpet; the seat-cushions were worn, and in several places she saw that the cotton stuffing was coming through. Instead of glass the windows had panes of tin pierced with little holes, such as she had seen in so many broken windows in town. When Darren got in and closed the door, the two of them sat almost in the dark.

The horse started. Celia bumped, and caught the seat on either side of her. "Where are we going?" she whispered.

"I can't answer," Darren whispered back, and added, "You trust me, don't you?"

"Yes, of course," she returned hastily, thinking that if she had not trusted him she would have been scared silly. Darren said, "Here's your supper." He took up a picnic basket from a corner and put it on her lap. With a feeling that none of this could possibly be real, Celia opened the basket. Inside she found a napkin, and buttered biscuits holding slices of ham and chicken breast, and a corked bottle of water. Darren said it was all for her, he had finished his.

Celia ate her supper. In spite of the jolting of the coach this was not hard to do, for the biscuits were crisp and flaky, the meat was good, and she was hungry. When she had dampened the napkin and washed her hands, she put bottle and napkin back into the basket. "It's sort of a long way, isn't it?" she ventured.

"Celia, I can't tell you anything at all," Darren answered in a voice of apology. "It's not safe to talk. Put on your cloak—pull the hood up around your face. Here, I'll help you."

As she put on the cloak he told her to keep it wrapped around her when she got out of the coach, and take no chance of being recognized. Then he put on his own, and since men's cloaks had no hoods he pulled down his hat like the driver's.

Celia had a spooky feeling. It was all so strange. She did not know where she was going or why she was going there. She did trust Darren, she told herself—of course she did, she had no reason at all to be scared. But she was scared all the same.

The horse stopped. Saying "Wait for me," Darren left her and closed the door behind him. A minute or two later he was back. "All right," he said softly, and held out his hand. Celia got out, hidden as well as possible inside her cloak and hoping she would not have to wear it much longer because it was far too warm.

She had a glimpse of a dark alley between two brick walls. Nothing else, for Darren led her quickly to a door in one of the walls. The door opened at his touch, and Celia guessed that he had left her to get it opened so she would not stand waiting outside. She wondered if this was because he did not want her to be seen, or because he did not want to give her time to look around and see where she was. Maybe both.

They went into a pitch-black entry. Celia thought of the storybooks the girls at school used to smuggle in and read secretly, with delicious shivers at the plight of the maiden lured to a ghostly castle for a fate worse than death—oh stop this, she ordered herself. Imagining things. But she had not imagined that strange ride and she was not imagining the black entry where she stood now, nor the tremor that ran over her nerves as she heard the door shut behind her. Now I'm here, she thought, and I don't know where I am and I can't get out.

In front of her, about the level of her hip, she saw a slit of light. Beside it she made out the lines of a female figure. The woman carried a lantern with a panel that could be moved to change the size of the opening through which the light shone, and she had set it for a tiny beam. She was holding the lantern at her side, so that Celia could see the floor but not the woman's face. Darren whispered that they were to follow her.

The woman turned and they walked behind. Celia made out that she had a dumpy little figure, and that she wore a blue dress with a white kerchief and cap—details that would have fitted about a thousand women within a mile. They went down a short flight of brick steps, along a passage, around a corner, and then to a door. The woman opened the door.

A dim diffused glow came out into the passage. In spite of its dimness, the woman kept herself in the shadow of the door so Celia still could not see what she looked like.

Inside, across the doorway hung a sort of curtain. It looked like a sheet, or rather two sheets overlapping each other so you could push one of them aside and go between them into the room. Celia felt so tense that she simply had to say something. She asked Darren, "Do I go in there?"

Darren said "Yes." Without saying anything else he held back one of the curtains so she could slip between them. Celia went in. She had thought he would follow her, but he did not. She heard this door too close behind her. She was alone.

The room was lighted by two candles on a table. Celia looked around. She saw nobody. She heard nothing. She felt goose-bumps on her legs, chasing up and down like ants. She twisted her hands together. This was creepier and creepier. She had never been in such a strange place. It was like being inside a box.

The room was small, about twelve by fifteen feet. The floor and walls were covered with cloth. The cloth on the floor was canvas such as Vivian had used on the ballroom floor at Sea Garden; and on all four walls, hanging from just under the ceiling, were curtains of heavy unbleached homespun. Looking up, Celia saw that more sheets of homespun had been tacked across the ceiling. She fancied now that she heard a faint movement overhead.

She thought back—the door from the alley had been at ground level, the strange woman had led them down a flight of steps—

this room must be a basement. The air seemed faintly musty but not oppressive. No doubt there were gratings at ground level which could be opened to let in air. But this was all she could guess. The canvas on the floor, the cloth hiding the walls and ceiling, would not only muffle sounds but would prevent anybody's describing the place so it could be recognized when the hangings were removed.

In the middle of the room stood a home-made wooden table about four feet by two, and on either side of it a backless bench. There was no other furniture, and there was nothing on the table but the two candles. They were common tallow dips, in candlesticks of plain metal, the sort you could buy anywhere. Nothing, Celia thought again, that would let her give away any clue to where she had been.

She heard a click. It came from her right. Celia turned her head sharply. She could feel her heart thumping. She heard another click. A door behind that curtain over there was being opened. Evidently that door also stood where two sections of the curtain overlapped—she saw a hand grasping the edge of one curtain to move it aside.

She stood tensely, her heart pounding, her hands clasped tight in front of her. The curtain was pushed back, and then she heard a low merry laugh as a voice of teasing humor said, "Well, Sassyface!"

Celia was so relieved to hear Luke's voice that sheer easing of nerves sent a sob into her throat, and tears came pouring down her cheeks. Fumbling for her handkerchief with one hand she covered her eyes with the other, trying to press back the tears, and almost instantly he was there beside her. She felt him grip her shoulder through her cloak.

"Stop that!" he said. His voice was thick with his effort to keep it low. "If you can't work without bawling—if you can't work without showing *anything* by your face—you're no good and we don't want you."

Maybe it was still the result of strain, but at any rate, though she did not know what he was talking about Celia found her sobs turning to laughter. Tears still on her cheeks, she choked out, "It's so funny, Luke—hearing you try to whisper!"

She heard him chuckle. As she dried her eyes he answered, "Anyway—" he spoke with emphasis—"I meant what I said about the tears."

Celia pushed back her hood. She looked up at his tanned face and his brilliant blue eyes, and her curiosity would wait no longer. "Luke," she demanded, "what am I here for?"

"To help win the war," said Luke. He turned toward the table, and she saw that he was carrying, tucked under his arm, an hourglass on a silver base—the same hourglass that had timed her conversation with Vivian the day she first called at the house on Meeting Street.

Luke was dressed in a heavy unbleached homespun shirt and leather breeches and thick high boots, and she guessed that he had a leather coat and gloves somewhere—the costume of a swamp-dodger. In peacetime a man would wear such clothes to go hunting in that wet tangle of forest; today he would wear them to hide there, himself hunted. "How did you get into town, Luke?" she asked.

Without answering, Luke drew out one of the benches by the table. It moved silently over the cloth-covered floor. "Sit here," he said.

Celia took off her cloak and obeyed. Luke sat across from her, moved the candles to the two ends of the table so he could look at her directly, and placed the hourglass by his elbow. Like a man with no time to spare, he came straight to the heart of what he had to say.

"Celia, what will you do to get rid of the redcoats?"

His words gave her a sense of liberty. Ever since that horrible day at Bellwood she had felt like an angry animal, but like an animal in a cage, with no way to fight back. "I'll do anything," she answered. She repeated, "Anything."

"Dear girl," said Luke, "there's no such thing as a job doing 'anything.' There's only a job doing *something*." He smiled a little. "Now tell me how much you're willing to do."

Celia considered. "If you want me to kill somebody—Tarleton, for instance—I'll be glad to."

"Don't be silly," said Luke. "You don't know how to fire a gun. What will you do that you *can* do?"

She thought again. "If you want me to go on an errand, a dangerous errand where I might get hurt or even killed, I'll go."

"That's better," he said. He leaned nearer. His blue eyes held hers in a hard straight gaze. "Will you lie, cheat, steal—"

"Of course," said Celia.

"I haven't finished," said Luke. "Will you do this, knowing that any day you may be caught and we can't help you?"

She did not quite understand what he meant, but she felt no hesitation. "Yes, of course," she said again.

"It won't be fun," said Luke.

"I haven't had any fun lately."

Luke was very serious. "Darren told me how you felt. I couldn't see you right away, so I sent you that message. Now I'm going to explain what you can do. When I've told you, think it over. Say no if you want to. Darren will take you home and you'll never hear about this again. I'd like to have you with us, but not unless you're with us all the way, not a single doubt. Now listen."

Celia had no doubts at all. If she could do something to get rid of the redcoats she wanted to start doing it now, tonight, right this minute. But if Luke wanted to talk, let him. "I'm listening," she said.

"All right," said Luke. "Some people have given in. That always happens when the going gets hard. But some people have not given in. We're still fighting. We're going to free this country or die trying. Some of us will die trying. One of them may be me, and one of them may be you."

He spoke with grim earnestness. But Celia was feeling pinpricks of pleasure.

"What I want you to do," Luke said to her, "is to be a spy. I'm asking you because I think you can do it. Not everybody can. There are plenty of patriots in Charleston, but they haven't got what you've got."

Celia was not sure what her special talents were, but he was telling her.

"For one thing," said Luke, "you notice what goes on around you. I remarked on that the first time I saw you—remember?"

She nodded. Luke went on.

"In the second place, you can keep your mouth shut. That's a rare gift, my girl. And another thing. You can smile sweetly at people you hate."

Celia knew she could do that. She did it every day.

"Now," said Luke, "I'll tell you what we want."

Celia was leaning forward, her lips parted, her hands clasped on the table before her. She could fairly feel herself coming alive.

"We want information," said Luke. "We want to know what the British are doing and what they're going to do next. We don't care how you get the facts. Listen at keyholes, read other people's mail—just get the facts. You'll have no reward. If you're caught —I've told you that already. What do you say?"

Celia drew a happy breath. "Yes. Yes. Yes."

"You're that sure?"

"Oh Luke, you don't understand!" she exclaimed. "What do you think I've been doing since that day at Bellwood? Just breathing. With no purpose, no reason—and this is a reason! Suppose I do get caught? What can they do to me? I've got nothing they can take away. I've got no future. Oh Luke, whatever you're doing—let me help do it!"

Luke gripped both her hands. He gave her a grin of comradeship. "Good." He glanced at the hourglass. "How that sand does run. I've got a lot to say so I'll talk fast. Listen, and remember."

Celia listened.

Luke said it was strange, how Fate worked things out. What seemed like a tragedy was sometimes a piece of great good luck. This had happened twice to the friends of liberty in South Carolina.

Remember when Francis Marion fell out of the window and broke his ankle, how distressed they were at losing him? But the city would have fallen even if he had been there. When the city was taken, every Continental officer in the garrison was made prisoner. Marion, in his home near Eutaw Springs, was not made prisoner.

Of course the British knew that so popular an officer would become a center of resistance if he was left at large. They had set out at once to capture him. Marion was still so crippled that he had to be lifted on and off a horse. But with the help of his devoted Negro Buddy, of soldiers like Luke who had escaped the British attacks, of friends like Herbert and Vivian who hid him in their homes, Marion had slipped around like a ghost. The British had not found him.

Then Marion went to join the army of Gates, and here came the second misfortune. Gates shoved him out of the way. But the result was that when Gates lost the battle of Camden, Marion was not there to be killed or taken. He was still free, Luke said triumphantly, to lead the men of the Lowcountry who wanted to fight.

And how they wanted to fight! Celia knew about Tarleton. But had she heard of a man named Wemyss?

Celia shook her head, so Luke told her.

As she knew, most of the Scotch-Irish farmers around Kingstree had stayed out of the war. Busy with their flax and wool, they had asked only to be let alone. But after the fall of Charleston they received Clinton's order that every man in South Carolina was now subject to call for the king's army, and if a man refused to serve he could be hanged for treason.

The Kingstree men got mad. If they were going to fight, it would be for themselves and not for a king three thousand miles away. They began to organize, and sent a scout to look for Marion and ask him to be their leader. It was this scout who had found Marion at the camp of Gates.

With his other followers Marion went to the camp of the Kingstree men and led them to destroy the boats as Gates had ordered. But after Gates' defeat Marion and his band—about a hundred and fifty men—had to go into a secret camp to avoid capture. At the same time Cornwallis, hearing that the Kingstree men were rising, sent troops of his own into that district. Their leader was Major James Wemyss.

Luke said Cornwallis had never shown himself unduly savage. It might be that he had not intended for Wemyss to do what he did. But anyway, Wemyss did it.

Along the road from Kingstree to Cheraw, Wemyss cut a swath seventy miles long and fifteen miles wide. In this strip, when they had emptied the houses of everything worth stealing, Wemyss' men set fire to every building, destroyed every loom and storehouse, killed every animal on the farms. When they got through, that whole stretch of country looked like what Celia had seen at Bellwood. How many girls were raped, how many babies and old people died, nobody knew.

Rumors of Wemyss' march came to Marion in his hidden camp on Lynches Creek. He sent scouts to find out the truth.

Luke spoke tersely across the table. "Celia, we saw those people skulking in the ruins like animals, eating things animals wouldn't eat. Half of those homes belonged to men who had never fought the king. They hadn't joined up with us because they still thought they could live in peace. They came out like crazy men, yelling 'Where's Marion?' Celia, you're not crying again," he broke off, for she had dropped her head on her hands, covering her eyes.

Celia shook her head. "No, I'm not crying. I was thinking— Agnes Kennedy. So that's why she's not back."

"Kennedy?" Luke repeated. "There's a lot of Kennedys through there, I don't know. Friend of yours?"

"She worked in the shop. Funny, I didn't even like her very much, but she never hurt anybody. She couldn't even swat a fly without feeling sorry for it. I wonder what they did to her." Celia looked up, resolutely calm. "Go on, Luke."

Luke had no more time for emotion. "Well, that was our start. Now men are coming to us from all over. But we can't fight a war with our fists." He spoke crisply. "We need guns, clothes, shoes. Some of those fellows came to us half naked. Wemyss had burnt up everything they owned. For something to fight with, we've raided sawmills and beaten the saws into sabers. In the farmhouses outside Wemyss' line of march women have melted their kitchen pans to make us bullets. We take guns and powder-horns from dead Britishers. But it's not enough. We need everything."

Celia wondered where she would get guns and powder-horns, and how she would send them to Marion's men if she had them. But Luke was still talking and it was her business to listen.

Luke told her the British expected to finish up the war in a few months, probably by next spring. They knew just how they meant to do it. Their plan, he added, was no secret. "We can read other people's mail too," he said.

As she knew, after Charleston surrendered, Sir Henry Clinton went to New York. The city of New York was the headquarters of the northern wing of the king's army, as Charleston was now the base of the army in the south.

Clinton had left Cornwallis in command of the southern army. Now that South Carolina (as they thought) was licked, the redcoats expected to have an easy time in the south. They had a strong fort in Florida, at St. Augustine; and they held Savannah, as well as other major points in Georgia. Cornwallis thought all he had to do was organize military government in South Carolina, then he could leave a small force to keep order while he, with his main army, marched northward.

"In the meantime," said Luke, "Clinton plans to hold enough men around New York to keep Washington busy, but to have a strong force from the northern army start south. The two armies expect to meet halfway, in Maryland or Virginia. They expect to meet about two months from now, say the end of November—anyway, before Christmas. If they do get together, it will mean that they'll hold everything from Florida to the Hudson River. Then, together, they can close on General Washington, at West Point or somewhere near by." He paused. "Get it?"

"Yes," said Celia, "I understand."

Luke smiled. "That's what I like about you, Celia. You're definite. You don't say 'I think so,' or 'Well, sort of.' You say yes or no." He glanced at the hourglass. The sand was still running, so he went on. "The trouble with this plan, Celia, is that it's good. Those two British armies together will be stronger than anything Washington can bring to face them. Now here's our job."

She nodded. "I'm listening."

"Our job," said Luke, "is to keep those two armies from joining. We're not strong enough to meet Cornwallis in open battle. But we can pester him. We can raid his outposts. Attack his supply trains. Slow down everything he tries to do. In the meantime the Americans in North Carolina will have time to get ready for him. They can slow him down some more. You see, we know Washington is negotiating with the king of France for more

Frenchmen to fight on our side. But the Frenchmen can't get here for six months, maybe a year. If those two British armies meet before the Frenchmen get here—well, we can't let them meet, that's all." He covered her hands with his, and spoke with a desperate earnestness. "Celia, every day we can delay Cornwallis is one more day for changing the Thirteen Colonies into the United States of America. Understand?"

"Oh yes, yes, yes!" said Celia. She added joyfully, "And we can always hold him back *one* more day!"

"One more day—that's it, Celia!"

"Go on, Luke! How do we do it?"

Luke began to speak more calmly. He said things would be easier if they were dealing with a clumsy fool. But Cornwallis was a smart man. Besides his two major bases at Charleston and Camden, he had set up British posts all over the state: at Georgetown and Beaufort on the coast, at Orangeburg, Ninety-Six, and other strategic points of the interior; at Quinby Bridge on the eastern fork of the Cooper River, Nelson's Ferry on the Santee.

"In fact," said Luke, "he's got us enclosed in a ring of redcoats. Sounds tough, and it is. But every one of those posts has got to have a steady stream of supplies or the men can't stay there. They have to send letters back and forth—make reports, get orders. We want those supplies. We want those letters. We want to take some prisoners so we can exchange them for our men who are prisoners now. We want a hundred little skirmishes, so they'll never know where we're going to turn up next. Then Cornwallis will have to use his troops to guard the roads instead of marching them north."

Celia said slowly, "I see what you meant a few minutes ago. A lot of men will get killed."

"A lot of them don't care," Luke said quietly. When she gave a start of disbelief, he said, "Miles Rand, for instance—he's with us."

She had no answer for this. So she asked, "Is Amos with you?" Luke said yes, and Big Buck too. Celia exclaimed, "Then you must get word to Marietta."

"She knows," Luke said smiling. "Now let's talk about you."

"Yes, let's," Celia said eagerly. "What can I do, Luke? *Me?*"

"Plenty," said Luke. "You're in a public place. Redcoats and Tories are coming into the shop all day. You can notice them, hear what they say, tell us. Also you can meet them socially, at Godfrey's."

"Luke, I'm ashamed of myself. I thought—"

"I know what you thought. People will think the same thing about you. Let them."

"What about Burton?" she asked.

"You know, Celia, I'm proud of that large pink brother of mine. He still hasn't taken the oath. He's standing there like a rock, pained at Godfrey, and we have to let it go on like that. We can't let him work with us."

"Why not?"

"My dear girl," said Luke, "you should know. Burton can't keep anything from Elise, and telling anything to Elise is like printing it in the paper. She'd have us all in that dungeon under the Exchange. Let's get back to you." He spoke carefully. "Whenever you notice anything that might be useful to us, let us know. For the present your friends will be Darren, Godfrey, and Ida."

"How do I tell them?"

"Some women," said Luke, "have used the scheme of putting a workbasket on the windowsill. This means they have something to tell. Somebody passes the window several times a day, and if the basket is there he passes the word to somebody else, to come in and get the message. Try that once or twice, then think of another code. Keep changing, that's vital."

"Suppose the shop is full of people? How do I give anybody a message?"

"Write it and have it ready. Write it in the fewest possible words, on the smallest possible slip of paper, so you can hide it inside a thimble or something like that. If it's that tiny, you can pass it over—say with a sample of cloth—and not be seen."

"Then how does the message get to Colonel Marion?" she asked.

Luke laughed softly. "You don't need to know that."

"If I should notice something," said Celia, "how do I know if it's important?"

"You don't. Tell us anyway. It's better we should get a hundred trivial messages than miss one that we need. And be as quick as you possibly can. Remember: men are going to live or die because of you."

For a moment they were both silent. Celia was realizing that this was no romantic escapade into which he was leading her. It was an enterprise hard and stern. To do it, she would have to be hard and stern. She asked, "Are there many others in town, spying for Marion's men?"

"Yes," said Luke, "but it's better you don't know too much about them. The fact is," he added, laughing a little, "I don't think anybody knows Marion's whole spy system except Marion himself."

She heard this with astonishment, and he went on.

"We don't know how he got news of Camden. He was with us in the woods, chopping up boats moored at the river landings. But one day he knew. He didn't tell a single man of us. He was afraid we'd lose our spirit. Instead he led us straight to Nelson's Ferry in time to attack a British force moving some American prisoners down to Charleston, and we set free the prisoners. Now how did he find out they were going to cross the river just then? We don't know."

"Doesn't he trust *anybody?*" she asked wonderingly.

"It's not that, Celia. But the less you have to hide, the easier it is to hide it." Again Luke glanced at the hourglass. "Sand's out. We've got to get you back on time."

Reluctantly, Celia pushed back the bench and stood up. She wanted to ask more questions. Also it seemed that there was something tickling her memory, but she could not quite get hold of it. Maybe it was about Sea Garden. Maybe it concerned Roy's mysterious visit. As Luke came around the table and picked up her cloak, she asked,

"I suppose Vivian told you Roy came to Sea Garden—do you know what he came for?"

"No, I wish I did," said Luke. "We've heard nothing about him since that day."

He held out her cloak. Celia put it on and drew up the hood, still trying to catch whatever it was at the back of her mind. She had just learned so many strange and startling matters that her head felt like an overpacked trunk where it was hard to find anything. "Will I see you again?" she asked.

"Oh yes. Right now it's my job to organize the information system in Charleston, so I'll be here a while."

Celia was glad of that. She had felt so limp and useless, and his energy gave her a feeling of strength renewed. She wished she could find that memory she was looking for.

"I'll call Darren," said Luke. He caught both her hands in his, and gave them a squeeze. "So now you're one of us. Good luck, Sassyface."

Before she could answer he had turned and was crossing the room. Without looking back he disappeared between the homespun curtains on the wall.

## CHAPTER 24

*T*HE COACH was waiting at the entrance to the alley. Celia had expected that now Darren would let her see where she was, but he hurried her inside. As the horse started Darren leaned closer to her and said in a voice she could barely hear,

"We're going to Godfrey's. We want to give the impression that you've been there all evening."

Celia said "Yes, of course," and Darren added,

"But we may go in or we may not—I'll explain later."

Again Celia said "Yes." That was all she said, and she was glad that Darren too was silent, for she was trying to go over in her mind what she had learned tonight.

The coach stopped sooner than she had expected. When they got out she saw that they were on King Street, near Tradd Street where Godfrey lived. So the meeting-place had not been as far from the shop as she had thought. Evidently on their first ride the driver had taken a long zigzag route. If she had not chosen to join them, or if they had decided that she had better not be trusted with their secrets, he would have brought her back by the same long route and she could never have guessed where she had been.

The coach rattled off. The driver had let them out in a business block, where now in the evening the buildings were closed and dark. There was not much chance of anybody's being around to observe them. They walked to the residential neighborhood of Tradd Street.

Here the windows were lighted, the gardens were fragrant, and from several of the houses came the sound of dance music. Celia remembered what Sophie had said at Sea Garden last summer, that Charleston had never been so gay. But now she did not feel the helpless disgust she had felt then. Now she knew about the secret war.

At Godfrey's door, Darren put a key into the lock and drew her inside. Later he told her that Ida had arranged a signal for him by her manner of draping the curtain at a certain window. The two officers billeted in the house had gone out tonight to a party, and the curtain had told him they were still out. If they had returned he would have taken Celia directly back to the shop.

Godfrey and Ida were waiting in a room off the front hall. Godfrey shook her hand with warm welcome, and Ida said, "Sit down, here's your dessert." She uncovered a dish on which there was a fruit pudding piled with whipped cream. Celia had always thought of Ida as a colorless person, but tonight Ida was fairly twinkling with mischief. She whispered to Celia, "I'm so glad you're with us."

Speaking in careful undertones, they told Celia they talked about their undertaking as little as possible, even among themselves. You never knew when somebody might overhear. Ida remarked that she planned to come into the shop soon to order some kerchiefs, and she was going to ask that Celia make them because Celia had done such beautiful work for Vivian. Her eyes met Celia's with gay conspiracy, and Celia smiled at her across a spoonful of pudding. The pudding was marvelous.

They all three walked with her to the shop, chatting about the weather. At the door Celia said, "Thank you for a lovely evening." As she went toward her room she met Miss Perry, about to ring the nine o'clock bell. "Did you have a good time?" Miss Perry asked, and Celia smiled and said "Yes ma'am."

In the bedroom she took a quick look at the pen and inkhorn on the side table. The pen had a good point and there were several sheets of paper in the table drawer. If she heard anything of use to Marion's men, she had material at hand for writing a note. She could get more paper next time she went out.

When she woke in the morning the room was gray with dawn. Her eyes felt sandy from lack of sleep, for she had been so excited that she had lain awake long after she went to bed. But for the first time in months she had the delicious feeling that this was a new day full of promises and she was eager to begin it. She sat up and threw back the covers.

It was a bright sunny day and the shop was full of people. Celia smiled prettily at them all, showed them samples, went upstairs on their errands, and between times sat hemming a cap-frill, and listening. She listened till she could almost feel her ears ache. But though they talked, they said nothing. They talked about clothes, and parties, and who was flirting with whom. By noon she was ready to cry with exasperation.

A little past noon Mrs. Torrance came in, escorted by her husband and two redcoats. She said she wouldn't be a minute, she was just going to run up and see how her dress was coming along, so the gentlemen sat down outside the balustrade to wait for her. Celia opened the gate. Mrs. Torrance went through, carefully not giving her any sign of recognition.

Mr. Torrance, a pleasant round-faced young man who looked like his sister Sophie, asked Celia if she had a copy of the *Royal Gazette*. She handed it to him, and the three men began lazily to discuss the day's news. Celia resumed her sewing. One of the Britishers said the war could not last much longer. In places where American money still circulated, the American cause was rated so low that Continental bills were worth only two cents on the dollar. The others laughed, and Celia bent her head over her work, trying to look as if she did not care. The redcoat fanned himself with the newspaper, remarking that the day was getting hotter every minute.

Celia started. Her needle made a crooked stitch. For a moment she could not move to take the stitch out, for her hands were trembling and waves of excitement were rippling through her body.

Now she knew what it was she had been trying to remember, last night when she talked to Luke. She had a message for Marion's men.

.~.

She could almost see and hear it. Those other redcoats last week, complaining about the hot weather; Mrs. Torrance saying it was not the heat that bothered them, it was their heavy uniforms; and Mrs. Kirby— "They've got a shipment of lightweight clothes ready for Camden right now . . . leaving here the first of October and that's *definite*."

This was real information. And that was exactly how Luke had told her to get it.

Celia thought fast. Today was Wednesday. The first of October would be next Sunday. She still had time to send the message. In a little while one of the other girls would come to take her place for the dinner hour, and she could go to the bedroom and write a note. This afternoon she would send it out. And somewhere on the road to Camden, Marion's men would pop out of the swamp and attack the supply train.

Celia unthreaded her needle, took out the crooked stitch, threaded the needle again and put the stitch in straight. Her heart was bumping. She glanced up. The three men were asking one another how much longer Mrs. Torrance was going to make them wait.

The time dragged. Mrs. Torrance finally appeared, and her party left. Two elderly ladies came in and asked Celia a hundred questions about materials and prices, and then said they would not decide on anything today. At last Pearl Todd came to mind the parlor for the dinner hour. Pearl had already had her dinner, and she whispered, "It's shrimp pie today, and it's good!"

Celia managed to smile. She folded her sewing, put it into her workbasket, and hurried up to her bedroom. Becky was not here yet. Celia drew a chair to the table and opened the inkhorn. Tearing off a slip of paper, she wrote her message in the smallest handwriting she could manage.

"Wagons carrying clothes and shoes leaving Charleston for Camden October 1."

She wondered if she should add her source of information, and decided no; they would understand she had heard it in the parlor, and Luke had told her to be brief. But Mrs. Kirby had known about this because of her husband. His name had better be there, so they could check the statement. She added, "Purchase arranged by Mr. Robert Kirby."

There were footsteps on the stairs. The girls were coming up to their rooms to get ready for dinner.

The ink on her note was still wet. As fast as she could, she slipped the paper into the drawer, closed the inkhorn, and laid down the pen. She pushed back her chair and started for the washstand. Behind her the door opened and Becky's voice said, "I thought Miss Loring would *never* let us go! I'm starving."

Celia poured water into the basin and began to wash her hands. She had a blot on her finger. Scrubbing at the blot, she said, "Pearl told me we're having shrimp pie." The way her temples were throbbing, she was surprised that she could say anything.

She had to get her note out of the table drawer. If Becky would only go downstairs! But Becky washed her hands, took off her cap, smoothed her hair, put her cap on again, said she was going out Sunday with two perfectly charming men. Redcoats, but really it was all wrong what some people said about redcoats, they were just as nice as anybody else once you got used to the funny way they talked. Didn't Celia think it was all right for a girl to go out with them? Celia, remembering the part she was playing now, said, "Oh yes, of course it's all right." The dinner-bell sounded. They both started for the door, but Celia bumped against a bedpost and stumbled.

"Oh dear!" she exclaimed. "I've torn my kerchief. I'll have to change it. Go on down, Becky, I'll be there in a minute."

Becky went out. Celia changed her kerchief, hiding the old one so nobody would see that it was not torn at all. She dashed to the table. The ink on her note was dry now. She folded the paper over and over till it made a tiny wad, slipped the wad into her handkerchief, put the handkerchief into her pocket and went downstairs, reaching the dining room door just in time to stand aside and let Mrs. Thorley go in ahead of her.

The shrimp pie was good, but Celia ate so little that Miss Perry asked if she did not feel well. Celia said oh yes, she felt fine, and she hurriedly swallowed a morsel of shrimp. But her throat was tight, and she was glad when it was time to leave the table.

She went back to the parlor. As she opened the door she felt a tremor. Suppose there should be redcoats here? Some of them might be on the lookout for spies.

But the only visitors were a placid plump couple named Duff, examining samples of men's shirting which Pearl was showing them. Dutiful and bored, Pearl was glad to have Celia take her place at the balustrade.

Mr. and Mrs. Duff were not people who had a great deal to do. Selection of material for half a dozen shirts was an interesting event in their lives. Besides the question of material, there was the decision of how the shirts should be made—with tucks down the front, or the little frills that men were wearing this year? These details were so important, they said to Celia.

Celia said tucks and frills were both fashionable, but the frills were more expensive because they took longer to make. Mr. and Mrs. Duff went into a conference. They compromised by deciding to have three shirts made with frills and three with tucks. And now, said Mrs. Duff, they would like to choose the buttons. Celia produced a box holding a variety of buttons, and set it on the counter. Her hand was shaky and she wanted to scream. For where, oh where in all this was there a chance for her to put her workbasket on the windowsill?

The basket stood on the table as she had left it before dinner, its straw top neatly in place. She had expected that when she came into the parlor she would open the basket and take out the cap-frill she was making, sit by the window and sew, and put the basket on the sill as if by chance. But she could not say, "Excuse me, while you're looking at the buttons I'll put my workbasket in the window." She had to stand here, smiling and answering questions, while this very minute some messenger of Luke's might be passing the shop, looking at the windows and going on in the belief that she had nothing to report because no basket was there.

Mrs. Baxter came in, accompanied by her sister from out of town, Mrs. Sloan. As they had an appointment Celia opened the gate in the balustrade, and when they had gone upstairs she returned to the Duffs. She told them that one of the senior seam-stresses, Mrs. Woods, was in charge of making men's shirts, and it would be better to discuss further details with her. Mr. and Mrs. Duff agreed, but they lingered awhile longer over the button-box. At last, however, they said they would like to speak to Mrs. Woods; and Celia, trembling with impatience, went to summon her. As men were not allowed upstairs where the ladies' fitting-rooms were, Mrs. Woods led the Duffs into a side room off the parlor so Mr. Duff could take off his coat and wig, and be measured.

At last, Celia was alone. Going to the table she opened her workbasket. She took out the frill, placed her chair by the win-dow, and set the basket on the sill.

Her heart bounced like a ball rolling down a staircase. She was as conscious of the wad of paper in her pocket as if it had been a coal of fire. Desperately, grimly, she went on sewing.

The Duffs finally finished their business and went home. More customers came and went. The sun moved westward over the Ashley River. Mrs. Baxter and Mrs. Sloan came downstairs, and lingered in front of the balustrade to look at the fashion dolls. A few minutes later the front door opened again, and Celia looked up to see Godfrey Bernard.

Hat in hand, Godfrey paused an instant and gave a quick glance around. This was long enough for Mrs. Baxter to catch sight of him, greet him effusively, present him to her sister, and ask about Ida. Courteous as always, Godfrey said he was happy to meet Mrs. Sloan, and Ida was well, thank you. They ex-changed more pleasantries, but at length the ladies returned to the fashion dolls and Godfrey came to the balustrade.

Celia was sure he had come for her message, and she was scared. She had thought working for Marion would be exhilarating; she had not expected these stiff lips and shaking knees, nor the squeaky little voice in which she said, "How do you do, sir."

When she had been Vivian's guest she and Godfrey had called each other by their first names, but she thought this was hardly proper for the shop. Evidently he agreed, for he said, "How do you do, Miss Garth. Remember my wife said she wanted to order some kerchiefs? She asked me to make an appointment for her. Friday or Saturday, preferably before noon."

Celia wondered if he too was quaking within. He did not look like it. Godfrey's hair—he still had enough of his own not to need a wig—was neatly tied behind with a silk ribbon. He wore a dark blue linen coat and tan breeches, and a white lawn cravat. Godfrey looked like himself, a man who had the habit of success; he showed none of the slack discouragement she had seen when the weather ruined the meat supply last spring. No, right now Godfrey knew what he was doing and he had no doubt that he could do it well.

Behind him, Mrs. Baxter was saying the cap worn by one of the dolls was too elaborate for the dress she had on. The thought came to Celia that Godfrey's confidence now meant that he also trusted her to do her part of the job. She said, "Certainly, Mr. Bernard. I'll go up and speak to Miss Loring."

"Thank you," said Godfrey. "And Miss Garth—" he looked at her directly—"will you ask her to give me a written reminder of the time? I have a wretched memory for these things." For the barest instant his eyes flashed to the basket on the windowsill.

"Certainly," Celia said again. She turned and opened the door to the staircase. As she put her hand on the banister she asked herself what on earth she was scared of. She was sure Mrs. Baxter had not come to the shop to look for rebel spies.

In the sewing room, Miss Loring said Mrs. Bernard could come in Friday morning at ten. She noted the day and time in her book, and at Celia's request she clipped a corner from a page and repeated the note for Mr. Bernard.

Celia started downstairs. Halfway down she paused. Taking her little wad of paper from her pocket she put it under Miss Loring's note and held it there. The last of her quakes had left her; she felt strong and sure of herself. She went on down and with her free hand she opened the parlor door.

Mrs. Baxter and Mrs. Sloan were still talking about the displays in the cabinets. Godfrey stood by the balustrade. But also standing by the balustrade, his elbow on the counter and his hat beside him, was a good-looking young British lieutenant.

For an instant Celia felt paralyzed. Ideas rushed through her head. She must not show fear, she had to speak and act normally, redcoats came into the shop often and he was just another one. Godfrey was waiting; this showed that he expected her to give him her message somehow. She would attend to the redcoat first —that was it, ask what he wanted and get rid of him. Smiling pleasantly, she went to the counter and spoke to him. "May I help you, sir?"

The redcoat smiled back. "This gentleman," he said, politely indicating Godfrey, "was here before me."

Again Celia's thoughts buzzed. Maybe she should give Godfrey only Miss Loring's note, and let him come back later for hers. But how could she know that there would not be redcoats here again, next time he came in? And Luke had told her speed was vital. She must get her message out now, not later. She noticed how well tailored were the young Britisher's red coat and white doeskin breeches, how shiny his boots, how properly powdered his hair; and she thought of what Luke had told her, that many of Marion's men were half naked. They needed those wagon-loads of clothes. She had to give Godfrey her message and if she kept her wits about her she could do it. She remembered what Vivian had said long ago: "You can do anything you *have* to do."

Godfrey had acknowledged the soldier's courtesy with a slight inclination of his head. Following this lead, Celia said, "Very well, sir." Turning to Godfrey she held out Miss Loring's three-cornered slip of paper, her thumb on top, her fingers hiding her own little note underneath. "Here you are, Mr. Bernard."

Godfrey closed his hand so that her wad was hidden but Miss Loring's note was held between his thumb and forefinger. He read as though to himself, "Friday morning at ten—good. Thank you, Miss Garth." He dropped his hand into his pocket, and with his other hand he picked up his hat. "Good evening, Mrs. Baxter, Mrs. Sloan," he said, and went out. Speaking as calmly as possible, Celia asked the lieutenant how she could serve him.

In his smooth British accent, he told her his name was Meadows. He had brought a note for Miss Becky Duren, about a change in their plans for Sunday, and he asked Celia if she would be kind enough to deliver it. Celia felt so happy that she gave him a smile more friendly than she had ever thought she would give a red-coat, and told him she would be glad to deliver his note. Lieutenant Meadows bowed, thanked her, and took his leave.

Mrs. Sloan called Mrs. Baxter's attention to a pair of gloves in one of the cabinets. Celia returned to the chair by the window. She took her basket from the sill, opened it and took out her scissors, and put the basket on the table beside her. Her thoughts were singing. I did it, I did it, I sent a message to Marion!

•～•

Becky exclaimed joyfully when Celia gave her Lieutenant Meadows' note that evening. She said she had promised to take a walk Sunday with Meadows and another officer named Captain Cole, but the note said Captain Cole had sprained his knee and could not go out. Meadows said if it was agreeable with Becky, the two of them would join a party who had engaged a carriage for Sunday. They would all go for a drive, and stop for refreshments at the new tea-shop on Cumberland Street.

Becky had not been to the new tea-shop and she was delighted at the prospect of going there Sunday with a party of elegant people. She said she was sorry about Captain Cole, but his injury was not serious. And anyway, he was billeted at the Baxters' and they had a lovely home.

Friday morning Ida came to choose the material for her kerchiefs. Miss Loring said it was all right for Celia to make them, and Celia felt elated. This would give Ida an excuse to come in often, and receive a message if she had one to give.

However, by Friday night Celia had begun to feel discouraged. For though she had listened as hard as she could, she had heard nothing more that could be of use to Marion's men. She told herself the best spy on earth could not hear what people did not say. But the fact remained, it had been more than a week since she had caught that remark of Mrs. Kirby's, and it did seem that she should have picked up something else.

On Saturday, though the shop was full and the parlor was chatty and gay, she had hardly any chance to listen. Everybody wanted something. Celia went upstairs so many times that by afternoon she ached all over. And finally, just as she was wearily thanking heaven that it was almost time to close, Mrs. Baxter and Mrs. Sloan dropped in. Just looking, they said. They began to admire the displays, many of which had been changed since the last time they were here.

They stayed, and stayed, and stayed. They were still there after everybody else had gone. Celia got tireder and tireder, but the two ladies, sitting by a table with samples spread out before them, were too much interested to leave. The supervisors were supposed to notice the time, and when customers forgot to go home Miss Loring or Miss Perry would come in and tell them the shop was closing, but Celia could not do this herself. She had to wait.

So she waited, and the end was worth it.

Too tired to sew, she sat with her hands in her lap, thinking about how her legs ached from all that stair-climbing. Mrs. Sloan said this gray-and-yellow striped silk was beautiful, but she simply could not wear any shade of yellow. This plain gray, though, it would be lovely combined with this dark green. She asked if Mrs. Baxter remembered the dark green dress Emily Torrance had worn to church last Sunday. Mrs. Sloan said she had noticed it particularly when Mr. and Mrs. Torrance were standing outside the church after services, chatting with Captain Cole. It was too bad, said Mrs. Sloan, about Captain Cole's accident.

"I don't think," said Mrs. Baxter, "that he minds it too much." She sounded amused.

"Why not?" asked Mrs. Sloan.

Mrs. Baxter laughed softly. "He had been ordered out of town on outpost duty, and you know how they all dread that. Now he can't go, at least not for a while."

Mrs. Sloan laughed too. "How do you know? Did he tell you?"

"Not exactly—I mean—" Mrs. Baxter gave a half-embarrassed giggle. "Oh, I can say it to you, you'll understand. Lieutenant Meadows came by this morning to see him, and while they were both in Captain Cole's room I happened to pass and I noticed that the door was open. Of course I don't make a habit of listening at doors, but I do like to hear if Captain Cole has any complaints. If your billets like you they can do you so many favors. It doesn't hurt to hear what they say."

"Of course, I understand," said Mrs. Sloan. "He wasn't complaining, was he?"

"Oh no, they were laughing and talking, and Captain Cole was saying that now he couldn't go up to Lenud's Ferry next week. It seems he was to lead a troop there to guard the crossing. But they're to leave Tuesday, and he won't even be able to stand up by then. Another officer will have to take his place. And I must say I was glad to hear what Captain Cole said about it—he said duty was duty, but he was so comfortable with us, he wasn't sorry to stay longer. I didn't know he'd been ordered out. I suppose they aren't allowed to talk about their orders."

In her dim corner, Celia sat with every nerve strained lest she miss a word. Lenud's Ferry was on the Santee River about twenty miles from Sea Garden, close to the church of St. James Santee. It was an important crossing, which would be used for men and supplies going from Charleston into the country back of Georgetown. And a troop was leaving for Lenud's Ferry next Tuesday.

The ladies had gone back to their discussion of the samples. Mrs. Sloan was saying, "It's a beautiful shade in this light, but I'm not sure how it would be in bright sunshine."

The door from the staircase opened and Miss Perry came bouncing in. She told the ladies she was oh so sorry to disturb them, but really the shop had to close. The ladies were oh so welcome here, their patronage was an honor, but Mrs. Thorley made the rules and she was quite strict and wouldn't they come back Monday?

Mrs. Baxter and Mrs. Sloan said they had had no idea how late it was, and they did not know what *became* of the time. At last they left, and Miss Perry bounced out again, and Celia began to lock up. Tired as she was, she heard herself humming a tune. She had no way to get a message out tonight, but she could do it tomorrow.

Pushing back the curtains of a front window she looked out at Lamboll Street. The sun was going down, and the street was striped with shadows and sunlight. Not far off she saw the little hairdresser Hugo, carrying his bag of pomades and curling-tongs. It was the first time she had seen Hugo since the day he had taken the bullet from Jimmy's leg, and the sight of him sent a painful memory shooting through her. As he came nearer she watched him, her eyes held to him by the memory. Hugo looked very spruce with his cocked hat atop his curly white wig, his fine purple coat, and the last rays of the sun flashing on the buckles of his shoes. As he passed he caught sight of her in the window, and doffed his hat in an elegant gesture of greeting. Apparently the day she remembered with such pain had been for him only another day. Celia managed a stiff little smile in return, and Hugo pranced along. He walked into another ray of sunlight, and Celia caught her breath.

Her hands on the sill, she leaned farther out, her eyes following Hugo. No doubt about it. Hugo had on fancy lacework stockings just like those that Luke had been wearing the first time she saw him.

Celia drew back from the window. It had been here in this very room that she had noticed those stockings of Luke's. She remembered herself asking, "Mr. Ansell, who made your stockings?" She remembered how startled he had been, and how he had recovered his poise so quickly that she almost thought she had imagined it.

But she had not imagined it. Engaged in dangerous business on the wagon track, Luke had had many secrets to keep from the king's spies in Charleston. Those stockings had been a signal, like the basket on the windowsill. And they still were. Hugo, doing ladies' hair, heard the talk of the town. Like herself, he was in a perfect situation to hear what Marion wanted to know.

"He's one of us," Celia said to herself. As she closed the window she said it again. "He's one of us."

One of us. Where had she heard that phrase before?

In the letter written to her by Mrs. Rand, about her own engagement to Jimmy. Celia remembered how warm and friendly the words had made her feel.

But she had lost all that. In these past months she had felt so unwanted and alone. Now she did not feel that way. She had heard the same phrase again somewhere, not long ago. After a moment she remembered.

Luke. The other evening, when he told her good night in the curtained room, he had said, "So now you're one of us." She was not alone any more.

## CHAPTER 25

As THE NEXT DAY was Sunday and Celia had no excuse to put her workbasket in the window, after breakfast she walked over to Godfrey's. She did not need to ask permission, for on Sundays the girls were allowed to do about as they pleased, so long as they did nothing improper for the Sabbath quiet. It was still so early that there were not many people out. One or two redcoats spoke to her, but she hurried on and they bothered her no more.

As she reached Tradd Street she heard a peal from the bells of St. Michael's. She walked on to Godfrey's house, and from the doorstep she looked across the roofs to the steeple, black on the sky. "Lighten our darkness," she whispered as she knocked on the door.

The maid showed her into the reception room, and summoned Godfrey. He was surprised to see her. "Don't tell me why you've come," he said in a barely audible voice, and added clearly, "Glad you dropped in. I'll take you up to see Ida, lazy girl's not dressed yet." He led her upstairs to Ida's sitting room, which opened from their bedroom. Looking pretty and frail in a boudoir robe of misty blue, Ida was finishing her breakfast egg.

In her low voice Ida explained to Celia that in these two rooms she and Godfrey could be sure of privacy—something not easy to achieve with two redcoats billeted in the house. Major Brace and Captain Woodley were courteous guests, but they were loyal to the king and it would not do to have them suspect what their host and hostess were up to.

Glancing from Ida to Godfrey, and keeping her own voice as low as possible, Celia asked, "Shall I tell you why I've come?"

They shook their heads. Godfrey cupped his hands around his mouth, bent close to her ear, and said, "I'll send you to Luke."

Celia smiled involuntarily. Before she thought what she was saying she asked, "Where is he?"

Ida looked at Godfrey. He nodded. Whispering into Celia's ear as he had done, Ida said, "Mr. Westcott's tea-shop on Cumberland Street."

Celia started. The new tea-shop—a fine place to hear the talk of redcoats, but for Luke, how terribly dangerous. Yet where in town would it not be dangerous for one of Marion's men? Godfrey had drawn a chair close to hers and was telling her something else.

"I'll send for Darren and he'll go with you. When a girl goes walking with a bachelor nobody pays any attention. But I'm a married man and somebody always notices that. Besides, we go to church on Sunday mornings."

"I think it's sacrilegious," Celia said shortly, "for us to go to a church where they pray for the king."

"So do I," said Godfrey, "but we're pretending to be Tories now, and we figure the Lord will understand." He went out, saying he would send a servant to bring Darren from the inn where he lived. Ida said to Celia that while they waited she would send for a pot of tea.

"Tea?" Celia repeated. "I—I don't like tea any more, Ida."

Ida smiled wisely. "If you're one of us," she said in her sweet soft voice, "you'll *like* tea."

Celia burst out laughing. The maid brought the tea, and they sipped like any other Tories until Darren arrived. He and Celia strolled uptown, Darren's cane tapping on the sidewalk.

The tea-shop occupied a building near the powder magazine from which Darren and Miles had helped move the gunpowder that night during the siege. Next door to the shop was a warehouse, and between them an alley—Celia could see now how she had been brought here in the dark. The place was well chosen.

This time, in the bright light of mid-morning, they paid no attention to the alley. They went up the front steps and into the shop by the main door. The air was rich with the smell of baking.

They were in an entrance hall, which had a door at each side and another door at the back. Through the side doors Celia saw a large room on either side. In one of these rooms, Darren told her, Mr. and Mrs. Westcott served gentlemen only; in the other, gentlemen accompanied by ladies. In the first room several men were having late Sunday breakfasts of buns and tea. But since it was mostly single men who took breakfast out, there were no customers in the other room.

A boy about twelve years old came into the hall carrying a plate of butter. Darren spoke to him. "Morning, Ricky. Tell your mother I've brought a young lady to try her nut-bread."

Ricky grinned alertly. "Yes *sir!*" he said. He carried the butter into the bachelors' room, and Darren led Celia into the room where ladies were served. A pleasant room it was, with fresh cloths on the tables, and at one end a counter, draped with a white net to keep off flies, where Celia saw and smelt a fascinating array of tarts and buns and fancy breads. Beyond this counter, leading toward the back rooms, was another door.

This door opened and a woman came in, a nice little woman with a dumpy figure, wearing a blue dress with a white cap and kerchief—plainly the woman who had carried the lantern the other night. Darren introduced her as Mrs. Westcott.

Mrs. Westcott spoke cordially. "I've got a fresh batch of nut-bread that ought to be coming out of the oven about now. Want to see it?" She stood aside for them to go through the doorway toward the back.

Darren glanced around to make sure nobody was observing them. Quickly he led Celia through this doorway. Mrs. Westcott did not follow. She closed the door behind them, and Darren led Celia along a dim hallway to another door, which he unlocked with a key from his pocket. Ahead of them a staircase led down to the cellar. Darren murmured, "I'll go first, I know the way."

The staircase was dark and steep. With one hand Celia gathered her skirt around her, keeping the other hand on the rail. Reaching the foot of the stairs they crossed the brick floor of the cellar to another door, barely visible by the glimmer from a sidewalk grating. Darren opened this door, beyond which she saw a home-spun curtain, and they went into the same muffled room where she had seen Luke before.

Though the sun outside was bright, the curtains covering the sidewalk gratings made this room nearly dark. Drawing a bench out from the table Darren said, "Sit down. She'll send Luke." He rested his cane across the table and began to rub his knee.

Celia sat down. A strange business this, but how proud she was to be part of it. Today was the first of October. She thought of Marion's men, creeping silently through the silver-green light of the swamps this very day, to attack the wagons carrying clothes to Camden. They knew where to lie in wait because she had sent word when the redcoats would leave Charleston and where they were going.

Luke came in, carrying a candle. With what looked like a single movement he strode across the room and set the candle on the table and grabbed both Celia's hands in his.

"The gallant dressmaker!" he greeted her. "More news?"

Luke's vitality had a grandness about it, like a forest wind. Celia said, "Yes, I heard something in the shop yesterday."

Luke sat on the edge of the table and swung his legs. "Tell us."

Celia recounted what she had heard Mrs. Baxter say about Captain Cole and the troop for Lenud's Ferry. Luke listened intently.

"Good," he said. "Good." He leaned nearer, his elbow on his knee. "Now tell us again."

Celia repeated her story. Luke asked several questions. At length he turned to Darren.

"Got it, Darren?"

"Yes."

"Start it out now."

"Right." Darren picked up his cane and left them. From his perch on the table Luke grinned down at Celia.

"You're doing a good job, Sassyface."

"Oh, and I'm so happy doing it!" she exclaimed. "This is the first time I've ever felt that I was doing something really important."

Luke smiled gravely. "It *is* important, Celia."

Their eyes met. More than Darren, more than Godfrey or anybody else, Luke made her understand that their task had greatness; they were not merely getting rid of the redcoats, they were making a nation. Celia said eagerly, "Luke, when Marion's men act on a message I've sent—how do I know?"

Luke shook his head. "Sassyface," he said quietly, "you don't know."

"What! You mean I'll just have to—to *hope* that I'm doing some good?"

"That's it. You won't know if they get your message at all. Some letters don't get through, some arrive too late. Even if you should hear definitely that a troop on its way to Lenud's Ferry has been attacked, you won't know if it was because of you. Six other people may have heard the same thing and sent it out."

Celia tried not to show her chagrin. "Well, if that's the way it is, I'll have to get used to it." She smiled up at him and shrugged. "Not knowing—I suppose that's the hardest part of this job."

"No it isn't," said Luke. He spoke grimly. "Harder than that, is knowing—knowing, and not being able to do anything."

"What do you mean?"

"Sometimes we get a message like yours. We come close to the track they'll have to take. We send scouts ahead. They climb trees and look. They bring back the word. We're outnumbered six to one. And the redcoats are all armed, and a lot of our men are not. We don't dare attack. We have to sit, and let them go by. Wagons loaded with barrels of gunpowder, barrels of beef, crates of guns and shoes, letters telling about their plans."

"I should think," said Celia, "when that happens—you could practically *hear* your heart breaking."

"It does seem like that."

"I'm glad you told me," she said thoughtfully. "Still, it is sort of disappointing, not to know if I'm doing any good."

Luke put his big hand on her shoulder. "What you do know,

Celia," he said, "is that it's folks like us, all together, who are keeping Cornwallis and Clinton apart. So long as the job gets done, it doesn't matter who does it. Right?"

Celia nodded. "Yes, that's right. Now can I ask you something else?"

"Go ahead."

"The Westcotts. What they're doing—isn't it very dangerous?"

"Sure it is," said Luke. "But they've got three sons in the swamp with Marion."

"What sort of place is this?" she asked.

Luke chuckled merrily. "This is a profitable tea-shop, my girl. Mrs. Westcott makes the best pastries in town, Mr. Westcott is a shrewd manager, and they're doing fine. They used to run a shop like this in Georgetown. When I was on the wagon track two of their boys were in my outfit. You must try Mrs. Westcott's nut-bread, Celia, it's great."

"Nut-bread," said Celia, remembering the grin of Ricky Westcott. "That word is a signal, isn't it?"

"It is this week. Next week we'll choose another."

"Like your fancy stockings."

Luke laughed as she told him about recognizing Hugo's stockings yesterday. "I'm glad you're on our side, Sassyface," he said. "With your habit of noticing things, I'd hate to have you working against us. You nearly knocked the breath out of me that evening. I did make the stockings on the track just as I told you, and after my first trip it occurred to me they could be used as a signal to my friends. But do you know, you were the first person who had ever asked me about them?"

Celia crossed her arms on the table before her, laughing too. "Who taught you to knit?" she asked.

"My father. His folks were Scots, and in Scotland men don't think of knitting as a strictly feminine art, any more than tailoring. A lot of Scotsmen knit their own waistcoats and stockings. He taught me once when I fell out of a tree and was laid up with a bad leg."

"Were you very fond of him?" Celia asked.

Luke nodded. "He was grand."

He spoke so warmly that for a moment she felt the old chilly sense of lonesomeness. She wished she could remember her parents. Hurriedly she brought herself back to present concerns. "What did the stockings mean when you wore them?" she asked.

"That I had supplies coming in, needed help to get them to my hiding-places, things like that."

"And how does Hugo use them now?"

"To say he has something to report. Like your basket in the window." Luke brought one knee up under his chin and wrapped his arms about it. "Not many rebel women can afford Hugo these days. Nearly all his customers are friends of the king. You know how long it takes to give a lady a stylish coiffure. So they like to have their friends in, to drink tea and chat while he works, and the ladies aren't always careful what they say. Like your Mrs. Kirby."

Celia nodded. Luke added humorously,

"Also, some of Hugo's customers are not ladies in your sense of the word. They're the girl friends of men like Tarleton and Balfour, and when they have other girls in they don't pour tea. They pour firewater." Luke shrugged. "Those beauties sometimes drink quite a lot during a hairdressing session. And while they drink, they talk. Hugo listens."

Celia spoke contritely. "I guess I've misjudged Hugo too. I never thought he was a real patriot."

Luke's bright sapphire eyes flashed reproachfully toward her. "Sassyface, Hugo is no 'real patriot.' I don't mean he's a Tory—he'd like to see us win the war. But Hugo never did any work in his life that he didn't get paid for."

Celia remembered the gold doubloons with which Darren had induced Hugo to take care of Jimmy. But she did not want to think about that. Again she brought herself back to the present. "Who pays him?"

"We have our friends," said Luke. "Men like Godfrey." He added with a short laugh, "And we do need them. Hugo isn't the only one who won't work for anything but money. What pretty hair you've got. Blond hair and brown eyes, I like that. We'd better figure out a few more signals for you. Mustn't use the basket in the window too often. Can you think of any?"

"Yes," she said, "I've just thought of one."

She spoke quickly. His remark about her hair had given her a twinge of strangeness. Her shock at Bellwood had been so stunning that she had felt washed out of life for good, and Luke's words reminded her that she was still, in spite of Bellwood, a girl that a man could find pleasing. The reminder was a little bit frightening, like taking the first step after an illness. She hurried to answer his question.

"I could give a signal with my cap-pin. I have several. One is a silver butterfly—I could change to the butterfly when I have something to report. It couldn't be seen from the street, but Ida is having some kerchiefs made at the shop. She can come in as often as she likes, to see which pin I'm wearing."

"Not bad. Try the butterfly pin."

"And when Ida's kerchiefs are made," Celia said, "could we tell Madge to order something?"

Luke shook his head, laughing again. "Madge is no good at anything subtle. Just naturally too straightforward."

Celia understood. An affectionate, candid person, normal as a loaf of bread, Madge was not made for adventures.

There was a tap at the door, and Darren came in. "Report's on the way," he announced blithely.

Celia felt a shiver of pride. No doubt Madge was a happy woman, but Celia was glad she was not made that way herself. Darren was crossing the room, and as he came near she gave a cry of astonishment. "Darren!"

He stopped. "What's the matter?"

She heard Luke laughing, but she did not look at him; she was staring at Darren. "Your cane!" she exclaimed. "Your limp—"

Darren held his cane in his hand, but he had not put it to the floor since he came in. He laughed too, a little shamefacedly, and Luke said, "I told you she noticed everything."

With a sigh, Darren laid his cane on the table. "Miserable thing. Walking stiff-legged makes my knee so sore that I'm likely to be really lame before this war's over. Here in the Westcotts' cellar I can walk naturally and it's such a relief, I forgot you didn't know." He sat down on the bench across from Celia and rubbed his aching knee.

"But why do you pretend to be lame?" she demanded.

"To keep out of the king's army," Darren said mirthfully. "I'm just what they want—healthy and under twenty-five, so since Clinton revoked the paroles I'd either have to fight for old George or be in trouble. But I did get a leg-wound during the siege, I've got a scar to prove it. All right now, but if I say I'm still lame they can't prove I'm not."

They all laughed together. It was such a simple trick, and yet so effective that it gave them a feeling of triumph. It occurred to Celia that she had laughed more this morning than during the whole time since she came back to Charleston.

Flexing his knee, Darren said, "I want to go with Marion, but they say I'm more useful in town. Just a born errand boy, that's me."

He and Luke went on to tell her more about the work they were doing and how they did it. How notes were hidden in cabbages, in the hair of farm girls who brought eggs to town, even in Mrs. Westcott's fancy twists of bread. How Marion's men slipped through the swamps with the silence they had learned in years of hunting there, sometimes coming so close to British camps that they could steal guns and powderhorns without rousing the guards. One of their best swamp-dodgers was Amos. Most Britishers were not used to Negroes and knew very little about them. Amos could, whenever he felt like it, drop into a fieldhand dialect and give the impression that he didn't know nothin' about nothin'.

Luke told her how a scout, hidden in a tree, would signal his comrades with a low soft whistle that could be heard for a remarkable distance. Marion himself had devised the whistle. It was so much like a bird-call that only a trained ear could tell the difference.

They talked and talked. They forgot the passage of time until they heard another tap on the door and in came Mr. Westcott, a round little plump fellow who evidently enjoyed his wife's cooking. Mr. Westcott said "Howdy, ma'am," to Celia. He told them that there were several couples here now, in the ladies' side of the tea-shop, and this would be a good time for Darren and Miss Celia to come up by the kitchen way.

He toddled out to wait on his customers, and Luke told Celia that Mrs. Westcott made it a point to be proud of her kitchen. She invited the customers to come in whenever they pleased, to see how spick-and-span it was. Celia and Darren could go up the stairs, but instead of turning toward the refreshment rooms they would go to the kitchen. Celia would give the proper compliments on its neatness, then they would go into the tea-room and order some of Mrs. Westcott's dainties. The kitchen visit would justify their coming into the tea-room by the back door.

Leaving Luke in the cellar, Celia and Darren climbed the stairs again. The kitchen was dustless and gleaming, with big brick ovens watched over by maids in shiny white caps and aprons. The odors were so luscious that Celia did not wonder at the size of Mr. Westcott's paunch. Another couple came in, a ruddy middle-aged pair, the housewife admiring the kitchen while her husband sniffed with appreciation. They all four went together from the kitchen to the tea-room.

Several tables were occupied. As Celia crossed the room she saw Mr. and Mrs. Leon Torrance, but they did not appear to see her. Observing the round innocent face of Leon Torrance, Celia thought again how much he looked like Sophie. She recalled that it must be about time for Sophie's baby to be born. Probably that was why she was not in town, taking part in the gay life she enjoyed so much.

Darren chose a table by a window, and Mrs. Westcott bustled over to serve them. The nut-bread was delicious.

# CHAPTER 2 6

*J*OHN CRUDEN, the man in charge of confiscating rebel estates, went seriously about his work. Two days after Celia's talk with Luke, Mr. Cruden chose the residence of Charles Cotesworth Pinckney, a rich American officer now a prisoner of war. Colonel Pinckney's wife and children were told to go and live with any friends who would make room for them. Mr. Cruden let them have their clothes, but they had to leave everything else.

The family moved out and Mr. Cruden moved in. Having taken care of himself, he was now ready to take care of other people.

It was a bright October and business was good. The town was full of people. Besides the Britishers, merchants from the West Indies were here to buy and sell; men had come from the country to take orders for army supplies; Tories had poured in from other colonies to reap the rewards of their Toryism. Day after day as she minded the parlor Celia listened to their talk, and she had never known there were so many ways to pronounce the English language.

Some of the talk was heartbreaking. She heard of plantations confiscated by Cruden and sold for a fraction of their value to friends of the king. She heard that half the men in Washington's army had no shoes, and winter on the way. She even heard that Cornwallis had started on his northward march.

"Is it true, Luke?" she asked despairingly, next time she saw him.

Luke, however, was not concerned. "Yes, it's true," he said. He smiled as he added, "It's a lot easier to start somewhere than to get there. You keep on listening."

So she kept on listening, and sometimes—not often, but sometimes—she heard items of real value, items that might help win the war.

They had no more news of Cornwallis, but Luke kept his merry courage. "I don't believe," he said, "that Cornwallis will get far. In fact," Luke went on serenely, "it wouldn't surprise me if we made things so tough that instead of his going north to help Clinton, Clinton should have to send more men south to help Cornwallis."

Celia gasped. "Oh Luke, we don't want any more!"

"Oh yes we do, Sassyface," he assured her. "We want all we can get. The more men here with Cornwallis, the less chance Clinton has to close in on General Washington."

He laughed so confidently that Celia laughed too. No matter how dismayed she might have been, Luke always made her feel that they could do anything.

And then Luke was gone.

Celia learned of his departure one morning. She had finished the last of Ida's kerchiefs the day before, and Miss Loring had told her to deliver them after breakfast. The maid who answered the door led her upstairs to the little sitting room, where Ida told her Luke had left town. Ida said Ricky Westcott had come by yesterday to tell them. Ricky did not know when Luke had left; he knew only that his father had sent him to say that Luke's work in town was done, at least for the present, and he had slipped out in secret to rejoin Marion's men.

Before Celia had time to think about how much she was going to miss him, Ida was saying, "Now I have a surprise for you. A nice one." As she spoke she crossed the room to the bedroom door. Celia heard her say, "You may come in now," and through the doorway came Marietta.

With a joyful cry Celia sprang to her feet. Marietta ran to

meet her and they hugged each other. "Oh, Miss Celia," Marietta exclaimed, "I'm so glad to see you!"

"When did you get here?" Celia asked eagerly.

"Last week. But Miss Ida said I'd better not go to the shop to see you, I should wait till you came here."

"And what are you doing in town?"

Marietta glanced at Ida. "It's all right to tell Miss Celia everything, isn't it?"

"Oh yes," Ida said, "only keep your voices down, both of you."

She left them, saying she wanted to speak to the cook about dinner. Celia and Marietta sat side by side on the long chair.

Marietta said Amos had come to Sea Garden several times, bringing letters to be passed on. He had told her about Marion's men. Marietta wanted to help. She had felt so useless, polishing silver and arranging flowers, things like that.

"I know just what you mean," Celia said fervently.

"So Miss Vivian said, if we could figure out some way for me to come to town, I could work for Miss Ida, and do things to help Amos."

"How? Oh never mind, we'll come to that. First tell me how you got here."

Marietta said a redcoat troop had come by Eugene Lacy's plantation some time ago, and had taken a lot of meat and fodder, and his best horses. They had given him one of those promissory notes in payment. But not only did Eugene Lacy have a son who had fought with the Continental Army and was now on the prison-ship in Charleston harbor, also Eugene himself had given aid and comfort to the rebels whenever he could. He could not get a pass to come to Charleston and cash that note on Queen Street.

However, since it was better to have a little money than no money at all, Eugene had asked his friends, if they heard of any Tories going to Charleston, to say he had a note that he would sell at a discount.

"And Miss Celia," said Marietta, "you'll never guess who bought it."

Celia felt a tweak of misgiving. "Not my cousin Roy Garth!"

"That's right, Miss Celia. He and Miss Sophie came by Sea Garden again, and asked if they could spend the night on their way to Charleston. They have a baby boy now, did you know that? Mr. Herbert told them about Mr. Eugene's note, and Mr. Roy said he'd be glad to oblige. He bought it for a very small discount, I don't know how much but I know Mr. Eugene was surprised, he said he hadn't expected any Tory to be so generous."

Celia remembered what Herbert had said of Roy last summer. "No honest man needs to be *that* charming." She wished she knew what Roy had in his mind.

"So then what happened?" she asked.

"Well, Miss Vivian told them her daughter-in-law Mrs. Bernard needed some extra help now that she had two officers staying in the house. She asked if they would take one of the maids from Sea Garden to Charleston with them. Mr. Roy said of course, glad to be of service. So I came to town on their boat."

"Now tell me what you do here," said Celia.

Marietta said Major Brace and Captain Woodley often had visits from other officers. Marietta brought them tea or drinks, came in to open or close the windows. They were not so careful of their talk around a colored housemaid as they were around Godfrey and Ida.

Marietta helped hang out the laundry, on a clothesline that had been arranged so one end could be seen from the street. Ida had some kerchiefs with blue borders. If Godfrey had a message to send but could not take it himself without attracting attention, Marietta hung a blue-bordered kerchief at that end of the clothesline.

"And as time goes on," said Marietta, "we'll find other things I can do."

Celia had heard all she said, but at the same time Celia herself was thinking of Roy. "Marietta," she asked, "where are my cousins staying?"

"With Miss Sophie's brother—Mr. Leon Torrance and his family. They've got a big house on Church Street."

Celia felt uneasy; she did not know why. She was of age now, there was nothing Roy could do to her—unless he found out she was a spy for Marion, and this was a risk she faced every day from everybody on the king's side.

The door of the sitting room burst open and Godfrey's voice exclaimed "Ida!" He stopped on the threshold. "Oh Celia, I'm sorry—didn't know you were here. Where's Ida?"

He spoke jerkily. Something was wrong. "Ida went out to the kitchen," said Celia. "Godfrey, what—"

"Marietta—please go and find her," said Godfrey—"ask her to come up here."

Marietta gave him a glance of concern as she went out. Godfrey slammed the door and stood there, softly beating one fist on the palm of his other hand. Celia stood up.

"Godfrey, shall I leave? Do you want to speak to Ida alone?"

"No, it's no secret. Everybody in town will be talking about it before night." He ran his hand back over his hair, and took two or three breaths to steady himself. "Celia," he asked, "did you ever hear of a man named Benedict Arnold?"

The way he spoke the name, it seemed to rattle around the room. Celia began, "I'm not sure—I believe I have—" and Godfrey said shortly,

"He's commander of the fort at West Point. I mean he was."

"What's happened?" she exclaimed.

Godfrey walked across the room to a window and stood looking out. "A ship has just come from New York with the news. Wait till Ida gets here. Then I won't have to tell it more than once."

A moment later Ida arrived. Evidently Marietta had told her that something seemed amiss, for they were both out of breath from running up the stairs. Ida's slight figure was tense with alarm. "Godfrey, what is it?" she asked anxiously. She added, "Major Brace and Captain Woodley were hurrying out of the house so fast they didn't even see me as we passed in the hall."

"They want the details," he said through his teeth, "hot and fresh. You needn't go, Marietta—might as well hear it now."

He sat down in the nearest chair. It was a little boudoir chair of French design, so slim and frivolous that it seemed to emphasize the heavy load of what he had to say.

He told them Major-General Benedict Arnold was one of the

most brilliant leaders in the American army. Arnold's battle record was heroic, and twice he had received serious wounds. But he felt that his country had not given him the recognition he deserved. Brooding over his wrongs (and his debts), he decided to sell his talents to the other side.

He wrote secretly to Sir Henry Clinton. Arnold had a scheme.

The British held the city of New York, but they had not been able to get control of the country above. Fifty miles north of New York, the fortress of West Point guarded the Hudson River valley. Clinton knew that if he could take this mighty stronghold he would have a good chance to surround Washington's army, maybe even to end the war without waiting for Cornwallis to come up from the south. But without the troops of Cornwallis he was not strong enough to take it.

Arnold knew this too. So he asked: What would the British give him, if he gave them West Point?

In delighted amazement, Clinton replied that they would give him almost anything he wanted. A vast sum of money, a commission in the king's army; and there were hints that the king might even make him a lord.

Arnold set to work. Shortly after the fall of Charleston he asked General Washington to make him commander of West Point. He said one of his wounds was troubling him, and until his health improved he could serve his country better in the fort than on the battlefield. Because of Arnold's valiant record Washington consented.

When Arnold was quite ready, Clinton sent an officer, Major John André, to meet him. In the woods several miles from the fort, Arnold and André worked out details.

On a certain day at a certain hour, the British were to move toward West Point. Arnold promised that just then the defenses would not be adequately manned. When the attack came, he would give vague and contradictory orders, confusing his men, scattering them so they could be easily picked off. Hundreds of Americans would be killed, the rest made prisoners, and the British would take the fort.

Arnold gave André written plans for the attack. André started back to the British lines. But on the way he was captured and the papers were found. On the very day that the king's men were to have taken West Point, Arnold fled to the shelter of a British man-of-war.

Major André was executed as a spy. But Arnold was safe. The British gave him six thousand pounds in cash and made him a brigadier-general in the king's army. They would have given him more if his plan had succeeded, but he got that much for trying.

．～．

As Godfrey talked, once Celia thought she was going to burst into tears. Another time she thought she was going to throw up. She did not do either. She merely sat and stared at him.

The others talked about it in shaky voices. Celia said she had better go.

As she walked back to the shop the streets were buzzing with excitement. Groups of people stood about, talking, arguing, gesturing; even housemaids leaned out of the windows talking to their friends on the sidewalk. Celia had reached the shop and opened the side door before she realized that for the first time since the army had occupied Charleston, she had gone through the street alone and not a single strange man had spoken to her.

She would have liked to sit down quietly and calm her thoughts, but she could not. All she had time for was to throw some cold water on her face before she went back to work. She was about to take out her sewing when the door opened and Mrs. Kirby came in with Mrs. Sloan. Mrs. Kirby was chattering.

". . . and do you know what Captain Cole said? He said that's what comes of making a major-general out of a horse trader. Yes, my dear, that's what Mr. Arnold was before the war, a *horse trader*—oh Miss Garth, I know I'm late for my appointment but so much has been happening I just couldn't get here any sooner, do run up and tell Miss Perry I've simply got to have my fitting—" She sank into a chair. "With so much going on and with all the responsibility I have, I declare I'm quite worn out—"

Celia escaped. She arranged for Mrs. Kirby's belated fitting. Rena Fairbanks, as usual escorted by a group of redcoats, came to order some gauze aprons. Rena went upstairs, the redcoats waited, and while they waited they talked about Benedict Arnold.

All day, everybody talked about Benedict Arnold. Some people laughed, some of them sneered. Some repeated Mrs. Kirby's statement that Arnold had been a horse trader, others said he had been a peddler of drugs. But they agreed that he was common as pig-tracks, like most of the men who were leading the rebel army. They further agreed that Mr. Washington was a monster for having let Major André be executed. They said that although Arnold had not succeeded in giving up West Point, he knew all Washington's plans and now would tell Clinton what he knew, and the American insurrection would be crushed in a month.

Celia tried to remind herself that not everybody in town felt like this. There were many people who were as stricken as she was. But as Luke had reminded her, most of the patriot women had little money to spend; they could not order clothes in a fashionable shop. She told herself this, but it did no good. The patriots were silent. All she could hear was the laughter of those who had yielded to the king.

She wanted to sob, to scream, to order them out of here. Instead she sewed, she ran up and down the stairs, she smiled and curtsied, she said, "How do you do. Certainly, sir. Yes ma'am. No indeed, it's no trouble at all." Silently she prayed, "Please God, help me live through this day!"

That afternoon there was a shower. During the rain no more customers came in, and by the time the sun appeared those who were already here had finished their business, so they went home. For a blessed few minutes the parlor was empty.

Celia let her sewing fall into her lap. She was stitching the waistband for a gauze apron; she wondered if the thing would be fit to wear. The room was close. Laying her work on the table she went to the nearest window and pushed up the sash. After the rain the air was clean and cold, and gave her a feeling of refreshment. It must be nearly closing time—maybe nobody else would come in today. But even as she thought this, she heard the front door open.

She wet her lips, put on her professional smile, and looked around. As she did so she heard a little gasp of surprise. The customer was Sophie, and Sophie had seen her minding the parlor, and Sophie did not like it.

"Why Celia," cried Sophie, "I didn't know you were working here again!" Her childish voice was shrill with astonishment.

"Yes," Celia said, still with her professional smile, "I've been back some time now."

They met at the balustrade. How pretty Sophie looked, and how pampered. Since the birth of her baby her figure had regained its soft young lines, and she was becomingly dressed in a fall costume of tan and dark green. Her neatly gloved little hands fluttered on the ledge of the balustrade. "But I thought," she said —"I thought you were with Mrs. Lacy."

Keeping her voice as level as she could, Celia answered, "I couldn't stay with Mrs. Lacy forever."

"But—" Sophie protested helplessly—"but she would have been so *glad* to have you!"

Celia's hands, out of sight under the ledge, gripped each other. "Really," she answered, "I'd rather be independent."

"But working here—right out in public—meeting all sorts of people—oh Celia, it's hardly right! Nobody in our family would think of working in a public place—" Sophie paused plaintively.

Celia wondered which really caused more trouble in the world, villains like Benedict Arnold or fools like Sophie Garth. Still doing her best to speak evenly, she said, "I'm sorry you and I have the same name. But I won't tell anybody your husband is related to me. I promise."

"But people always—" Sophie began, and caught herself. She did not want to be so tactless as to say what she had almost said: People always find out embarrassing things like that. Her hands fluttered again, her eyelids quivered over her soft gray-blue eyes. She smiled hopefully. "Now don't you worry. I'm sure we can do something for you. Roy is so fond of you. He and I were talking about you last year, we wanted to do something for you then, but about that time we heard you were planning to be married—oh that was such a pity about Mr. Rand—but don't you worry, I'm sure we can—" Her voice fell off into an uncertain silence—probably, Celia thought, because she herself was looking as stony-mad as she felt.

Celia said, "I'm perfectly all right, thank you. I don't need anybody to 'do something' for me. I'm earning my—"

The door opened again. Sophie turned around, plainly glad to have Celia's speech interrupted, as she would not have known how to answer it. The newcomer was Sophie's hostess and sister-in-law, Mrs. Torrance, who had paused on the front steps to speak to her husband. Celia heard a carriage drive off, and Mrs. Torrance said to Sophie that Leon would be back for them in a little while. Sophie exclaimed,

"Oh Emily, you didn't tell me Celia Garth was working here!"

"We've had so much else to talk about," Mrs. Torrance said with a quick smile. Brushing the matter aside as if they could gain nothing by discussing it, she spoke to Celia with formal politeness. "We have no appointment, Miss Garth, but will you ask Miss Loring if we can see some nice soft muslins, to make clothes for a small child?"

Celia replied, "Certainly, Mrs. Torrance. Will you and Mrs. Garth sit down for a few minutes, please?"

She curtsied, and went toward the door to the staircase. Mrs. Torrance was several years older than Sophie and had two children of her own, so now she enjoyed giving Sophie some big-sisterly supervision. Celia heard her saying that they outgrew their baby-clothes so fast, you simply had to have a few more things made for them right away.

Celia went upstairs, told Miss Loring what the ladies wanted, and came back to tell them they could go up now. She opened the gate in the balustrade and then the door to the staircase. They went through and she closed the door after them.

For a moment she stood with her hand on the doorknob, thinking. Sophie was such a buttercup of a child, though she was a grown woman, a wife and mother. It was puzzling. Celia had been told that the experiences of love and motherhood were tremendous. And yet Sophie, and so many other women who came through this parlor every day, had had all this, but still seemed to have experienced nothing at all.

Right now she was too tired to try to understand it. She pressed her hands to her head. She did not often have headaches, but now she had one, a dull weary feeling more like a heaviness in her head than like actual pain. She thought of Sophie's words. "I'm sure we can do something for you . . ."

Anybody hearing her, Celia reflected, would think I was a puppy sitting up on my hind legs begging. I don't want anything of Sophie or Roy or the Torrances. All I want is for them to let me alone.

Her head felt as if she were carrying a rock in it. She could not help feeling that they were not going to let her alone.

# CHAPTER 27

*D*URING the next few weeks Sophie came into the shop several times. But she was always accompanied by Emily Torrance or some other friend, and she followed Emily's example of addressing Celia as "Miss Garth." After that first visit she made no more personal remarks.

Sometimes Leon Torrance came in with them, but Celia did not see Roy at all. From their conversations she gathered that Roy was busy elsewhere, running British errands. He seemed to be doing a lot of traveling these days.

Celia went on with the work Luke had told her to do. He had warned her that it would not be fun. He was right. It wasn't.

Now that the first excitement was over, she found that spying was a hard and thankless job. She had to be alert for a thousand trifles before she found one that might be of any use. When she found it she had to use all her wits to report it without being observed. And while she was doing this she also had to do her day's work; she had to be quick and obliging and sweet, though her legs ached and the customers often made unreasonable demands, especially the new-rich Tories who were not used to the heady sensation of ordering people around.

She passed her notes in many ways. She passed them to Ida, Godfrey, Darren, the Westcotts. How any note went out of town, or if it went out at all, or if it did any good, she never knew. Now and then she would hear of a skirmish, but she had no idea if she had had anything to do with it, or even if the report was true. In general, people in Charleston did not know much about what happened out of town. The *Gazette* published only what Balfour wanted them to read.

But in November, they got a piece of news that Balfour had done his best to keep from them. The rebels of the Upcountry had won a resounding victory. At Kings Mountain on the line between the two Carolinas, they had defeated a crack Tory troop led by a British colonel. And Luke's prediction turned out to be right: Cornwallis had hastily reversed his northward march and had brought his army back to South Carolina.

The news of Kings Mountain, five weeks late, was brought to town by a Negro servant of John Rutledge, the exiled rebel governor of South Carolina. Godfrey was too shrewd to rejoice openly, but Burton invited his rebel friends to a dinner-party. In the shop, behind her sweet professional smile, Celia was thinking how mad Colonel Balfour must be. From what she had heard of him, she guessed that he was drowning his wrath in a bottle. She hoped that tomorrow morning his head would hurt terribly.

Perhaps it did, but his temper hurt worse. Balfour could not take away knowledge of Kings Mountain from the Charleston rebels, but he could punish them for knowing. A squad of red-coats knocked at the door of the house on Meeting Street and told Burton that he was under arrest and would be shipped to St. Augustine. At the same time, other squads of redcoats were at the doors of some twenty-odd other prominent men who had not taken the king's oath, telling them that they also would be shipped to St. Augustine. The men were marched through the streets and hustled aboard a British ship in the harbor. Two days later the ship sailed.

The next time Celia saw Darren, he told her that Cruden had confiscated Burton's plantation and sold it for almost nothing to a deserving Tory. Cruden had not taken the Meeting Street house, possibly because it was not grand enough to be tempting. So Elise and her children still had a home, and Godfrey would see to it that they did not lack anything they needed.

*319*

There were now sixty exiles in St. Augustine, all of them leading men of South Carolina who had refused to take the king's
oath. At first Celia was distressed that Burton had to be one of
them. But as she thought it over she felt sure that he was not
distressed about himself. Burton was a yes-or-no man; he was
simply not capable of leading a double life, as Godfrey was doing now. Burton had always tried to do the right thing, and this
time he had no doubt about what the right thing was. He had the
approval of the best people. As long as he had this, Burton would
not be miserable.

•~•

After Kings Mountain, Balfour tried to keep Charleston shut
up tighter than ever. But as long as food had to come in, he could
not keep out all the rebel news, nor even all the rebels themselves.
So it happened that on a Sunday morning shortly after breakfast,
the maid came to tell Celia that Mr. Darren Bernard had called,
and wanted her to walk with him to the tea-shop.

When they reached the tea-shop they found Godfrey and Ida
already there. Mrs. Westcott told them Luke had slipped in last
night from a fishing-boat. She said he had a grand tale to tell.

She led them down to the muffled room, where Luke had just
finished a breakfast of hominy and fresh mackerel and hot buttered raisin rolls. Beside him on the table stood Vivian's hourglass
and a lighted candle. Mrs. Westcott took the tray and went upstairs, while the others gathered around Luke to hear his story.
Luke strode up and down, talking with big vivid gestures that
made the little room seem even smaller than it was.

He was talking about General Marion. Yes, general now, he
said, no longer colonel. From his hiding-place in North Carolina,
Governor Rutledge had sent couriers to both Sumter and Marion,
bringing them commissions as brigadier-generals.

"Here in the Carolina Lowcountry," said Luke, "we swamp-
dodgers have been making pests of ourselves. We pop out of the
swamp, we attack, we disappear. Tarleton hollers that we 'won't
fight like gentlemen.' I suppose he's right. Tarleton went to Ox-
ford, and most of us are not gentlemen in his sense of the word.
Quite a few of us can't read Latin. To tell the truth, quite a few

of us can't read English. But every man of us can shoot the eye out of a squirrel at the top of a pine tree."

Luke's eye caught Celia's, and he grinned. Thrusting his hands into his pockets he said to her, "The swamp-dodgers have a proverb. They say, 'A Carolina fightin' man, sir, owns all the ground within shootin' distance of where he stands.' And that's just about the way it is." Celia laughed, and Luke went on.

"Well, as you know, Cornwallis left Camden and started north to meet the troops Clinton was sending south. But the word had gone out—delay him, make the going hard. His men were sniped at from behind the fences. Boys and girls went out with hatchets and chopped up the road signs, or sometimes turned them around so the men went miles in the wrong direction and had to march back and start over.

"They had trouble getting food. In that country above Camden, Tarleton and Wemyss had been busy in ways you already know about. People who still had corn, or meat animals, burned the corn and killed and buried the animals, to keep Cornwallis from getting them. And behind him, we were attacking the wagon trains that were bringing supplies for his men.

"Then those heroes in the Upcountry won their victory at Kings Mountain. When that happened, Cornwallis had been on the march a month and he had gone only fifteen miles past the South Carolina border. He brought his army back as fast as he could.

"When he got settled in camp he had still more reports on Marion's men. He decided Marion had to be captured. He sent an order to Tarleton.

"Tarleton was aching for glory. He's ambitious and extravagant and he has a pile of gambling debts. When Cornwallis told him to get Marion, he was delighted.

"I don't know where Tarleton was when he got the order. But the main body of his legion was at Camden. He was in such a hurry to get after Marion that he wouldn't wait for the legion— he sent them word that he was riding toward the Santee River and they were to catch up with him. He set out with a few horsemen and rode toward Nelson's Ferry.

"Marion got word from his informers—don't ask me who they

were, I don't know. They told him Tarleton had set out with a small escort. We had about five hundred men, and Marion figured that if we could meet Tarleton before his legion caught up with him, we could make him prisoner. So we got orders to ride toward Nelson's Ferry.

"We rode hard. The night of November tenth—it was a Friday, I'll never forget it—we had had a long day's ride and were mighty glad when Marion told us to halt. We were in a grove near a plantation owned by a rebel officer named Richardson.

"While we were making camp, Marion saw a glow on the sky over toward the Richardson place. He told a guard to see what was on fire. Pretty soon the man came back with Colonel Richardson—he'd been home sick and was barely strong enough to walk.

"Colonel Richardson said Tarleton's men must have caught up with him some time during that day. He said Tarleton and the whole force had come riding down the road toward his place not long before dark. They were looking for Marion, but when Tarleton saw a rich-looking country house ripe for looting, he couldn't resist it.

"The men stormed through, helping themselves to whatever they wanted. They even dug up the dead body of Colonel Richardson's father, to see if anything worth stealing had been buried in his grave. When they had taken as much as they could carry they started the fires. The glare of the burning was what Marion had seen on the sky.

"Now that Tarleton had his legion with him, Colonel Richardson said we were outnumbered two or three to one, and also they had brought along a pair of cannon. We've got no field-pieces. And what was most heartbreaking—Colonel Richardson said we had an Arnold right along with us. One of our men had deserted to Tarleton and had told him where we were camped that night.

"There just one thing for us to do. We had to move fast.

"So we did. We went through a swamp the like of which I hope I never have to go through again in the black slimy dark of a night in November. Six miles of it that night, and we'd already had a hard day. We sloshed on till we had passed a mill-dam on a little branch called Jack's Creek—that's around the bend of the Santee, upstream from Nelson's Ferry.

"But Marion knew exactly what he was doing. At the end of that six miles, he had put a bad swamp and a millpond between us and Tarleton. We had come to some big trees on high dry ground. He let us stop here, to eat whatever we had in our saddle-bags—mostly cold roasted sweet potatoes—and fall down for some sleep."

Luke let out a tired-sounding sigh, as if remembering his own exhaustion after that night's escape. He went on.

"Tarleton sent some fellows to spy out our campsite. They came back and reported that we weren't there any more.

"They didn't have any trouble seeing which way we had gone. We had had to move in such a hurry that we had left a clear trail. Tarleton ordered his men to their horses and they set out after us.

"Marion expected Tarleton to follow. We were sleeping like pigs, but it seemed like no time at all before he was waking us up. I had time to eat half a sweet potato while my horse got some grass, and that was all before we were moving again.

"Marion led us. It was broad daylight now, but under the trees where we were there was hardly enough sun to make shadows. Just that green swamp twilight. Do you know that country?— cypress trees hung with moss like gray curtains, vines thick as tree-trunks growing from tree to tree, swamp-water black from the cypress drippings. All around us birds and butterflies and a million flying things biting our faces and getting into our eyes, and little animals scurrying under the brush and sometimes an alligator in the water. Everything teeming with life, and yet there's a silence—I don't know why. The noises get lost.

"We went on and on, splashing through water or picking our way along the ridges, our horses so tired they could hardly move, ourselves slapping and scratching and sweating and shivering and too tired even to complain. Marion was leading us northeast, toward the Black River. We rode, we stopped and cut the way through, we mounted again and kept riding. We had no stops to eat or sleep. You munched what you had, as you rode. When you couldn't stay awake any longer you fell out for some sleep. When a man fell out nobody waited for him. The rest kept going, and he had to catch up when he could.

"We rode to the river. Then we rode downstream.

"Tarleton was right behind us. Every now and then Marion would tell one of us to climb a tree, and wait there to see what could be seen, and come down and catch up and report. So we knew. Marion was moving so fast that some of our men couldn't keep up. They straggled at a distance, following our trail. Tarleton was so close that his foremost men were making prisoners of our hindmost.

"Some of the men didn't want to keep moving. Miles Rand, and other men who had had experiences like his. They wanted a battle. They wanted to get at Tarleton right now, tear him to pieces. But Marion kept his head, like always. He expected a battle, but he wanted to choose the place.

"And he had chosen it—I know that country pretty well, and it was plain where he was leading us. Benbow's Ferry. Ten miles above Kingstree. Right there, the swamp meets the river, then there's some safe high ground. It's the only spot for miles where you can cross the river safely. Once we got there, we could turn and make a stand on the high ground, and we would have command of the crossing. Since we had to meet a force so much larger than ours, at least there we would have a fighting chance.

"We had left Richardson's place on a Friday night, and now it was Sunday. For a while we'd been riding along fairly dry ground. Now we came to another bog, about ten miles above Benbow's Ferry. Folks thereabouts call it Ox Swamp. It's a mess of mud. Wide and miry, trees growing thick in the water.

"Marion sent for me, and several other fellows who had been with him long enough to be well trained in his ways. He told us he could lead the men around the swamp, but it would take longer. He was going to lead them straight through.

"He wanted us to stay behind, to see if Tarleton went through the swamp or around it. As soon as we made sure, we were to catch up and report, so he could know how much time he had to set up his defenses. He was leaving several of us as lookouts so if one man was caught, or two, there would still be the chance that another man would get through.

"So he left us. We each chose a tree, and climbed up and waited.

"It was bright sunshiny fall weather. I had picked a big tree with moss hanging around me like a tent. Before long, I saw Tarleton's Legion. And Tarleton.

"They were an impressive lot. Tired as we were and spattered with mud, but still a great array. Fine men, fine horses, fine weapons.

"And a fine leader. Tarleton's a good-looking man, green coat and white breeches and knee-high boots, and on his head a tall hat with black plumes—a shako, they call it.

"They were coming over the dry ground where we had crossed a little while before. They were riding right in our tracks, Tarleton at the head of them. And there I sat in the tree, almost scared to breathe, waiting to see which way he would lead them.

"They came near. As the ground got softer the men slowed down. Tarleton rode up to where the bad mire set in. He reined his horse, looked around. The leaders of his troop rode up. They all looked at that mess in front of them.

"Tarleton knew Marion's men had just been there. If Marion could get past the swamp, Tarleton could get past it too.

"The men were waiting for orders. Up in those trees, we were waiting. Tarleton rode a few yards in one direction, then in the other, and back again. Then all of a sudden he stopped with a sort of disgusted snort, he wheeled his horse and shouted his order. He said,

" 'Go back! We can find that gamecock Sumter, but as for this damned swamp fox, the devil himself couldn't catch him.' "

Luke stopped. His hearers burst out laughing.

"Swamp fox!" said Godfrey.

"Swamp fox!" said Celia.

They all said it, merrily, with appreciation. Celia was thinking that while she had never expected to thank Tarleton for anything, she did thank him for inventing so apt a name. Marion the Swamp Fox.

"And he really turned back?" she said. "So close!"

Luke smiled and shrugged. "He did. I saw him. He quit, and rode up toward Camden to look for General Sumter."

Godfrey gave an exclamation. The sand had run out. It was time for church. He and Ida had been so dutiful about attending and affecting to join in the prayers for the king, that they did not want to stay away now. Ida drew her cloak around her, laughing softly as she said, "And today we really have something to thank the Lord for."

They went out, and Luke told Darren to bring some pens and paper. Tarleton's unsuccessful chase of Marion had been noised all over the country outside Charleston, and now, to spread the the story in town, Luke said he would write a summary that could be quickly read. Darren and Celia would make several copies, and Darren would take these around to other friends of Marion who would make more. Tonight—or rather, early tomorrow morning—all these copies would be posted on walls and fences about town. They would be put up by people whose business took them out before dawn: a fisherman going to his boat, a doctor on the way to a patient; an old woman who kept hens, delivering eggs for breakfast.

Of course the redcoat guards would pull down the notices as fast as they saw them, but no matter. The tale of the Swamp Fox would be out.

When the papers were ready Darren went to distribute them, telling Celia that when he came back they would go to the refreshment room. "Mrs. Westcott's making crackling-bread today," he said.

As the door closed Celia smiled happily up at Luke. He stood by her, resting one hand on the table.

"I feel so much better than I did," she told him.

"Has it been hard going?" he asked with sympathy.

She nodded. "I've been so tired. Ever since that business about Benedict Arnold."

Looking down at her, Luke smiled slowly. For a moment he did not answer. With his rough homespun clothes and thick boots, his face so weatherbeaten that his skin was darker than his hair, his bright blue eyes full of devilment, Luke looked like an embodiment of all he had been telling her. She thought of Marion's men, tough and fighting mad, living on sweet potatoes and water, slogging into battle with two rounds of ammunition apiece, and many a man with not even a gun until some other man—friend or enemy—dropped and he could grab the gun from the falling hands. Such men had to have the kind of strength she saw in Luke.

They had to have absolute faith, like his, in the rightness of their cause. They could not do what they were doing if they had had anything less.

She had spoken of Arnold. With his untroubled grin, Luke answered,

"Celia, when we lost Charleston, lots of people said, 'It's all over.' After Camden they said, 'It's all over.' After Arnold the same. And it's not over yet."

"I wish you had been here the day we got the news," she said, "to tell me something like that. I've never had such a day." She told him what it had been like, the sneers and shrugs and Tory laughter. "And then that little fool Sophie, gabbling that she wanted to 'do something' for me! I suppose she'd like to have me move into her house and do her dressmaking for nothing, instead of disgracing her by working for wages in a shop." Celia gave a shiver.

Luke's big rugged hand dropped on her shoulder. "My dear," he said in a low voice, "I can't protect you from the sneers, I can't protect you from fools and Tories—how I wish I could."

His hand closed on her. His other hand gripped her other arm and lifted her up to meet him as he bent forward and kissed her.

Celia was so taken by surprise that for an instant she made no response at all, either of yes or no. But then her back stiffened and she pushed herself away from him, violently exclaiming, "No, Luke, no! Don't do that!"

He still held her. "Why not?" he asked simply.

"Because—" With an effort Celia pulled one arm free, and put up her elbow in front of her face. "Because I don't want you to! Not you or anybody—after Jimmy—"

"Oh, bosh," said Luke. His hands closed on her as before. He kissed her again, hard and almost roughly, and let her go. Taking a step back from her, he spoke. "There. I didn't want to fall in love with you! But I knew I couldn't help it if this kept up."

He walked away from her and stood looking down. His big heavy-shod foot kicked at a seam of the canvas that covered the floor.

Celia stood where she was. She was astounded. Luke had never, by any word or gesture, indicated that he might be in love with her. On the contrary, his manner toward her had been studiedly casual. As for herself, she had thought she was through with love. She felt now that she wanted to be through with it, she did not want Luke or any other man to come near her. After a moment to catch her breath she said shortly, "I don't know what you're talking about."

At the sound of her voice Luke turned around and faced her.

"I'm talking about you, dear," he retorted, "and about me. Everybody wanted you to work with us—Mother, Godfrey, even Hugo said, 'Miss Garth has got the nerve, I have seen it.' But me—I wanted you too, because I liked you so much, and I didn't want you for the same reason. I knew I'd get into trouble —and I did." Luke gave a mighty sigh.

Celia did not know how to answer. The way he spoke was so different from the way he had ever spoken to her, and so different from the way she had ever heard anybody talk. She stood twisting her hands together, hearing him and not understanding him, and he seemed still more strange when he said,

"You see—the fact is, I've been in love with you ever since I've known you."

This at least she could answer. "Oh no you were not!" she exclaimed. "When I first worked for Vivian you could have seen me any time you pleased and you ignored me utterly. That doesn't seem like love—"

"It was, though," he said. But she rushed on.

"When you found I was engaged to Jimmy—that night of the ball—you were glad to hear it!"

"My dear girl," said Luke, "I was delighted. I thought I was getting rid of you."

At her gasp of shock he laughed, softly and with a sound of pleasure.

"Maybe," he said, "you were slightly in love with me too, right from the start, or you wouldn't have been so conscious that I was avoiding you—a man you'd never seen but once in your life."

Now she was getting angry. "What *do* you mean?" she demanded.

"I'm trying to tell you," Luke said patiently. "The first time I met you, I liked you. There was a communication between us—a sort of 'deep calleth unto deep,' as the Bible says in another sense. Remember?"

She did remember. He had been so easy to talk to. Luke was saying,

"When I left you I thought, Now *there's* a girl—and right away my common sense told me, Look out! If one chance meeting has scorched you like this—let go, before you get burned by the real fire."

The tone of his voice changed. It became earnest, almost pleading.

"Can't you understand that, Celia? I was doing one of the most dangerous jobs of the war. There wasn't any room in my mind for a girl—"

"Oh yes there was," said Celia. "That first evening I thought, He's got a girl in every town between Charleston and Philadelphia. And I still think so."

"Oh no," Luke protested, "not *every* town." He took a step toward her, and stopped. "My dear, if you don't know the difference between girls and *a girl*, you know even less about love than I thought you did."

Celia spoke with a breathless anger. "What are you—"

But Luke had not paused. "Of course, you were not in love with Jimmy—"

"Oh, stop!" cried Celia. "How can you say I didn't love Jimmy?"

For a moment Luke did not answer. She felt his strong direct gaze, and when he spoke there was a quiet wisdom in his voice. "You loved him, Celia. But you were not in love with him. There's a difference."

Celia's throat felt as if she had a marble in it. She wanted to scream at him, and tell him again to stop this, but she could not. She could not say anything. His bright eyes held her and she had to hear what he was saying.

"You loved Jimmy, yes. You loved his mother, and Miles, and you loved the feeling that they loved you. Nothing wrong with that. Plenty of women settle for less. But my dear—" again he spoke earnestly, in a low voice—"that's not being in love with a man."

With a great effort Celia managed to free her voice. "Stop it, Luke! I won't hear any more." As she spoke she ran to the curtain that covered the door. She started to draw it aside, but she felt him gripping her elbows, forcing her to turn around and face him.

"Don't be a fool," he said shortly. "Do you want to put us all in that lockup under the Exchange? Don't go blundering out of here till you know it's safe."

Celia was trembling with rage. "Let go of me!"

He did not obey. His hands were so tight that he hurt her. "Keep your voice down," he ordered. "And listen. Don't leave this room till Darren comes here to get you. I'll leave. Is that what you want?"

Celia wished he would stop *looking* at her. He had such vitality that his eyes seemed to shine at her with a light of their own. "Yes, yes," she said breathlessly. "Go away. I don't want to hear any more of what you've been saying. About love."

Luke began to laugh. "All right, Sassyface. I'll leave you now. But one of these days I'm going to teach you what I mean about love, whether you like it or not."

He let go of her, and with one hand he swept aside the curtain that hid the door. Celia stood rubbing her elbows, trying to ease the ache of his grip. Over his shoulder Luke grinned down at her.

"And my darling," he said softly, "you'll like it."

# CHAPTER 28

*N*ow Celia was so confused that she hardly knew what was happening around her. Day after day she went through her routine in the shop, almost without thinking about it. She tried to listen as before, and pick up hints that might be of use to Marion's men. But after a minute or two she found her mind back where it had been, concerned with herself, and with Luke.

He says he's in love with me. He says I was somewhat in love with him from the first. He says I was not in love with Jimmy.

What does he mean? Jimmy was so warm and strong! I knew I could count on him. I loved him. But—

But Luke was talking about something different.

She tried to be practical. It would be easy to say, "Why yes, Luke, if this crazy talk means you're asking me to marry you, I'll be glad to do it. Any girl as poor as I am would grab the chance to marry into a rich family like yours." Of course she would say it in prettier words than this.

But these days there was no counting on wealth. Look at what had happened to General Sumter, to Burton, to hundreds of other rich men. No matter who won the war, at the end of it Luke might not have a penny.

Or she might say, "Yes, yes! I'll take you rich or poor. Anything is better than being a dried-up crosspatch like Miss Loring."

But she knew she was not really in danger of turning into a dried-up crosspatch. Now that she no longer felt the hopeless despair with which she had come back to the shop, Celia knew that here she did have a future. She had proved that she could become a famous dressmaker. She could be a woman with a career, proud of herself.

No, she had no reason to pay attention to Luke. No reason at all. Unless she was in love with him.

There she was, back where she had started.

Day after day her mind followed the same circle. She would sit behind the parlor balustrade, sewing and thinking, until her thoughts were cut by a peevish voice. "Miss Garth! Can't you hear me? *Please* open the gate!"

Celia would spring up, saying, "Oh, I'm so sorry, do come in." But as soon as she went back to her sewing the circle of her thoughts would start again.

The war seemed a long way off, though there were signs of it all around her. Luke had done his work so well that now the spy system reached every corner of town. Marion's helpers were rich men, laborers, tavern maids, peddlers calling shrimp and oysters in the street. They gathered information, they passed notes, or they engaged the attention of the British guards so other people could do so. More items about Marion's men were posted in the night, to be read in the morning. Gradually, to redcoats and rebels alike, Marion was becoming a figure of legend, a ghostly hero who came out of nowhere and went back into nothing.

But to Celia, this seemed to be no concern of hers any more. Always she was thinking, Luke may be back any time. What am I going to say to him?

Ida sent Marietta over one day with an invitation to supper. After supper, when they gathered in Ida's little sitting room, Godfrey said, "We were getting worried about you—hadn't heard from you lately."

Celia said with Christmas so near, the shop had such a rush of business that she had hardly five minutes at a time to sit and listen for what the customers might say. "I'm sorry," she added.

She felt guilty. She felt even more guilty when Godfrey urged,

"Don't apologize! That wasn't what I meant. You're doing a great job."

Ida said she had thought of a new way to pass the next note across the balustrade. She would write to the shop ordering five yards of pink ribbon, and would ask them to have the package ready so that she could have a maid pick it up. Little packages like this were customarily put into a drawer of Celia's worktable. Next time Celia had a note to send out, Ida continued, she was to give a signal by way of the window. Marietta would come in to ask for the ribbon, and Celia could hand the package and note together across the balustrade.

And they really must think of a new window-signal, said Ida. Now in winter the parlor windows were kept closed, so the signal must be one that could be seen through the pane. Celia had already used the special draping of the curtains.

Celia said she would try to think of a new signal. She bit her lip, telling herself that she *must* keep her mind on Marion and not on Luke, or she would have no more notes to pass.

Godfrey and Ida walked with her back toward the shop. They had not gone far before they sensed an unusual excitement around them. It was a chilly evening when you would expect people to be more comfortable indoors than out, but the streets were crowded. Men stood in groups, talking angrily. The redcoat patrols were telling them to move on and not block the sidewalk, but as soon as one group broke up, another began to cluster near by. A little way past the home of old Simon Dale on Meeting Street, Celia caught sight of Mr. Dale himself. Striking his cane on the pavement, he was announcing to a gentleman of his own age that this was an outrage, sir, an outrage, and he'd gladly say so to the king himself.

Godfrey paused to ask what had happened.

Simon Dale gave a growl. Speaking so vehemently that his breath was like the smoke of cannon in front of him, he exclaimed that he hardly liked to discuss this matter in the presence of ladies. That's how disgraceful it was.

Ida took Celia's hand and drew her gently back into the shadows. Pretending to think that only Godfrey could hear him now, Simon sputtered out the story. Celia had felt inclined to giggle, but as she listened she felt like that no longer.

Simon said Balfour had ordered the arrest of two women of good reputation—unmarried sisters, named Sarazen—and had put them into that dungeon under the Exchange. The Misses Sarazen had been told that they were suspected of sending out rebel information. They had not been told who accused them, nor what information they were supposed to have sent; nor had there been any trial. All that had happened was that a few hours ago a red-coat party had appeared at their home, and the leader had told them they were under arrest. They were led through the street to the Exchange, and locked up in the vault with the criminals.

This vault was called the Provost. It was the only place where criminals were kept nowadays, for the town jail was being used as a barracks for British soldiers. The Provost was a stone-walled room, damp and almost airless, crawling with vermin. The place was already jammed with fifty-six human beings. These were men and women, white persons and Negroes; they were killers, drunkards, prostitutes, street-brawlers, some of them suffering from loathsome diseases. There was no separation by sex, day or night. There was no privacy at all, not even for what Simon Dale referred to as "calls of nature."

As he talked, Simon nearly choked with fury. He said he knew the Misses Sarazen. They were *ladies,* and Simon made it clear exactly what he meant by a lady. Also, said Simon, the fact that the Sarazen sisters had never been married made the whole business even more of an insult. It was an insult, he added, to every decent woman in town.

Celia felt Ida pressing closer to her. Ida carried a fur muff; she took Celia's hand and drew it into the muff and held it, as though for security. Celia returned the grasp. They were both trembling with the thought, This could have happened to me.

"Now, now, good people," said a tired young voice with a British accent. "Walk on, don't crowd."

"Very well," said Godfrey, and turning to Simon Dale he said good night. By the glow of the street-light Celia saw his face. Godfrey looked sick. He too was thinking, It could have happened to anybody. To my friends. To my wife.

Simon Dale was right, thought Celia. It's an insult to every decent woman in town.

For the next few days, everybody talked about the affair of the Sarazens. People on both sides were shocked. They said it was just about what you would expect of Balfour.

Balfour knew—how could he help knowing?—that rebel news had been going out of Charleston. But they said, and had been saying for a long time, that he was too drunk and lazy to carry through an efficient plan of stopping it. His guards had arrested a few boys posting news on fences, a few fishermen smuggling notes written by other people. These fellows were usually thrown into the dungeon until they paid a fine.

This procedure, no matter how often repeated, did nothing to dig up the roots of the spy system. The rebels had scoffed at Balfour. So had some of his own subordinate officers in Charleston. Many of these men had given years of real service to their country, and they did not enjoy taking orders from a fellow who had used Balfour's methods of getting ahead.

Prodded to do something about the informers, one day Balfour angrily shouted the order to throw the Misses Sarazen into the dungeon. People in general agreed with Simon Dale that he had chosen them because he thought the indecencies there would be especially painful to women used to living in maiden isolation.

Balfour's own officers waited on him with such violent protests that after three or four days the Sarazen sisters were allowed to go home. They were besieged by visitors. Some of these were busybodies panting to hear a sensational tale, others were genuine friends. In their state of distraction the sisters could not tell the difference. They locked their door, and refused to discuss their days and nights in the dungeon. What had happened to them there, nobody ever knew.

Nothing was proved against them. This might have been because there was nothing to prove, or because the British authorities were so eager to forget the episode that they did not try.

After her first shock, Celia found that she was not so much scared as she was just plain mad. She felt a burning defiance. For the first time since Luke had kissed her, she was thinking of something besides Luke. She was wondering, Does Balfour think this is the way to stop us? I'll show him.

She found herself again keeping her ears alert. With no effort at all, she thought of a new signal she could give from the side window. Because of the gloomy weather she suggested to Mrs. Thorley that they brighten the parlor with some potted ferns. Mrs. Thorley said it was a good idea, and Celia then suggested that the pots be of different colors, such as red and yellow and white.

When she saw Darren again she told him that next time she had a message to send she would put the white-potted fern at the window. The white pot could be easily seen through the glass.

She felt refreshed, glad she was back on the job. In spite of the rush of business she managed to listen. December ended, the year 1781 began, and in January her attention was rewarded. She heard Mrs. Hendrix bragging to another stout overdressed woman that Mr. Hendrix had been *so* busy lately, collecting wagons to take barrels of gunpowder up to Camden.

Mrs. Hendrix had a great deal to say about her husband's importance in this matter. Celia guessed that all he had done was guide some British officers to plantations where they would find the sort of wagons they needed, so the British could take these and give the owners promissory notes, which Mr. Hendrix would then buy at a discount. Many Tories did this. They were most helpful, leading the way to supplies of all kinds. Naturally they took care to recommend that supplies be bought from people who for one reason or another could not come to town to cash the notes for themselves.

However, this did not matter right now. What did matter was that in the course of her bragging Mrs. Hendrix clearly said the wagons were gathering at Dorchester, and would start very soon unless it rained again.

Celia thought it was likely to rain again, for the winter so far had been a mushy one and she saw no sign that it was drying up. But sooner or later the wagons would start. Meanwhile, some bright fellow could be sent to Dorchester to keep an eye on them. Now at last after her weeks of uselessness she had something to report.

Everything went well. She thought of a new excuse to get up to the bedroom alone and write her message. Putting some wood on the parlor fire, she smudged her arm; raising her arm to push back a lock of hair, she wiped the smudge on her nose. So she had to step out and ask that somebody take her place while she went up to get washed.

When she came down she had her note in her pocket. As soon as she had a minute alone she took hold of the stand holding the fern in the white pot, and moved it to the window. Before anyone came in she had returned to her sewing.

She waited serenely. Odd to remember how jittery she had been about this at first. All she felt now was a cool triumph. Balfour thinks he can scare us, does he?

Late that afternoon Marietta came in. Curtsying politely, she said to Celia that she had come to pick up a package of ribbon for Mrs. Bernard. According to plan, Celia handed her the package and the note together. Marietta went out. She would deliver the note to Godfrey, who would start the news on its way. Celia had learned by now that many of her messages were passed by a certain bartender at a tavern on the highway. As Marietta went out, Mrs. Baxter came in. Celia smiled at her pleasantly, and Mrs. Baxter said she wanted to order some gloves.

The shop continued to be busy. Celia had expected a quiet period after the turn of the year, but there was none; trade at the port was good, so the Tories had money and were spending it. Celia ran up and down the stairs until she thought her leg-muscles must be as hard as those of an infantry soldier.

On a Sunday morning late in January she decided to rest by staying in bed. Becky and Pearl went to breakfast, as they were both going out for the day with their boy-friends; and Becky brought Celia the glass of milk that had stood by her plate. Celia drank it gratefully and lay down again.

She had a restful morning, dozing and reading. It was nearly noon when a maid knocked on the door and gave her a note. The maid said the boy who brought it was waiting for an answer.

The note was signed "Sarah Westcott." Mrs. Westcott asked Celia to be her guest at a little private luncheon today. She said Ricky, who delivered the note, would walk with her to the tea-shop.

As soon as she saw the signature Celia's heart began to thump. Sunday was the Westcotts' busiest day. Mrs. Westcott had no time for a little private luncheon. This was a summons.

Luke must be here. Her heart thumped harder, and it seemed to be up in her throat instead of in her chest where it ought to be. She wet her lips. Trying to speak to the maid as if she was merely pleased at having a chance to go out, she said, "Tell the boy I'll be down in a few minutes."

With Ricky, she walked uptown toward Cumberland Street. It was a silent walk, for she could not talk about Luke and she could not think about anything else. Ricky led her to the family living quarters at the back of the shop, and saying, "I'll call my mother," he left her there.

When Mrs. Westcott came in, she laid a warning finger on her own lips. Silently she led the way along the back passage, and pointed down the cellar stairs. Celia nodded, and Mrs. Westcott bustled back to her customers.

Celia crept down the dark staircase and felt her way to the door of the muffled room. Here she paused. Her mouth felt dry. Luke was there, on the other side of that door, she was sure of it. He was going to remind her of what he had said. Six weeks ago—she should have made up her mind by now, but she had not. She was scared. It was a strange sort of scaredness, not the way she would have felt if she had heard somebody tiptoeing behind her on a dark street. Not that, but—what? She did not know. She thought, I've got to go in, I've got to speak to him, answer him, I've *got* to—

The door opened and two imperative hands grasped her and pulled her in between the curtains, and his voice said roughly, "Thank God you're here! I've never been so worried in my life —tell me, Celia, are you all right?"

One hand still gripping her shoulder, with his other hand Luke pulled the door shut and dropped the curtain across it. All Celia could think at the moment was that with Luke, nothing was ever the way you thought it was going to be. In a voice thin with astonishment she answered, "Of course I'm all right! What did you think was wrong?"

Luke strode across to the table, where stood the hourglass and a candle. He struck the table with his fist, so hard that the shadows leaped crazily around the room. "You little fool," he burst out, "what made you send that message about the wagons at Dorchester?"

Celia's knees felt weak. She made her way toward him and grasped the table with both hands. "Oh good heavens—did I make trouble? Weren't the wagons there?"

"Oh yes, yes, the wagons were there—but Celia, you half-wit, you reckless imbecile—what made you send any message at all? After what happened to those Sarazen women—suppose you'd been caught?" Luke was pacing up and down. His voice and gestures were so violent that the room seemed like a cage too small to hold him. "Balfour might have put you in the dungeon, or sent you to St. Augustine, or anything else his evil mind could dream of—didn't you think of that?"

Celia shook her head.

"Well, I thought of it!" roared Luke. "I haven't had a night's sleep since—"

Celia felt a wicked amusement. "Luke!" she cautioned. "Keep your voice down!"

Luke tried to. "I'm sick with worrying!" he said. "If you weren't thinking about yourself couldn't you have had some consideration for me? Away out in the swamp, not knowing—"

Celia began to laugh. She could not help it, and she could not stop laughing until Luke grabbed her shoulder and gave her a shake.

"What's the matter now?" he demanded.

Her lips still quivering with merriment, Celia managed to answer. "Now you know what other people have borne because of you."

"What?" said Luke.

He spoke blankly. Celia thought with sudden understanding, We're like each other. He hasn't thought of that, any more than I thought of it.

"But this is war!" said Luke. "I'm a soldier. Soldiers always—" He broke off again. "Oh, stop talking about me. I want to talk about you. Celia, didn't you know—"

"No I didn't know!" she retorted. "It never occurred to me

that I was in any special danger. I was just so mad with Balfour, for doing such a vile thing to those two women, and thinking he could scare us that way—"

"Well, maybe he didn't scare you but he sure did scare me," said Luke. "And now you listen." He was trying to speak calmly but he did not sound calm at all. "Here's what I came to tell you," he went on. "You're getting out of Charleston. Right now."

"What?" gasped Celia.

"Yes," said Luke. "You're going to Sea Garden. To my mother. Sea Garden isn't safe—there's not a square foot of South Carolina that's safe now—but if anything really bad threatens, you can always get out by that passage you saw General Marion use. Mother will show you."

"But I'm useful here!" Celia protested. "That shop is a perfect listening-post. You said so yourself."

"No!" Luke insisted. "You're going to Sea Garden."

She tried to answer reasonably. "Luke, it's not right for me to quit! I'm not a soldier but I'm as good as one. Don't you remember what King David said, those who stay by the stuff are as important as those who go into battle! You told me yourself."

"Stop telling me what I said myself. I talk too much."

Celia pushed the bench back from the table to give herself more room. "Don't you want me to help win the war?"

"No!" Luke exclaimed. He walked to the end of the little room and back again. "When I think of you I don't care what happens to the war. Celia—" Luke planted his hands on each side of his waist and blurted—"Celia, when a man gets to the place where he doesn't care about his country nor his character nor his sense of duty, where he doesn't care about one single thing but a woman—then, Celia, he's got it bad. And my dear, that's the way I've got it. You're leaving this town if I have to tie you and gag you and bury you under a load of live mackerel in a fishing-boat."

Celia stood between the bench and the table, staring at him. Luke said,

"Well, that's how I feel about you. It's not important how you feel about me, not now. You go to Sea Garden now. You can make up your mind about me later." He stopped to catch his breath.

Celia heard her own voice speaking.

"But I've made up my mind. I'm in love with you."

She had not planned to say that. Swept along by his torrent of talk, she had not been thinking of an answer. The words simply came out of her throat.

Luke stared at her. For once in his life he was speechless. Still to her own amazement, Celia heard herself speaking. It was as if a pixy in her mind, hidden under her confusion of the past weeks, had been doing all the thinking that needed to be done. And now the pixy spoke, clear and sharp, without any doubt.

"I'm going to marry you. As soon as you can find a minister you can trust, not a British chaplain who might think it was his duty to turn you in. I don't know any of the things I ought to know about you, what you did before the war or what you expect to do afterwards—I don't know, and it's strange but I don't care."

Luke stood where he was, listening. Celia went on.

"This is no way to start a marriage. I'll be at Sea Garden and you'll be in the swamps and we'll only see each other once in a while. I don't care about that either."

She heard Luke laugh softly. She did not pause. The words poured out.

"I know this is crazy and foolish of me but I've never done anything crazy and foolish in my life and now I'm going to start. Because I know now, this is the way I'm made. I want things to happen to me—I don't want every day to be like the day before! And that's what I'll have with you. You're headstrong and reckless, you'll worry me and exasperate me and drive me wild—but that's what I want! Luke, I'm in love with you!"

She stopped, trembling with excitement at what she had just found out about herself. Luke strode across the room and with one big sweep he gathered her into his arms. She had been kissed by Jimmy, many times. But like everything else about Luke, this was different.

# CHAPTER 29

*T*HIS TIME, it was all different. Everything went well.

Celia left Charleston in February. The weather was bright and crisp, and in the courtyards the pear trees were blooming, like piles of white cloud against the clear blue sky.

Godfrey arranged for her to travel with a family named Pritchard, friends of the king who were going up to their indigo plantation on the Santee. Godfrey had known the Pritchards for years, and his ships had often carried Mr. Pritchard's indigo. But though they were friends, Godfrey did not care to strain Mr. Pritchard's loyalty to the king by telling them that Luke, a scout for the Swamp Fox, could be expected at Sea Garden in a few days. Instead, he said that when Celia had worked at Sea Garden before, his mother had found her both useful and congenial, and now wanted her there again.

The Pritchards were glad to take Celia along, as Godfrey had known they would be. They could not reach their country place in one day. They would have to stop somewhere for the night, and now they could stop at Sea Garden, a pleasant break in their journey.

Even Celia's qualm of conscience about giving up her part in the war, was there no longer. The war was going well. In the upper country, at Cowpens, Tarleton had taken the worst beating of his career.

Tarleton was no coward. He fought like a madman and had one horse shot under him. But his men were scattered, and Tarleton himself had to gallop for his life. Godfrey told Celia about the victory. He also told her Congress had finally sent a first-class commander to coordinate the troops in the south. This was General Nathanael Greene, the man Washington had wanted to send last year when Congress had overruled him and sent Gates.

As Mr. Pritchard's schooner moved away from the wharf in the early morning light, Celia heard the bells of St. Michael's. She smiled. The steeple was black, but the bells were as lovely as ever. It was as though they were saying, "We wish you happiness." She saved that up in her mind to tell Luke.

As the schooner sailed up the coast Celia sat in her deck-chair, dreamily happy. The Pritchards, in spite of being Tories, were nice people. Their two older children, boys about ten and twelve, were playing jackstones. The two little girls were listening while their mother read to them from a storybook. One little girl was wrapped in a blue cloak, the hood of which had fallen back. Her hair was blowing in the wind like soft golden-brown silk. Looking at her, Celia thought, I'm going to have a little girl like that. Even prettier than that. Little girls look like their fathers. My little girl will have those gorgeous blue eyes of Luke's, and his thick ripply light hair, and his aliveness. What a beauty!

Once Celia had not liked babies, but now she wanted a family. She had made up her mind that she was never going to be alone again.

Godfrey had told her that on his way back to the camp of Marion, Luke would stop at Sea Garden and tell Vivian and Herbert their plans. So when Mr. Pritchard's crewmen rang the landing-bell, Herbert rode to the wharf to welcome them. While they exchanged greetings Celia stood aside like a nice working-girl who knew her place.

When they reached the house Vivian and several maids were waiting on the steps. Vivian welcomed the Pritchards, admired their children, and said to Celia, "I've missed you!—Mr. Pritchard, how kind of you to bring my favorite dressmaker." She asked one of the maids to show Miss Garth to her room.

Celia expected to be led upstairs, to the bedroom she had occupied before. But instead she found herself at the first floor back, in a dark little room that she had never seen until now. The maid left her, saying she would bring some hot water. Celia looked around.

Her room was very dim. In the outside wall were two windows, but they were set so high that she would have to stand on a chair to see outdoors. They gave the place the look of a storeroom, but she thought it could not have been meant for one because it had a fireplace. There was a neat stack of wood by the hearth.

Celia wondered if she had been put into this unwelcoming little place because Vivian did not approve of her marriage to Luke. Vivian liked her, but Luke was his mother's darling and maybe she would have begrudged him to any woman on earth. Celia had not considered this until now, and the thought sent shivers over her. Before she could calm them she heard a knock on the door, and Vivian herself came in, carrying a candle.

"The girls are busy with supper," she said briskly, "so I brought you a light." She set down the candle, closed the door, and took Celia into her arms. "My dear," she whispered, "I'm so glad!" With a sound of surprise she added, "Celia, you're not crying!"

Her head against Vivian's shoulder, Celia nodded.

"Well, stop it," said Vivian. "You've got nothing to cry about."

Celia lifted her head. "You're really glad, Vivian?"

"Certainly," said Vivian. "Luke is twenty-eight years old—time he was getting married. I like you and I'm glad he's chosen you." Her hands on Celia's shoulders, Vivian looked at her straight. "Celia, I'm not *that* kind of mother-in-law. I mean it."

She laughed, and Celia laughed too, through her tears. Vivian gave her a kiss, and went out.

The dusk was gathering. Celia climbed on a chair and drew the curtains over the windows. The maid brought the hot water, and she dressed for supper.

When she had knotted her kerchief on her bosom she stepped back from the dressing-table. The candle threw long shadows over

344

the walls. As she saw the pattern of the shadows, Celia gave a start.

On three sides, the walls of this room were made of plain boards. But on the fourth side, the side where the fireplace was, the wall was paneled, and the paneling was exactly like that in the ballroom.

In the fuzzy gray of twilight she had not noticed it. But the candlelight outlined the structure: the wide panels, every alternate one standing out above its neighbors.

Now she understood. This little room was to be her bridal chamber, because this room also had a way to the secret passage.

•~•

When the Pritchards had left, Vivian sent a message to the Reverend Mr. Warren of the church of St. James Santee. They had no means of knowing when Luke could get here again, so she asked Mr. Warren to come to Sea Garden and wait for him.

A likable man in later middle age, Mr. Warren was a long-time friend of the Lacys. They had often attended services at his church, now locked and empty by British order because Mr. Warren had a son in the rebel army and had refused to pray for the king's victory. But he was an ordained clergyman, and they could not take away his right to conduct marriages and baptisms and funerals.

The morning after Mr. Warren arrived, Vivian came to Celia's room and explained about the passage. Curled up on the bed, the pillows piled behind her shoulders, Vivian asked, "Did you ever hear of the Yemassee massacre?"

Celia, sitting on a hassock by the fireplace, bit her lip. The Yemassee massacre had been an Indian uprising, long before she was born, and she knew very little about it. She said hesitantly, "I've heard of it, yes."

"Sixty-six years ago," said Vivian. "I was a tiny child, not quite two—" She laughed a little as she added, "Now you know exactly how old I am." But as she continued, again she became deadly serious.

"The Indians had their tomahawks and scalping-knives, and

345

also they had guns provided by the Spaniards in Florida, who didn't like having a British colony so close. We never did feel safe until Florida became a British colony too. But that was years later."

She moved a pillow, and went on grimly. "The massacre was well planned. Bands of savages moved through the country, burning and butchering as they came. We lived on Goose Creek, at the plantation where my brother Dan lives now. I was a small child, as I told you, and Dan wasn't even born yet, when the Indians started toward the Goose Creek plantations.

"My father didn't try to save his possessions. There was no time. He threw a few bundles of food and clothes into a wagon and we started toward Charleston. The road was full of people, women carrying children and men carrying guns, or sometimes a child on one arm and a gun on the other. We got to Charleston—not everybody did—and Dan was born there while my father was off fighting the Yemassees.

"There was terrible fighting that summer. The Indians were finally put down, and since then they've never been a danger to the coast country. But nobody knew this was going to happen. For months, we all lived in terror."

Vivian shuddered as she paused.

Celia shuddered too, but she spoke incredulously. "Vivian, you don't *remember* all this!"

"Celia, I don't know," Vivian returned. "It was all over before I was three years old, so it doesn't seem possible that I could remember anything much. And yet, it seems to me that I do. I think small children absorb the atmosphere around them even when they don't actually remember the events. And for months, I lived with fear. I breathed it in."

Celia nodded, and Vivian went on,

"So now you want to know what this has to do with Sea Garden.

"There were a thousand stories of horrible things that happened during the massacre. I heard how the Indians chased helpless people from room to room of their homes, and finally cornered them and cut them to pieces. When I was a little girl

I used to think, some day I would build a house of my own and I would build it with a secret way to safety."

She laughed and added, "I didn't know that scores of people, maybe hundreds, were thinking the same thing. A lot of the country homes built after the massacre had secret exits. Last summer when Luke was helping General Marion hide from the redcoats, he was surprised to find how many there were." Vivian raised herself from the pillows and put her feet on the floor. "Now come with me and I'll show you."

Celia had the same creepy feeling that she had had the evening Darren took her to the mysterious room to meet Luke. But Vivian was quite matter-of-fact.

"Lock the door," she said, and laughed again as she added, "The ballroom doors have been kept locked ever since the night you went in there and saw Luke with General Marion." She had brought with her two pairs of old gloves, and she gave one pair to Celia. "You'll need these to protect your hands on the guide-rails. Now watch."

She showed Celia how to move a brick at the left side of the fireplace. The brick was high up, so it could be moved whether a fire was burning or not. Behind the brick the wall was recessed and lined with metal. Set into the metal were two levers. You moved the left lever to open the passage, the right one to close it; and Vivian said there were two others inside the passage so the panel could be moved from within as well as without.

"You must keep the screws well oiled," said Vivian. "I'll show you how to do that. Now come along."

She turned the lever. To the left of the fireplace, one of the panels slid across the panel next to it. They stepped through the opening, and Vivian waited to let Celia look around.

They stood on a landing about eight feet wide. In front of them were five or six brick steps going down. Celia went down the steps and paused again.

The floor and walls were brick. The ceiling—which had slanted downward above the steps—was made with heavy beams. The wall on her left was solid, but at intervals along the right wall she saw gratings where light came through. These were over her head, but Vivian told her how the light got in. The house stood on a raised brick basement, and the passage here ran alongside the basement. It had the same thick brick walls, and openings guarded by iron gratings like the others that let light and air into the ordinary storerooms under the house.

Celia and Vivian went on until they came to more steps leading down. Ahead of them they saw only blackness. Vivian said this part of the passage went underground. "There's a wooden railing along each side," said Vivian. "Keep your hand on it."

Celia obeyed. After a few steps she could not see anything. The air was dank and horrid. Out of the darkness she heard Vivian's voice at her side.

"We try to get air in here. In windy weather we open both ends of the passage to make the wind blow through. It helps some, but not much."

To Celia, their journey seemed to go on and on. She heard their footsteps on the brick floor, and the rustle of their clothes. The little sounds seemed enormous in the dark. She heard Vivian's voice, low and serene as always, telling her to hold up her skirt and walk carefully, for time and damp had made the floor uneven. Celia gathered her skirt with one hand, keeping the other hand tight on the rail.

But after a little while the tunnel was no longer absolutely dark. What she perceived was not really light, but it was a lessening of black. A few steps more, and the black continued to lessen; looking down, Celia could make out the ends of her white kerchief. The black turned to gray, and now she could see her own hand on the rail. She turned her head and saw Vivian, walking as easily as a lady going to call on a friend.

Looking ahead, she saw a grating just under the ceiling. The light from this grating showed them another flight of steps, this time leading up.

At the top of the steps they came to another landing, and another wall, and another pair of levers. Vivian turned a lever. A panel slid back, and there was a rush of air and light.

They were in a boathouse. Not the big boathouse where Herbert kept his schooner, but a smaller one, solidly built and opening on a wharf. Celia saw several small rowboats ready for use.

But as her mind went back over the distance they had come, she was sure this boathouse was nearer the main dwelling than the other. "Where are we?" she asked. "This can't be the river."

Vivian smiled at her acuteness. No, this was not the main stream that flowed past Sea Garden. This was a little creek, too shallow for anything but the smallest boats, one of countless little creeks that laced the countryside and flowed into the larger streams. Unlocking the door of the boathouse she told Celia to step outside, and see how it was hidden by the forest growth.

The morning was sunny and the temperature by now was well into the sixties, but here under the trees they stood in a chilly shade. The boathouse was well hidden. But Vivian said that just in case somebody did see it, and wondered what it was here for, she had taken care to build several other boathouses like it on other little creeks like this one. All the houses held rowboats, which now and then were taken out for fishing or errands.

As they went back inside, Vivian said these boathouses were exactly alike even to a panel in the wall of each one like the panel that had moved to let them in, but in the other houses this panel was merely a fixed part of the wall. And the other houses had stout brick corners like this, but only in this one could a certain brick be turned—she showed Celia which brick it was—to reveal the levers that moved the panel.

So this was how Luke came and went. "It's wonderful!" Celia said with awe.

"It's mighty convenient," Vivian agreed. With a smile she added, "And now that I'm telling you all our secrets, here's one more. In all the boathouses there are wall compartments for tools. In one of them—we'll walk over there one day and I'll show you which one—we use a certain compartment as a letter box. We put messages there for Marion's men, and they leave notes for us. Now if you've had enough fresh air, we'll start back."

They walked through the passage again. On the way, Vivian told Celia that the windows of her bedroom had been set high, so that if by chance the curtains had not quite been drawn together when the panel was open or the screws were being oiled, nobody outside could look in and see that there was anything unusual about the room. As they came near the steps leading up to the bedroom, Vivian pointed toward a side passage, dimly visible here by the glimmer from the wall-gratings.

"That leads to the ballroom," she said. "I had it built because the ballroom is used only on special occasions, so it's ideal for a secret door."

"Can we go out that way?" Celia asked eagerly. She wanted to see everything.

"Why yes," said Vivian, and they turned into the side passage, where they felt their way along the wall and up another series of steps. At the top Vivian said, "Maybe you can't see it, but I know it all by heart—here's the recess with the levers. Put your hand on this one—that's it—turn the lever to the right, and we'll go through into the ballroom."

Celia felt a thrill. This was the opening where she had seen Francis Marion and his servant leave the house. She put her hand on the lever. Vivian stepped behind her to make room, and Celia gave the lever a turn.

Silently, the panel moved. Ahead of them was light—dim, for the ballroom curtains were closely drawn. Turning her head, Celia gave Vivian a questioning look. Vivian smiled and gestured for her to go in first. Celia stepped through the opening into the ballroom, and stopped short.

She was standing at one side of the fireplace. Opposite her, between two of the long windows, was a sofa. On the sofa, serene as a baby, Luke was lying asleep.

·~·

This was her wedding day. Luke told her he had slipped into the house about three o'clock this morning. He had ridden day and night to get here, for he could stay such a little time. When he came into the ballroom he was so sleepy that he had tumbled down on the sofa, and this was all he remembered.

They were married that afternoon in the parlor. Mr. Warren read the ceremony, and the witnesses were Herbert and Vivian, and the house-folk. The sunset streamed through the parlor and fell on them like a blessing as Luke put on Celia's finger the ring his father had given Vivian when they were married.

*350*

It was so quiet, so simple, so beautiful, that they could almost forget how closely the house was locked and barred, so Luke could escape by the secret passage in case some Tory informer had found out he was here and had told the king's troops.

But nothing happened to disturb them. After the ceremony they all gathered for a wedding supper, and Herbert poured wine he had been saving for some grand occasion. After supper, Herbert and Vivian and Mr. Warren moved into one of the guest-houses, and left the big house for Luke and Celia.

In ordinary times Luke and Celia would have been given one of the guest-houses for their honeymoon. These were charming little hideaways, designed with Vivian's distinctive skill. But the times were not ordinary. Day and night, Luke had to be near the secret passage.

He had three days to spend here. It seemed to Celia that the time went by like a flash, though when it was over she could remember so much that it did not seem possible for them to have crowded all this into so short a space. They had said so much, had loved so much, had given each other so much joy.

In the daytime they walked outdoors under the ancient moss-hung trees. The nights they spent in their odd little room with the secret door. As she lay with Luke's arms around her, Celia said to herself and to him, over and over, with a happiness so great that she could hardly believe it, "I am not alone any more. I am never going to be alone again."

At night Luke kept his weapons on the bedside table. All day he wore his pistol, and when they went outdoors they stayed in sight of the house. It was the last week of February. The jonquils and violets had begun to bloom; in the fields the Negroes were cutting mustard greens, and the mustard plants were brilliant with golden flowers. Luke and Celia talked and talked, and Celia was astonished at how much she had to say, now that she had a listener who understood her so well.

She told Luke she had found out something. It used to be that she had clung to the future as so many old people clung to the past. Now she had learned that one was as foolish as the other. She had made up her mind to live in the present. She was interested in the future, of course, but she was not going to lean on it. She was going to count her happiness in terms of here and now.

"Does that make sense?" she asked him.

"Of course it does," said Luke. "The here and now—that's all we've got." They sat on a bench under one of the great oaks. He looked at the beauty around him, and back at her. "And as far as I'm concerned," he said, "it's plenty."

But there was something about the future that he wanted to tell her. It had been arranged long ago that he was to have Sea Garden. Vivian's other children had been amply provided for by their fathers. But Luke's father, though a prosperous rice broker, had not owned land.

Luke had been born at Sea Garden and he loved every stick on the place. The Lacys raised only what they used, but the plan had been that he should turn Sea Garden into a working plantation. The war had interrupted him, but this was still what he meant to do.

"And this will be my home," Celia said in a half-whisper, "as long as I live. Oh Luke, why didn't you tell me?"

"There was so much else to tell you!" he answered. "Fact is, I hadn't thought of it until you said you didn't know what I had done before the war or what I meant to do afterwards."

But all this lay ahead. For the present, Luke said he did not know when he could be with her again. But he would be able to send her an occasional note, placed by some other scout of Marion's in the boathouse compartment Vivian had told her about.

He said General Greene, with the main body of his troops, was now in North Carolina. Cornwallis was there too. Cornwallis had been in North Carolina before, Luke reminded her with a chuckle, but had had to come back southward when he heard of the defeat at Kings Mountain. Now he and Greene would probably meet any day for another battle. "And in the meantime," said Luke, "have we been busy in the Lowcountry!"

He grinned proudly as he talked.

"There are more of us now, so we don't just attack the supply roads. The whole Santee country is overrun with Tory bands who live by plunder. Marion's scouts bring him word of where the Tories are, and we ride. Many a time we've caught them in the middle of a raid. How many homes Marion has saved from looting, how many women he has saved from being raped, nobody knows." Luke smiled as he added, "Nobody knows either how many grateful parents have named their little boys 'Francis Marion.' Must be hundreds. Those people on the Santee nearly worship him."

Celia felt the same way. It was because of Marion that none of those Tory bands had been able to come as far as Sea Garden. It was Marion who had made it possible for her and Luke to be married. She thought it likely that one of these days she too would have a little boy named Francis Marion.

Luke told her good-by in the black hours between midnight and dawn. They stood by the open panel in the bedroom, Luke's arms around her. He said, "I love you and I'll think of you every minute. And don't worry about me."

"I won't," Celia promised. "I'm not going to be licked by anything that hasn't happened."

Luke kissed her again. "You've got gumption, my darling."

Then he was gone. The panel slid into place behind him.

Celia sat down on the bed. She took Luke's pillow between her fists and put her face down into it and let go the sobs she had kept back while he was here. But even in this minute she did not feel utterly desolate. She had Luke. He loved her and belonged to her. And maybe she was going to have somebody else. A little girl with eyes like Luke's, or a little boy to be named Francis Marion.

## CHAPTER 30

$\mathcal{S}$HE FOUND that she was not going to have a baby. She was disappointed, but perhaps it was just as well, for she had so much to do.

Vivian told her Luke needed clothes. He had worn out most of his hunting-shirts and had little left now but parlor finery, which would not last a day in the swamps. Vivian said she had plenty of cotton on hand—they raised it at Sea Garden to make work-clothes—and one of the colored men was a good weaver, but it took several spinners to keep one weaver supplied with yarn.

"I can spin almost without looking," said Celia. "I'll do that in the evenings, and in the daytime I'll make a shirt for Luke."

Vivian gave her a piece of thick homespun made by the Sea Garden weaver. Celia made the shirt with a collar that could be brought up close around his neck to keep off mosquitoes, and cloth ties that would keep it on without need for buttons. Next she planned to make him a pair of breeches. She had never made men's breeches—Mrs. Thorley would not have considered this a genteel occupation—but she could learn.

Before she could make the breeches she had a visit from Luke. When she went to her room one night two weeks after he had left her, she found him sitting on the bed. With a cry of delight she tumbled into his arms and asked how long he had been here and how long he could stay.

Luke said he had been here about fifteen minutes. He could stay tonight and tomorrow, but as soon as the dark came down tomorrow night he would have to go on. "What a way to be married!" said Luke.

"I've never been so happy in my life," Celia told him.

She gave him the new shirt. Delighted, Luke gave her the one he was wearing, to be washed and mended before he came here again. When would that be? Luke had no idea.

He brought news. Not about the war—he had had no word of Greene and Cornwallis, and he was forbidden to say where Marion was headed now. But he said Herbert's grandson Tom Lacy, captive on a prison-ship since the fall of Charleston, was now with Marion's men. Along with some other prisoners, Tom had pretended to yield to the blandishments of the guards, and joined the Tory troops. Then at their first skirmish these fellows let themselves be taken by the rebels, and were now fighting for their own country again. Luke said so many men had used this trick that now the British would not accept a deserting prisoner unless he would join a regiment bound for the West Indies. No more would be turned loose on their home ground.

Later, Celia asked him about Miles Rand. Luke said Miles was still with Marion. He fought like a demon. If he lived through the war, Miles had said he would never rebuild Bellwood. He would go west, into the mountains or even beyond.

Celia thought how fortunate she was. Her despair had been so hopeless, and now she had so much. She hoped it would be the same for Miles. She could understand his not wanting to go back to Bellwood, but the world was wide.

Luke had to leave the next evening. But this time, when the panel closed behind him, Celia shed no tears. He had shown her how easily he could come and go. Any time, he might be back.

She started the breeches. Eager to be useful, she would have liked to sew all day and spin all evening, but Vivian insisted that she must spend part of her time outdoors. So Celia tended the flowers, and with Herbert and Vivian she took turns walking to the boathouse in which was the compartment they called their letter box. One of them went there every day, to see if a scout of Marion's had left a letter. If they found one, they knew they could expect another scout soon, to carry it on.

But then the news stopped. Three weeks went by and no scouts appeared. The letter box was empty.

They tried to hold up their spirits. Herbert and Vivian said the best thing to do was keep busy. Fields must be cared for, cotton must be seeded, soap and candles must be made. So everybody at Sea Garden kept busy. But white and colored, they all felt—and they felt it harder because they did not talk about it—that these silent weeks were like those weeks last year, before Darren brought news of the dreadful defeat at Camden.

Celia tried not to worry, but she could not help it. In the daytime she had work to keep her occupied, but at night when she was alone, all sorts of possible tragedies went through her mind. Marion's men could have been defeated. They could have been trapped in a swamp and cut to pieces. And in defeat or victory, always some of the men engaged were hurt, some were killed. When Luke was with her it was easy enough to be brave. But not now.

Sea Garden might be raided by some plundering band. It was far from the main roads, but it was rich and tempting. Celia had once looked up Vivian's birthday Bible verse. Vivian's birthday was the sixteenth of June, and the sixteenth verse of the women's chapter of Proverbs read: "She considereth a field, and buyeth it; with the fruit of her hands she planteth a vineyard." A fitting verse for Vivian. But for her dear Sea Garden to be destroyed like Bellwood—Celia shuddered at the thought.

And Luke, Luke—

Night after night, Celia clenched her teeth and doubled up her fists. "I won't give in," she said to the dark. "I'll keep smiling if it kills me."

So she kept smiling, and she worked as hard as she could. Herbert and Vivian did the same, and they were all grateful to one another.

At last, on a bright April morning, a Negro man rode in from Pinevale, the plantation of Herbert's son Eugene. The fieldworkers recognized him as he rode out of the woods, and one of them dropped his hoe and ran to tell the folk at the big house. Herbert and Vivian and Celia hurried out to the back porch to ask what news he brought.

But the man brought no news. He brought only a letter from Eugene Lacy to his father, in which Eugene was begging for news himself. He said he had received one note from Tom, telling how Tom had escaped the prison-ship. But this was a month ago. Had Herbert heard anything since?

Sadly, Herbert told the Negro to go into the kitchen and get a meal. Shaking his head, he walked back indoors.

Celia saw Vivian biting her lip and trying not to show how bitterly disappointed she was. Taking her hand, Celia spoke in an undertone.

"Maybe there's a letter in the box. Shall I walk over there?"

Vivian nodded. "I wish you would."

They smiled at each other with desperate cheerfulness.

Celia went through the room that they used as an informal gathering-place. Her sewing lay on a chair, where she had left it a few minutes ago. By the fireplace stood her spinning-wheel, and on the table lay several bound copies of the *Gentleman's Magazine*, which Herbert used to receive regularly from London. Celia smiled. What a comfortable, welcoming room it was. Here at Sea Garden they had made her feel so pleasantly at home. If only she knew Luke was well, how happy she could be.

She started toward the boathouse. This was not the boathouse that had the exit from the secret passage; this one was nearly a mile from the big house, on another creek that flowed into the river farther upstream. Celia hurried along the path and opened the door.

As she went to the compartment where letters were placed, she felt a glow of hope. The silence could not last forever. One day she would find a letter. Maybe today. She opened the compartment.

The box was empty.

Celia choked back a sob. She wondered if any certainty could have hurt much more than this long pain of suspense. From the trees outside she heard the twitter of birds. They sounded so gay in the sweet spring weather.

Then she heard something else. The clang of the landing-bell.

She started with a cry of joy. At last, somebody from outside! Not Tories sneaking in to loot and burn, but visitors who sailed openly up the river, who rang the bell to announce their arrival. These would be friends. They would bring news.

Catching up her skirt, she began to run. She ran out of the boathouse and through the woods toward the main landing, but before she had gone far she stopped and told herself not to hurry so. Whoever the callers were, Herbert would go to meet them at the landing. In the meantime Vivian would open bedrooms, order refreshments, summon maids and house-boys to give service.

And she herself was now also a lady of the house. It was her place to stand beside Vivian to welcome their friends and help with the duties of hospitality. She must not run like a child, and arrive all breathless and damp-faced; she must walk in fresh and smiling, like a person who knew her manners. This would be her first experience at being a hostess in her own home. Vivian might appear to be giving all her attention to the guests, but Celia knew Vivian would also be observing her, to see what she was doing and how she was doing it.

With an effort Celia curbed her impatience and began to walk sedately along the path toward the house. She would smile at the company, explain that she had been taking a stroll when she heard the bell, and say how glad she was to see them. She hoped they would be people she knew.

Surrounded by the woodland growth, she could not see the visitors, but by now she could certainly hear them. They were a mighty noisy group. She heard men shouting. There seemed to be a great many. Some of them sounded like men giving orders. Celia stopped again. Those men did not sound like friends. They sounded—she wet her lips—they sounded like an army.

Whoever they were, they had terrified the Negroes. A woman screamed, an instant later there was another scream, and a man's voice cried out, "Oh Lord have mercy on us!" Celia broke into a run.

She ran as fast as she could, panting, more than once nearly stumbling over clumps of grass. She felt her armpits suddenly wet. In front of her she was holding up her skirt so as not to trip on it;

she saw drops of sweat on the backs of her hands. Oh, what a long way it was—the boathouse had never before seemed so far from the big house, and the shrubbery was so thick! If only she could see what was going on. She heard more noise, shouts of men and cries of women and rushing footsteps and a general confused commotion, and then at last she came out of the woods.

She saw the beautiful dwelling-house of Sea Garden. She saw the oaks around it, and the flowerbeds, and among the flowerbeds she saw men in red coats.

There were thirty or forty men in red coats, or maybe more— in her shock Celia was no good at counting. She saw the Negroes huddled in groups, around the house, on the front steps, on the piazza. As she went toward the front of the house she saw a British officer standing on the top step, facing the main door. In his hand he held a large official document with a red seal.

Before the front door, Herbert and Vivian stood facing the officer on the step. On the piazza, between the door and the steps, stood Roy Garth. At his side was Sophie, and with them a colored nurse holding the baby. Near by stood a group of about twenty Negro men and women, evidently servants they had brought with them.

Roy was very grand in a black cloak with three overlapping shoulder-capes and a gold buckle at the neck. Sophie had on a rose-colored cape of thin wool, thrown back to show a printed silk dress. The British officer wore tall headgear, looming a foot and a half above his wig; his red coat was held by white shoulder-belts crossing in front, and his red coat-tails hung behind him to his knees. His breeches were white doeskin, his boots black and gleaming. He had opened the document with the red seal, and now he was reading aloud.

"Know all men by these presents: In the name of George the Third, by the grace of God king . . ."

Celia crept nearer. She tried to walk softly on the grass. The other soldiers were quiet, standing at attention, and the Negroes were now too awed to speak. The reading went on.

". . . John Cruden, Commissioner of Sequestrated Estates for his majesty's province of South Carolina . . ."

Celia's heart sounded like thunder in her ears. She felt as if she were making an agonized effort to wake up from a nightmare, wake up and find that this did not mean what she knew it did mean.

". . . In consequence of the powers in me vested, by the right honorable Earl Cornwallis . . ."

From somewhere above her Celia heard the squawk of a jaybird. The officer went on reading. In her agitation Celia missed some of the words. It did not matter, for many of them were long legal words that she would not have recognized anyway. But she heard enough.

She heard ". . . confiscated . . . the owners having given aid and comfort to traitors during the late insurrection . . . confiscated and sold . . . therefore the estate known as Sea Garden is hereby declared the property of his majesty's loyal subject . . . [Celia tried to pray, but the words would not come] . . . Sea Garden is hereby declared the property of his majesty's loyal subject, Roy Garth."

•~•

When Celia looked back, it seemed to her that she had considered every possible disaster but this. She had tried to steel herself to face any blow that might come. But she had not thought of the chance that Roy might take Sea Garden.

And yet it seemed to her now that this had been in front of her all the time.

Roy's plantation was small, run down, in debt. From the day he married into a rich Tory family he had done his best to take advantage of his status as a friend of the king. Since the British marched in, Roy had been always ready to give aid, to act as guide or courier. He had been constantly on the move. Now she knew why. He had wanted to look the country over and choose his own prize.

She remembered his visit to Sea Garden last summer. How solicitous he had been about taking Sophie for a walk, so he could see more of the property. At that time the confiscation order had not been publicly issued, but men of the inner circles no doubt knew it was going to be. She thought of his return a few months later, the time he had so graciously bought Eugene

Lacy's promissory note—to see the place again, to compare it with others, to be sure he was getting the best. Roy was no foreigner. He would know, as well as Vivian had known, how to read the signs of trees and wild growth telling which was the richest soil.

So now he had it. He had obtained the confiscation order after the battle of Guilford Court House. This was the battle they had been expecting in North Carolina, and the redcoats were happy to tell them all about it. The Americans under General Greene had met the British under Cornwallis and Tarleton, and they said the Americans had taken a walloping defeat.

When news of the great British victory reached Charleston, they said cannon roared and church bells rang, and everybody put lights in the windows as a sign of rejoicing. John Cruden, Commissioner of Sequestrated Estates, celebrated by giving a grand ball in the residence he had confiscated for himself. He further celebrated by issuing more orders confiscating estates, so Tories who deserved the best could buy them for tiny prices. One of these orders conveyed Sea Garden to Roy.

After attending Cruden's ball, Roy and Sophie made ready to go to Sea Garden. A detachment of British troops had been ordered to go up the coast by ship, under command of the officer, Major Edmore, to whom Roy had made himself useful on several occasions. It was not difficult for Roy to get permission for Major Edmore to escort him to his new estate.

Major Edmore was a kindly soul who tried to do right. While he knew traitors must be punished, he felt sorry for these misguided folk who had to lose their homes. Herbert would have to leave the horses in his pasture and the schooner in his boathouse, but Major Edmore said he would take Mr. and Mrs. Lacy on his ship to wherever they expected to live now. And Roy, not to be outdone in kindness to his fallen enemies, said they might each choose one personal servant to take with them.

As the man bringing Eugene's letter had arrived that same morning, Herbert counted himself fortunate to know that Eugene still had a home—or at least had had one two days ago when the man started. He thanked Major Edmore, and said they would go to the plantation of his son. The Negro man would be sent ahead to tell Eugene to expect them. Major Edmore said they would leave tomorrow.

Through all this talk and movement, Celia had kept silent. At the beginning, both Roy and Sophie had greeted her with perfunctory smiles, but after that, with so much else to be noticed, they seemed to have forgotten her. The sun grew hot on the outside, so they all moved into the parlor, where Major Edmore said he would give further orders. Celia followed, but she stayed out of the way, moving aside when anyone came near her, keeping as inconspicuous as she could.

Here in the parlor she and Luke had been married. It was a beautiful room, its long windows giving a fine view of the oaks. Herbert and Vivian stood listening to the instructions of Major Edmore. Roy and Sophie were walking about, looking over their new possessions. Celia stood by the wall, trying to be as quiet as a leaf that lay on the floor, fallen from a vase of flowers.

She had heard everything they said, and her thoughts supplied what they did not say. General Greene, Washington's own choice as commander, had been defeated. No doubt Cornwallis and Tarleton were triumphantly marching north right now, at last on their way to join Clinton for the final push that would win the war. And Marion's men? Maybe they too had met defeat. But even if they had not, what use now to attack the supply roads and ferries? They could delay Cornwallis no longer. He was marching north. And Luke?

From outside, she could hear the Negroes wailing. They had been told they would have to stay and work for the new owners. Nearly all these Negroes had been born at Sea Garden, and had never worked for anybody but Vivian and her family. The house-folk, as well informed about the war as the white people, were appalled. Through one of the windows Celia could see two women, sobbing. She was glad Marietta was in town.

She looked at Herbert and Vivian, standing side by side before Major Edmore. What dignity they had. Expecting nothing unusual to happen today, they were both plainly dressed. Herbert wore a suit of unbleached homespun; Vivian a white muslin house-dress and cap, her only ornament the silver filigree pin that held the cap to her beautiful blue-white hair. But they looked regal. Celia had never admired them as much as she did today. And she was glad, oh she was glad she belonged to them, could go where they went. The preacher spoke a few words, he wrote your name in a parish register, and what a difference it made!

Herbert was saying that with Major Edmore's permission he would have the servants bring the trunks, so he and Mrs. Lacy could set about packing their clothes. Herbert spoke with icy calmness. There was a white line about his lips.

Major Edmore cleared his throat. He was doing his duty, but plainly he wished somebody else had to do it. He said Mr. Lacy need not call the servants to bring the trunks, the servants were —ah—upset. This could be done by some of the private soldiers. He would send for them at once.

But though Major Edmore was uncomfortable, Roy and Sophie were quite at ease. Roy was walking from window to window, surveying his new kingdom. Now he paused by the marble mantelpiece, running his hand over it as if calculating what it must have cost; now he lingered by a window to take a look at the oaks—Celia guessed, sick with anger, that he was counting what they would bring when cut for timber.

Sophie was fluttering about, noting the furniture, the rugs, the crystal vase that held the flowers. Clearly, both she and Roy considered that they were as much entitled to Sea Garden as if they had bought it in a broker's office. They had no concern about the former owners.

Herbert said he would show the soldiers where the trunks were kept. Vivian went to lay out her clothes for packing. Celia went out after her, to do the same. As she left the parlor she heard Herbert asking if he would be allowed to take any of his books.

She went to her room. Opening her wardrobe, she began to lay her dresses across the bed.

She moved slowly. Her arms and legs felt heavy. She thought how Vivian had built Sea Garden with her dreams and her love. Every brick and board and pane of glass, every tuft of flowers, every wind from the sea, brought her dear associations. And now —why didn't they cut off her right arm instead? It would hurt her less than this.

Celia thought of herself. In taking Sea Garden they had taken her own future. This was where she and Luke would have lived, where their children would have been born. She wondered what she was going to do now.

She heard a knock. Stiffening herself to meet the men with her trunk, she opened the door. But her caller was Vivian.

Vivian's face looked like something cut out of a rock. Without speaking, she closed the door and turned the key. Taking Celia's hand she drew her away from the door.

"Celia," she said in a low voice, "you've got to stay here."

Celia gave a start of horrified protest. Vivian went on.

"Luke doesn't know Sea Garden has been taken! What if he came through the passage and met Roy instead of you?"

Celia gasped. Of course she had to stay. Luke would be taken prisoner, maybe shot as he tried to escape.

"I guess I was too shocked to think," she said. "But—what will I do? I'm married to Luke. Won't they expect me to go with you?"

But Vivian had thought quickly, and as usual her thoughts were practical. "They don't know you're married. Take that ring off until after we're gone. When they saw you this morning they took it for granted that you were here as before, a dressmaker. Our servants will say something about your being married, but they're so confused that they won't say anything for a while. It won't make much difference. Roy and Sophie think your husband is a fool clinging to a hopeless cause. When this is over he'll have to dig ditches for a living, so you're just a poor relation to be ordered about."

Celia wet her lips. "Is it a hopeless cause, Vivian?"

"You know as much about it as I do," Vivian returned crisply. "Now listen. Write a warning and put it in the letter box. If a scout comes by maybe he can get it to Luke."

"I'll do that," Celia promised.

Vivian managed a little smile. "Thank God you have a steady head, Celia."

Celia's head did not feel steady. It felt dizzy. She swallowed hard, and caught her lower lip between her teeth.

"Sea Garden!" Vivian said softly, and covered her eyes with her hand.

Celia's throat had closed up. She could not speak, but she put her arms around Vivian and held her.

Vivian shook her head. "Don't give me any sympathy, Celia. I can't bear it right now." But she stood there, her head on Celia's shoulder, fighting for self-command.

Celia thought, Vivian is losing Sea Garden; she doesn't know how Burton is faring in St. Augustine; she doesn't know what's happening to Luke. How much do people have to put up with in this world?

Vivian raised her head. "I'm all right now." She straightened her shoulders and looked around. After a moment she kissed Celia quickly, as if a long embrace was more than she could bear. "Good-by, dear girl."

Celia said, "Good-by." She could say no more.

Vivian went to the door and unlocked it, and went through without looking back. Celia heard her footsteps dwindling off, down the hall.

# CHAPTER 31

Celia had heard that the real trials of life are not the great tragedies. Not these, but the small vexations that come back over and over till you think that one more day like this will turn you into a screaming maniac.

She had heard it. After a month with Roy and Sophie at Sea Garden she knew what it meant. Ever since Aunt Louisa had told her she had no dowry, Celia had trembled at the thought of living on Roy's charity. Now the fate she dreaded had caught up with her.

Here at Sea Garden she was the poor relation, allowed to stay here because of course, as Sophie explained to her friends, Roy wouldn't be unkind to his own kinfolks. Naturally, since they were giving her a home, they expected her to show some gratitude. In fact, they thought she should be *glad* to help around the house a little.

"Celia, you won't mind darning the stockings. You haven't anything to do."

"Celia dear, you'll take care of the baby today, won't you? I want the nurse to help with the ironing."

"Celia, Sophie has some gauze that she bought in Charleston for caps and kerchiefs. I'm sure you'll make them for her."

Day after day, Celia did as she was told. She did it grimly, and usually in silence except to say, "Yes, Sophie." "Yes, Roy." "Certainly, I'm glad to help." "No, I don't mind at all."

Day after day, she reminded herself that this was how she guarded her husband's life. She had tried to warn Luke about keeping away from Sea Garden. But he had not received her warning—the letter she had written was still in the secret letter box. Whether or not Vivian had managed to reach him she could not tell. All she knew was that she had to stay here, to meet him if he came in, and tell him what had happened. The only way she could be sure of staying was to make herself the meekest and most useful servant on the place.

Vivian had been right—Roy and Sophie had forgotten about her and had been surprised to find her here. Celia said she had thought they meant for her to stay. She had no claim on Eugene Lacy, and she was Roy's cousin.

Roy, in the midst of his new wealth, was in a genial mood. Yes, yes, he said, glad to have her. But when Sophie told him her maid had heard from one of Vivian's maids that Celia was married to Luke and Luke was with Marion, Roy became stern. He ordered Celia not to embarrass him by speaking of this. He was expecting some friends, officers who had been ordered from Georgetown to Charleston and were going to stop here on their way. He would introduce Celia as Mrs. Ansell, but if anyone asked where her husband was, he would say Mr. Ansell was with the Tory troops. She was to do the same. Was that clear?

Celia doubled her fists and hid them in the folds of her skirt. She replied, "Yes. Quite clear."

She foresaw that she was not going to have much chance to say anything, one way or the other. A poor cousin like herself was kept in the background. Celia got used to hearing Sophie say, "I do think you'll be more comfortable if you don't come to table this evening, Celia. The ladies will be elegantly dressed, and I know you haven't anything—I mean—"

Celia said, "I understand. I won't come to table. No, I don't mind at all."

She preferred staying away from the dinner-parties. It made her sick to watch Sophie preside over Vivian's silver while Roy poured Herbert's wine.

The guests came and went: Aunt Louisa, Roy's silly sister Harriet and her rich husband who looked like a fish; Sophie's rich family, other rich Tories, and of course, redcoats. Celia stayed in her bedroom—luckily this room was so small and dark they were glad to have her keep it. Or she sat in one of the back rooms with a book, or with the sewing they were always giving her to do; or she took long walks, taking care to go by the boathouse where the letter box was.

But the box still held her own letter, placed there for any scout who might come by. She had written: "Give this message to Captain Luke Ansell," and followed with a statement of what had happened at Sea Garden. Then she added, "This letter written by Mrs. Ansell. Whoever takes this, please leave a line telling me how Captain Ansell is but do not leave any more messages after that. Not safe."

She quaked lest Roy find the letter box. He had ridden over the place and looked into every building, including all the boathouses, but he had not opened the tool compartments. Some day he would examine the property more carefully, but right now he was busy being a host.

He had been at Sea Garden a month when he demanded her emerald necklace. He had an imposing group of visitors just now: the Torrances, a number of redcoat officers, and some pretty girls with their Tory parents. This evening there would be dancing— no longer was the ballroom shrouded with canvas. Emily Torrance was going to wear a set of pearls, heirlooms in the Torrance family. Sophie said she had nothing to wear that would impress her relatives, then she remembered. "Roy darling, hasn't Celia been keeping a necklace that really belongs to me?"

Roy sent a maid to summon Celia. He did not say what he wanted, but merely that she was to come upstairs at once.

Roy and Sophie occupied the master suite on the second floor front. They were now in the little boudoir next to the bedroom. Vivian had designed this suite, and as Celia opened the door of the boudoir she could see Vivian's taste in every detail, so clearly that she almost expected to see Vivian herself. But instead she saw Sophie, in a robe of apple-blossom pink, reclining on the long chair with Roy sitting beside her.

Standing in the doorway, Celia said, "You sent for me, Roy?"

Bluntly, Roy told her he had sent for her because he wanted the emerald necklace.

Expecting this, Celia had hidden the necklace in the passage, behind the secret panel in her room. "I won't give it to you," she retorted.

Roy was astonished at her manner. When she had lived in Uncle William's home, Celia had talked back to Roy, but here at Sea Garden she had been so docile that he thought she had at last learned her place. However, though he was surprised he was not daunted. He told Celia sternly that her impudence would do her no good. He wanted the necklace. Now.

"I won't give you that necklace," Celia returned. "I mean it."

Sophie began to cry.

Roy's dark eyes narrowed. He set his well-shaped lips in a line of exasperation. Handsome and angry, he told Celia he had been patient about this. He had wanted to give her a chance to do right, and return the necklace of her own accord. But she had not done so, and his patience was at an end.

Celia said nothing. Sophie gave a little sob, and Roy patted her gently. He asked, "Where is that necklace, Celia?"

"It's put away," she said.

Sophie sobbed louder.

Roy was angry. He intended to impress Sophie's rich brother. If Leon Torrance could give his wife heirloom pearls, then Roy Garth could give his wife heirloom emeralds. Roy stood up.

"Celia, if you don't bring that necklace here at once, I'm coming down to your room. I'll tear your bed apart, empty every bureau drawer, shake out every garment you own, until I find it."

Suddenly Celia began to tremble. When she put the necklace into the passage she had felt confident. But now, her thoughts were ticking as if there was a clock in her head. They were saying, Give it up. Give it up. Suppose he finds the passage.

It could happen. Roy was mad. He would tear up her room like a pig rooting in a potato patch. He might, he just accidentally might, stumble against that brick in the fireplace and see it move. Or, suppose his heel struck the panel and he noticed a hollow sound. He would not hesitate to knock a hole in the wall. Sea

Garden belonged to him. He could do anything he pleased here.

And if Roy found the passage, and then if Luke came here to see her, he would never get safely away.

Roy was standing over her, glowering. Celia said, "All right, all right. I'll bring you the necklace."

Sophie looked up eagerly through her tears. For a terrifying instant Celia thought Roy might say he would come downstairs with her, but he sat by Sophie again, putting his arm around her as if to assure her that this was only one more example of how he was seeing her through the troubles of the world. Turning to Celia he said, "I'll wait fifteen minutes. Right here."

Celia went to her room, locked the door, climbed on a chair and drew the curtains over the high little windows. Opening the passage, she brought out the purple velvet case that held the necklace.

She closed the passage and took the necklace upstairs to the boudoir. The door stood ajar, and she pushed it open. Roy and Sophie were sitting together on the long chair, Sophie cuddled against him while he played with her soft light brown hair.

Celia walked over to them. "Here it is," she said.

She felt, rather than saw, Roy take the case from her hand. She turned on her heel and walked to the door. Behind her she heard Sophie's squeal of delight as Roy opened the case.

Celia did not look back. She thought if she did she might cry, and if they saw her cry she simply could not bear it. She went downstairs and out of the house.

It was a warm afternoon in May, and most of the guests were indoors. Celia hurried toward the woodland path. There might be something in the letter box. Hope of a letter was the only thread she had to hold her to the world outside of this nightmare island of Sea Garden.

The woods were beautiful. She smelt honeysuckle and the bursting buds of sassafras, and she heard the joyful buzzing of bees. She was glad to see that the lush spring growth had almost hidden the path that led to the boathouse.

The inside of the boathouse was dark and damp and cool. Celia went to the compartment where the letter box was. "Please, God, please!" she whispered. "I can't stand it much longer!"

She put her hand on the little door. For seven weeks—three weeks before the Lacys left, four weeks since, day after day she had done this without finding anything. For the past four weeks, when she opened the box she always saw her own letter giving a warning to Luke. The letter was getting grimy, and curling at the edges.

She drew the door open. Her letter was gone. There was another letter in the box.

Nearly sobbing with relief, her hand shaking, Celia reached in and took the letter. She closed the compartment door.

There was one sheet of paper, but on it were two messages. The upper message was the sort she used to write herself in Mrs. Westcott's basement so other patriots could post it around town.

"To lovers of American freedom: Cornwallis won the battle of Guilford, but he lost one-fourth of his troops. Greene retreated but saved his army to fight again. Marion's men have taken Fort Watson at Nelson's Ferry. Praise God and keep fighting."

These lines nearly filled the page, but in the space at the bottom somebody had squeezed in a few words more. The first message was clearly written with good pen and ink; the second had been scrawled with some sort of makeshift, by a hand more used to a gun than a pen.

"Mis Ansell dr madam sory for yr truble yr husbin wunded Ft Wotsn but beter now he will be tole."

So this was why she had heard nothing for so long. Fort Watson was on the far bank of the Santee, miles from Sea Garden. And Luke was away up there, wounded.

The month of June came in, beautiful, but in Celia's small-windowed bedroom, almost unbearably hot. Tossing in bed one night she wondered if it would be safe to tell Sophie she wanted another room. She could get it by the simple expedient of refusing to sew any more until they gave it to her. But there was always the chance that Luke might not have received her message. The scout who had taken her letter might have been killed or captured on the way. No, she had to stay here, guarding the panel, locking the door every time she went out. She had to stay if she smothered to death.

She got out of bed and went to the washstand, and threw some water over her face. The water was almost warm. Through the high little windows the moonlight came in. She could not feel any wind at all.

Standing there in the deep night silence, she heard a sound. It was a soft, silky sound. It was so faint that in the daytime she might not have heard it, but tonight she heard it and she knew what it was. The oiled machinery behind the wall was moving.

The instant she heard the sound, she knew she had been expecting it and waiting for it. She knew, she had known all along, that no warning would make Luke stay away. By the moonglow she could see the panel sliding open. Luke came through and saw her, and he said, "My dear Sassyface," and the next instant he had his arms around her and she was shaking and sobbing against him.

• ❧ •

It had been so long! Luke knew exactly how long—eighty-seven days. He had received her letter and it had sent him nearly out of his mind because he could not come to her at once. He had been lying in bed in a farmhouse near Fort Watson, his left side ripped open by a British gun.

He still had on a bandage, and he was not yet able to fight, but he was getting well. As soon as the surgeon would let him move, he had obtained permission for Tom Lacy to row a boat for him. They had made their way to Eugene's place at Pinevale. Yes, Herbert and Vivian were there, courageous as you'd expect them to be. Vivian had made him take a day's rest, after which Tom had rowed him down to Sea Garden. Right now, Tom was asleep in the woods.

Luke had to leave her before daybreak. But he had brought her a clear and practical plan. He could not fight, but he and she were going to work together again, for Marion.

Luke would live in a cabin several miles away, which in happier days he had used as a hunting lodge. Celia was to stay at Sea Garden, and make herself useful, and listen. At intervals a scout of Marion's would pick up Luke and row him to Sea Garden.

Luke would slip through the passage to this room, and she would tell him what she had heard.

For the rest of the summer they followed Luke's plan. Celia wondered how many people there were who, like herself, led a secret life. People who seemed colorless, but who actually were walking hand in hand with glory.

Roy continued to entertain prominent Tories, and officers on their way up and down the coast. Celia waited on men as well as women, offering to mend a torn shirt or sew on a button that had come loose from a red coat. She worked quietly. Sometimes she had to decline the attentions of an eager young soldier, but except for this she hardly opened her mouth. She was surprised at how much she learned. Men and women who would never have talked too much in a public place like Mrs. Thorley's shop, were less discreet in the home of such loyal Tories as Mr. and Mrs. Roy Garth.

Luke came to see her as often as he could. The summer was rainy, and sometimes the creeks were so swollen that the strongest rower could not manage a boat. This meant that sometimes her information was too late. But just as often, she knew about troop movements in time for Marion to act upon them.

About midsummer the British and American authorities arranged for an exchange of prisoners. But the men in the fort at St. Augustine, being civilians, were not released to the American army. They were herded on a boat and taken to Philadelphia, where they were turned loose to get along as best they could. At the same time, in Charleston, Balfour ordered their wives and children, along with the families of several other leaders of the rebellion, to be loaded on several small ships and sent to Philadelphia also. What they were going to live on when they got there was no concern of his. As he ordered that their homes should be given to Tories, many of the women sent him humble letters begging his permission to sell their shoe-buckles or other personal articles, so they would reach Philadelphia with a little cash to buy food.

However, Luke said he was sure Godfrey must have given Elise whatever cash he could spare, to take care of herself and Burton and their sons.

"This war," Celia said with admiration, "has been hard on Godfrey!"

In the darkness she heard Luke laugh. "Hard? Why?"

"I meant hard on his fortune."

"My dearest," said Luke, "Godfrey can make money out of anything. Right now he has several British officers investing in his trade with the Indies. It's honest, they get their share every time a ship comes in. But he hasn't told them how much of his own share goes to pay spies for Marion's men."

Celia smothered her laughter with her head in the bedclothes.

But it could not last. Late in August Luke told her his visits had to cease.

When she started back in fright, he said he had gone on meeting her longer than he had any right to expect. His wound was well and he was fit for active duty, but Marion had found him more useful getting information from her. Now, however, he was needed to fight.

His lips close to her ear, he told her a British fleet had recently reached Charleston, bringing war supplies and fresh troops. This was no secret. But also, General Greene had received a letter from General Washington's headquarters.

"Remember," said Luke, "I told you the French king was going to send us more men and ships? Well, at last they're on their way. They're coming up from the French West Indies."

In spite of her fear Celia gave an exclamation of glad surprise. Luke hugged her to him.

"Honeychild, we've done a good job. Ever since they took Charleston, and that's a year and three months ago, Cornwallis has been trying to meet Clinton's northern army and he hasn't done it yet."

"How far has he gone?" she asked.

"Nearly to Virginia," said Luke. "That's where Washington is headed now."

"Yes, yes—go on."

"The redcoats have spies," said Luke, "and good ones. They've certainly heard that the Frenchmen are coming, and that Washington is marching south. So Washington's orders are: Don't let the redcoats in South Carolina go to help Cornwallis. Draw them into battle, right here. That's our job now. Understand?"

She understood. She understood with a pain in her throat and a stiffness in her back and quivers in her knees. Luke was going into battle again. Last time, they had nearly killed him.

She threw her arms around him and buried her face. He held her close. For a while they did not say anything. At length Luke stroked her hair, and kissed her. "This has to be good-by," he said. He kissed her again, long and hard. "I love you, Sassyface," he whispered.

She had to let him go. She was alone again.

Over and over in the next few days she asked herself desperately, Is it always going to be like this? Am I always going to be alone? Those people have taken everything. Sea Garden. My emerald necklace. My friends. Jimmy. And now maybe Luke. They leave me nothing. Always, I'm alone.

And then, in those warm blue days of late summer, she found that she was not alone. She was going to have a baby.

At first she would not believe it. She felt so lost and frightened, and it did not seem possible that anything good could be happening to her now. But as the time went by she was convinced. It was really true.

At last, at last, she had something of her own. This they could not take away.

# CHAPTER 32

HE MONTH of September was long and lonesome. Day after day the landing-bell hung silent. Roy was busy overseeing the fieldhands, but the work went slowly. Indoors the maids were slow too. In fields and house alike the Negroes resented Roy and Sophie, and hated the British for making them serve these trespassers. They worked because they had to, but nobody could make them work well.

Celia said nothing about her coming baby. After her first joy, she had a reaction of fright when she remembered that she had no way to reach anybody who cared what became of her. She went on as before, darning the stockings, making clothes for Sophie's little boy, and yearning for news.

At last, one afternoon late in September the landing-bell rang. The visitors were Sophie's brother Leon Torrance and his family. For some weeks the Torrances had been at their indigo plantation, but now Leon had left the place in care of his overseer while he took his household to Charleston.

Leon Torrance was an earnest man, a Tory by pocketbook conviction; he had never hurt anybody and did not want to. He merely wanted to live in peace and comfort, but this, he said with a hurt anger, was getting harder every day. The rebels under that man Greene had attacked the British at Eutaw Springs. There had been no real victory for either side, but the king's commander had withdrawn his men to a camp near Moncks Corner. As this troop was the major British force outside Charleston, now there was nobody to protect Tories in rural homes.

Sitting in the parlor with the rest of them, Celia listened with a tenseness that made her muscles ache. Leon had said in passing that Marion's men had taken part in the battle. She twisted her hands together in an agony of apprehension. Would there never, never be an end to this torture of not knowing what was happening to Luke?

Leon urged Roy and Sophie to come to Charleston too. But Roy said no. The idea of abandoning his new property was more than he could bear. He said Sea Garden was a long day's journey from anywhere, and such remoteness was protection. If there should be any danger he could always go to town, or to Kensaw; his schooner, he said (meaning Herbert's schooner), was ready in the boathouse. Leon nodded thoughtfully, and said yes, this was true.

The Torrances went on to town. The weather grew cooler, with a tang of autumn, but Celia was miserable. She was worried about Luke and worried about herself, and she felt a thousand small discomforts. She had dizzy spells, and aches in her breasts and her legs, and sometimes nausea, all reminding her that her body was adjusting to a new state of things and that she wanted, more than ever, love and security and peace. But after what seemed like an endless time, on a starry October midnight Luke came through the panel into her room.

Celia was asleep when she felt his arms around her and his kiss on her hair. She opened her eyes, and in the starlight she saw him kneeling by her bedside, and she could not speak, she could not even kiss him back. She simply burst into tears. Luke did not know why her nerves were so on edge, but he drew up the coverings and smothered the sound of her sobs until she could get quiet again.

But she was still too choked up to talk, so he talked first. He had been at Eutaw Springs, and a fierce fight it was, but he had not been hurt. He said Marion's plantation, almost in cannon-shot of the battlefield, had been utterly destroyed. Marion was a bachelor, and had left his home in care of a foreman who had kept it in good condition.

"But I guess they decided," said Luke, "that if they couldn't catch him they could punish him. They wrecked everything he owned. I mean everything—what wouldn't burn, they broke up."

Luke was now on his way to Marion's new camp on the Cooper River. He had a few hours' leave, only long enough to let Celia know he was all right and to make sure that she was. "And you *are* all right, Celia?" he begged.

Celia spoke breathlessly. "I'm going to have a baby."

Luke was startled, he was thrilled, he was scared. He asked a hundred questions.

Now at last Celia could talk. After all these weeks of silence she talked and talked, and lying in Luke's arms she was not frightened any more.

"Do you want a boy or a girl?" Luke asked after a while.

"I don't really care," said Celia, "except—oh, I'd have such fun dressing a girl!"

"What a lucky girl," Luke said laughing. "To have the best dressmaker within a thousand miles for her mother."

Celia laughed too. It was such fun, this sharing of anticipation. This was what she had been missing.

Luke became serious. "Celia, you can't stay here."

"Oh no, no, I can't!" she agreed in a desperate whisper. "But what can I do?"

"My mother will take care of you."

"How can I get to her, Luke?"

"I don't know. But I'll manage it." He spoke with a deep earnestness. "Celia, I'm going to manage it. Wait here. Put up with Roy just a little while longer. I'll be back. I promise. So help me God."

⌇

Celia promised to wait. She waited, and waited, and waited.

She sewed and mended. She went for walks, and shook her head at the half-hearted look of the flowerbeds. Vivian would have been clearing the beds and planting bulbs. You should put in the bulbs now, before the frosts, if you wanted snowdrops and tulips in the spring; but if Sophie did not know this or was too lazy to do it, Celia was not going to remind her.

The weather was clear, and sailing up the coast would have been easy, but again they had no visitors. Sophie was cheerful enough around Roy, for she stood somewhat in awe of him and knew he would not like her to find fault with his new paradise. But when he was out she complained to Celia all day long. She was so bored! She wished to heaven they were in town, or at least at some plantation on a main river. Even Roy grew irritable at the long isolation and the long wondering about what was happening outside. The remoteness of Sea Garden was protection, but this remoteness also meant that they were the last to hear the news.

The days went on and still Sophie did no planting. Finally, one morning in November, Celia woke to find that overnight the air had chilled, and the roofs and lawns were white with the first heavy frost. There was nothing anybody could do now to make the flowers bloom next spring as they would have bloomed under Vivian's care. Celia felt an angry little triumph.

She dressed and went into the breakfast-room. Unless they had guests she usually had breakfast alone. Roy's custom was to go out early and give orders in the fields while Sophie yawned and dozed again; then after an hour or so he would come in and join her in the boudoir, where a maid brought trays for them both. Celia liked it this way. The less she saw of Roy and Sophie the easier it was to put up with them.

After breakfast she went out and walked through the grove, wondering if Roy would leave any of these mighty oaks. The sun mounted and the frost melted, and she thought she had better go in before the damp soaked through her shoes. She did not want to complicate matters by catching cold.

She went indoors, into the big room where she used to spin and sew for Luke. Her spinning-wheel was still there by the hearth, and on the table lay the bound copies of the *Gentleman's Magazine*. Celia put her fingers on the table and saw her fingerprints in the dust. She went to a window and looked out. The panes were dingy. Things had not been like this when Vivian was mistress here.

As she turned from the window she heard a dull noise from a

long way off. With a start, she listened. The sound came nearer and she heard it more plainly, a sound of rippling thuds—the hoofbeats of many horses.

From somewhere near the front she heard a scream from one of the Negro women. There was a rush of footsteps on the stairs. Celia was out in the hall now. She saw Sophie running down the staircase, wailing in fright and pulling a shawl around her with shaking hands. Behind her came the nurse with the baby, and several maids, all wailing like their mistress, while the baby, catching the fear of his elders, was squalling with all his might. Raiders, Celia thought—maybe I can get out by the passage before they can put their hands on me. The thought brought her a wave of sick dizziness, and she clung to the newel-post till it passed.

There was a great deal of noise outdoors, in front of the house. Celia could hear shouts of men and stamping of horses, and the cries of the colored women, and the shrill scared voice of Sophie. They had left the front door open as they ran out. She went through the doorway and paused just over the threshold. The fieldhands had rushed up, and were crowded at one side of the lawn. She saw Roy, riding in from the fields, trying to calm them, telling them he would ride to meet these men and find out what they wanted. Celia looked toward the front, at the pack of horsemen. Surprised and puzzled, she moved forward, and stood staring.

A raiding band? They did not look like it—or what did raiders look like?

There were about fifty men, making noise enough for a thousand. Moving their horses with splendid skill they were forming a semicircle on the lawn, four or five rows deep. One man near the front had on a green coat, like a Tory. Several others wore coats that had once been British red, and had been re-dyed with some stuff that made each coat a patchwork of brown and rust and purple, with spots of red showing through. Other men had on any sort of coat they could find, often in tatters; some had no coats, but shirts and breeches of homespun, or leather, or the fine doeskin breeches of British officers, once white but no longer.

As for footgear, they wore British boots, or buckled shoes, or heavy homemade clumpers; some in good condition, some tied on with rags. They carried shotguns and muskets, rifles, pistols, hunting knives, even the sabers their blacksmiths had made out of log-saws. But to Celia it was not their clothes nor their weapons nor the racket they made that was most striking—it was the impression they gave her of being violently, almost frighteningly, *alive*. She had never been aware of such vitality. Their strength seemed to reach out even to her—a minute ago, clinging to the post at the foot of the staircase, she had been weak and sick; now suddenly she had never felt better in her life.

A bewhiskered rider leaped off his horse and ran toward her, and Celia cried out in delight as she recognized Luke. He met her on the front steps, and caught her to him and kissed her, and she gave another little cry of joy. This was November, the first time since March that she had seen him by daylight, and his eyes were such a dazzling, joy-giving blue.

Over his shoulder she saw his companions, bearded and dirty and glorious, and she loved them every one and would have gladly kissed them all. Marion's men.

⁓

This detachment was commanded by Major Osborn, a sturdy fellow dressed in coonskin cap and thick homespun shirt and breeches, and a pair of knee-high boots captured from some British supply train. Spokesman for the band, Major Osborn advanced his horse a few paces in front of the others and called out that he wanted to speak to Roy Garth.

Without hesitation Roy rode to meet him. Roy was erect, defiant. The Negroes looked on in silence, but Sophie, somewhere near by, gave a plaintive moan. Luke drew Celia down the steps and to one side. His arm around her waist, they stood on the brown grass. Major Osborn said,

"Mr. Garth, we are here by authority of General Francis Marion. You are ordered to return this property to Mr. and Mrs. Herbert Lacy. Mrs. Lacy's son Captain Ansell will receive it."

Sophie made a sound like a scared chicken. One of the Negro men, in a deep low voice, said, "Praise the Lord."

Roy looked almost too shocked to speak. But he spoke. He spoke with angry contempt.

"Do you think," he asked, "that I, a subject of his majesty the king, will obey a traitor like Francis Marion?"

"You had better, Mr. Garth," the major retorted. He gestured toward the men with him. "Otherwise, I must remind you that we can force you to do so."

"So you can," Roy answered. He was furious, but Celia had to own that he had dignity. Roy continued, "You can, of course, put me out of my home at gunpoint. How long you can keep me out remains to be seen. Let me remind *you*," he said clearly, "that I am owner of this property by British command, under authority of the Earl of Cornwallis—"

Roy's voice had a carrying quality, and Marion's men had not the disciplined calm of the British regulars. At the mention of Cornwallis a rustle of laughter ran through the band. Major Osborn and the men just behind him—who appeared to be officers also—kept their soldierly composure.

"Apparently, Mr. Garth," Major Osborn said quietly, "you are not aware that Cornwallis surrendered to General Washington—"

Celia gasped. Again she felt a dizziness, but this time it was like a swirl of rainbows. If Luke had not been holding her close to him she thought she would have fallen down. She heard Major Osborn as he continued,

"—Cornwallis surrendered to General Washington on the nineteenth of October, in Virginia, at the port of Yorktown."

Celia did not hear what Roy answered to this, or even if he answered. All she heard was her own voice, weak with excitement.

"Luke—Luke—then we did what we set out to do! We kept Cornwallis back—long enough!"

Luke's arm tightened around her. "Yes, Sassyface," he said. "Long enough."

•~•

When Sophie understood what the order was, she burst into hysterical sobs, calling upon heaven to protect her and her helpless child as they were thrust out into the world. Roy, however, behaved with a self-possession that both Luke and Celia had to admire. He finally persuaded Sophie to go to her room, and led her up the staircase.

Major Osborn ordered the men to make camp on the grounds.

Luke, who had promised them a banquet of the best that Sea Garden could offer, went to give some directions to the Negroes. Celia sat down on the steps to wait. Major Osborn had placed guards by the steps, and others at various lookout points. The guard nearest Celia, a lanky fellow with red hair and big knobby hands, looked up at her with a companionable grin. She smiled back at him.

When Luke returned, he sat by her on the steps and told her about Yorktown. How Washington, to honor the Carolina patriots who had made the victory possible by their long delay of Cornwallis, had chosen officers of the defense at Charleston to receive the surrender. And how Tarleton, quaking at what the American militiamen might do if they got their hands on him, had begged for—and received—special protection.

Major Osborn asked Luke where Roy was. Luke told him Roy had taken his wife to her room, and would be back in a few minutes to ask where he was to go now and how he was supposed to get there.

Hearing him, the red-haired guard by the steps jerked up his head with a snort. Celia heard him remark that when the British set fire to his farm up Kingstree way, they had not let him ask such a question. If it hadn't been for some corn in the field, too green to burn, he would have gone to the graveyard.

Major Osborn spoke over his shoulder. "That will do, Mac-Nair. Leave this to me."

Celia sent a glance of curiosity toward the guard. MacNair, Kingstree—the names had a familiar sound. After a moment's thought she remembered. Agnes Kennedy, soft-voiced Agnes from the shop, had been engaged to a man named Robert Mac-Nair who had had a farm near Kingstree. They both had lived right in the way of that terrible path of fire that the British had laid from Kingstree to Cheraw.

Celia went down the steps and spoke to the guard. "Is your name Robert MacNair?"

He smiled, and answered politely. "Yes ma'am. And you're Mrs. Ansell? Pleased to meet you, ma'am."

"Then you know one of the girls who used to work with me in Charleston," said Celia. "Agnes—"

The name caught in her throat. MacNair's whole appearance had changed. The muscles tensed around his mouth and eyes; his body tensed too, and his big hands tightened on his gun. Celia guessed what he had to say before he said it.

"She's dead, ma'am."

"Oh," Celia said softly. It was not a word, more an instinctive sound of shock and pity. Gentle Agnes, who had had her life all planned—the flax, the nice children, the cat with kittens. Celia managed to add, "I'm so sorry."

Through his teeth MacNair said, "Would you mind not talking about it, ma'am?"

Celia answered, "Of course, I understand." She wondered if MacNair knew how well she understood. She did not know what they had done to Agnes, but she had the scar of Bellwood and no matter how kind to her the future might be she would always have it, the scar and the knowledge of horror that it had brought her. Turning away, she went back to sit on the top step.

Roy came back out to the piazza. Addressing Major Osborn, he said he had come to ask for orders.

Major Osborn told Roy he could go to Charleston as so many other Tories had done, or to his own country place, Kensaw Plantation. Captain Ansell would make him a present of one of the Sea Garden vessels—not the big schooner, but a small sailboat that could be operated by Roy and the Negroes he had brought here with him. Roy would leave, the major said, tomorrow morning.

His lips tight with fury, Roy answered, "Very well." He turned on his heel. Some guard nearby gave a chuckle.

Roy stopped. He looked at the guards. He looked at Major Osborn and at Luke. His handsome face was dark with anger.

"Laugh if you want to," he said clearly. "The war is not over." His voice rose, piercing and sure. "Nobody but Cornwallis has surrendered," said Roy. "Sir Henry Clinton is still here. The rest of the king's men are still here. *They won't leave.*"

# CHAPTER 33

*A*ND THEY DIDN'T.

For the first few days Celia was so happy that she did not think of what Roy had said. She knew there were thousands of redcoats who had not surrendered, but she forgot about them.

Roy and Sophie and their servants left Sea Garden. Luke made them return Celia's necklace, though he told her he was pretty sure they had tucked into their trunks various other articles that had caught their fancy. But this he could not help. Marion's men had not time for small details. Get rid of Roy, that was the idea, and several men of the detachment went along on the boat to make sure he kept going till he was beyond the lines guarded by Marion, so he could not come back.

After a day or two the rest of the men left for other missions. Luke stayed until Herbert and Vivian came home, but then Celia had to face the fact that the war was not over and he had to leave her again.

Cornwallis and Tarleton had seemed so important that it was hard to realize they commanded only part of the king's troops. But the northern army under Clinton still held New York; while the troops Cornwallis had left behind him, along with the new troops who had arrived last summer, held Charleston and Savannah and several smaller posts. Luke told Celia that after Yorktown,

Washington had begged the Frenchmen to stay and help him capture Charleston, but they refused and went back to the West Indies.

"This means we've got to take care of ourselves," said Luke. "But the king's men in South Carolina hold only one place that we can't force them out of. That's Charleston. So our plan is, force them all *into* Charleston. Squeeze 'em there, till they'll *want* to leave."

Celia ached with disappointment. She dreaded the long lonesomeness ahead, the days and nights when she would want Luke so much and he would still not be there. She was so tired of all that.

But they had Sea Garden again, and her nausea and dizzy spells had disappeared. She could not make the beautiful baby-clothes she had dreamed of, for they had no fine muslins and no way to get any, but Vivian gave her an armful of old sheets and towels, soft from many launderings. "Baby won't know the difference," Vivian said laughing. Celia laughed too. Everybody was making her feel so important. Herbert and Vivian, the colored folk, Luke and the men he brought with him on his visits—they all made much of her. After seven months as Roy's poor relation, the change was like wine after swamp-water.

Vivian was very busy this winter. She said she had never seen such a jumble as Sophie had made of her household. Watching how smoothly Vivian got things organized again, Celia looked ahead, and quaked. Vivian was certainly going to expect her to help with the housekeeping, and she dreaded it. Aunt Louisa had taught her about household affairs, but Kensaw had been no such establishment as Sea Garden, and Vivian's habits of perfection were terrifying.

However, she did not expect to be given anything to do until after the baby was born. She was astonished one morning when Vivian came to the sewing room and interrupted the cutting of diapers.

Vivian was about to make her regular morning round of the household. Her keys, a great important-looking bunch of them, hung by a chain from her waist, and she carried one of her record-books. She told Celia to come with her.

"Oh dear," said Celia. "Now?" She glanced down at her figure. That was as good an excuse as any for putting it off.

"You're perfectly well," said Vivian. She sat on the arm of a chair. "I'd have taken you with me before this, but I did want to clear up after Sophie."

Celia laid down her scissors. Her fingers began to fidget with the ends of her kerchief. Vivian's dark eyes looked her over.

"Are you still scared of me, Celia?"

"Yes!" Celia answered. She knew she would feel better if she told the truth.

"You've learned one trade well," Vivian said quietly. "You can learn another."

She sat on the arm of the chair, one hand on the back, the other lying in her lap. Will I ever, Celia wondered, be so calm, so sure of myself. She said, "If you'll teach me, I'll try to do things the way you like them. I do want to help you."

Vivian glanced down at the bunch of keys. After a moment she raised her eyes. "I'm not teaching you to help me, Celia," she said. "I'm teaching you to get along without me."

Celia started. "You mean—what *do* you mean?"

Vivian laughed a little. "Celia, my health is good. I've probably got many years ahead of me. You don't want me to spend those years bossing you around."

"But you wouldn't do that!"

"Oh yes I would," Vivian returned coolly. "I'm not capable of living in the house with another woman and *not* bossing her around." She paused a moment. Then, with an odd intentness, she said, "Celia, the day you came here to get married, you were afraid I wouldn't like it."

Celia had forgotten that moment of doubt. It was so long ago, and Vivian had been such a dear. But now, under Vivian's steady gaze, she had to remember. "Yes," she said hesitantly. She did not know what else to say.

"You were quite right," said Vivian. With a smile she added, "I told you I was not 'that kind of mother-in-law.' I'm not, but I could be—oh, so easily. Celia my dear, about Luke I'm a fool. You know that. Long ago I made up my mind that when Luke brought a wife to Sea Garden, I would leave. I only prayed he'd choose a girl who would love Sea Garden and take care of it, and I think he did."

Celia felt a lump of pain in her throat. She did not want to cry, but these days it was hard not to cry when things touched her. She could not speak. While she fought for control Vivian went on.

"Herbert and I have been talking this over. We'll stay until Luke can take charge, then we'll go to town. I understand that ever since Burton and Elise were sent to Philadelphia a pack of Tories have been living in our town house—I hope they don't wreck it before they have to leave."

Still fighting back her tears, Celia felt such a rush of gratitude as she had never known before. Vivian was smiling, her voice was steady, her manner was calm. But Celia knew that this was a moment of great renunciation. Right now, Vivian was holding out her two greatest treasures, Luke and Sea Garden. She was saying, They are yours now. Take them.

Aloud Vivian went on, "I'm assuming that if I behave myself like a nice person I'll be welcome here when I want some country air, as you'll certainly be welcome in my house when you come to town. But this will be your home and that will be mine, and we won't interfere with each other. Oh, cry if you feel like it, Celia—don't be ashamed. I've been in your state several times and I know how the tears rush out at the most awkward moments."

Celia had a feeling that she could not have put into words. It was not knowledge, it was a deep instinctive grasp of the fact that she did not know yet how much Vivian was giving her. She would not know until she had been mistress of her own home and her own life, until after she and Luke had been let alone to work out their own marriage in their own way. Maybe she would not really appreciate Vivian's gift for years to come, not until she herself gave up a son of her own to another woman. She felt this, and she did not know how to say it. She turned her head, and put her hands over her burning eyes, and stood there feeling young and clumsy, until at last she pulled out her handkerchief and scrubbed at her tears and managed to say, "You'll never know how much I love you for this."

Vivian stood up. Celia stumbled into her arms and sobbed on her bosom, and Vivian held her gently until she was quiet again. At last Celia raised her head. Vivian smiled at her, and Celia smiled back.

"Now," said Vivian, "go to your room, and wash your face, and get a wrap—it's chilly in the halls. I'll wait for you."

Celia's baby was born on an afternoon in May. When the time came, Vivian summoned the Negro midwife from the quarters. The midwife was old and wise, and knew her business, but Vivian promised that she too would stand by. Celia had expected this to be a hard day, though she had not dreamed it would be as hard as it was, nor that any day could be so long. But at last it was over and she heard Vivian say, "You have a beautiful little girl," and through Celia's head went a confused vision of lace and ribbons and fine lawn. The colored woman brought her the baby, wrapped in garments made of an old sheet. Celia drew a happy breath and her eyes fell shut.

Her little girl was a week old when they heard a horse's hoofs clattering up the driveway. Celia, lying in bed planning a baby-dress of white silk with pink shirring, raised herself on her elbow and said "Luke!" But the rider was Burton Dale, back from exile in Philadelphia.

Though she was disappointed, Celia was glad Burton had come safely home. Vivian brought him in to see her. Celia had not seen Burton since Balfour shipped him to St. Augustine eighteen months ago, and to her astonishment he seemed all the better for his experience. His clothes had been mended and re-mended, but he no longer looked as if he had been stuffed into them. Not only was he leaner, he was tanned and muscular (she did not wonder at this, when she found that he had alternately walked and ridden horseback all the way from Philadelphia). Also, he had an air of jaunty confidence, which for the first time made Celia notice that he looked rather like his half-brothers Luke and Godfrey.

Herbert joined them in Celia's room, and Burton sipped a glass of wine and told them about his adventures. As Luke had surmised, Godfrey had given Elise money to help her get along in

Philadelphia, but it was not enough to support the family indefinitely and they had had no idea how long they would have to stay there. So they rented rooms in a boarding-house, and Burton went out and got a job.

Vivian said, "Heaven help us, doing what?"—for Burton had never done any work in his life except supervise his rice crop. Burton chuckled, rather proudly, and replied, "I taught school."

Vivian and Herbert together flashed him a look of startled admiration. Burton continued.

At first, he said, the situation had scared him. Besides day-to-day living expenses, the boys were growing out of their clothes; also winter was coming, a northern winter, and nobody among the Charleston exiles had clothes warm enough. Burton thought over his accomplishments. These, he readily admitted, were few. But he recalled that he had kept careful plantation accounts, which meant that he had years of practice in arithmetic.

"I went to the headmaster of a boys' school," said Burton, "and told him I'd like to teach the fellows to do sums. He put me to work. And do you know," Burton said with a grin, "I enjoyed it."

He went on to say that on the whole they had managed very well. "The boys ran errands, held horses, did all sorts of odd jobs. And Elise worked hard. The churches collected second-hand winter clothes for us—imagine!—and Elise patched them and made them over. A real helpmeet she was."

"The grace of the Lord," murmured Vivian, "can do wonders. How did you get home?"

Now that, said Burton, had been a problem. They had been free to leave as soon as the exchange of prisoners was officially accomplished, but the snows were deep, and the country through which they would have to travel was demoralized by years of war. He had waited till spring, when he had joined several other families to buy horses, and two wagons for their scanty belongings. By slow stages they had traveled south. They had spent the nights at inns, when they could find any; but oftener they had slept in deserted barns or farmhouses whose owners had fled the redcoats, or sometimes they slept in the wagons outdoors.

As they neared home the party scattered. Burton headed for

the plantation of Elise's brother Gilbert Arvin, north of the Santee and easy to reach. As they rode through the desolation, Burton and Elise prayed with every mile that Mr. Arvin's home would still be there.

What they found was bad, though not the worst possible. The property had been confiscated for some good Tory; but the new owner had not cared to live on the place. All he wanted was fast money. He had stripped the plantation of everything that could be sold. As redcoats and Tories fled into Charleston, Mr. Arvin had brought his family home. Their dwelling and the other buildings were empty, but they were still there.

The Arvin family had returned shortly before the Dales arrived, and the house gave shelter to Elise and the boys. They had to sleep on the floor, but by this time they did not mind. Burton was now on his way toward Goose Creek, to see what was left of his own plantation. He spent a night at Sea Garden, and went on.

It was another two weeks before Luke appeared. Celia was up now, and sat on the piazza with the baby beside her in a little cart made long ago for Vivian's babies. Leaning back in a big chair, she was lazily enjoying the summer day when she heard the sound of horses' hoofs. Again she started eagerly, and again she said "Luke!"—and this time it *was* Luke. He had brought Amos with him, and the two of them rode up the driveway.

Before his horse had halted, Luke was off, tossing the bridle to Amos and bounding up the steps in what looked like a single leap. He grabbed her in his arms with a force that took the breath right out of her, and to her own disgust, Celia found that she was crying again.

Later, when they were alone in their room, she told him she wanted to name the baby but had been waiting for his approval. "I want to name her Vivian," said Celia.

Luke smiled as he glanced at the crib. He still marveled that the baby could be so small, and yet be human, and his. "I like that," he said. "And Mother will be mighty pleased."

"Then it's all right?"

"Of course. I'm glad you want to. What gave you the idea?"

"I'll tell you sometime. But I don't think you'll understand."

"Why not?" Luke exclaimed in surprise. He was not used to being told there were things he could not understand.

"Because you're a man," said Celia.

"Oh, good Lord," said Luke.

Celia gave a shrug. "All right," she said, and told him about Vivian's plan to leave Sea Garden.

Luke smiled broadly. "Mother's a grand person, isn't she? But Celia, what made you think I wouldn't understand that?"

"I meant," said Celia, "the way she loves Sea Garden, and loves you—" She paused. It was no use to try to explain.

Luke began to laugh. "Celia, I know some women want to baby their sons, and hate their sons' wives. But Mother isn't that sort. Anyway, now that they're getting older, I think she and the governor will be happier in Charleston. They like people and parties, and town life in general. But I do think it's fine that you want to name the baby for Mother. I'll go right now and tell her."

He gave Celia a kiss. Leaving her to take the afternoon rest that Vivian said she must have now, he went off. Celia heard the clump of his great boots in the hall.

The baby's name was Vivian. But Luke did not understand what she had understood when Vivian had talked to her that day. How could he be expected to? He was a man.

## CHAPTER 34

$\mathscr{B}$UT VIVIAN UNDERSTOOD. When she saw Celia in the parlor later that afternoon, she said, "Thank you, dear. You make me very happy."

They smiled at each other. But they said no more, for they had gathered to listen to Amos. He had slipped into Charleston several times recently, carrying messages for Marion.

Amos said the town was jammed. The rebels in South Carolina had been doing their job well. They were pushing into Charleston not only the king's soldiers, but also the Tory civilians, who did not dare stay home without British guns to protect them. Rich Tories were paying fantastic sums for rooms at inns or private homes. Others were sleeping in stores, warehouses, anywhere they could. Nobody, rich or poor, could get enough to eat. The British troops had killed their horses for lack of fodder. They had a new commander, General Leslie, and he was trying to keep order, but he could not do much to ease the nightmarish state of things.

Celia thought of the Hendrix family, putting on airs as they spent other people's money. She hoped Mr. and Mrs. Hendrix and Miss Dolly were very uncomfortable now.

Vivian spoke with concern. "But Amos, people who are not Tories—my children—can't they get away?"

Amos said it was harder than you'd think. General Leslie

wanted people to leave town, for every person who left took his mouth with him. But there were no horses, and the general himself had taken most of the boats so his troops could raid nearby plantations for food. However, Amos knew that Godfrey and Lewis Penfield were both trying to get boats. Marietta had told him this.

Herbert and Vivian began to ask about friends in town. Luke suggested to Celia that they sit on the piazza. As he drew out a chair for her he asked,

"Celia, would you mind very much doing without Marietta?"

"I'd miss her, certainly," Celia said. "After what we went through together, she's more like a friend of mine than a maid. What do you mean?"

"She's still with Ida," said Luke. "Amos has seen her whenever he's been to town. He says they want to be married, and go away with Miles Rand."

"Go where?"

"To the mountains. Wherever Miles goes."

He said Miles was still resolved to dispose of Bellwood and go west, to the frontier. He would take Amos with him, and Big Buck, the other Negro who had escaped the fury of Tarleton's Legion. Luke had bought some of Miles' outlying land, and Miles had offered some extra acres as compensation for Marietta's services.

Celia spoke doubtfully. "Does Marietta want to go out to the frontier?"

"Amos says she does. Why?"

"Because I shouldn't like it," said Celia. "Sleeping on the ground, and being scared of Indians—let me talk to Marietta. I'll ask her how she feels about it."

Luke said this was fair enough.

He had to leave the next day and go back to Marion's camp. They had no more news from Charleston until August, when the landing-bell clanged violently one afternoon, and kept on clanging while Herbert and his men mounted and rode to the river-bank.

At the landing was a boat—a scrabby boat, ramshackle and creaking and patched and miserable—and on the boat were Godfrey and Ida and Darren, with Marietta and Godfrey's servants. They were hot and tired. Their nerves were torn to pieces from their dread that their boat would not last to get here, and they were so hungry that they were nearly frantic.

Vivian and Celia hurried to call the maids, and set out a meal— "Cold rice will do," said Godfrey, "stale bread, anything." The kitchen boys dragged a long table out to the back porch, while Celia and the girls ran to the pantry and brought whatever they could bring fastest. They put it all on the table helterskelter, and Godfrey's group fell upon the food like animals.

Between gulps, Godfrey told them that Madge and Lewis Penfield and their children had joined another family going up to Goose Creek, where Lewis' brother had a country place. Celia wondered if they were all as hungry as this. She sat down on the back steps. After a while, when Godfrey's party had had enough to eat, with little embarrassed laughs they began to apologize for being so ravenous. Marietta came over to Celia. "You'd think we were a bunch of pigs!" she exclaimed.

"You forget," Celia said laughing. "I know what it's like to be hungry." She patted the step beside her. "Sit down, Marietta."

Marietta obeyed. "Miss Celia," she said, "I'm so happy for you and Mr. Luke, and your little girl."

"My little girl has big blue eyes," said Celia. "And Marietta, I've heard about you and Amos. I'm happy for you too."

"Thank you, Miss Celia," said Marietta, and by the look of her she was happy for herself.

"You're mighty brave," said Celia, "not to mind going out to the mountains."

"But why should I mind, Miss Celia? Amos—and Mr. Miles and Big Buck—they all want to go. So I want to go with Amos."

"You're sure you'll like it?"

"Oh yes," Marietta returned with conviction. "Amos wants to go."

Celia reminded her that there would be hardships, even actual danger. Marietta was surprised that Celia should be worried about such things. She said Amos was all excited about going west. And since Amos was so happy about it, why naturally she was happy too.

Celia began to understand that Marietta was one of those rare women who could lose themselves completely in the lives of the people they loved. She was happy to go with Amos, but she would have been equally happy staying at home with him. To Amos and her children Marietta would give her life, and she would not even know that she was giving anything.

Celia smiled with a thoughtful wonder, for she knew very well she was not made like that herself.

A few days later Miles and Amos got leave to come to Sea Garden, and Mr. Warren was summoned again to marry Amos and Marietta. After the ceremony there was a supper in the quarters for the colored people. While Amos and Marietta were receiving the good wishes of their friends, Celia drew Miles aside and gave him the case holding the bracelets of gold roses that Jimmy had given her.

Miles looked at the bracelets with tender affection.

"I've seen my mother wear these so many times," he said in a low voice. "I'll keep them to remember her by. Thanks, Celia."

Celia said, "You're welcome, Miles." She was thinking, You won't keep them to remind you of your mother. You'll give them to a girl. You don't know it now, but you will.

As Miles closed the case, hiding the bracelets from her sight forever, she felt relieved. Miles would give them to a girl, but Celia was glad the girl would not be here in the Lowcountry. If she had to see those bracelets they would remind her of Jimmy, and she did not want to be reminded. It would hurt too much.

•～•

A month later, in September, three hundred British ships sailed into Charleston harbor. They had come to take the redcoats home.

Not only the redcoats, but as many Tories as wanted to go with them. Some Tories, who had nothing to apologize for except that they had taken the losing side, intended to stay and make up with their old friends. But there were others who knew they would never have any American friends again. Also, there were some who said frankly that they did not trust the future of the little new nation that would be made out of the Thirteen Colonies. They thought it wise to get away.

So the king's army and the king's friends made ready to go. It still seemed to the weary patriots that they were never going. But at last, in December, 1782, a year and two months after Cornwallis had surrendered at Yorktown, they left.

First the king's friends went aboard the ships: Tory families and their Negro servants, nine thousand men and women and children. They went under protection of the king's guns, while bad boys shouted dirty words at them from trees and windows.

The next morning the king's soldiers marched to the wharf and went aboard. That afternoon the American Continentals marched in. The bad boys, the old people, all those who had not been able to get out of town during the dragging months just past, leaned out of the windows and over the balconies, calling, "Welcome home, gentlemen! Welcome home!"

Celia, still at Sea Garden, wondered if Roy and Sophie had gone with the redcoats or had chosen to stay and make the best of Roy's little property at Kensaw. She did not know, and when she thought about it she did not care either.

Luke came back to Sea Garden. He put his horse into the stable, changed his swamp-clothes for some gentlemanly apparel, and said now he was home for good.

However, that first evening he did not say much more than this. He walked around, sat by the fire, got up and walked around again. As they went in for supper, Vivian said softly to Celia, "Don't try to make him talk. He needs to get used to being home."

Celia obeyed, and asked him no questions. But the next day, while she sat alone by the fire turning her spinning-wheel, Luke came into the room. It was a dark winter day, dripping with rain. Celia looked up, her hand on the wheel, but Luke said, "Go on, I like to watch you." She went on turning, while he walked up and down between the ruddy fireplace and the gray windows. After a while he began to talk. He told her how it had been, under the great cedars that sheltered the camp, when Marion said good-by to his men.

As he talked, Celia turned the wheel more and more slowly. At length she forgot it altogether.

"We didn't have any formal mustering-out," said Luke, "because we had never had any formal enlistments. I guess Marion's men were never really soldiers at all."

He was looking at the rain as it streamed down the window-panes. After a moment he went on.

"Well, there we stood, under those big cedar trees, and there he stood. He made a little speech."

Luke stopped again. The pause was so long that she prompted him.

"Go on, Luke. What did he say?"

As if startled by her voice, Luke turned from the window. "Why—he thanked us for staying by him. He said for us to go home now, and get back to work. Said this was what he was going to do. Though only the Lord knows what he's going to work with. They've left him nothing but a patch of weeds and cinders. He doesn't own even a hoe to chop up the weeds."

Luke looked down. He kicked at the corner of a rug. After a while Ceila asked,

"What else did he say, Luke?"

Again, Luke seemed to start. "Why—nothing much. He just made a little speech. He's not much of a talker."

The wheel was still. Celia did not remember when she had stopped turning it. Luke looked out at the rain, and back at her. He spoke with a half-embarrassed bluntness.

"I don't know what else he said, Celia. I didn't hear him very well. I had my head down. I was blinking, I was swallowing, try-ing not to let anybody see that I was about to bawl. But then I sneaked a look up, and every man I could see was blinking and swallowing like me. We stood there like that, and he told us good-by. Then when he finished, we said good-by to each other."

Luke looked down at his shoes, and out again.

"We shook hands. We turned our backs on each other and coughed. We turned around and shook hands again."

Celia sat very still. Luke's mind was back at the camp under the cedars. The fire gave a snap. As if this had roused him, Luke went on.

"We tried to talk. To say what it had meant to be such friends, to fight such a fight together. We said, 'Well, we've been through a lot, haven't we?' Or, 'It'll sure seem funny to live under a roof

*398*

again.' Or, 'If you ever get up our way, drop in, glad to see you any time.' Things like that. Stupid things. We didn't know what to say. We had such a feeling—it was over, and we were glad it was over, and yet while it lasted it had been the grandest thing that ever happened to us. It's hard to explain." He paused a moment, and added, "I don't think you'd understand anyway."

He stood fiddling with the curtain. The fire snapped again, and a log rolled out of place. As if glad to move, Luke came hurriedly to the fireplace, put the screen aside, and knelt on the hearth to rearrange the logs. As he stood up and put the screen back into place he repeated,

"I don't think you'd understand."

Standing by the mantel, he watched the fire. Celia put her fist to her mouth and bit her knuckles, thoughtfully. Maybe she would not understand. Maybe, in spite of all he could ever tell her, she never would understand, not as he understood it—that comradeship of war, the strange brotherhood in killing that made men like war while women hated it so. She remembered the exhilaration she had felt when she watched the guns of Fort Moultrie shell the king's fleet, and her joy at sharing the effort of Marion's men. But this did not go down deep into her instinct about what she wanted to do in the world. It was behind her now, and she was glad of it.

Not long ago she had told Luke that some things were beyond him. Now he was telling her. The fellowship of women, the fellowship of men.

There was no use in pressing him to tell her more. He could not.

•～•

In January the weather cleared. Herbert told his men to get out the schooner and make it ready for the trip to Charleston. Godfrey and Darren were already there—borrowing horses from Herbert, they had ridden into town on the heels of the American army, for Godfrey wanted to get his affairs in order. But Ida and her servants had waited at Sea Garden, and they went down on the schooner. Also Luke and Celia went along. They wanted to see Charleston without redcoats.

All the way, Celia was restless. She cuddled Baby Vivian to sleep, and left her with the nurse while she herself went on deck. She walked up and down. She thought of Charleston as she used to know it—the warm sunlit city, bright with flowers and musical with church bells. How long, she wondered, would it take for Charleston to be like that again?

A long time. Battered by the guns of a siege, occupied for nearly three years by a foreign army—no town could get over that in a hurry. But the time would not be so important, if only you knew the wounds were healing. Celia wondered if the redcoats had left any wound that could not heal.

It was dark when they reached town, and she could not see much as they drove through the streets. Godfrey had brought some firewood into the Lacys' home on Meeting Street, and he and Darren had awkwardly spread sheets and blankets on the beds. Tired after her long journey, Celia slept soundly. But in the morning she walked around the house, and her heart felt sick.

For more than a year this house had been occupied by a Tory family. They knew they had lost the war, and every room was bruised with their resentment. Vivian's furniture was scuffed and dented, ringed by wet glasses, scorched by careless smokers. The rugs were spotted with spilt food and drink. All through the house Celia saw broken hinges, peeling wallpaper, and a filthy army of cockroaches.

After a breakfast of provisions they had brought with them, Vivian called a conference of the servants. Celia offered to help, but Vivian smilingly shook her head. "You mind your own business. This is my house, remember?"

Luke and Herbert said they would go out and hear the news. Celia stopped Luke at the front door, to beg him, if he saw any nice muslin for sale, to buy it so the baby could have a pretty dress. She was so tired of old sheets and homespun.

Luke said he had never bought any such stuff in his life, but he would see what he could find. He and Herbert went out. As Celia turned from the door she saw Vivian in the hall giving the maids instructions about cleaning up. If Vivian shared her own apprehension that Charleston might have any incurable hurt, she was not saying so.

But Celia still felt her foreboding of yesterday. She started up-stairs. First she had to feed the baby, then she wanted to go outside and see what the town looked like now.

When the baby fell asleep again she put on her cloak and went down. In a sitting room at one side of the hall, a colored man was making a fire while a girl dusted the chairs. That was like Vivian, to make one room comfortable at once. Celia opened the front door and went outside. On the sidewalk by the steps she paused and looked around, and as she looked she smiled, and told herself she had been foolish to feel such misgivings. Charleston was in an ugly muddle, to be sure. But everywhere she turned, she saw people busy putting it back in order.

The morning was full of wind and sun and the noise of rebuilding. All around her Celia could hear saws and hammers. On the roof of Simon Dale's house next door workmen were making repairs. Across the street a man was replacing the broken lantern over a door. Farther down, another man was painting a wall blackened by a British shell. A hand-cart came down the street, pushed by a peddler calling that he had fine raw shrimp.

What had she dreaded? The redcoats were gone, and before long there would be scarcely anything to remind you that they had been here. Nothing but a few scars to be pointed out to children, scars of honor.

Celia had turned her head toward Broad Street. As she saw the steeple of St. Michael's she started with pleasure. They had built a scaffolding around the steeple, and on the scaffolding men were at work. They were scraping off the black paint.

How good it would be to have the spire of St. Michael's white again! At night the beacon would shine again over the town. And the bells would ring, the beautiful voice of Charleston.

She saw Godfrey and Darren coming down the street toward her. They waved, and Celia waved back. How well they looked.

Godfrey gave her a package of coffee, and she exclaimed with delight, for she had not tasted coffee in months. They accepted her invitation to come in by the fire, and Celia threw her cloak over a newly dusted chair and went to call Vivian.

Vivian came in, saying they were interrupting her housecleaning, but that task would take six weeks or maybe six months, and she couldn't wait so long to hear the news of the town. The four of them sat around the fire. Darren told them about the gunpowder.

Remember, during the siege, they had moved ten thousand pounds of gunpowder from the magazine on Cumberland Street? They had stored the powder in a vault under the Exchange, and secured it with a hurriedly built brick wall. Well, when the redcoats were gone and the Americans marched in, the gunpowder was still there.

All the powder the redcoats used was brought in by ship. They would have been glad to pay for the powder hidden in the Exchange. But though many people knew it was there, nobody had told them.

Celia thought of the Charleston patriots—the rich ones impoverished and exiled, the poor ones struggling to feed their children by any job the British would let them hold. It would have been so easy. "What will you give me if I tell you where to find ten thousand pounds of gunpowder?"

She smiled with astonished gratitude. After so much cruelty and nastiness, it was good to learn how really magnificent people could be. She said so, and the two men agreed with her, but Vivian was laughing.

"What's funny about it?" Godfrey demanded.

"Why so surprised?" Vivian asked. "You conceited creatures. You knew, all three of you, and you didn't tell. What makes you think you're so much better than the average?"

There was an instant of startled silence, then they all laughed too. Vivian had such a way of making sense.

Celia leaned back in her chair, stretching her feet toward the fire. Godfrey told about the deserters, hundreds of them, who crept out of hiding as soon as the British ships had gone across the horizon. He had found three of them hiding behind boxes in his own attic. They had not taken anything or done any harm. They liked America and wanted to stay here, that was all. One of them said he was going to be married to an American girl, a young lady named Becky Duren who worked at Mrs. Thorley's shop. He was a private soldier, had been a farm laborer at home, and when they were married he was going up to her father's farm and help with the work. Celia wondered if Becky really meant it this time.

The front door banged, and Luke's voice shouted, "Where's everybody?" Godfrey called an answer and Luke strode in. "Morning, boys. Celia, is this what you wanted?"

He dropped a bundle into her lap. Celia drew out a length of fine cambric, soft and silky—such cloth as she had not seen since she used to make clothes for Tory women. She sighed with ecstasy. "Oh Luke, it's beautiful! Where did you get it?"

"Mrs. Thorley's," said Luke. He went to the hearth and held out his hands to the fire.

Celia gathered up the cambric and held it against her cheek. This was what she was born for. She had never known it so well as during the months when she had had to do without it. As long as she lived she would thrill to beautiful clothes as some people thrilled to painting and poetry. "I'm so happy," she murmured, "to have things getting right!"

Vivian smiled at her. "We all are."

"It will be so good," Celia went on dreamily, "to have the church steeple white again, to hear the bells—"

The three men all gave a start. Godfrey and Darren sat up straight in their chairs. Luke, still standing, struck the mantelpiece with his fist. Godfrey said something to him, a question—in her shock Celia did not hear what it was, but she heard Luke answer, "Yes, I heard about it, at the Exchange."

Celia had sat up too, frightened. The cambric slid out of her hands to the floor. It was as if a voice inside her was saying, I knew it! This is what I was afraid of. They've done something terrible to us, something we can't make right.

She heard Vivian ask in alarm, "What's the matter? Luke, Godfrey—what's happened?"

At the same time Celia begged, more definitely, "Luke, what did they do?"

Luke's eyes turned to Celia. He answered her question. "We'll never hear the bells again. The redcoats took them."

Vivian caught her breath. Celia put her hand up to her throat as if she felt herself choking. As so often when she was deeply moved, she had no words. But Vivian spoke, though her voice was strained with a sense of disaster.

"You mean—the redcoats—stole the bells of St. Michael's?"

The others nodded. Celia looked from Luke to Godfrey, from Godfrey to Darren, and back again, as if hoping that one of them would tell her it was all a mistake. She felt almost as if they had announced the death of a person she loved, someone who had seemed to be getting well. She could not think of Charleston without the bells of St. Michael's. Everybody in town reckoned time by the bells. Everybody, of whatever faith, loved the music of them as the morning came up or the sun went down.

Helplessly, Vivian asked, "But why?"

Godfrey pushed back his chair and stood up. "To sell," he answered curtly. "Those bells are worth a lot of money."

Luke began to poke the fire. He poked it viciously, as if he was beating something. They had borne so much, had lost so much. And now when they had thought it was over, the theft of the bells had come like a new insult. It was so cruel and so needless, this last indignity.

Godfrey stood leaning his elbow on the back of his chair, talking as if it was a relief to talk. He said it was lucky the redcoats had had to take all those Tories with them. Their ships had been so crowded that there had not been room for much loot. But they had taken all they could stuff in—fine furniture, silver, much public property. And the bells.

Luke set down the poker. "Stop talking about it."

Godfrey gave a harsh little laugh. "I know how you feel," he said. "It hit me the same way."

Luke said he was going out again, to order some plantation tools. He wanted to get his mind off the bells. The others felt the same way. Godfrey said he and Darren had to check a shipment of goods, and Vivian said she would go back to her housecleaning. Celia picked up her cloak. "I think I'll go out too. I'll feel better if I take a walk."

Luke went out with her. In front of the house he said good-by, and started toward King Street.

Celia walked toward St. Michael's, past a knot of boys watching the work of repair on the steeple. Losing the bells was like losing part of her life. She remembered hearing them that morning when Jimmy told her Vivian needed a dressmaker; and again that gray evening when Jimmy had first kissed her. She had not forgotten Jimmy; she never would.

Luke had said, "Of course, you were not in love with him."

But she had been!

The minute she owned up to it she had a feeling of release. Pausing on the sidewalk she looked up at the steeple. She had loved Jimmy, she had been happy loving him, and the bells had been part of that happiness. What she had felt for Jimmy was not what she felt now for Luke—this was a different love because she herself was different. When she had realized her love for Luke she was no longer the young girl Jimmy had kissed. But she had loved Jimmy. Luke must know this. Only—she understood now, as she walked on—Luke did not want to know it.

Vivian would understand this. Vivian had loved Luke's father best, but he was not the only man she had loved. But—if he had wanted to think he was, a woman as wise as Vivian would have been wise enough to let him think so. ·

All of a sudden, as she walked along the busy street in the bright winter chill, Celia knew that her aloneness was not gone. In some ways she was alone and so was everybody else. This dream of being completely one with another person—well, it was a beautiful dream. Everybody had areas of silence.

But maybe you were better for this. For if you had lonely places in your heart, you knew other people had lonely places too.

Even Luke?

The thought struck her sharply. She walked faster, thinking. There was a great deal about Luke that she did not know. They had never been really married—they had said "Yes" to a wedding ceremony and they had had a child, but they had not lived day after day in the intimacy that made people really know each other. Maybe they would find it hard to get used to that. Luke would, certainly. He was reckless, daredevilish—the change to being a peaceful citizen was going to be a hard change for him.

She remembered how the bells of St. Michael's had rung when

she was sailing out of Charleston harbor bound for Sea Garden to be married to Luke. It had seemed to her that they were saying, "We wish you happiness."

The bells would remind her of so much. They would remind her—men like war, women don't. Women like being peacetime homemakers, men don't. Be gentle, Celia. Be understanding. You've got a rough road ahead of you and so has he. Everybody has lonely places. Even Luke.

She stopped and turned around, and looked back across the housetops to the steeple. This was what the bells would say, but they were not there to say it. The steeple was silent.

Celia wanted to cry out, No! It must not be this way. She could not, she simply could not, accept the idea that she would never hear the bells again, that her child would never hear that lovely whisper of music. Standing on the sidewalk, she looked up at the silent steeple.

"Please," she whispered, "please don't let it be always silent! Please God, give us back the bells!"